SHOES OF OCTOBER

June Crosby Jackson

Pen Press Publishers Ltd

First published in Great Britain by
Pen Press Publishers Ltd
39, Chesham Road
Brighton
BN2 1NB

ISBN 1-905621-05-1
978-1-905621-05-7

Printed and bound in the UK

A catalogue record of this book is available from
the British Library

Cover design by Jacqueline Abromeit
from a painting by Hannah Victoria Simmonds

About the author

June Crosby Jackson is a published poet. She also had a play
'*Ayesha 2000*' successfully staged locally, and published short stories.

June is widowed and has one son, three daughters and five granddaughters
and lives in Greater Manchester.

'*Shoes of October*' is her first novel.

Dedicated to my husband Alfred James Jackson
many thanks for beautiful memories.

For my children: Robert, Valentina, Elizabeth and Rebecca

and my five stars:
Kelly, Katie,Emma, Hannah and Sophie

To: Andrea.

With Best Wishes

June Bosly Jackson

Acknowledgements

For my good friend Marry Barry
thanking her for all her kindness, help
and heartfelt generosity during the writing of my book.

For my son-in-law Alan Rowe
Thanks for everything across the years.

For Thomas and little India Hollywood
Just for being who you are.

Prologue

Held in the man's grip, tantamount to a vice, she was conscious of snow resembling soft down, falling first on her hair before drifting down on exposed skin, chilling her pale features.

Aware also, of smoke, which, as it lifted from recently ignited explosives, rose and fell on the spring air, screening the rubble that had originally been buildings. The whole atmosphere had an unreal feeling about it, as if she were some unwilling participant in an evil charade. The part she was acting out made her thoughts unclear, leaving her impervious to the screeching of cars and the screams of people in what appeared to be abject fear.

To her tortured senses, compared to the hatred she felt for the man in whose arms she was now imprisoned, the rest became insignificant. The clamour going on around her merely enhanced a feeling of loathing for a double adversary: one that had long haunted, not only her childhood dreams, but taunted her unmercifully, through out her youthful years.

Yet, beneath such enmity, lay something deeper, more urgent. An act, she knew, she had only seconds left to accomplish. That she must play her cards with a cool hand if she wished to succeed her goal in the final moments left to her. To document all that remained – revenge!

Well and truly conscious she was about to die, like any other human caught in such harrowing circumstances was aware of her own fragility. She wished for time. Time to kiss her husband. Her son. To comfort a recently returned lover who now lay dying at her feet. But she would not sacrifice her pride, nor would she beg for mercy or a stay of execution from an enemy in whose power she now lay. Instinctively, she knew such a request would not be granted.

Though she was in a sense spellbound by her captor, mesmerised in the fashion of a rabbit confronted by a stoat, a strong and devious plan was already at work in her mind... how to repay her captor? Then the answer came swiftly. Magically! And, though she was not sure if it was heaven sent or a solution from the devil, a revelation came to mind. She had a plan that would surely have the affect she so desperately sought.

Also, try as she may to dismiss it, was the knowledge that, when a person drowns, their whole life floats before them. And, that when a man holds a gun to the heart... the sensation is exactly the same.

Part One

One Foot in Spring

We walked by seashores.

Loved aimlessly in gentle spring.

Made vows by tumbling falls.

Imagined our love as a never,

Ending thing.

Chapter One

The late March wind raced across the city more like a predatory lion than the proverbial lamb, bulldozing all before it, causing trees to sway, chimneys to topple, doors to creak and windows to rattle. It continued to clean streets of Manchester city with more efficiency than a hundred Corporation dustcarts before spiralling, fickle fashion, out of control; changing course, sweeping and bustling its way through the Cheshire suburbs. In so doing, attacking the beeches that painfully rustled their objections where they stood sentinel on either side of Sandy Wilson's garden.

Jedda, awakened from a dreamy sleep, stretched her arms above her head, expanding her body as she did so. Her face, flushed pink from the warmth of slumber, portrayed an innocence only present in the very young. Her spirit, filled with eager wonder, at odds with a body reluctant to leave the warmth of a cosy bed and explore the garden below. Just one thought occupied her mind. It was her birthday. She was seven.

Inquisitive by nature, she knelt up in her small bed adjacent to the wall and leaned her elbows on the white painted windowsill while studying the scene portrayed in the garden below – one that addressed winter rather than spring, depicted by a covering of snow, willing plants to thrust their way to earth in a dogged fashion. Gusts of wind, keen and sharp, rose and fell like a fragile dress of silk refusing to be anchored, causing trees and bushes to moan constantly.

Too young to be interested in counting the days, Jedda was nevertheless aware by the quietness below stairs it was Sunday. She was also conscious of the cold beginning to bite into her small frame, making her shiver. All thoughts of celebration speedily pushed aside, she returned to the warmth of a recently vacated bed, snuggling down decisively.

Dwelling there, her thoughts on the lovely party she had shared with her young friends only yesterday, specially arranged with them in mind, she considered that tonight was the turn of the adults. Meditating on what other surprises might be in store for her she wondered if her grandmother had made another birthday cake. Would there be more presents?

Unhesitatingly, enjoying the luxury doled out by a comfortable bed until, becoming bored – zero conditions or not – she decided to brave the elements by making her way gently down the stairs. She tiptoed her way diligently. Quietly.

Her feet sinking into the thickly carpeted stairs and, having reached the hall, opened the door that led into the morning room.

Seated by the fire, her willowy form draped unceremoniously into the plush interior of an easy chair lounged Zizzie, her maternal grandmother. Cigarette poised in one hand, cup of coffee balanced in the other. She smiled as Jedda made her way forward, offering a cheek to be kissed. Returning the kiss, Zizzie was consciously aware of the excitement surging in waves through her granddaughter's thin body. She wished Jedda a happy birthday, handing over both a gift and card, delighted by her eager acceptance of both.

Jedda read the greeting, a smile playing on her lips; an expression that changed to a beam once she had opened the parcel and a pretty watch came into view. Expressing her thanks she threw her arms round her grandmother's neck, almost strangling her.

Zizzie felt gratified by the immense pleasure Jedda derived from her gift but begged her to desist.

"You're choking me, Jedda!" Nevertheless, she continued to smile.

Zizzie stubbed out her cigarette in the tall ashtray placed by the side of her chair, pressed a small button and the offending end disappeared with a flop through a small space. Rising from the comfort of her chair yet unwilling to desert the heat of the fire she stated, "I had better make a start on the breakfast."

Jedda jumped into the vacated place left by Zizzie's absence, snuggling down contentedly into the warmth left by her grandmother's recent presence.

"Be in my grave as quick," was Zizzie's parting shot.

Like a beacon, the smell of bacon and eggs sizzling soon drew Sandy and Sally to its source and, guided by its aroma, they ventured into the kitchen where they always breakfasted in a lazy Sunday fashion. Minus Jedda, they indulged in adult conversation, some including Alex, the other politics.

Jedda, eventually joined them, but for only cereal and toast. She hated eggs and bacon – they made her squeamish. Zizzie often complained that she would never put meat on her bones eating that kind of stuff. Chicken feed, she described it.

Sally, still sleepy, wished her daughter a happy birthday, whilst Sandy stroked his granddaughter's hair, congratulating her in the same fashion, both of them showering Jedda with kisses as they handed her cards and presents. A box of oil paints from Sandy. A beautiful doll from Sally. The doll had dark hair and joints that moved. Jedda named it Marina after the Duchess of Kent, more than pleased with her mother's gift.

"We've much to do. We have company coming tonight," said Zizzie, fussing in her usual fashion.

"It's not even lunchtime yet and you're acting like a worried hen, already," said Sally. "Calm down."

"The news doesn't sound very good," said Sandy, his ear half-cocked to the wireless.

"Oh, never mind the news," said Zizzie. "What will be will be! I'm more concerned with thinking up a menu."

"We said that in the last war and look where it got us then," continued Sandy, in a vexed fashion.

"What? How to think up a menu?" Zizzie pursed her lips, teasing him and at the same time spreading marmalade on crispy brown toast.

"No! Not thinking up a menu, you naughty woman! I meant you couldn't trust the Germans! And our own government even less if the last fiasco was anything to go by. Murderers! The lot of them! This fellow Hitler seems a bit of a tartar to me, you mark my words," said Sandy, exasperated by Zizzie's lack of interest.

Zizzie scraped a crumb up from the cloth and put it onto her plate, "Well, he seems very popular with his own people, that's more than you can say for those in power over here."

"I dare say you have a point there, my love; nevertheless, it's a worry. I don't want my son going off to war! Not if he's going to return with his lungs full of poisoned gas like I did during the last romp."

Quite unusually, for a change, Jedda ignored what she assumed was "grown up" talk, more concerned about her own well being and at how disappointed she would be if Alex did not come to her party. She so wished her father lived with them; however, it seemed to have a disastrous effect upon her mother whenever he stayed around for too long. She would notice how Sally's chin would set in that determined way of hers, especially when her grandparents implored Sally and Alex to get together. "For the child's sake" they'd say, meaning her, and she'd feel terrible for being the cause of such upheaval. Just the same, she wanted more than anything for Alex to attend her party. Her birthday wouldn't be the same without him; but on the other hand, all those endless rows made her feel dreadful and gave her a headache and made her feel guilt-ridden into the bargain, as though she, and she alone, were the cause of the break-up of her parents' marriage.

She always knew whenever they told her to go and play in the garden that it was some kind of ploy on their part; young she may be, silly she wasn't. "They" meant grandma and granddad, and they desired her absence because they were going to have one of their discussions, of which she herself was the subject in question.

Sally must have had a psychic blip for her next words were, "Go and play in the garden Jedda. Get some roses in your cheeks."

Outdoors the sky was a bright, cold blue with clouds, fluffy and silver-edged, scattered here and there.

Seated by a stream that ran merrily at the bottom of the garden she wistfully studied her grandparents' large, eight bed-roomed, rambling property built on the crest of a hill.

Lacks Brow had been purchased by Sandy previous to the Great War and he had brought Zizzie here as a bride, along with Sally who had been only a child at the time.

The house was situated two miles from any other properties – dwellings much smaller and all of a modern design. What had once been country had turned into suburb. Only the village green and small tracks of farmland remained.

She smiled happily at a seagull, obviously lost in flight, circling above before nosing its way home to more familiar shores.

Wandering round the garden was fine for a while, before it became too cold to linger. In spite of her being well wrapped up against the elements, the wind whipped wickedly through her coat and bonnet so viciously it even made her ears tingle.

A period spent in grandfather's shed entertained her for a while as she rooted eagerly amongst all the junk Sandy stored there. Zizzie saw no reason for such an accumulation. "We'll get rats!" was her constant complaint.

She scoured amongst Sandy's gadgets diligently until boredom set in and they ceased to interest her. Even seated on Sandy's cosy bamboo chair with its chintz cushions – the comfort from which she allowed herself to gaze through a small side window – eventually became monotonous. Not one to put up with any form of nonsense for long she made her way back to the house.

Her feet echoing on the tiles as she skirted the large kitchen, she crept up the thickly carpeted stairs silently to avoid adult confrontation.

Reconciled beyond her years to the behaviour of her elders, once inside the private domain of her bedroom she picked up a book, reading its contents with interest until her eyelids became heavy. She drifted towards sleep, the sound of voices below fading steadily away until, suddenly, as if conjured up by an unseen hand, strange faces appeared on the wallpaper. Terrifying faces that threatened at every turn. Dancing figures started to float about in the curtains before joining the others on the walls until, finally conquered by sleep, the room gradually disappeared as she drifted into the mists of slumber.

Still seething at what she considered her daughter's stupidity, Zizzie placed a ham on the chopping board; one cooked early that morning, now cooled and made easy to slice. Cutting it into an assembly of plate-sized portions, she went through the same motions with cold roast beef and chicken; after which she transferred them to individual platters, placing them in the larder before starting to prepare a winter salad of cold, mixed vegetables. To these she added her own recipe of mixed pickles and spices. Tasting the liquid with a small spoon she sighed, "Delicious" because she much preferred her own concoctions to those purchased in shops.

Before continuing with further preparations for the buffet, she made a brew of strong black coffee and seated herself down at the kitchen table. The coffee, strong, sweet and with a dash of rum, steadied her nerves. After a "tangle" as she always referred to it when rowing with Sally, it took a long time for her to really cool down. Worry over Jedda, whom she loved beyond all reason, resulted in extreme palpitations. Sandy was always saying, "Calm down you'll have a heart a attack," But what was she to do? She couldn't help but be anxious where her granddaughter was concerned.

Reaching for a small bowl she filled it with ingredients for a mayonnaise and, once whipped up and perfected to her satisfaction, she spooned the creamy liquid into a pretty glass bowl and placed it in the larder along with the rest of the preparations.

For sweet she had decided on a choice of fresh fruit, plus cream for those who wished it. This, to be followed by a selection of cheeses and accompanied by a nice bottle of Alsace Riesling – being both French and German, it offered the best of both worlds. Add a box of Neapolitans and the strong, steaming odour of coffee – well, how better to round of a meal? Zizzie had to admit that even she cheated at times. She kept a store cupboard full of tinned fruit, salmon, jams, corned beef, hams, and a selection of vegetables for emergencies.

Sandy often teased her about her hoarding saying that she had enough sugar to run a sweet factory and that the bathroom cabinet didn't need so many soaps and shampoos, nor did the kitchen that was overloaded with soap powders. He also added she had enough stock to keep a dozen Chinese laundries going for years.

"Never mind," she had argued. She remembered the last war. If another was on the horizon she did not want to be caught napping. Eking out meals compliments of Mr Austerity was not her forte! She did not care for a load of unwashed linen.

Sandy had given her a look of utter amazement, "You never do any laundry. You send it for the poor Chinese to cope with and let them get their hands all wrinkled."

"Well, they wouldn't be able to live otherwise, would they?" had been her tart reply, as if she were doing them a favour.

Jedda, unaware of how long she had slept, stirred lazily. Night or day, time eluded her. It was something she never questioned. She was young and had all the time in the world.

Now her mother was shaking her by the shoulder telling her, "You've been asleep for ages and you'd better take a bath." Sally also pointed out that she had placed her party dress on the back of a chair. "You've missed lunch, and so if you want a snack, it will have to be a small one. Our evening meal is at seven-thirty. We don't want your appetite spoiled, now do we?"

Jedda said she wasn't hungry and, making her way to the bathroom as instructed, once bathed, dressed herself ready for her party, praying all the time that Alex would soon arrive.

Zizzie's friend, Viner, would be there. To everyone's amusement she would sing, "Speak, speak, spoke to me Thora" with her odd habit of mixing her tenses. Apart from this, Jedda was delighted that uncle David and her beloved aunt Dora were also coming to her party.

From the hall below her mother's voice coolly informed her that Alex had arrived. Jedda caught her breath. He'd come then? And so soon! Happiness complete, regardless of her safety, she scaled the first flight of stairs, reached the second, sailed down the banister, reached the hall and ran swiftly to meet her father.

It was four o'clock and Alex had arrived ahead of the others, desiring an hour's privacy with his daughter. He stooped and picked her up as if she was a feather, stepped into the living room and walked over to the nearest chair. Holding her close, he settled her upon his knee and handed her a brightly adorned package.

Jedda opened it expectantly and from its wrapping retrieved a musical box of carved wood lined with silk. It had many different compartments in which to place jewellery. Alex inserted a key in its tiny lock and wound up the mechanism several times. A lovely melody sprang forth. The theme was the Viennese Waltz.

"It's lovely. What tune is it daddy?" Jedda held the box tightly.

"Tales from the Vienna Woods. It's by Strauss," said Alex.

"I prefer Liszt. Especially Lebensraum," said Sally, entering the living room followed by Sandy and Zizzie.

"Not a patch on Puccini, none of them," said Sandy, his eyes bright with interest.

Jedda slid down from Alex's knee and stood first on one foot, then the other, restlessly. "I like them all," she said, at her most tactful.

Zizzie's eyes misted over, "I love Richard Tauber best. Especially when he sings Franz Lehar or Victor Herbert tunes. Do you remember taking me to see him in the opera *Turandot* in Dresden? Nineteen-twenty-six, wasn't it Sandy?"

"Yes," said Sandy. "The man's a wonderful singer. In fact he's a wonder at everything. And dresses so smartly."

Zizzie gave him an agreeable smile. "I wore grey silk, remember, and that lovely pearl necklace you bought me. We had a lovely second honeymoon, didn't we?"

"Yes, but I don't think we'll be going to Germany in the near future dear, not as things are."

"But the people are lovely, aren't they Sandy?" Zizzie was feeling nostalgic.

Sandy frowned deeply. "Yes, except they go funny every twenty years, and feel the urge to polish up their cannons."

8

"I like Viner singing 'Speak, speak, spoke to me Thora' best," said Jedda insincerely, trying to add a little lightness to the conversation.

"Don't you dare say anything, Jedda," said Zizzie, noticing Jedda rolling about laughing. "We don't want her feelings hurt, even if our ears do."

"No, I won't," said, Jedda. "I love aunt Viner; it's just that her singing voice makes me laugh."

"I wish you'd tell her, Zizzie," said Sandy. "Especially the 'spoke' bit. I know she'll sing it again tonight after she's indulged herself in a few drinks. I won't be able to contain myself. Nor will the rest of us, for that matter."

"She won't notice if you smirk, anyway. After six gins she's well away. It's her drinking that bothers me more than her voice." Zizzie bit her bottom lip, concerned.

Aunt Dora was first to arrive, breezing in, flinging her fox fur onto the sofa with a dramatic gesture all the while complaining about the weather.

Jedda hated dead foxes, their snarling mouths, even more their false beaded eyes. If ever she met a live one she knew she'd detest it even more.

Uncle David arrived late; business had held him up, which was often the case and, though Dora was far from pleased, she did not choose to argue in company. Besides, there was Jedda's birthday to consider; also, the fact that there was enough tension between Alex and Sally without adding to an atmosphere so electric, which, as the night drew on, generally ignited even further.

Zizzie, displeased by David's late arrival shook her head knowingly, but kept her counsel. She loved her son – he was her only child by Sandy – but found him to be very thoughtless at times. Sally's own father existed only as a photograph in a silver frame placed upon the dresser, an eternally young hussar, whose body rested in far off India.

Jedda lounged comfortably in a large, green tub chair close to the sitting room fire munching peanuts, nuts which Zizzie had warned her against dropping behind the cushions. "Once they slide down," she declared, "they are difficult to retrieve." That had been her complaint.

Jedda felt a sudden urge for music and said to Sandy, whilst popping peanuts at the same time, "Can I listen to the wireless? Are there any songs, do you think?"

Sandy looked amused. "I don't know, old dear," he mocked. "We'll just have to try it and see."

He twiddled the knobs from station to station. "There you are," he said, as a selection from the Merry Widow seeped through. "Will that do you, madam?"

Jedda said that would do fine. Sandy left the room smiling, leaving her at peace with the world. Nodding happily, the firelight shining on her face and reflecting in her sloe-dark eyes she listened to the music, entranced by its harmony.

David came in, joined her by throwing a cushion on the floor close to her feet, stole some of her peanuts and began to tickle her unmercifully. He loved his little niece unreservedly and, as he teased her, gales of laughter were soon heard coming from the depths of the sitting room; a sound that soon carried to the ears of amused adults talking in the living room, making them smile and shrug their shoulders.

Aunt Viner floated in an hour later in a hail of endless chatter – mostly on her part – declaring that it was cold enough to frighten an Eskimo.

Upon hearing her wild acclaim, David decided it was time Jedda and he joined the rest of the guests.

Three other friends of Zizzie's arrived later, whose names all began with an "E" – Edna, Edie and Erica respectively. They threw down their pelts along with the others already lying on the sofa, which was gradually becoming camouflaged by a succession of discarded skins – furs of all shades, crawling all over like beasts on the rampage.

They were all too much for Jedda. She viewed them with fear and distaste. Soon, they began to cause havoc with her imagination, which caused her climb on Sandy's knee and snuggle close. She was especially fearful of Viner's black pelt. Terrified of its beady, pale glass eyes – hypnotic and vicious, as if ready to strike. It lay on top of the others, its head half across the sofa arm in a primed position, as if about to pounce and destroy her. She was so horrified she turned cold.

Sandy, noticing the terror reflected in her eyes, held his trembling granddaughter tightly, acting quickly to dispel her fears. "Move those blasted furs, Sally! They're frightening the child to death."

Sally came forward and swept the furs up in her arms. "She's just being silly. She'll have to learn to be braver," was all she said as she made her way out of the room in a huff.

Sandy gave her a parting shot, "Not with her imagination, she isn't. Anyway, she hasn't a cowardly bone in her body," he parried, holding Jedda close and comforting her. "Those nasty foxes have gone now! Your mother's taken them to her room. Just don't make the mistake of going in there."

Dora helped Zizzie to bring fare previously prepared that morning into the dining room. They placed the assortment of food on the long mahogany table and everyone chorused "How beautiful!"

It did look quite charming with the sparkling cut glass bowls, silver candlesticks, light flickering from tasteful white candles, and rose bowls filled with spring flowers.

Viner, for her part, ate huge amounts of vol-au-vents declaring they were whisper light and, "How did Zizzie manage it?"

The three "E's" followed suit, the food becoming more and more sparse as they went on the offensive. Erica was plump and red-haired and should have been advised to eat less. Edna was dark and Edie blonde, but both were slim, so greed on their part did not matter. They ate like the troupers they used to be when once they had kicked their heights as Tiller Girls along with Zizzie and Viner in their youthful days so long ago.

As if by magic, cooked meats, salad and sweets disappeared, consumed with much appreciation. Wine was quaffed with equal vigour and once the party reached its peak Viner sang "Thora" with gusto and her usual "speak and spoke", her voice pitched high as she became "La Viner", her fingers like long red talons twisting and tugging her amber beads.

When adult attention was elsewhere, Jedda purloined a bottle of wine from the sideboard and drank steadily, hidden away under the table away from prying eyes, a hideaway which allowed her to listen with interest to Zizzie and her theatre friends talk of the good times. The ones they had in Germany and Paris.

"...and wasn't it terrible the way Maisie died. Getting in trouble like that, poor girl!" A sound fact, but little understood by Jedda who was steadily becoming inebriated by the minute. Something that went unnoticed by her elders until she deserted her hiding place in favour of a dance – the effort of which caused her to fall over.

"Jedda looks tired," said Dora, innocently.

"Jedda's drunk," said Sandy, knowingly.

"Drunk! Goodness! How did she steal the wine without being noticed?" declared Sally, upon discovering the empty bottle. "Shall I send for a doctor? Or shall we run her up to the hospital?"

"No," David intervened. "I'll fix her. Give me some warm salt and water. That'll make her sick!"

"Seems cruel," said Dora.

"It works," said David.

"You should know," said Dora, sarcastically.

David ignored her, continuing with the job of washing out a crazy child's stomach, feeling afraid and guilty for allowing her such easy access to liquor. The rest of the company looked on in a worried fashion as he proceeded with the salt and water treatment, the ladies pulling faces and looking quite squeamish at times.

Morning proved David had accomplished what he'd set out to do. His cure had worked and the culprit, as Jedda's presence at breakfast showed, though if somewhat defeated, was not completely bowed.

The meal was a subdued affair. Viner, Dora, David and the three E's had stayed overnight and all looked the worse for wear, especially Viner, who kept complaining about a headache.

"You shouldn't drink so much then," said Sandy unsympathetically. "It's also fortunate we have so many bedrooms, because I for one, had no intention of sleeping on the floor last night."

"Tush!" said Zizzie. "Like as if! No one expects you to!"

Seated next to an equally listless Jedda, who lolled rather than sat, Sandy laughed as he analysed the situation.

"Serves you right! Learn young that hangovers aren't pleasant." He turned to Zizzie. "I was listening to the news after you'd all gone to bed last night. That man Hitler's full of crazy talk. Germany's rearming like mad. You'd have thought nineteen-eighteen would have been enough for them."

"And so close to Jedda's birthday, too!" declared Zizzie. "Nineteen-thirty-five doesn't look like being much of a year. The things governments get up to."

Sandy threw up his hands in exasperation. "What has Jedda's birthday got to do with it? Must I send Adolf a telegram and say, 'Leave it till next week. It's Jedda's birthday?'"

"I like Germans," piped up Viner unexpectedly.

"Oh, you're alive then?" said Sandy. "Welcome to the world."

The three E's giggled, but Viner ignored him, as always finding his feckless wit at her at her expense tedious at times. She continued, "I was in Germany last year. Very clean and most hospitable they are; absolutely love the English, but hate the French! Have never forgiven them for Versailles." She tugged at her beads in an exasperated manner. "Come to think of it, I'm not too keen on the French myself. Always eating horses and frogs' legs. Ugh!"

Sandy liked to torment her, "Different nations like different things – different people like different things. Different animals like different things – different women like different men. Diff..."

"Shut up!" said Zizzie, hitting his hand with a spoon, "and stop trying to aggravate poor Viner."

"It gets him nowhere," said Viner. "Not with me."

"I wouldn't want to get anywhere with you," quipped Sandy.

"I think he fancies you on the quiet," said Zizzie.

Not to be outdone, Sandy reached forward and placed Viner's hand in his. Fondling it! Kissing it! The three E's giggled again. Sandy gave them a look that suggested they were mental.

"There! I told you so," said Zizzie, laughing.

The three E's giggled even louder. Viner merely sniffed and withdrew her hand, outwardly shrugging her shoulders with displeasure, secretly pleased within.

David stretched his legs and reached for a cigarette. "Pass the matches, will you, Jedda?"

Jedda complied with his wishes.

"You shouldn't ask children to touch matches," said Dora. "Jimmy Smith got burned playing with matches."

"Jimmy Smith's daft to begin with. Jedda's sensible beyond her years." David lit a cigarette and inhaled appreciatively.

"She got drunk, didn't she?"

David did not answer.

"Take me for a walk will you please, uncle David," said Jedda, at her most beguiling.

"Later. In about an hour," said David. "When I've come round."

Jedda frowned thoughtfully? Come round? What was it about grown-ups that they always had to come round?

Viner toyed with her amber beads. "I really must be going. The weather doesn't look too good. Can I give you girls a lift?" The three E's giggled more outrageously and accepted her offer. Viner slid into her coat, wrapped her fox fur close to her throat and leaned down to kiss Jedda. The fur tickled Jedda's cheek as she did so and Jedda pulled away, quickly!

Viner was quick to apologise, "Sorry, Jedda! I forgot you hated fur." She smiled apologetically. "You had better dress up warm if you're going for a walk. And by the way, thank you for inviting me to your party. Most enjoyable." She turned and hugged Zizzie before leaving. Sandy hurried towards the kitchen to escape any repetition on his part. He quite liked her really, just not the fuss she made.

After lunch and an hour later than promised, David took Jedda for a walk. A faint powder of snow had just begun to fall – a fact that delighted her as it cascaded down in endless profusion covering her hat and coat. She prayed it would never stop, hoping it would become deep enough to build a snowman.

Once David and Jedda had taken their leave, the general conversation turned to Alex. Dora was the first to speak. "Alex looked in quite good health. And so handsome."

Sally stuck out her beautiful chin. "I'm thirty-six years old and know my own mind." She looked furious. "So it's no use going on about Alex and I ever getting together again. We won't! That's final!"

"I wasn't assuming you would. None of my business anyway," said Dora, somewhat huffy.

"Precisely!" Sally turned her nose up in a manner solely peculiar to herself. "I'm going for a long soak in the bath. Think I'll try out my new bath salts."

"Do just that," said Zizzie, "and while there, think about Jedda and the pain you're causing her."

"You don't understand. What's more, you never will! You just can't seem to get it into your heads, any of you. I no longer want Alex. And what's more – I don't think I ever did."

She flounced out of the room closing the door sharply behind her.

13

David and Jedda returned from their walk cold and exhausted, but spiritually and physically invigorated.

Zizzie, concerned as ever, fussed over them like a worried hen, plying them with hot drinks and biscuits declaring that dinner would be at seven, and that she did not want their appetites spoiling. She folded her arms in a determined fashion.

"Don't eat too much," she warned. "Viner will be coming later, too."

"We didn't have much lunch," complained Jedda.

"You won't die for once," Zizzie was adamant. "Anyway, Mrs Parker is due to clean the place up and I don't want it untidy."

"I don't know why you employ someone to clean up for you if you do it all beforehand," said Sandy.

"I don't," said Zizzie looking vexed. "Mrs Parker – Ruby – that is, gives the place a good bottoming."

"So it's Ruby now, is it?" Sandy mimicked her and made her lose her temper.

Zizzie stamped her foot. "So? I'm no snob! Ruby is very interesting to talk to."

"No need for tantrums," said Sandy amused. "But why pay for a lady to clean if you're going to do the cleaning yourself."

Zizzie made a glum face. "That's right, sneak off to bed at a moment's notice just because you're losing the argument."

"I wasn't aware that I was," said Sandy and made his way towards the stairs, laughing to himself.

Jedda, having eaten enough to satisfy youthful hunger, went into the sitting room to play cards with David. After a while, noticing the bored look on her face, David decided on a change of venue, placed a record on the turntable and took Dora in his arms. They danced away to the tune of "La Paloma" and Dora sang the words, "White dove though you fly ahead over one I love... white…"

Jedda thought it most romantic and that Dora and David made a handsome couple. Jedda decided to join in the dance and took to the floor in the abandoned fashion of a Pasha dancer – an action mimicked from having seen it performed at the pictures. Much to the amusement of David and Dora she became too giddy and tripped over.

"I see you still can't manage to dance even when you're sober?" said David.

Dora laughed and said, "Leave her alone, hasn't she been punished enough already after yesterday?"

Resting from the dance, Jedda began to wonder where her mother had disappeared to and when she inquired of aunt Dora she was given the answer that Sally had gone for a nice long bath and wasn't to be disturbed; nor was granddad who was having a catnap.

Seated on the window seat, Jedda gazed wistfully through the large mullion windows, beguiled by the falling snow. After a while, restless and in need of a new

14

form of distraction, she rose and walked over to Sandy's desk, first opening a drawer and then removing a magnifying glass.

Because Zizzie would not allow the French windows to be opened on cold days due to a loss of heat she was obliged to make her way to the kitchen and sit on the back stairs. Being close to the porch allowed her to snuggle down into a tartan rug poached from the sitting room sofa. Feeling warm and cosy she delighted in letting snowflakes settle on her hands while placing the magnifying glass across the palms of her hands to reveal the magic of each individual flake. All pretty, each with a fingerprint of its own. Just like real people.

With something new to entertain her she remained content for a while, the capricious ways of adults forgotten; nevertheless, not for long or before she had formed her own opinion of them. I'd hate to be an adult, she thought. Always making a fuss over things that did not matter: war and all that kind of thing. Being cosily wrapped up and involved with nature was by far the better.

Minus the three E's, Viner arrived at seven o'clock in the evening, bastioned against the icy weather in a fur coat that offered protection against the onslaught of the bitter weather; having shook herself like a naughty puppy, letting snow fly all over the hall. Once removed from her slim form, she gave the coat an extra shake before hanging it on the coat stand. Considerate. Away from Jedda's haunted eyes. She then floated into the living room to the sounds of Richard Tauber singing "Vienna Mine".

"It's freezing!" she declared whilst removing her scarf and gloves. "Cold enough to freeze an Eskimo."

She was wearing an ensemble of many colours that included a green skirt topped by a yellow jumper, her feet encased in a pair of bright red shoes.

Sandy studied her image in mock dismay. "You look like a set of traffic lights, Viner."

Viner retaliated, the tone of her voice acid with reproach. "What shall it be then? Stop, caution or go? Though I suppose its only men who go in for flashing."

"Very good," conceded Sandy. "Very good, indeed!"

"Oh, go back to bed, you monster," said Viner, laughing in spite of herself, before joining Zizzie in the far corner of the living room.

"For goodness sake! Don't tell him to go to bed! It took me all my time getting him up," said Zizzie. "Anyway, I must prepare the table for the evening meal."

Much to Zizzie's obvious amusement, Sandy swept Viner into his arms and started to waltz her round the living room.

"There! I told you he fancied you, Viner."

Viner plopped a large kiss on Sandy's cheek. "I know. No man can resist my sex appeal."

Sandy laughed, "So that's what they call it."

Viner slipped from his grasp. "Dance with your wife, Romeo."

15

Sandy gripped Zizzie's waist. "The pleasure's all mine." They danced together like young lovers and brought tears to Viner's eyes.

"I'll just get myself a drink," she said going towards the sideboard.

Sandy and Zizzie, each entranced by the other, failed to notice her knock back three gins.

More people were beginning to arrive so the ball was over.

Sandy smiled at Jedda during dinner and asked her to pass the potato salad, amused by her efforts as she tried to manoeuvre the large dish across the table. Zizzie restrained herself from helping knowing Jedda liked to be independent. Good or bad, it was also one of Sally's characteristics.

Alex, Jedda noticed, was looking far from happy. She loved her father so, but her mother, she knew, was content to keep them apart.

Viner ground her teeth together, conscious of the animosity between Alex and Sally, surprised by Alex's unexpected early arrival.

"I have a new song in my repertoire for tonight. Wings of a dove." She fiddled with one of many of the gold chains adorning her neck, exchanged for her usual amber beads.

Sandy smiled secretly to himself when beholding her many gold rings and large gypsy earrings thinking she resembled a walking Fort Knox. He winked at Zizzie, but she did not smile back. In spite of her placid nature, Viner was no fool, and Zizzie had no intention of losing her friendship on account of one of Sandy's frivolous observations.

David said, "Turn the wireless on. I want to know if Tokyo has rejected an alliance with Germany."

"They already have," said Sandy. "I heard it early on."

"Must we have politics round the dinner table?" complained Zizzie. "It drives me mad, apart from giving me indigestion." She reached for her tenth olive. "One can never have a meal in peace in this house."

Sandy said, "You must have the constitution of a horse the way you devour food. Why you don't put weight on, I'll never know."

The assembled company continued with their meal, keeping to topics in general.

"I'm going to see that new film that's just come out," said Dora by the way of light relief. "Jean Harlow's in it. It's called *Dinner at Eight*. I hear it's quite good – very amusing. As a matter of fact, would you like to come with me, Sally?"

Sally, about to devour a piece of cucumber, looked up from her salad. "I might. When are you going?" she said and forked a new potato onto her plate from the round, blue dish.

"Tuesday. I want David to come too, but he won't."

"I don't like Jean Harlow. Don't care for brassy blondes." David pulled a face.

"She's quite glamorous. They call her the Blonde Bombshell," said Dora.

David twisted one of Dora's glossy auburn curls round his fingers. "I prefer ginger nuts," he said.

Dora blushed, embarrassed. "I'm not a ginger nut. Just a few auburn highlights in my brown hair, that's all."

In the midst of unusually frivolous conversation Jedda observed Alex nervously, worried by his silence. All evening he had barely spoken, eaten little and when he did, it was slowly, almost methodically. He seemed preoccupied either with his food or thoughts in general. Jedda wasn't sure.

Everyone else seemed relaxed by comparison; even her mother seemed at ease for a change.

The meal finished, Zizzie rose from her chair saying, "If everyone's eaten enough, we'll clear the table. Are you sure you're all satisfied?" Everyone thanked her and said they were.

"Who's for cards?" she added.

Dora, intent as she was on playing the role of peacemaker, helped Zizzie with the chores. It was an act noticed by David, that and the complete absence of Sally's desire to assist in any form of domestic activity – a fact that annoyed him immensely

Jedda liked having aunt Dora around. Without the family blood or temperament, she was placid and unassuming by comparison to the firebrand mentality of the rest.

Once everything was neat and all to Zizzie's liking, wine and chocolates were placed on the sideboard for all to indulge in. Where the liquor was concerned – for adults only.

Dora, Viner, and Zizzie wiled away the time playing gin rummy round a small card table in the living room. David and Jedda were located in the sitting room, free to make as much noise as they chose, allowing the rest of the family to enjoy their pastimes in harmony: Alex and Sandy having departed to Sandy's small, cosy, book-lined study for a chat, Sally retired to her room to read a book – a deep intellectual book – about left wing activists.

The evening drew on and the whole company joined forces round the piano in the drawing room. Everyone had become more at ease after several drinks, even more so when Viner sang "Oh for the wings of a dove", bosoms heaving, taking her gold bullion for a ride.

Sandy was afraid he might choke on his own laughter, but one look from Zizzie's ice-blue eyes kept him in check. And all went well, until, having finished one song, Viner, immediately launched into her favourite, "Speak, speak, spoke to me Thora", whilst batting her eyelashes. Sandy, unable to contain his emotions any longer, was forced leave the room in case he shamed himself in front of Zizzie.

Once the music ceased Jedda glanced through the window, distracted from the rest of the company by gazing at the magic unfolding in the garden. The trees surrounding the front lawn had a fairytale air about them, their frozen branches resembling white arms imposing grace upon the world, bringing to mind *The Snow Queen*, one of her favourite fairytales. David noticed her change of mood and asked her if she was tired. She said, "No, but could you perhaps read me a story? *The Snow Queen*, maybe?"

David reached over to the bookcase, took down the desired book and began to read to her at a steady pace, only to find after twenty minutes had elapsed she had fallen asleep, stretched out on the window seat.

First, carrying Jedda upstairs, he slipped into Sally's bedroom to inform her about her daughter's falling asleep and then he made for Jedda's bedroom, Sally tripping unwillingly behind. She said Jedda was in too deep a sleep and to remove only her shoes and socks.

"She looks like angel, doesn't she, David? Wouldn't it be nice if she could stay young forever," said Sally.

David nodded in agreement. "Yes, it would indeed. No one can though, and you must come to terms with the fact." He frowned and crossed his arms in front of his chest. "You could do with growing up yourself, if only for Jedda's sake." He nodded his head in despair. "Stop dreaming about past events. You can't recapture what's gone before."

Sally shrugged her beautiful shoulders. "Well, Alex wants me to play happy families, something I can't do! I just can't do it!"

"What's finished, is finished," continued David, "You should never have married Alex. It wasn't fair on him when the only man you ever loved went to war and died." David looked bemused. "Though, had he returned, he would no doubt have changed. They all did. Live for now, not then."

Sally's chin began to jut out in a mulish fashion and David knew he was fighting a losing battle. "If only Alex had given me some encouragement," she said. "We could have been good friends." She straightened her back. "He's like the rest of you men, though. He wants me banished to the kitchen! Well, I refuse to concede!"

"It's a waste of time talking to you, Sally. You just won't give an inch." David shrugged his shoulders despairingly.

"If you and Alex have been discussing me during your little get-togethers, you've both been wasting your time. It's pointless him asking for you to intercede on his behalf. I don't want him any more, and that's it! Matter closed!"

Both descended the stairs, and when they reached the hall Viner was just leaving. Wrapped up in her furs, protection against the March winds, Viner refused Zizzie's offer to stay the night.

Zizzie was making a fuss, telling her to drive carefully, and that it was icy, and would she change her mind and please stay over.

Viner thanked her for her concern, but refused to be coaxed by her good friend. She marched towards her little car, revved up noisily, and sped off into the night.

Alex followed immediately after, but more quietly, glum-faced having had a few harsh words with Sally. Zizzie had waited by the door once Viner had left, and offered him the same advice in return. After kissing her cheek he had entered his car and driven smoothly away, not wishing to disturb his sleeping daughter.

Jedda, the object of the adult discussion and the main bone Alex's contention, slept innocently on. Unconscious of what destiny may hand out to her, locked in the kindness of sleep.

Once she had waved Alex off, Zizzie went indoors, feeling sad. Depressed by what she considered badly laid plans gone astray. Frowning, she let the bolts slip into place in the large front door, solid oak and firm enough to dispel a band of invaders. Relieved to note that the rest of the household had retired for the night she levered herself gently down into a large armchair, lighting her last cigarette of the day.

Chapter Two

Spring was far behind. May almost over. The daffodils had long since waned, but the tulips still soldiered on, bright goblets of colour drinking in the rain.

Whisked by a sturdy breeze, the blossoms of the flowering cherries, apples and plum trees fell like confetti in pink and white array.

"Reminiscent of the flower scene in *Madame Butterfly*," declared Sandy, shaking blossoms upon Jedda's head as she ran laughing around the garden. When she asked him to explain about *Madame Butterfly* he ushered her indoors, placed a record of the score on the turntable, unravelling the plot as he went along.

Jedda thought it sad and disliked Pinkerton very much for deserting Butterfly. "Why did he do it?"

"That's the way some people are," replied Sandy and played more music. He said he did not want her to grow up as an "ignoramus".

Jedda nodded in agreement, not having the slightest idea what an ignoramus was. Aware only that it was easier to play along. Just nod and accept the strange things adults said.

Zizzie and Dora, with Mrs Ruby Parker's help, resembled a spring breeze – full of gusto – turning the establishment upside down and leaving it smelling as sweet as a rose.

Secreted away from the house at the bottom of the garden - as far as possible from the human eye for Zizzie did not care for lines of washing hanging close to the house - an array of household linen floated in the breeze in the form of curtains, cushions and rugs; anything that was removable.

Light fittings and lamps came under the same scrutiny as did larger items of furniture, devil take the hind most.

Sandy groaned through all these chaste female actions. He shuddered as the ladies disinfected and sanitized the place; sterilizing every nook and cranny it was possible to reach. He thought his son a lucky man to be away on business and have "escaped from a fate worse than death" as he referred to it. "I'm surrounded by a bunch of heckling banshees," was his war cry and wished he'd joined David until it was all over – done with! "Women! Always wanting to be doing something! And God! How they did it! Like a gaggle of geese!" He went through the hall, fell over the cylinder Hoover and stubbed his toe in the bargain.

He was so outraged the whole household could hear him as he bellowed on about "the dratted thing!!!"

The females, as he liked to think of them, were in the kitchen grouped round the table, chattering and giggling at Sandy's mishap with the Hoover, indulging in coffee and crumpets oozing with butter.

"More coffee Ruby?" asked Zizzie

"Yes, please, Zizzie," replied Ruby. "It's most delicious, and these crumpets are rather more-ish, too"

"Well, there are plenty more," said Zizzie, pushing a plate full of steaming crumpets towards her.

"Is there anything for Jedda and me?" said Sandy, pursing his lips doubtfully upon entering the kitchen.

"Oh, don't be such a baby and stop feeling sorry for yourself. After all, we're the ones doing all the work. Surely you can toast a few crumpets for yourself and Jedda," she declared, pouring more coffee and patting her mouth with a napkin.

After coffee break the ladies transported themselves upstairs to make a concerted attack on the bedrooms. Dora fluffed up the eiderdown on Zizzie's bed and said, "What time will Sally be back?"

Zizzie shook out one of her many silk shawls and wrapped them in tissue paper. "I don't know, to be precise. Once she attends these Labour Party meetings she's so keen on, one never knows."

She folded another shawl. "I think I'll put these all away in a trunk. I don't wear them much any more."

Dora agreed, pliant as always in the presence of her mother-in-law. She loved Zizzie and knew her emotions were returned. She also thought it sad that Sally did not treat Zizzie in the same loving fashion as she herself did, thinking her sister-in-law stubborn and extremely difficult at times.

Zizzie sighed as if reading Dora's mind. "I do wish Sally would give over with this left-wing business."

Dora smiled in a conciliatory fashion. "She'll grow out of it," she said, as if speaking about a wayward teenager rather than a grown woman. "She may have a left-wing attitude, but she definitely has a capitalist stomach and their way of dressing up, too."

Zizzie laughed, "You can say that again. Can you imagine Sally digging in the fields with the peasants... Why! She won't even wash a pot!"

Chapter Three

The end of June was swift. "As swift as a boat flying over the rapids," Zizzie had declared, as always.

Jedda knew this, because Zizzie was always saying, "Doesn't time fly!" and she'd looked "fly" up in the dictionary and found it expressed there in no uncertain terms. Anyway, she liked words. Any words, and the more complicated, the better. But then again, Sandy had warned her not to be too pretentious and that the words in the Bible were beautiful ONLY because of their simplicity. She had tried to read the Bible but it was all about people getting and begetting, which she didn't understand, and when she asked the grownups about it they said they didn't understand either, which was odd. She thought grownups knew about everything because they were always saying they knew best.

Sandy, when she had asked for an explanation of "getting and begetting" had told her to ignore that part of the Bible and read the Psalms. These she had found to be poetic. She had also read the Songs of Solomon, which she had thought beautiful, but difficult to understand also. One of her school friends had giggled and thought it rude. All about bosoms and breasts and things and they'd both giggled until Sandy explained to her it was Christ's love of the Church and quite poetic if read in the right context. Then she had had to look "context" up in the dictionary because she hadn't known what that meant, either.

Basically, it was a pleasant time for all the family, and in a sense, euphoric. The depression had not affected them as badly as some. True, Sandy had been forced to depose of much of the property handed down from his parents, but most of the proceeds from the sale he had invested wisely. A good rate of interest allowed the family to live comfortably, if not with the same luxury of previous years. On the whole, Sandy had doubts about the future, and suspected that if the government didn't keep on their toes, that the dark clouds of war were steadily gathering momentum. In the present climate though, he was aware that, as things stood for them financially, this was not their summer of discontent, nor would it be their winter.

Viner had been invited for afternoon tea. This made very little difference; she often arrived unannounced. The weather was extremely warm and Sandy was wearing a very light fawn suit with a matching, wide brimmed hat.

Viner commented on his appearance declaring, "You look like the godfather, Al Capone. I'm none too keen at being asked to tea, certainly not if 'Al' here had a hand in arranging it. That's the trouble with taking tea with the Mafia – is it safe to drink, Zizzie?"

"You two hate one another so much, I'm sure you must be in love!" said Zizzie, laughing and reaching for an olive and hurting her tooth on a stone. "That's the trouble with black ones," she said rubbing her lips. "Green ones are so much easier to manage." Then as an afterthought, "You do look rather Italian though, dear. Why people nickname you Sandy, I have no idea. You're slim, six-foot tall, and your hair was black before the grey crept in," she continued, smiling. "I know your parents were Scots, but you were born here in dear old England, just like me... Oh, I do so love to be English and I feel so sorry for the rest of the world for being otherwise."

"Now you've stopped for breath at last, all I can say is it's a matter of opinion," said Sandy wryly.

"Well, I don't suppose being a Scot is too bad. If I weren't fortunate enough to be English, I suppose I'd choose to be a Scot."

"I'm sure the Scottish nation must be in deep mourning regarding that particular issue. I can hear them all discussing it in the Highlands. 'Do you know brethren; Sandy's Zizzie is not a Scot. For shame how can we bear it? How can our Nation hold up its head without such a magnificent creature consenting to be one of us'." Sandy's face was a picture of mirth. "Anyway, you married me as a favour to them, didn't you? In future all the Celtic nations will celebrate it – call it St Zizzie's day!"

Zizzie straightened her back, feathers ruffled, "There's no need to be facetious, Sandy."

"And there's no need for you to be so pompous," was his tart reply.

Jedda was seated at the garden table, an eye on the parasol, fascinated when it swayed as the breeze caught it, an ear cocked towards adult conversation. She loved listening to her elders talk. It was an education in itself. As in all things, it was life – good or bad. It was what formed people and created writers and she, though unaware of it, was one of them – a complete observer.

Sandy placed a record on the gramophone, one he had brought out onto the veranda and extracts from La Boheme echoed forth, enchanting to the ear, uplifting to the soul.

Sandy had formed Jedda's ideas about music for all time. Her taste would never change. Nor would her love of reading, because she had been so well instructed by David. First Hans Anderson, and the Brothers Grimm, then Dumas, Baroness Orczy and Jeffery Farnol which in time would set her on the road to Shakespeare, Dickens, Thackery, and the Brontes. Also many more works of genius, at first, not always understood, but evolved in childhood and read in a time of quiet promise.

"Is daddy coming today?" she asked Zizzie wisely, noting Sally's absence.

"I don't know," said Zizzie, aware of Jedda's worried frown. "I shouldn't bank on it." She gave her hand a squeeze.

"What about uncle David and aunt Dora?" Jedda persisted.

"Uncle David is busy, so I doubt it. Not all people are retired. Not like grandfather and me. Perhaps they'll call at the weekend." She began to twist her rings round her fingers, something she did when perplexed. She wondered at times why life was so complicated, and in such an unnecessary fashion. If people behaved in a more exemplary way life would be so much easier, not leave her having to make excuses to vulnerable children.

Jedda moved away from the table and lay down on the three-cushioned garden seat. She sank into its plush upholstery comfortably, lulled by its intermittent swinging and Puccini's soulful music, at the same time studying Zizzie and Viner from the corner of her eye. It was getting unbearably hot and the two of them looked as it they were about to melt. She surmised that someday she too would grow old, and though she loved them both dearly, she was in a sense relieved she was only yet seven.

Sandy, having jumped into his car and ridden down to the little hut situated in the park down the lane had returned loaded down with ice creams, in his possession a large lump of ice, charmed out of the lady who owned the hut. First, having crushed the ice, he added it to the ginger beer and a large jug of Zizzie's freshly made lemonade ready for Zizzie to pour once the liquid had cooled.

Jedda stirred among the cushions and studied the faces in the flowered awning above her head. Some appeared pretty, some ugly, almost sinister; strange faces that appeared without warning in the form of gargoyles and other unnerving creatures. Faces that made her tremble and fired her imagination in a most unpleasant fashion. She blinked her eyes to make them go away, only to find they returned to haunt her once they were fully opened. She had long come to the conclusion that, no matter where, if she lay too long and stared at objects, they invariably took on a life of their own; features that materialised in the most unlikely places. Even if she lay on Zizzie's bed with its soft satin quilt they would appear without notice. Grinning faces, twisted with evil in the flowers of her grandmother's hats – hats that hung in profusion from a selection of pegs; or in shawls, Spanish or otherwise – sometimes so grotesque, that she almost felt forced to scream, but she never did. It would seem foolish somehow. She had long suspected adults wouldn't understand – certainly not her mother! She always shook a finger at her and said it was her imagination. Her grandparents were kind about it and promised her she would grow out of it. How she wished she could hurry up and do so, then she could sleep without fear. Fear of evil, and fear of being laughed at!

Jedda heard the clink of ice against glass as Zizzie poured lemonade from a large cut-glass jug, combined with the rustle of her grandmother's silk dress as she came towards her in the breeze. A glass of lemonade in one hand, treat enough to cool anyone and a bowl of ice cream in the other.

She thanked her grandmother and drank the lemonade slowly, letting it slide down her throat, relishing its sharp lemon taste, whilst retaining a piece of ice in her mouth for several seconds before letting it slip back into the glass.

From the round wicker table where she was seated, Zizzie remonstrated her severely. "Don't do that Jedda, it's rude. Very, very, rude! Do be more polite!"

She desisted in an instant. Grandmother was always correcting her, amending her behaviour immediately. "Sit down lightly Jedda," she would caution her. "Float down, you're not an elephant," and "Sit up straight," and "Don't fiddle." She always had to watch her posture. "You can tell a lady by the way she sits and stands," her grandmother would say. Permission to leave the table was always required of her and her table manners severely checked. "Only because I love you," Zizzie would say. "You'll thank me one day."

She ate slowly, savouring each small mouthful of ice cream. It was sweet, enjoyable to the senses. If the presence of Alex, David and Dora were inconceivable, ice cream would have to do.

The garden was dressed at its best in high summer. On the north side, where the lawn dipped into the shade, camellias were beginning to fade, being replaced by a succession of different shrubs – deciduous, white as spring brides, they now bloomed in the summer haze side by side with hydrangeas – pink, purple, blue, pale pink and even deeper pink. Whilst on the south side, beneath the beeches, roses – a myriad of colours – sided friendly with the deep blue of the ceanothus, which slept next to the tea myrtle.

The sweet scent of lavender, mixed with roses, and the ever-vigorous honey suckle, rode on the breeze and assailed her nostrils. She basked in its fragrance peacefully, until her tranquillity was sharply interrupted by the sudden appearance of a face, whose features formed foxy-evil, stared threateningly back at her from the middle of the ceanothos bush. Baleful blue eyes gleamed pale through the colour of the flowers causing her to freeze, becoming incapable of any form of movement until, at last, her grandmother's voice was asking her did she want any more lemonade, and, quick as a flash, the animal disappeared, non-existent, as if it had never been there.

She ran quickly to her grandmother, who had just that very second vacated a wicker chair in preference for the sofa. She lay down beside her and rested her head on the soft upholstery of Zizzie's shoulder. Zizzie sensed something was wrong, but felt unable to communicate.

Sandy did. "Come and sit by me, Jedda." He patted his chair and said to Zizzie, "I think she's been seeing faces again."

25

Grandfather was so clever, seemed to sense her every need. She left Zizzie's side and climbed onto his lap, safe again. That horrid fox was bound to be afraid of Sandy – everyone else was.

Viner raised her arms above her head and said she wished it were cooler and could Sandy put another record on. He obliged and placed Richard Tauber's version of *Girls Were Made to Love and Kiss* grinning to himself as he did so. Half way through the melody Viner rose to go indoors and he chased her up the garden steps, catching her by the waist, synchronising with Richard Tauber, "Girls were made to love and kiss... and who am I to interfere with this?"

"I don't know," said Viner, slapping him playfully on the cheek. "As long as you don't interfere with me."

"Be careful what you say, you two. There's a child present!" declared Zizzie.

"She doesn't understand, Zizzie. I wouldn't have said it otherwise," said Sandy.

Jedda was too busy laughing at their antics to care one way or another.

Sally returned from a meeting at the Labour Party's headquarters just after three o'clock. She pointedly ignored Sandy's protestations at her having been absent on such a fine day; also, for neglecting her daughter's needs.

After Sally's return, Alex arrived half-an-hour later. David, accompanied by Dora, arrived at five-thirty and Jedda said goodbye to boredom whilst Zizzie refused to cook saying that it was too hot and they would eat at seven. A salad and shellfish would have to do, and couldn't Sandy try and get one of those icebox things they have in the American pictures. That way she could keep the food fresh without begging ice from the woman at the hut.

Zizzie watched David remove a box gramophone from the boot of his car and told him how much she admired it. She liked anything new and modern. David placed the contraption on the smaller of the two tables that stood on the terrace, placed a Bing Crosby record on the turntable, wound it up by its small handle and led Dora towards the wide square of concrete beside the lawn. Once the strains of "where the blue of the night meets the gold of the day" echoed out, they began to sway, holding each other lovingly.

Jedda wished with all her heart that Sally and Alex would act in the same tender fashion; but she knew an icy stare from Sally's blue eyes, so like Zizzie's, would have stopped such a request before she had ventured half way through her sentence.

Alex, the main object of her thoughts, was standing at the end of the terrace, his back to everyone; like a sailor looking out to sea and, by the set of his shoulders, expecting stormy weather. She turned her attention to her mother, whose rigid spine was also far from friendly, her eyes gazing coolly through the dining room window. Jedda leaned back against the upholstery and visualised Sally and Alex coming together in some romantic Waltz such as the Merry Widow. It became too much and she asked Zizzie if she could go to the park. Zizzie argued it was too far away, and then relented with, "Just for an hour then."

The old men were playing bowls when she arrived at the park. She climbed up a tree close to the green and watched them at play, amused by the sunlight reflected on the men's bald heads; intermittently changing her glance from bald men to flowers growing in profusion in the beds below, dahlias and asters being amongst her favourites due to their brilliant colours, especially the bee haunted dahlias with their cabbage-shaped, fleshy leaves.

In the distance, unknown to her, a school friend named Marjorie was watching her, puzzled by the intensity of Jedda's gaze; the way she studied things was sometimes beyond Marjorie's comprehension.

"Why do you stare at things so much?" she would inquire of Jedda, knowing full well she would never explain in any way that made sense.

Jedda found such questions annoying. It was not that she did not want to give an explanation; she was completely unaware of why she scrutinised things. Sandy would often remark, "Jedda's dreaming again."

Her teachers often took note of it. "Do concentrate, Jedda," they would say. Jedda always answered that she was, as far as she could tell.

Jedda climbed down the tree, lightly and at high speed. Marjorie, eyes wide, was mystified by the way Jedda changed one mood for another, altering from dreamer to tomboy in seconds as she started across the grass balanced on her hands only to land gracefully into the splits. She could twist her body in such a procession of strange angles and to an observer it was quite unbelievable. Marjorie wondered if she ever gave up, became tired, aware that, if this were true, she had never noticed it. If her body wasn't moving, her mouth was – or her imagination. She also sensed that Jedda was unhappy, but never said as much. She liked her friend too dearly to impinge on her inner most thoughts and feelings.

They went on the swings, the helter-skelter being forbidden territory. Jedda had almost fallen off it once and Sandy had found it unbearable. It was now strictly out of bounds.

With his little box perched on the front of his three-wheeler bike, the ice cream man sailed through the park. They each bought a snow fruit, a delicious, three-cornered concoction, which they devoured slowly, enjoying its sharp flavour.

"I have to leave now," said Jedda. "My hour's up. Grandma will shout if I am late."

Marjorie agreed, "It's too hot for play, anyway." She pushed her hair back from a damp forehead. "We're only having salad. My mum says it's too hot for cooking."

"You like salad. You know you do. You're always saying, 'I hope its salad for dinner.'" She tugged Marjorie's hair playfully and ran off mad as a hatter through the park gates with Marjorie close behind her, giggling.

Upon arrival home and reaching the garden path, still running, Jedda made for the terrace, landing on Alex's knee in a heap.

Zizzie, red faced and uncomfortably hot, vowed it was too hot for chasing about and asked why Sally didn't keep Jedda in check once in a while.

She ran her fingers through her hair - the heat was getting to her, she said, and she wished she lived in Norway.

Alex remained cool, avoiding a row. Getting in Sally's bad books was not his idea of heaven. Anyway, he wanted to take Jedda to see his mother in Chester next week, and had no wish to rock the boat more than necessary.

Once they all settled down to an evening meal, the sun was still strong. A slight breeze fanned their cheeks, helping the situation a little.

" I love eating out," said Viner.

"So do I," said Sandy, being his most amusing self. "I just love midge butties."

Viner laughed and flipped him with her napkin. "I hate you," she said.

Sandy's dark eyes twinkled. " I bet you say that to all the boys."

"Does anyone want any more salad?" said Zizzie. "There's lobster, as well. By the way, I haven't seen much of your new boyfriend, Viner. When are you bringing him round to see us?"

"Oh, quite soon. Rodger will be more than pleased to meet you all, I'm sure." She wafted her napkin across her cheek. "As I've already told you, he has a beautiful voice and will sing for us after dinner."

Sally had gone to a Socialist meeting and Viner, David, Dora, and Alex had returned to their respective homes. Sandy, Zizzie and Jedda spent the rest of the evening seated on the terrace watching the evening sun go down. Sandy and Zizzie held hands while Jedda sat on a pouffe and rested her head on Sandy's knee. Richard Tauber sang, "When we were young one day" and Zizzie and Sandy were in a romantic, nostalgic mood. They kept smiling at one another, and Jedda felt peaceful, content as Sandy stroked her hair from time to time, and she wished that things could be like this forever.

Viner, as good as her word, visited them a week later. One arm was tucked proudly under that of her latest beau, Rodger. "This, everyone, is Rodger," she said imperiously.

Sandy was less than delighted, referring to him as a "pompous oaf", or "Rodger – Viner's latest lodger" more than pleased when the evening eventually drew to its boring close.

Rodger went through a whole repertoire of songs "in a voice like crushed glass" was Sandy's estimation. Jedda quite enjoyed the presence of a new guest;

it helped with the deteriorating state of her parents' marriage. She noted the rest of the audience were too polite to comment.

Zizzie wished the weather would break. It was so heavy, she could hardly breathe, but Jedda was in her element playing in the sun. David declared everyone looked so brown they resembled Spaniards instead of English people.

Sally said she hoped he didn't mean Franco's Spaniards and everyone started to look depressed. Jedda went in the garden in case they started talking politics again.

The garden was filled with the smell of roses, lovingly planted by Sandy, and of honeysuckle, spreading recklessly, perfuming the evening air. Jedda was filled with a sense of absolute joy and wanted to cry at the beauty of it all. David, watching her from the window, smiled when a butterfly landed on her shoulder. From the open French windows the music of Strauss echoed across the terrace, reached her ears in the garden below, and completed her fantasy, until Rodger decided to sing again, which made her laugh.

Autumn arrived, turning the leaves of the beeches from green to gold. Colours, which blended with the flame of the Japanese maples. Jedda found the fallen leaves to be a crispy delight beneath the feet, trampling on them for good measure. Sandy kept trying to sweep the elusive remains into mounds for burning on the fire alight at the end of the garden, but the wind kept blocking his efforts.

It was Saturday and guests would be arriving for dinner at seven. Zizzie was making it a party affair.

Viner was bringing her Rodger along again. "My latest," as she referred to him. She had had a procession of them across the years, but none of them long-lasting.

Sandy, as usual, was less than pleased because everything Roger owned, said, or did, was either bigger or better than anyone else's. He had so many gold teeth Sandy declared he must sleep with his head in the safe.

"Your hollyhocks are nice, Sandy," Roger would say, much to Sandy's annoyance, "but they are not as big as mine." Also he would place an arm round Sandy's shoulder "buddy, buddy" fashion in a familiar way that irritated Sandy even more.

Sandy would squirm to one side declaring he must water his plants, or make up some excuse or other. "Where does Viner find them?" he would say to Zizzie when once Rodger and Viner had departed.

Viner had been married once, until her husband Henry had run off with a waitress. It was a well-known fact the anger she had felt was not so much that Henry had deserted her, but that the woman who had replaced her in Henry's affections had been one who waited on tables.

Sandy had declared, "What's wrong with being a waitress? It's an honest living. You were only a Tiller Girl, anyway."

Zizzie had stormed back at him, "Tiller Girls are the best! The crème de la crème of dancers."

"They're mere stage folk," he had argued. "At least when waitresses are out of work, they are honest about it. What do Tiller girls say? 'I'm resting darling' instead of 'There's nothing on offer,' or 'I'm past it!'"

Zizzie did not speak to him for weeks. Nor did she like it when Sandy said, "Henry, having worked for the Co-op, must have liked sharing his divi."

Viner arrived in the late afternoon accompanied by Roger, who informed Sandy that he had a positively stunning new compost bin, and wouldn't it be better if he, Sandy, swept the leaves into little bundles first.

As this is what Sandy had been trying to do all afternoon, Jedda had a problem trying not to laugh out loud at the wild, furious expression on her grandfather's face.

Dinner was a sumptuous affair and once the family, guests included, had dined on Zizzie's delightful meal of fillet steak in a light pastry, followed by chocolate cream pudding and a selection of cheeses, everyone relaxed; contented as kittens nestling in a cat's bosom. The adults sat around in little groups, the ladies separate from the men.

Dora and Sally discussed topics in general amidst sips of wine. All about the impending doom they feared was about to engulf the world. Jedda sat and listened intently as they addressed the fact that Jewish people in Germany were now completely banned from the taking part in any form of special activity, and that marrying outside of their race was condemned. Snuggled up on her favourite place – the window seat – she viewed the rain as it began to fall. She was in a pensive mood, conscious she had not seen her father for a long time. Gazing across at her mother's animated face she wished she would give her a cuddle, worry more about her instead of the world.

To get closer to Sally she walked over to the sofa and lay down, resting her head on the arm, trying to draw attention to herself. She soon did, but not for the reason she had ventured there. Then it happened! An awful something that chilled her very being; something soft, yet evil, caressed her face. It was not so much the feel of it once she had turned her head to inspect it, but more about how it stared back at her with cold pale orbs. The foxes were awful, all of them...but none so fearful as the black one, the one with the ice blue eyes. For only the briefest of seconds the persona became human, then just as quickly, changed, but not before she had sensed its purpose – to attack her! Destroy her!

Noticing the whiteness of Jedda's face, Sandy was furious.

Thinking Jedda was about to have a fit she had turned so pale, he raced across the room and picked her up, glaring at the company in general. "I've told you before," he said angrily, pulling Jedda onto his knee. "Zizzie! Zizzie! Zizzie! If people must wear furs, for goodness sake tell them to take them and hang them somewhere else. In a butcher's shop, perhaps!"

"Jedda gets upset too easily," Sally remonstrated. "It makes no sense."

"You must certainly be lacking in it if you don't know terror when you see it!" declared Sandy, holding Jedda even closer

Jedda squeezed his neck tightly. "It was the black one! It had a man's face!"

Sandy knew he had to make her stand up to her fear and picking up the red fox, holding it around the neck and pretending to choke it, he said, "There, its dead now."

Jedda even smiled slightly, appreciating his efforts, until he picked up the black one and tried to reason with her. She stiffened, so much so, that he gave up trying to placate her, at the same time suggesting to Viner that she did not bring the dratted thing anymore.

Viner nodded in agreement.

As usual, once dinner was over, and everything ship shape, they gathered in the drawing room for a singsong round the piano, a usual autumn and winter pursuit, the cold keeping them all indoors. Zizzie had asked Sandy to build up the fire and was busy offering everyone hot punch, with the exception of Jedda – a lesson learned from her granddaughter's recent encounter with liquor.

Sally played List's Lebensraum first then Roses of Picardy and everyone joined in the singing.

Roger was next to perform, stating he would sing Maud and saying in a most pompous fashion to the gathered company, "The ladies at the Women's Institute found my rendering of Maud most unbelievable."

Sandy said sarcastically, "I don't doubt it."

Roger answered by what he assumed to be a compliment, with a flash of gold teeth. He was so thick- skinned; even Zizzie was forced to smile.

"Come into the garden Maud…" he trilled away, "and the Woodbine spices are wafted abroad..."

"I could just enjoy a good Woodbine," whispered Sandy, aside to Zizzie.

She kicked his foot giving him an ice-blue stare for good measure, knowing too well he smoked another brand.

Sandy offered his rendering of The Road to Mandalay. He would have preferred to sing Your Tiny Hand is Frozen but it was quite unsuitable for his baritone voice.

Dora and David performed a pleasing duet of Only a Rose and Viner ended with a grand finale singing her usual, "Speak, Speak, Spoke to me Thora," before everyone moved into separate little groups. Each individual spent the evening discussing their favourite topic – arguing, as was their want – whilst Jedda and David sat on the window seat and played cards. Happily, while the autumn leaves swirled past the window.

31

December brought a cold spell and with it, a virus from which Sandy's chest never recovered. A Christmas of plenty made sad by a future unsure. In spite of his illness, Sandy was becoming very concerned regarding world events. In Germany, Jewish doctors had been forced to resign from private practice. Mussolini had already invaded Abyssinia – the Japanese, Peking. As for the Germans – the French had been right – the power to arm should never have been allowed in Germany. They were the reason for his dying. Mustard gas had invaded his lungs during his time with the Ambulance Corp in nineteen-seventeen. He had been attending the wounded in the trenches when it had struck him down, weakened his lungs beyond repair.

He was no fool in spite of Doctor Marsh's assurances to the contrary, that all would be fine. Sandy was as positive as the day was long that he was heading for his maker. It would all be over for him, he told himself; but what of those left behind? Especially Jedda. She was his greatest worry. Though not his flesh and blood, she might as well have been, he absolutely adored her.

Christmas was spent quietly. Jedda stayed with Dora for most of the festivities, though they all gathered at Zizzie's for Christmas dinner. To Jedda's surprise everyone behaved in a most civilized fashion, such politeness on her family's part left her feeling perturbed. And, when Viner didn't even try to sing, she became even more concerned, especially when the only carols to be heard came from the wireless.

She played in the garden hoping for snow, yet, in spite of bitter weather, none arrived. Still, a distinct heaviness hung around the sky, and also around the house. Granddad kept to his room and a fire was constantly kept alive, mainly to stop any further complications. The doctor visited constantly, it was so serious. Jedda was only allowed minutes with him in case it tired him too much.

Sandy died in January, along with King George V and Rudyard Kipling, the family weeping uncontrollably as they stood around the bed together. Zizzie held his hand in his final moments and his last words were, "I love you Zizzie."

In the days that followed the house dwelt in complete darkness. No blind was drawn back and a strange smell pervaded the atmosphere. Jedda sensed it was flowers! Not the delicate perfume of spring lilacs or summer roses, but the heavy scent of lilies and chrysanthemums.

The day of the funeral arrived along with a light sprinkling of snow. On the far side of the room, placed against a wall – amidst what appeared to be the whole of a florists shop – waited a cross of flowers from Zizzie: to be placed on Sandy's coffin when the time came.

Zizzie, Sally, Dora and Viner lounged around red-eyed, each in different poses of grief. Jedda sat dried-eyed in what appeared to her to be an unreal situation.

Jedda had stayed with Dora during the final days of Sandy's illness.

"Granddad is seriously ill," Dora had informed her: then the news came of Sandy's death and this morning she had arrived at Zizzie's dressed in a black reefer coat, wide-brimmed black hat and black patent shoes.

To complete the ritual, uncle David lifted her up to kiss Sandy a last farewell; an experience of complete shock – like kissing a very cold stone. Stranger even than that, instead of his usual cardigan he was dressed in a white suit and satin shirt. David did not like Sandy's ensemble either and he said as much to Zizzie, who was standing across from him on the other side of the coffin.

David had shaken his head in complete denial when confronted with his father's burial suit. "Christ mum! He looks like a bloody band leader!"

"Don't use language like that in front of your father," cried Zizzie imploring David to be more respectful. "Anyway, it isn't my fault. I left the arrangements to the undertaker."

"The consequences of which dad's gone to his rest looking like the head waiter at the Savoy," said David. Why the Savoy and not another hotel puzzled those gathered there.

Jedda was more concerned with Sandy's moustache, which, according to where the smoke had tinged it, had once been varying shades of brown. It was now a perfect shade of white.

Everyone was shocked when Viner suddenly rushed forward and threw herself on Sandy's coffin, sobbing and moaning, resembling an Indian widow about to be put to the torch with a dead spouse.

Zizzie stood trance-like for several seconds before going up to her beloved friend, leading her gently away, thinking to herself, "Poor Sandy. Even in death there was no peace. What would he have thought of such a carry on? Viner! Of all people, making a fuss like that?"

Jedda didn't quite understand peoples' reactions with regard to death or indeed its trappings. She sat silently, white-faced, immersed in her own thoughts, feeling detached from it all. She did not like death nor could she relate to it. It was a mysterious, yet frightening thing that made grownups sob uncontrollably. She did not quite understand why this should be. She wanted to ask why, but was unsure of what their response might be. Grownups were strange creatures.

She enjoyed the ride to the church because she loved big cars. A fact that made up her mind she would never be poor. Not if she could help it. In spite of an excess of imagination and sensitivity she had not inherited her mother's desire to save the world. She had a practical side to her nature and would be of the same persuasion throughout the whole of her life. Sandy controlled her mind to this extent and Sally would never be able to alter his early teachings.

The scent of flowers filled the church with a heady perfume, an array of blossoms offering a prayer to God's House.

33

Jedda, seated between Zizzie and Dora, viewed it all with interest. The candles as they flickered were "symbolic of death" she'd often heard Zizzie say. So this is what her grandmother must have meant? So this was death? The figures in the stained glass windows of the High Church looked down in solemn procession. Heavenly saints and angels accompanied by a dirge coming from the organ. To her mind they didn't seem to relate to Sandy's laughing love of life. The earth! The here! The now!

The minister started to tell everyone that grandfather was with God and the angels. This brought a lump to her throat that hadn't been there before. She started to sob, uncontrollably the way grownups do. Zizzie grasped her hand but it did not help. She could feel herself becoming angrier and angrier for a reason she could not understand. She only knew she didn't want grandfather to go to heaven and kicked the back of the pew. It made a thumping sound and people began to stare. Zizzie's cold, sideward expression hinted she had better behave and she quietened down as always when given that certain "look" by her grandmother.

The minister continued with the service until it all became too tedious and she started to swing her legs. Zizzie checked her once more, squeezing her knee and Viner sang "Abide with me," instead of "Speak to me Thora" as a last salute to Sandy.

They left the church, a silent procession behind the coffin. David was one of the pallbearers. Zizzie, Jedda and Sally walked close behind followed by two mournful ladies, Dora and Viner, joined by a mixture of close and distant relations and friends adding to the grieving assembly. Alex had arrived from Chester with his mother. Jedda had a fondness for her grandmother Markham, and wished she could see her more often. Not having granddad around was going to be hard and an extra ally would always help; tears filled her eyes at the very thought of life without him.

Gathered around the graveside, the mourners stood shivering and weeping in turn as a faint powder of snow traced their garments, bringing light relief to their black garments. A sharp wind threatened to turn the weather into a blizzard and bit into the bones of those standing there. The vicar's black cassock blew about in the wind, untamed, giving him the appearance of a deranged rook. Pausing from time to time in the midst of prayers he would remove a large, white handkerchief from his pocket with which to wipe his face, made damp from the melting snow.

Jedda skipped from one foot to the other, trying to bring warmth to her frozen feet, to rub hands whose gloves gave little in the way of protection. Her nose, unprotected from winter's cruel blast, resembled a bright cherry above lips frozen blue.

The vicar closed his prayer book, a signal for the grieving to throw a handful of earth into the open ground. Jedda, precocious as ever, hid a small bunch of snowdrops behind her back, a last gift to Sandy, which she refused to relinquish. They seemed too pretty to part with. Zizzie frowned, but knew Sandy would have laughed.

The company arrived back at the house, in drifts, like the snow itself. The banging of car doors, and the solemn greeting of Ruby, who had obliged Zizzie by helping with the funeral treats, completed a sorrowful picture that in time would turn into a regular pilgrimage to Sandy's grave mainly attended by close family.

The large dining table groaned with food, heavy with sundry funeral fare and plates. Sandwiches of ham, salmon and chicken, vol-au-vents and meat pies resting next to a whole assortment of cakes, plain and fancy. The ladies flitted about with offers of food and drink while the men talked in low voices respectful of the occasion.

Meanwhile, Jedda remained subdued, less conscious at last of the sadness involved. In spite of their sorrow everyone ate something, the cold having sharpened their appetites. Jedda noticed Sandy's cardigan still hanging on a hook, as if on hand for him to slip into anytime.

"We must save some of these pies for granddad for when he comes back," she said. "He's bound to be hungry."

David smiled. Zizzie looked alarmed. The rest of the company said nothing. Sally resolved to talk to her daughter later.

The guests took their leave amongst commiserations to Zizzie combined with manifold handshakes and kisses. Grandmother Markham hugged Jedda donating Sally a sharp look as she did so. She said she hoped it would not be long before Jedda visited her because she didn't see her very often.

Zizzie told Ruby not to bother with the remaining dishes and that they would do in the morning. It was late, she said, and she was sure everyone must be tired. Her head ached and she couldn't wait to be alone.

David and Dora were staying the night, a fact that comforted Jedda.

To the amazement of those left behind, Sally brewed tea for a change. She even poured it out, handing it round in an agreeable fashion.

"What do you think of that carry on with Viner?" said Sally, in the midst of playing hostess. "I didn't know what to make of it." She started to titter nervously, "I'm sure Sandy wouldn't have, either."

Everyone glanced her way, a smile lighting up their faces. A smile that turned first to a titter, then an outright laugh. Dora started rolling about. "Oh, dear whatever would he have thought? Viner, Sandy and the funeral pyre?" She brought her knees up to her chest in a fit of raucous agony. "Oh dear, oh, dear..."

All joined in the merriment; laughing uncontrollably. An action that broke a dam of tears that had been long kept in check, laughter turned to the sobs of the broken-hearted.

Mr Grimes, Sandy's thin, ingratiating solicitor, read the will the very next day. David said he always reminded him of Uriah Heep, but he was most proficient at his job. Sandy had left the bulk of his money to Zizzie, with a clause: it was to be divided between Sally and David upon her own death. In the meantime, he had left Sally and David five thousand pounds each to do what they so chose to do with it. A slip-up on his part, as Zizzie soon found to her sorrow, it allowed Sally to spread her wings...fly away, taking Jedda with her.

In the ensuing weeks after Sandy's death, Zizzie found her worst fears came to light. Sally's restless attitude in the past weeks had not been without cause. She informed Zizzie that she was going to buy a small business in a poor part of a dockland area and, in spite of Zizzie's distress, remained adamant.

Alex and David joined Zizzie in the fray against her, but Sally remained mulish. She had no intention of backing down.

Even Alex's threat of court proceedings to take Jedda away from her had no effect whatsoever. She was determined to go her own way.

Grandmother Markham journeyed up from Chester to add fuel to Zizzie's cause, but it only seemed to make Sally angrier.

David called Sally all the fools under the sun and said he had a "nut case" for a sister. Dora tried to placate everyone in turn. Jedda, listening in to all the commotion, began to sob, her actions causing everyone to feel guilty, each blaming the other for "upsetting the child".

Next morning, Sally packed cases for herself and Jedda ready to make the journey to Salford. She had decided they would ride in the van with the removal men, and they would take their bedroom furniture with them, along with necessary linen and clothes.

"I've already ordered a suite," she told Jedda. "Also, some dining room furniture – all to be picked up from a store on the way down to their new home."

Jedda had cried all night knowing this would be the last one she would spend in her grandmother's house. She had come the end of an era. One full of cherished memories she would never forget.

Chapter Four

The removal van had already left the outskirts of Cheshire, leaving behind a heart-broken Zizzie. David and Dora were beside themselves with grief, the loss of Sandy was still painfully deep and now Jedda – their beloved Jedda – would not be with them.

"And now this," David had stormed, losing his temper with Sally. "Dad must have been mad to leave you all that money!"

Alex had been in absolute turmoil, even his laid-back attitude deserting him. "How can you take my daughter to live in a dump like that! A dock area of Salford? Of all the places in the world, why there? If you must live on your own, at least find somewhere suitable."

"Someone has to live there!" Sally had retorted. "She'll come to no harm, having to rough it. Help her stand on her own feet. Anyway, it was the cheapest business I could find."

"Business?" said Alex. "What do you know about business? A sweet shop is hardly representative of a way in which to make money. I doubt if the people living in such terrible circumstances will be able to afford many toffees." He nodded his head wisely. "They'll end up asking for tick, and you'll soon be in bad straights allowing them to do that!"

Sally merely cocked her snoot and called them a bunch of snobs stating, "Those men have fought for the country the same as anybody else. And it isn't their fault they're on the dole."

Now here they were, racing along, just the two of them, jammed in between two removal men. Sally, with jaw gritted and ready to face whatever life threw at her, Jedda slumped next to her, gazing through the van window, becoming glummer by the minute. She took note that it had been a long time since she had seen even a particle of anything green, her surroundings becoming greyer with each receding mile.

Eventually having reached a warren of never-ending streets of rows upon rows of identical terraces huddled together in monotonous uniformity, not even a flower basket between them, Jedda thought it as barren as the moon! Such was her first encounter with the city and its docklands.

Upon arriving at their destination, Jedda beheld a very small shop, the front windows displaying sweets and groceries, and, once they had entered the premises, to her mind it appeared even smaller. At the back was a dining room come lounge with a small kitchen situated next to it. The removal men placed a table, four chairs, a sideboard and three piece suite in this small interior; carefully, in respect for its good quality; their eyes questioning – why would a well-brought-up woman venture here alone with only a daughter for company?

The rest of the furniture consisted of two beds, two wardrobes and two dressing tables, which the men just about managed to squeeze into the two small bedrooms. They accepted Sally's payment gracefully and, when she gave them a tip in respect of their good work, they saluted her with raised hats before going on their way.

Sally unpacked the items necessary for their immediate use and, after a light supper, they made their way to bed, tired from their subsequent hassle of a long journey.

Awakened by a clacking noise, before rising from her small bed to make her way downstairs, Jedda first took a look through the small bedroom window towards the houses facing opposite – houses even smaller than the shop in which she now resided. Casting a quick glance at the pretty glazed china clock on the dressing table – a gift from Zizzie – it showed five-forty-five.

Why so early? What had been that strange noise, one that she was, as yet, unfamiliar with? Clogs making a quick tattoo on cobbled streets, along with the tapping on windows by the "knocker up" as he was referred to – hired by dozens of customers who had no desire to oversleep. Jobs were hard to come by in the height of the depression, so being late on arrival for work was a thing to be feared. The street lamps still glowed, and cast an eerie yellow-green glow through an equally yellow fog, giving the streets an eerie, unearthly appearance. Zizzie's household had slept at least two hours later, even longer during her school holidays.

Hating intensely the view recently witnessed, she jumped back into bed and pulled the sheets over her head in the vain hope she might fall asleep, wishing, that when she woke again, she would find it had all been a bad dream. An hour later she was still awake and had to admit, a nightmare it might be, but one based on reality.

She heard Sally open her bedroom door and descend the stairs, rapidly, as always, and noted it was still only six-forty-five. An hour later Sally called for her to come down to breakfast.

She could hear Sally in the shop actually serving someone. Jedda frowned as the reality became clear. Her mother out and about at so uncivilised an hour was something beyond her comprehension. Babylon!

Sally, the shop momentarily empty of customers, came into their living quarters and gave Jedda her breakfast. A doubtful cook, she emptied some cereal into a dish, and Jedda became even more forlorn when she realized that Zizzie's offerings of oranges and cinnamon on toast was amongst other things that she was going to miss in this dreadful place.

"We must sort you some kind of a school out," said Sally. "A lady customer who just came in said there was one close by. When things slacken off, I'll shut the shop for an hour," she paused to pour milk onto the cereal, "and we can pay them a visit... All right? Perhaps tomorrow, then?" she said more gently, noticing Jedda's crestfallen face. "Want some toast?"

Jedda stood in the little shop more out of boredom than a desire to be a part of it, certainly not from the delights of ownership. True, for such a small establishment, it was well stocked containing the usual gadgets necessary for running a mixed grocery business. Furnished with large white scales for heavier items and a small brass pair for weighing tobacco and snuff etc; it also boasted a machine upon which, should any child care to gamble and, if lucky enough to win, was on the road to obtaining a few extra sweets or even a bar of chocolate.

Jars of sweets almost covered one wall, whilst three others were filled with motley of tins and packets in many shapes and sizes. Under the counter smaller shelves, though wider in proportion, held loose cigarettes, these being one of the commodities kept there. It was from these items that Jedda made her first "almost" sale and met what was to be the first of a succession of new friends.

He introduced himself with the self-assurance of a thirty-year-old lord instead of his nine-year-old self.

"I'm Gingo Albertini," he said, with much dignity. Jedda suspected a bow would not have been out of place. "They call me that because of my red hair; also, because my father is Italian. I suppose if I were all English they would call me Ginger," he paused for a second, as though not sure which nationality he wished to be heir to," but my mother's English."

Jedda smiled at him, "My name's Jedda," she said.

"How do, Jeddo. Will you be going to our schoolo? County Council?" he asked her.

Jedda wondered, noting that there was only him standing there, why he used the plural "our".

Jedda merely said, "I don't know which school I'll be going to."

"You won't like it," he said. "Especially old Peppercorn. No class. Only been on some course or other, I'll bet." He wiped his nose with a handkerchief that was not too clean. "He's not like Miss Bevan. She's a lady and better as a teacher; he's a bully."

"Peppercorn?" inquired Jedda.

"Salt! His real name is Salt. We nicknamed him that. Just don't let him catch you using it, though."

He expressed himself in terms of "we" as though he were a solitary actor on a stage and quite unaware that the rest of the cast had gone missing. A habit of including non-existent others was something she would learn to appreciate as her acquaintance with him grew, most certainly so when she became familiar with his friends, who were what "we" were all about. Then the penny struck home. He would become close to her, as would her new friends, Addie and Mrs Tobias, in what were to be the worst of times, and even more dreadful ones to come.

The legendary Italian "O" was prevalent at the end of certain words he used: "We have a mirro in our parlo," he informed her with the same sense of dignity, the expression in his eyes distant, like a count musing over the majesty of his castle.

"Mamma has managed to get some bananos from the Co-op," he said. "You can have some if you like." He broke the fruit into two pieces and handed her half. "Mamma says if war comes we will be short of things, like in the last war, and bananos will be one of them."

She didn't much care for bananas but he behaved like a prince offering jewels, so she accepted his simple gift graciously. She wanted to offer him some sweets in return, but thought better of it in case she offended him, innocently unaware that, if she had turned her back on him, he would steal a whole jar full without a qualm. He gave her the sweetest of smiles before leaving and it was only when he'd gone that she realized he hadn't bought anything.

When Sally came in and asked who she had been talking to, she had answered, "A strange boy who spoke funny... is there going to be a war, mum? Is it true we won't get bananas?"

"Who's been filling your head with such nonsense? Don't take any notice of the news... bothering your young head about such things." Sally looked very concerned. "You know if you get upset you'll get a migraine."

Jedda thought that a bit much because nobody in this world upset her more than her mother.

Jedda enrolled at the County Council school one week later. It wasn't Sally's wish to have her head filled with religious nonsense at some Church school, channelling her mind into some kind of dogma. "All that's needed in there," she said, pressing her daughter's forehead, "are the three R's. Nothing else! The rest of your opinions, if any, can be learned at home."

Gingo turned out to be "cock of the school". A strawberry-headed, green-eyed, bossy kind of a boy. Yet, he had three things to his credit. He was both brave and generous but, much more than this – he could sing. It was the type of voice to put the angels to shame, so one was inclined to ignore his poverty. He certainly did. Never once did he seem to be depressed by the lack of the good things in life, having the confidence of ten kings, despite the fact that, never once was he ever seen garbed in other than a dingy grey shirt and pullover, one so "holey", the angels could have lived there. To complete his outfit he wore a pair of short trousers so grimy they more or less stood up on their own, and to make sure they stayed put, he had graced them with a pair of bright tartan braces...though he never seemed to have had any connection with the Highlands. He accepted life as it was, after all, one could hardly dress up like "Little Lord Fauntleroy" in the middle of a depression.

Gingo delivered newspapers on an old rusty bike, the creak of which could never drown his singing. The sweet strong sound of his vocal chords would echo through the murky streets, treating all and sundry to such refrains as Marta, Amapola, and many other songs in his repertoire. Trouble was his middle name, yet, at times, though he vexed many, all was forgiven once he started to sing. Even tough-minded Sally Markham could be swayed in his favour.

He was a bit of a thief at times – hardly in the Public Enemy Number One class – nevertheless, he would lift the doorbell, sneak into Sally's shop, reach under the counter and help himself to a pocketful of loose cigarettes. He was quite partial to a good Woodbine. Sally, having caught him in the act many times, would spank him, inform his father, who in turn would subject his errant son to a good walloping. After several sessions of double punishment, Gingo finally gave up filching Woodbines at Markham's, aware it was a poor option. With so much punishment meted out on his behalf, he decided to try his luck elsewhere.

One of his favourite haunts was the local Co-op. He found it quite easy to squeeze his thin frame through the gap in a sidewall close to the cellar; this he did with effortless grace in a way one would not have thought humanly possible. Once through the cellar window he would unlock the side door allowing access for his partners in crime: Fats, who could never have climbed through anywhere without difficulty, was followed by, Frogs, Ince and Cowboy.

Frogs wore thick glasses. Cowboy was film-struck, slow. Fats, the boy being corpulent, spoke for itself. Ince? No one ever knew the reason for this and Jedda certainly never questioned it; after all, Jedda wasn't her true name either. Once inside the building they would loot to their hearts content, cigarettes being their favourite booty, apart from Cowboy, whose main pastime was playing with wooden implements in the food department, patting butter into squares and oblongs and making patterns; imagining himself to be grocer Number One. Gingo would eventually be forced to clip his ear, declaring his daftness would land them all in gaol.

A quick visit to the gents clothing department seemed to send Cowboy even crazier, and whilst the others were stuffing their pockets with socks and hankies, Cowboy would pose in front of a full-length mirror, trying on tweed jackets and shiny black top hats. The boys would be bowled over with laughter while watching him posing. Ince said he had no taste. Gingo said he had no brains. Frogs, the intelligent one, said nothing, but thought plenty.

Not allowed access to any of their escapades, or into any of the secret places of a boys' world, Jedda was, nevertheless, included in all the conversations that took place in their hanging-out place – the corner of the concrete where the gang assembled nightly. Often, she would shake her head and warn them of the consequences their actions might bring about, only to have them laugh at her; and having no other friends at the moment with whom to converse, she was obliged to listen to their "boys will be boys" way of carrying on – then fortunately, she met Addie.

Addie was tall and thin – very much the same build as herself, yet lacking Jedda's dramatic looks. She had pale blond hair and large blue Betty Davis eyes. In personality and character she was very much the opposite of the imaginative Jedda. Commonsense was her forte.

Jedda, having arrived home from school one day dying of hunger, found Sally had not prepared any lunch. "That shop opposite is a baker's," said Sally. "They sell pies. Try there."

Jedda put her hand on the handle of the door of Tobias's bakery shop and made her first acquaintance with the Dionne Quins. They were depicted advertising soap on a poster at the back of the shop door. They were there upon her arrival at the shop and would still be there when she left years later, ever children, young and smiling.

Mrs Tobias came into the shop, plump, dark and motherly, arms covered with flour, so much the opposite of Sally. Milly Tobias greeted Jedda with a warm smile and asked her what she wanted. Jedda noticed the shop had a mixture of many aromas. It smelled of a delicious concoction of freshly-baked bread, vanilla, slab cake and a mixture of spices and, lingering somewhere between, pervading all else, was Mrs Tobias's special meat and potato hot pot. Jedda instantly fell in love with the place. It was the nearest she would ever get to Zizzie's motherly warmth again for many years to come.

When she asked how much the hot pot cost, Mrs Tobias informed her that it was sixpence for a plateful and that really she should bring her own plate, but as her daughter Addie was having her lunch, perhaps she would like to join her. "You are the new girl from across the road, aren't you?" she asked, while lifting the flap on the small counter and ushering Jedda in to the confines of the living room.

Jedda answered, "Yes," taking in the contents of the interior as she did so. It was a very small room, overcrowded with heavy furniture, which included a large sideboard that boasted bronze horses, a pianola and a large table surrounded by equally heavy chairs. Jedda was asked to take a seat on one of these worthy wooden objects. She thanked her host and did as instructed.

After she had been introduced to Mrs Tobias's daughter, Addie, Milly advised Jedda to order hot pot a day in advance in future and, once having tasted and eaten each delicious morsel, understood why. It was wonderful, the meat and gravy succulent, the square of pastry placed on top, light as a fairy's whisper.

From the start, she and Addie became close friends, finding they had many things in common.

They had only just finished their apple pie and custard when Milly's son, Billy, walked in. He resembled his mother in the physical sense – dark, robust, but much more quick-tempered, exhibiting a passion for the "blues". Jedda found it to be rather mournful music, but interesting. Several friends had accompanied Billy and much to Jedda's pleasure, he began to entertain them by placing a record on the turntable of the Tobias's large gramophone. "Went down to St James Infirmary and saw my baby lying there," moaned a crooner.

Milly returned from the small bakery adjacent to the dining room carrying a Russian Sandwich. She offered Jedda a slice of it "on the house" to compliment the hotpot and apple pie. "Just this once," she said. "In future, you must pay." Jedda thanked her, thought her kind and spent many lunchtimes eating there ... on the house!

"Miss Otis regrets she's unable to lunch today, madam," moaned the crooner. "Miss Otis regrets she's unable to lunch today."

Jedda found with jazz – though rather depressing – that the characters expressed in song, with many coming a sorry an end, were quite dramatic: "And from under her velvet gown, she drew a gun and shot her lover down, Madam. Miss Otis regrets she's unable to lunch today."

Jedda liked drama of any kind, but Addie was far from impressed with her brother's taste in music and asked Jedda if she would care to play whip and top on the concrete. It was something she had never done, but she soon got the hang of it and it became a habitual pastime.

Jedda borrowed a set of Addie's for the time being and they chalked rainbow colours round the surface of the tops. Once accomplished, they whipped them along at high speed. A simple pursuit in itself with which to while away many hours: an inexpensive pleasure and jolly good exercise, yet, as Jedda pushed the top along, thoughts of Miss Otis came to mind and she wished they had not "hanged her on that old willow, across the way."

Before both girls knew it, lunchtime was over and done with and each returned to their own separate schools. Addie was Church of England – Milly made Addie learn the catechism so that she might be confirmed – but confessed she did not like the vicar, he was always drunk. Jedda, having also been christened Church of England, at Alex's insistence, found it to be her only attendance there.

If school had "Old Peppercorn", it also had Miss Bevan. Jedda had been fortunate enough to be assigned to her class along with Gingo and co. Though, still being under eight years of age she was younger than the rest, but it was the only class in which there was room for her – besides, being in the same category as Gingo, was something that pleased Jedda no end.

Miss Bevan was an excellent teacher of English, with a passion for the classics.

She was to be the panacea for her loss of Sandy and David. Plump, with a magnificent carriage, she perpetually wore her hair in a bun, her strong face framed by a pair of tortoiseshell glasses from which small, intelligent eyes were ever vigilant.

One of Miss Bevan's favourite poems was *The Ancient Mariner*. She read it on a regular basis wishing to imprint it on the minds of her pupils. "What's taught at seven will be recalled at seventy," was her motto. "Catch 'em young, and you've got 'em."

Sadly, this was a misconception on her part, for it worked only on those who chose to adhere to it. Jedda did. Gingo did not. He hated poetry and thought it soppy. In a way that opposites often do, Jedda could not understand his lack of interest in the arts, nor him, her love of it. But either way it was no bar to their friendship and in reverse to his arty friend, Gingo considered maths and geography a passable pursuit. Jedda hated both. During the morning session taking maths with Peppercorn made her miserable; but come afternoon she shone as her imagination soured, her happiness complete as long as Miss Bevan reigned.

Clouds drew across the sky like a dark cloth in perpetual motion, promising rain. The March winds blew in from the east threatening to turn the rain to sleet, bending the trees in constant dance.

Jedda and Addie clung to the swings trying to bring about some form of control but the chains kept slipping from their grasp as they held on amidst peals of laughter. Still, they struggled continuously, refusing to be foiled even by an act of nature so savage it seemed to take away their very breath. The rain had come slowly at first before taking up momentum with such force that a mixture of rain and sleet stung their faces, pitilessly; while a gale force wind blew open their coats as they struggled keep up their collars. So much so, they were obliged to run to the empty band stand and shelter, but its open aspect offered little in the way of warmth; something neither of them were prepared to endure, and the moment there was a lull in the weather they decided to hurry to a more comfortable shelter – home.

They reached the Tobias's shop chilled to the bone, wet garments clinging to their small frames, the ache of young hunger gnawing at their stomachs making them appreciate the smell of good food. This was a pleasure combined with the living room fire, in front of whose warmth both were seated, relishing heat from flames that came alive from the coals that Mrs Tobias had heaped into the grate of the large, iron fireplace. They had, upon entering the living room, thrown themselves onto the sofa, removed shoes and socks, ones that squelched as they did so, and rubbed themselves down with a towel – proffered compliments of Milly Tobias. Their hunger rose and reached craving point, titillated by the inviting smells emitting from the bake-house.

Milly was busy with her lunchtime preparations: her special hot pot – amongst many of the delicious concoctions, which she magically conjured up with her large and capable hands – sold like wildfire. After she had managed to free herself from the bustle of serving her eager customers, she joined the children, placed a yellow gingham cloth on the huge table, while cajoling Addie and Jedda into adding mats and knives and forks. Jedda's presence was now so familiar to her that she had no compunction about asking her to take part in the domestic scene; noticing also that the child seemed to spend more and more time around their family than with her pretty mother. She felt flattered in a sense, but also a little concerned. The child seemed rather unsure of herself at times; she was aware of this, because she had often seen a lost, almost bewildered look in Jedda's eyes.

"It's my birthday today," Jedda informed her proudly.

"Is it?" said Milly, pretending disinterest.

Addie put a hand across her mouth to hide a smile and Milly did the same.

Eric Tobias and Billy arrived home for lunch from the cinema. Eric worked there as a doorman come odd job man, and Billy was the projectionist. It was a small, but recently built modern cinema and boasted a weekly showing of the most recent films, competing well with the stylish ones in the heart of the city. It was also more convenient for those living in the area because of its locality, and from the Tobias's shop, it stood only three streets away.

"It's an awful day. The wind almost blew me over," said Eric shaking rain from his cap.

"All right, Eric," said Milly. "There is no need to give us all a shower. Hang up your cap, or put it near the oven to dry."

Jedda and Addie giggled, and Jedda forgot about her sadness concerning her birthday.

Milly dished out hot pot that they practically devoured in appreciation, enjoying apple pie and cream for pudding. Milly stole away into the bake house and re-turned post-haste holding a round pink cake aloft, a cake upon which eight candles burned merrily lighting up the name, Jedda.

In unison, the Tobias's wished a blushing, delighted Jedda a happy birthday. "Your mother knows of this and has another surprise for you for after lunch, so when your ready I'll take you home, cake and all." said Milly Tobias.

"Can Addie come," said Jedda.

"She'll see you later on tonight, perhaps. Right now, I think there are other people you would rather see."

Jedda smiled, thanked the Tobias's for a lovely gift and made her way dutifully home with Milly.

Zizzie, David, Dora, and Alex arrived twenty minutes later, and it had seemed like forever since Jedda had last seen them. They brought her wonderful gifts and smothered her with affection as she sat contented on Alex's knee, arms around his neck. He declared how he loved her and she answered she loved him too and she'd missed him.

After a while she jumped on David's knee and told him she loved him too.

He said he loved her "Three."

She said, "Four."

She said, "A thousand."

He said, "A trillion."

She said, "What's a trillion?"

Zizzie said, "Shut up, David. You sound more like Sandy everyday." Then she looked sad. Everybody did.

The grownups were pleasant at first because it was her birthday, but it all ended on a sour note. She had assumed from the very beginning somehow, that it would.

Zizzie had declared the place a dump and that Jedda looked pale and asked were the children she played with clean. Jedda had been upset at the suggestion her newfound friends were unsavoury and had answered they were poor, but nice. Of what Zizzie would have thought of Gingo, she could only surmise. She loved her grandmother, but the Pied Piper had played his flute and Gingo had won the day!

Alex said, "It's not a very safe area to be in should war break out. Now Hitler's marched on the Rhineland, anything can happen and the French want action. We refuse to do anything and I think it's a mistake." He bit his lip concerned. "I think the French are right...we should act now!"

"I don't think he'll go any further. He's got what he wants," said David. "We've nothing to fight with, either."

"I agree with Alex. I don't think there will be any stopping him," said Sally.

"Praise from Caesar, is praise indeed. Not often my wife agrees with me," said Alex tartly. "Anyway, we're getting away from the subject of Jedda. What's to do about her?"

Zizzie intervened, "Come home, Sally, away from this dreadful place. Before Jedda succumbs to something," Zizzie, all but spat it out.

Sally laughed, "Don't be so dramatic mother. You left the stage years ago."

"No need to be cheeky!" said Zizzie, her face going red with vexation.

Alex sat next to Jedda holding her hand. He had missed her so these past months, but felt unable to express as much in words; feeling miserable with each passing moment by her lack of concern with what was going on.

He was completely wrong; the object of his thoughts was confused. Her mother was the boss; also, she conscious of her father's inability to get the better of Sally, especially when it came to rescuing his unhappy daughter.

The small gathering drank endless cups of tea, absorbed in conversation, deep in confrontation as always. Jedda began to wish Viner were there – even if her singing was dreadful and her black fox the bane of her life – at least she would have broken the monotony of what was going on.

Conversational wise, things were beginning to hot up far too much and Dora tactfully suggested it was getting late. She could see Jedda was becoming agitated by all the commotion and thought it tactful to withdraw and fight another day.

Apart from Sally, who appeared to remain unmoved, the family wished Jedda goodbye with tears in their eyes and she started to become inconsolable, clinging to each in turn.

Once the company had departed, Sally said she wished they'd never come. Jedda had become settled over the past months and now recent events had come back to haunt her.

Later that night Jedda cried and said she missed her grandfather. Sally told her to go to sleep and things would be better in the morning, being of little use when it came to child psychology.

Sally thought nineteen-thirty-six a most dreadful year. Hitler had embraced his Rhineland, Mussolini had achieved his empire and Civil war had broken out in Spain. England had lost one king, only to lose another because Edward, once declared King, had given up his throne for that awful American woman, Mrs Simpson.

Jedda listened all ears to the discussions taking place in the shop. Mrs "What do I want" and Mrs "Tut tut, I don't know", as Sally referred to them, were at this very moment being most opinionated and giving their complete attention to matters in general.

"Fancy Teddy doing that. Deserting us for that awful woman!" said Mrs "What do I want".

"Tut, tut! I don't know. Whatever next. Our Teddy! Well, perhaps they should let them marry though," said Mrs "Tut Tut, I don't know".

They discussed the matter in a most familiar way, as though King Edward were their favourite cousin; or even more, that they alone, should have control over passing events in Parliament as a whole.

Jedda found all her mother's customers interesting portraits of human nature. She was not necessarily conscious of the fact at the time, but this mix of colourful characters would be something to write about in the far off future.

Sally thought them silly because she hated a lack of intelligence in anyone, and though she endured it all diplomatically, was secretly aware that she would be relieved when nightfall finally allowed her to close the shop.

Not so, Jedda. She found them a perpetual delight no matter what they said or did; nor did she find her self put off by Sally's intellectual snobbishness.

Mrs "What Do I Want" had either forgotten or couldn't make her mind up about what to purchase. "Now what do I want... let me see. What shall I get for

Harry's tea?" she pondered her usual lament.

"Tut, tut, I don't know," said Mrs "Tut Tut", once Mrs "What do I Want" had left the shop. "That woman never knows what she wants."

Sally and Jedda exchanged smiles. Jedda kindly, Sally less so. Once closing time came and Sally drew the blinds on the little shop it was with the words, "Now what do I want? Tut, tut I seem to have forgotten."

Jedda laughed, yet told her mother not to be cruel.

Chapter 5

Two years passed swiftly and at the age of eleven Jedda's parents had divorced, and Sally and Zizzie were no longer on speaking terms and the hostile situation left Jedda even more isolated. Apart from her seeing little of Alex, Jedda began to feel at an absolute loss when uncle David and aunt Dora decided to emigrate. Canada, being their choice of residence, left her imagining that her whole family had fragmented. It also left her feeling not only dejected, positively rejected.

Desertion on their part, all those people she had ever loved, leaving one by one, made life difficult to bear at times, but she never mentioned the fact to Sally. Not to anyone in fact, but Milly Tobias was concerned by the sudden change in a previous bubbly Jedda.

Her relatives had been more or less so much a part of her existence; so much so, that it not only saddened her, it also left her feeling confused. The fun had gone out of her life and she began to become more melancholy with each passing day by being forced to dwell apart from what had, at one time, seemed a perfect existence. Only Addie and Gingo kept her on an even keel.

To add to her burden, school was being made more intolerable by the arrival of a Miss Smith whom she had come to detest. She was only a physical education teacher. A stand-in teacher, because with the incoming threat of war, many of the men teachers had been called to do duty of a different kind, known as his Majesty's Forces. Even Peppercorn was preferable, but he had two classes to teach, so the curriculum was split between him and Smith – only temporarily until a replacement came. Still, she was thankful that at least Miss Bevan still taught them English, if only for three days a week.

It was late August and things were looking ominous. The threat of war was looming closer and it was all the people seemed to talk about. Discussed it endlessly with worried frowns on their faces and fear in their hearts.

Sally said, "The Jewish people are leaving Germany quicker that bees from a whacked nest. I'm afraid our children need to be sent somewhere safer." She hated to admit Alex had been right; the docks were not a safe haven when it came to living through a war.

Milly Tobias, who had come across for a break and a chat with Sally over a cup of tea, quite disagreed with her where evacuating the children was concerned.

"I know it's a dangerous area," she said, "what with the docks and factories being so close; nevertheless, as I said to Eric only the other day, if we are to die we might as well all go together."

"But supposing we don't?" argued Sally. "What then? Our children could be maimed and we parents killed. I'm sending Jedda to the country if war starts."

Millie nodded. "She's your child, of course. You do have a point about the danger. But to lodge with strangers? No! Never!"

Miss Smith had legs like tree trunks and thick-cropped hair that grew in wisps down her neck and travelled under her chin. She had taken a distinct dislike to Jedda and the feeling was mutual. Miss Smith was not bright and Jedda, young as she was, sensed it.

Miss Smith did not like pupils to be ahead of each other and seemed to be of a new school named "equality". She belonged somewhere in the future, but unfortunately for Jedda, she had insidiously kept to her own time. Jedda's fine copperplate hand seemed to have an adverse effect upon her. She would bring a ruler down on her hands, hard, and say, "Print when I tell you! Print girl!"

It was quite impossible on Jedda's part; her hands would not seem to obey. If she had ever printed it was so long ago she could not remember. She was afraid to complain to Sally, but told Milly Tobias, who in turn told Sally, who marched off to school and made things hot for her tormentor.

"What an ugly, stupid woman," had been Sally's dismissive account of her.

Miss Smith joined the Land Army a week later and Jedda hoped a truck would fall on her! She was becoming hardened to life and certain people. Determined in future, and at all costs, not to be bullied. She was, she assured herself, going to make a success of her life whatever the circumstances. Adult power held her in its sway at the moment, but time would free her from its web.

It was hot in August, bees a buzzing, the clink of ice on glass for the more fortunate who drank home-made lemonade and swung in garden hammocks caressed by gentle music. People blessed such as this were only a delightful memory as far as Jedda Markham was concerned. In the hot grip of the city lay reality, heat reflected on brick and pavement, pitch melted on the cobbles and stuck to children's socks and sandals, as it was now doing to Jedda's and Addie's as they made their way to the cricket grounds.

They had crossed Trafford Bridge, but still had a good way to go before reaching Old Trafford; also, quite a walk after that. They passed St Dunstan's with Stretford to the left, walked through some side yards close by, using the railway lines as a guide and made their way to some large trucks standing silently in the sidings and traipsed slowly past them, their thin forms flagging under the intense heat. The sun was an orange ball beating down on their heads, and young and agile as they were, even they were beginning to wilt.

They had almost reached their destination when they came upon a hut adjacent to the cricket grounds. A man was selling pop, crisps and an assortment of biscuits. Not having a penny between either of them they asked the man serving behind the counter if he would oblige them with a glass of water. The man did as requested and, noticing their embarrassment through lack of funds, handed them a packet of biscuits each on the house, or hut, as was the case.

Across the years the memory of his kindness would come to Jedda when her generosity was not always at its peak, causing her to relent in a shamefaced fashion. At such times, she would try to remember his face and long to have known his name. She wished she could have secretly rewarded him in a time of plenty, though she suspected he would have been too proud to accept.

Standing there now in the cruel heat she vowed that when she grew to adulthood she would always be kind to children, they have long memories.

Jedda and Addie kept an eye on the bikes left outside by the visitors to the cricket grounds. Their job was to keep them out of thieving hands – of which there were very few – considering there was a depression on.

Addie's uncle Fred worked at the cricket grounds helping to keep the lawns in trim and it was he who had arranged for them to help out with the bikes. He also worked part-time at the billiard hall situated near Salford market.

Addie's father, Eric had a part-time job there also, and whenever the fair came to town and she and Addie ran out of money, they would call in on some pretext or other – never asking for money directly, but suggesting the fair was on in a beguiling fashion; a fact that always amused Eric Tobias no end as he placed silver in their small, beseeching hands.

The girls, both in their individual ways, had a knack of getting what they wanted. The fact served them well.

Addie's uncle Fred lived in a garden-fronted terraced house with a small front garden in which he proudly grew an array of flowers. Jedda and Addie had been invited to tea, a treat that always happened when they attended the cricket grounds, one they were more than pleased to accept being in the throes of exhaustion from the August heat.

Addie's aunt Jenny was small and dark like her sister Milly Tobias and just as fussy. She was an equally good cook, and, in spite of the heat, had baked that morning as per usual. She offered the girls a bumper menu of salmon salad, freshly baked bread, scones, potato cakes and an endless selection of cakes and fancies.

Uncle Fred was a sweet, contented kind of person, small of stature, so that his smile always seemed larger than himself. He had possessed a mop of bright red hair when young, but once he had started to lose his hair had purchased a very fine wig to match the original colour. But age had turned his natural hair snow white and now the top half, where the wig balanced, resembled a large marigold perched on a field of white daisies. Sometimes, it became detached, and teetered to one side looking even more daisy than marigold – much to the amusement of the girls.

Due to start their journey home, Jedda and Addie were loaded down with sweets compliments of aunt Jenny, along with a batch of thorough kisses and a warning not to dawdle in case it turned dark.

Their luck was truly in. Jedda and Addie had made five shillings each on the day and, to round things off to their advantage, Mr Tobias had promised them complementary tickets for the pictures; perks allotted to part-time doormen on some occasions.

Though it had been quite a profitable day, the sun was still unbearably hot and they decided to take a short cut through the back of what appeared to be a large, overgrown garden. Situated inside of this tumble of weeds was a small workshop, by all accounts deserted, until, suddenly, a slight rustle was heard by the girls coming from the undergrowth; a sound followed by a dark head suddenly popping up. This apparition was soon joined by the appearance of a brown one, a blonde one and last, but not least, one of flaming red – Gingo and co!

Gingo was carrying a large bunch of parsley, trying unsuccessfully to hide it beneath his coat; while Ince and Fats who sported bunches of flowers, were fruitlessly trying to do likewise. Not so Cowboy, lagging behind as usual, his face a picture of delight as he dragged an enormous sunflower behind him which, even by the most shortsighted policemen, could not have been missed.

Jedda and Addie started to giggle causing Gingo to turn round and find out the reason for their outburst. Vexed, he lashed out at Cowboy, reprimanding him with a thump on the spot. Cowboy sulked for a while, but relinquished his bounty in the end by throwing it behind a hedge.

Jedda said they would get in trouble if caught and should not be here. She told the boys to throw away their stolen goods, the advice of which they took no notice, and ran off shouting, "Girls are soft!"

Before making their way to the pictures the girls had something more to eat at Addie's. Milly Tobias laughed at Jedda's large appetite. "I don't know where you put it, Jedda? It certainly doesn't show."

It was in fact Mrs Tobias's food that made her eat; her famous meat pie and homemade pickles, followed by slab cake and cream horns, made such a delicious combination difficult to abstain.

The meal over, she and Addie cleared up after themselves and washed the pots by way of saying thank you.

Mrs Tobias was pleased and gave them a bag of sweets each.

They arrived at the cinema in great anticipation. George Raft, their favourite movie star, was on at the pictures that night. They were attending the first house in the hopes they could cheat and watch the picture twice; something most of the children tried to do if they could get away with it. They watched in agony as George was "done to death" by wicked Edward G. Robinson, and spent the night in tears because, even as he lay lifeless, George had been incredibly beautiful. Nor was he able to dance any more, which to them was the greatest tragedy of all. And what wouldn't they have given just for one tango with Latin George of the dark eyes and flashing smile?

Being flush, Jedda and Addie sat in the best seats, which gave them a better chance of staying on through the second house. They sucked the sweets Milly Tobias had given them with obvious relish as they sat through the *Three Stooges*, a Chaplin short, a Laurel and Hardy and two cartoons, all of which they loved, plus the news, which they hated.

During the interval they treated themselves to a choc-ice, a luxury of all luxuries. On nights less favourable, they had often sat in the tuppenny seats, minus an ice cream and so close to the front they had to sit upright, chin tilted, the head tipped back as they focused on the screen. It was often jokingly referred to as, "Go in the tuppennies too often, you'll end up looking at the sky and walking in dog-dirt." So went the expression when anyone was perceived to get a little bit above themselves or take on a haughty stance.

Jedda was more than pleased to be seated where she was, recalling quite categorically nights when one could be treated to a piece of tripe thrown haphazardly by certain characters who had no concern for where it landed. Or some child, restless on its mother's knee, inserting a carrot in one's ear. The motley selection of edible things people brought with them to the pictures were, at times, indescribable!

The lights dimmed and Jedda and Addie sat in the welcome darkness devouring their ices, mingled with the pleasure of seeing their adored Georgie Raft for the second time, even if it did bring tears to their eyes. Only an hour had passed when the picture broke down midst the stamping of feet and jeers.

The manager declared the film would soon be fixed and cried, "Patience! Patience! Please!" Then someone several rows away from where she and Addie were seated stood up waving a newspaper...

Gingo! Chips! He must have been eating chips. Fats, Cowboy and Ince were with him. Jedda gave Addie a sidelong look as they both slithered down in their seats eager to avoid detection. Neither of the girls were snobs, but somehow trouble beckoned. Ince was standing upright in his seat. Too late for them to take cover! Fats had spotted them. He nudged Gingo, then all four boys started to wave...

Jedda gave them a sickly smile accompanied by Addie's honest frown; then the attendant walked forward giving Fats a mighty whack before telling him to sit down. Once the man had walked away Gingo made a rude remark, so the attendant came back and asked who had made it. No one would own up to it, so the attendant declared he would not allow the film to start until the culprit made himself known; then people became more boisterous, the stamping of feet louder. The attendant told all four of them to take their leave. All four stood their ground. Some people shouted, "Leave the boys alone."

Others cried, "Throw 'em out!"

Fortunately the lights went down, the film came on, and the evening's entertainment was allowed to proceed avoiding an all-out fight.

It was almost nine when Jedda and Addie deserted the cinema having decided not to watch Georgie die.

Lon Chaney featured in a weir wolf picture next week so instead of sobbing themselves to death, they would be able to frighten themselves to death instead. Like last week, when they had watched *Count Dracula*, terrified, they had left each other on the corner whilst they ran each to her own shop, trying their hardest to find which one could arrive there the quickest.

They were never sure why they watched horror films because they frightened them so. But there was always a subconscious delight in doing so as they ran past black, mysterious entries, afraid in case Dracula should jump out on them from the terrifying darkness. A wicked, dangerous pursuit, even if it did lead in the end to having nightmares.

The thing that generally terrified Jedda even more though, was the thought of angels standing round her bed in the way that Miss Bevan kindly suggested they did. Just in case the soul departed in the night, she said. But she didn't want her soul to depart at all, not ever.

She had mentioned the fact to Gingo once. Ince had interrupted saying, "It must be most uncomfortable having wings sticking out of the back all the time. How do angels lie down?"

"I would hate to be an angel too," said Cowboy.

"How's that?" said Gingo. (Ask a silly question.)

"I'm allergic to feathers," he said. "The doc..."

Gingo slapped him before he could go any further, while the rest of them stood there laughing.

The last days of August were a time for laughter and a time for being young. In spite of the depression, life had its moments, and now there were signs that the darkness was lifting and the days for many spent on the dole were about to end. Remarkably, the government suddenly needed people and many were to comment bitterly, "Who needs to march from Jarrow now?" The grey days that had marked the thirties were certainly coming to an end, but sadly, even darker ones were soon to take their place.

In the same fashion as August, September too was a mellow month, yet followed by a sense of unease as people became extremely worried. Conscription, it appeared, had not been unnecessarily executed. In Paris already, sixteen thousand children had already been evacuated, now it was England's turn.

Sally decided it was time Jedda left for the country. "Dockland is hardly a place for young ones in these dangerous times," she declared once more.

Jedda ran across to the Tobias's in desperation to tell Addie the dreadful news. Addie said she wasn't going anywhere,

Milly Tobias repeated, "If the family must die, it must all be together."

Jedda mentioned nothing of her fears of being hoisted onto strangers to Sally. She seldom mentioned things that troubled her. Indeed, she found it difficult to tell her troubles to anyone, acquaintances old or new. Her mother's "don't be soft" attitude made her dwell deep within herself and made her stand on her own two feet. She missed David and Dora's cuddles, though, and now just when she was settling in again she was about to be uprooted once more. Sent to heaven knows where. Sent to heaven knows, who.

Continuing with their usual sense of play, but with a sense of foreboding subconsciously brought about by adults' continued depression by the news and threat of war, whip and top became a listless game, especially for Jedda.

Gingo was not his usual, cheery self, either. Worry about his father being Italian had put an end to his singing. Even his temper, with whom the gang were well acquainted, seemed to have fizzled out into smouldering depression.

Summer had more or less ended, yet the weather held deep in to September. Jedda, who had showed no previous interest in world events, listened avidly to the news with hopes of a peace settlement. This she did in between the *Third Programme* that featured classical music, opera and poetry – difficult to fathom at times, but pleasing to the ear. Sally said she thought Jedda was too serious about things at times. Not necessarily the wrong ones, but deep for one of her tender years.

Chapter Six

The second of September found the evacuees posted to a coach outside the school. Sandwiches were packed for the journey and each child had been issued with a brown paper bag filled with biscuits, corned beef and chocolate – compliments of the government – for those who were about to foster them. Gas masks were flung over shoulders, labels pinned to coats, and from the pavement, where the mothers stood, tears mingled with children's waves.

Studied bravery on Jedda's part kept her dry-eyed and she noticed that Sally was not crying either. Still, she had never seen her mother look so pale and worried. A lump came in her throat as she forced back tears that threatened to flow; nevertheless, she managed to restrain them, giving her mother a last brave wave. Once out of sight of Sally's slender form the dam burst and she joined others in howls of protest and the tut-tutting of the teachers.

Alighting from the coach, the children, under the protective eye of the teachers keeping them in line, like chicks farmers feared would escape, the children were made to hasten onto a train. In time, as the train rumbled on, the city smells, clanging trams and the whole hustle and bustle of the city were far behind them. Jedda studied the view from the carriage window,

Eyes fixed on each scene as it altered shape with every passing mile through town after town until, after what seemed a very long time, they reached flat lush meadows soon to be exchanged for slopes that gave way to sea and mountains. At last, they were in Cumberland.

The children alighted from the train in a disorganised fashion. Miss Lomax – head mistress supreme, and of the straight-backed Barbara Stanywick walk – took charge.

Miss Bevan stood behind her, eyes misty with surprise, wiping her glasses from time to time, as if to hold at bay whatever disaster was about to befall them. Eventually, a coach arrived to take them to their final destination, and a crowd of travel-weary children continued on what was not only the last lap of their journey, but the beginning of something that was in a sense, alien to them... country life.

The village hall was not very large, but with only a sprinkling of the children left and after what seemed hours of waiting, Jedda began to consider it a huge and frightening place.

She was standing next to Lily Adams, and though neither spoke their thoughts, their feelings were similar. Fear! Fear of the unknown! Would they be left in the hall alone, rejected? Jedda's imagination began to work in its usual over active fashion, overshadowed by visions of ghosts and goblins.

Accustomed by now to the city, and its closed community of several streets, she felt as if she were lost in some vast desert. Even living in Cheshire – which had been green and countrified – seemed flat by comparison to the wild hills and vast space that encompassed her new surroundings.

Apart from that, it was the isolation, utter loneliness and changeability of life itself; as though nothing in her young life ever remained constant.

Several other children had just been picked out for fostering, and it came to Jedda's notice that several of these grown strangers had first looked her way, spoken to Miss Bevan, nodded, then passed on regardless. Now there were just the two of them left – she and Lily...

A tight knot began to work its way down from her chest to her stomach, as it always did when she was tense; only this time, it was worse than she had ever known – then Mona came along.

She walked across the hall elegant and smiling. A fair-haired, beautiful, warmer version of Sally as she made her way towards them, at the same time waving to Miss Bevan who came over and joined them also.

Mona spoke to Miss Bevan in a light, breathy tone, "Are these the two children you mentioned? I'm sorry I'm late. I had to drop some food off at old Mrs Barnes's place, she'd starve otherwise." She smiled at Jedda and Lily pinching their cheeks gently, a salutary plea for forgiveness.

The girls' smiled back. Mona had appeared as an angel from heaven, but they would have smiled at the devil himself if he had come to rescue them from this place.

Miss Bevan had been aware of Mona's coming to pick up the children but completely unconscious of they're suffering, only too pleased that they would be staying at the vicarage where she too had been billeted.

Jedda and Lily idled over supper, exhausted by the days events, feeling intimidated by the proportions of the room that served as a dining area. It was obvious to them by the mounds of food and plates stacked on the large mahogany sideboard that previous diners had already eaten, but of whom there was no presence. Such spacious surroundings were unfamiliar to them, leaving them unsure of their part in the scheme of things.

The Vicar came into the room, first nodding to Miss Bevan, as if already acquainted with her, before introducing himself to the two girls.

"Hello, you two. You must call me uncle George," he said.

The girls looked up and saw a tall, well-set figure, above which beamed a kindly face. A face they would learn to love and trust implicitly – especially Jedda – in the way of lonely children longing for love. For the present, the gods smiled kindly down on them, but in spite of this, the girls began to yawn, dead on their feet.

The Vicar motioned to Mona. "I think we had better get these young ladies to bed." He gave them both a loving smile, bid them goodnight and left the room leaving them in Mona's tender care.

The Vicarage was light and airy, the walls decorated in soft hues with many prints and beautiful pictures placed here and there. The floors were nicely carpeted upon which tasteful furniture rested: not the abode of some poor vicar of God, but of one comfortably well off. The girls decided that morning would be a good time to explore further, especially when they would be feeling freshly restored from a good, sound sleep.

They had been allocated two rooms on the top floor; originally attics, which had been nicely arranged with extra comforts for the children's expected arrival. Already the large beds had been covered with chintz covers, which tended to soften the effect of the dark, looming wardrobes and solid dressers. Fine furniture for adults, but for young ones, somewhat spooky; certainly for those only used to terraced boxes. Jedda wished Lily and she could share a room, but was nervous of asking permission from so gracious a hostess.

The long night continued on, certainly, for Jedda. She lay in the great ship of a bed like the Ancient Mariner, all at sea. She had not shot an albatross, but it certainly felt so as she studied the room with its oblong windows, large and slanting inwards, allowing plenty of light to filter through. Mona meanwhile, had already unpacked her case, removing what little there was of her meagre belongings. Lily's worldly goods were even less, and had been left in the capable hands of Miss Bevan who was busy sorting them out in the bedroom next door. "There you are! All ship-shape!" declared Mona, missing the irony of it. "Have a good night's sleep." Her smile was like an embrace.

The bedroom door was prised open and the vicar stepped forward to comfort Jedda, "Thought I'd say a prayer for you. I know you must feel sad at this time," he said, "but God is with you and with your spirit."

Jedda was embarrassed, having never been acquainted with a vicar at close quarters before – except of course when sheltering from the snow in the back of the church with Addie, Gingo and the gang. Even then, she had always avoided contact with men of the cloth if possible. Now one was in her bedroom of all places. A vicar! What would Sally have thought about it? Her mother? Intent on bringing up her daughter an agnostic, to ignore the opium of the poor!

The Vicar took her hands in his and blessed her, his eyes kindly, filled with the essence of goodness. She had not the heart to withdraw them, a prisoner hemmed in by a big fat eiderdown, meek as a lamb on the surface, her thoughts within a

58

cauldron of emotions. The Vicar touched her hair with what seemed to her a form of blessing before leaving her to her own and Mona's devices.

Mona came over towards her, eyes quizzical, "Something wrong? Tell aunt Mona," she said.

Jedda wrung her hands together nervously. She had to tell the truth, Sally said only despicable people told lies. "I'm not supposed to bother with God. Mother doesn't like it. Will I have to leave here if the vicar finds out. I like it here! I like you! They won't send me back to the village hall, will they?

"I don't know who 'they' are?" said Mona, "but I most certainly won't. I'm a poet and believe in all the gods. George doesn't know though, our secret!" she winked, leaned over, and kissed Jedda goodnight.

Alone at last and tired from a long exhausting day, Jedda settled down, gradually feeling more secure and much more at ease in her surroundings. She liked poets, if poets were like Mona, that is; though she had never met one before she decided there and then not to tell the vicar about her own lack of godliness either; after all, there was such a thing as hurting peoples feelings. George?...So that was his name? Just like her favourite film star. She wondered if he could dance?

Mona had drawn back the curtains to let the moon shine in. It was her way offering some form of light, making Jedda less nervous? Though it was September, the moon was definitely August. It hung low in the sky, both yellow and mellow. Almost blood coloured in parts, mostly round the rim. That was eerie enough, but when the bats came, throwing their enormous bodies at the windows – or so it seemed to her – unaware that they were merely huge country moths, her terror knew no bounds. Fear began to engulf her. Soon they would get in! Hypnotise her! Suck her blood! Come morning, they would find her pale and lifeless. Sally would be furious!. Maybe one was in already, hiding the wardrobe. Maybe it had been there all along? Waiting! Waiting until the vicar had left: they were afraid of men of God. She wondered if he kept a stock of holy water, like what's his name? Van Helzing – or something like that? It became too much, fear was the spur that moved her into action... she let out one unearthly scream. Feet came running.

The curtains had been drawn across to hide the windows. Mona and the vicar had consoled her and explained the bats were only moths; nevertheless, she had achieved her objective. She now lay snuggled up next to Lily. Safe! Fast asleep! Mona had promised that tomorrow they would put two small beds in one room, that way, they would each keep the other company.

Lily had risen already, but Jedda had remained in bed, exhausted by so much travelling and the ensuing nightmares that followed. She was propped up on her pillow, half dozing when he entered.

"I'm... Flash Gordon!"

The voice interrupted her reverie, bringing her out of a dream state. At first she thought she had not heard it, then it came again, more strongly this time. "I'm Flash Gordon!!!"

Jedda peered out into the half-light obscured by the heavy curtains to behold a male figure, half child, half youth, standing before her. He was wearing a ladies pink bathing cap minus everything else.

She gripped the sheets, shocked not only by the intrusion of such an apparition, but also by the fact that he marched forward, whipped of her counterpane, and proceeded to wrap it around his naked form. Once done, he marched backwards towards the door and stood to attention. "I'm going to capture Ming in this," he said.

She did not answer, for the simple fact she was speechless, but he had plenty to say for them both. "Mona loves me. Mona loves me best. Mona loves Ferdie."

Young as she was, she was conscious that the statement had been directed against herself in the form of a threat.

A jealous statement, mainly: "I have no intention of sharing her with you." She was also aware that she was dealing with someone with whom she would have to be careful. Someone not quite as herself. Mongoloid.

Flash Gordon changed tactics, rushed towards the windows, and flinging back the curtains, opened them. He jumped on the bed and stood facing the open casement. Jedda moved quickly and dashed for the door, screaming.

Mona flew in as if on wings, spirited by some unseen hand, grabbed Flash Gordon's legs, and saved the day. "That's enough, Ferdie!" she cried on the verge of exploding. "Come down, and get into the bath! This minute! She wrapped the cover round him and turned to Jedda, who was cowering by the door. "He's quite harmless. Please excuse his nakedness. He's as innocent as a baby." She stroked Ferdie's head. "You won't do that again, will you, Ferdie? You can't fly! Your not Flash Gordon, and if you try anything like that again, we won't take you to see him at the pictures any more."

She smiled at Jedda, including her in the conversation. "He loves Flash Gordon, he's Ferdie's hero. Come on Ferdie, bath time. Put your new suit on, dear. We have two little girls for company today." Flash Gordon removed his bathing cap, and Ferdie went meekly for a bath.

Jedda collected her toothbrush and towel, made her way down the attic staircase and, upon reaching the third floor, worked her way along a wide corridor. She felt lost in this maize of a house until the sound of Ferdie's singing led her to her goal. "Oh, Mona you shall be free... e... eee," he warbled. A song she was to become well acquainted with as time went by and one with much significance.

She stood by the bathroom door, not sure if she should enter. A pair of eyes watched her – Matt's – as he strolled towards her an amused look on his face.

"Hello. What have we here this bright and sunny morning? A sprite?"

Jedda wasn't sure what he meant by a sprite, and frowned.

Matt noticed her confusion. "Elf! Fairy! It's only a compliment. Don't look so frightened! I won't eat you!"

She smiled quickly, dimples flashing. He was her slave.

"No need to be afraid. I'm harmless at this time of day," he added.

Jedda looked into eyes shadowed by a previous night's drinking, breath still heavy with the smell of whisky. "So you're our new lodger? No, guest," he corrected himself as an afterthought.

"No, I'm an evacuee," she said, rectifying his statement.

"I see you're the type to call a spade a spade. What's your name?"

"I'm Jedda. Jedda Markham."

"That's an unusual name."

"It's not my real name, it's Jennifer. People just call me that."

Matt grinned, mocking her, "I see. Thank you for letting me into your secret."

A woman came along the corridor pushing a vacuum cleaner. "That's Mrs Clayton. A bit snappy at times, but a heart of gold and quite harmless. Good morning, Mrs Clayton!" Matt shouted to her.

The woman nodded and made her way into one of the bedrooms close by, smiling at neither of them. Matt gave Jedda a "let's be pals together" look.

"She doesn't like me."

Jedda began to wonder why everyone referred to each other as harmless. She had never heard a word spoken so often, in such a small space of time; certainly not in conjunction with anyone she knew, and it made her nervous.

Matt knocked on the bathroom door. "There's a young lady out here waiting to beautify herself," he winked at Jedda in "I'm your best friend style".

Mona popped her head round the door. "Can't she use the other one?"

"George is bogged down in there. I've been trying to get in for ages. You know what he's like! Cleanliness next to godliness, kind of thing."

Mona laughed. "Don't be a fool. What if he hears you."

Matt smiled. "You know I love him, and that's the truth," he said, becoming serious, "but he does take a long time with his ablutions."

"We're almost done here, anyway. Lily had her bath ages ago. I didn't disturb Jedda, she had a restless night."

"Restless? said Matt. "And who's Lily?"

"Moths," said, Mona, relating last night's events to him. "She doesn't like moths and Lily is the other evacuee."

"I thought they were bats," said Jedda, as a protection against foolishness.

"Too much imagination, I'm the same," said Matt, tugging at her fringe.

"You! Imagination? That'll be the day!" said Mona as she ushered out a pink Ferdie – he liked his bath hot. She motioned to Jedda as she entered the vacant

61

bathroom. "Don't be too long, little one. Breakfast is almost ready."

Once bathed, Jedda's nose led her to the breakfast room.

To Jedda's delight Miss Bevan was there, seated at the table next to Lily. She placed herself down between Matt and George – as far away from Ferdie as possible. Ferdie gave her a mean look, which made her want to smile and feel sad at the same time. He seemed to sense it and lifted a spoonful of cornflakes, throwing them at her across the table. Something in her seemed to bring out the devil in him.

Mona smacked his hand, remonstrating with him, and he started to cry. Jedda felt terrible, thinking it not a very good way to start off her first day, but Matt squeezed her hand, and Miss Bevan smiled at her and said she was very mature not to bother about Ferdie and the vicar agreed with her.

Ferdie left the table with "the sulks" as Mona referred to them. "He's gone to the blue room," she said, "to play his favourite record. He always does that when he's upset."

"Blue room?" Jedda was intrigued.

"Well, he calls it that," said Mona. "Though only he knows why. It's more of a sunshine yellow, the walls, that is, and the suite and curtains are green."

"You and Lily can come over and see the church later, if you want too. Unless of course you wish to explore our countryside?" said George, offering them a choice.

Breakfast was finished by eight o'clock, the vicarage was kept to a strict routine. Mona had opened the patio doors and the mists of early Autumn promised a warm day. The heat of August had subsided along with the flies, though an odd bee could be found having its last drone amongst the flowers, happy in the September sunshine.

Jedda asked Lily to come outside and go for a walk and take in their newly found playground.

Lily answered, "Perhaps later. I'm feeling tired."

Jedda thought Lily ate too much, and at too rapid a speed, and wasn't surprised she was as wide as she was long and always out of breath. She quite liked her, but she was no substitute for Addie. Thinking of Addie made her feel fretful, because when she thought of her friend it automatically brought thoughts of home and Sally and of Gingo and co. This was a beautiful place, but home was where her thoughts and feelings were. She was sick and tired of being uprooted from one place to another.

Seated on a fence close to the vicarage she watched with interest the scene in the distance, beyond which a sea of grass moved to and fro in the warm wind. She studied mountains that formed a background upon which goats, sure footed on the rocks, clung on, the way flies cling to sticky paper. After a while, sitting became tedious and she abandoned the fence in exchange for a lane that veered to the left.

The wide path was empty both of humans and any kind of vehicle. A long path seemed to lead to somewhere, so she took it.

It had been ages since she had encountered nature in all its splendour. Her beloved Cheshire, in spite of its leafy lanes, paled once more into insignificance against the wild beauty of the Cumbrian scenery. Familiar for years with only the grimy city, painted in shades of black and grey – all that was to be found in the dark confines of the city – her senses had become stunted. Now they rushed to the fore as spread before her lay vistas, enchanting in their glory to her ever-searching eyes. As she meandered down the lane, to her left gurgled a stream pouring silver over stones and the sprightly watercress that flourished there. In the background, and protected by a fence, grew damson and plum trees overhanging their screen: purple, lush and hazy in the autumn sun. She found the soft bloom of their skins irresistible, tempting to little fingers that reached up and grasped at nature's bounty. First feasting on some there and then, she pocketed the rest for later. With the strange logic of a child, she gave no thought to the fact that it was stealing. Fruit to her was a gift from the gods, though playing the hypocrite was against her nature and she was shamefully conscious that Gingo would have had a field day laughing at her antics.

She strolled past cottages and low-lying bungalows, pretty and rose covered, like a scene on a chocolate box until her attention was captured by a distant gleam – the sea! Once reached, the end of the lane brought in horizons of blue and gold and only a level crossing barred the way. She waited until an oncoming train passed by and, once it had done so, waited for the safety gates to draw aside, allowing her to walk across the tracks. Now, only sand dunes stood between her and the beckoning sea. When she had started out on her journey it had been with less expectations than this. She had certainly not envisaged an ocean.

It was not a large beach and to her surprise, completely deserted. She wondered how could there be so beautiful a place in which people showed no interest. Boys, footballs, deck chairs, and paddling children were all obviously absent, and she could only suppose it was because the people lived there all the time. Still, it was early morning and perhaps they were all sleeping late.

Walking towards the water's edge, her untrained city eye beguiled by its vast expanse, she was reminded of another day spent with Alex. She had managed to get lost and Alex had been angry, more from fear of losing her than anything else. He had told her to stay put whilst he bought an ice cream, but foolishly on her part, she had followed some children having donkey rides and lost her bearings. She recalled how afraid she had been and how she had cried and a lady had given her a chocolate bar. Then Alex had come running up and found her.

Now, standing on a strange beach, in an even stranger place, she felt sad and alone, as if she were still seven, instead of eleven. Alex had not been to see her for ages and she missed him terribly.

She stood unmoving, mesmerised by the water lapping at her feet, deep in thought. A solitary figure, she became part of nature's painting as she studied seaweed floating Ophelia fashion so that it resembled the hair of drowned maidens. She was so deeply enchanted it was as if she had entered some magic world, one in which she was oblivious to the rest of humanity.

She daydreamed on, lost in her inner thoughts, within the quietness, vaguely aware of a sound in the distance behind her, but she simply ignored it. Then it came again, louder this time, accompanied by the sound of approaching footsteps attended by a man's voice, deep and sounding extremely urgent. Her brow puckered, her body stiffened defensively against the sound of feet becoming more thunderous, closer. Fear made her act and she started to run away from the sound: it was as if a clock had set off alarm bells inside her head. Sally had warned against such creatures. Strangers!

She ran faster towards the foam but was not allowed to damp a toe as fists, big as hams, grasped her from behind.

She was too shocked to struggle, fear held her in its grip, and as they moved from the water's edge the man's back was against the sun casting his shadow on the sand. She hung in a rag doll position, yet even in her terror, was aware of shells scattered on the damp ribbed patterns of the sands.

What was to become of her. Her mother's face flashed before her. Sally would be furious! All her warnings had come to naught! Unexpectedly, as quickly as she had been picked up, she was released and set down on the sand dunes, made aware of the coarse grass as it bit through her clothes and into her thighs. She closed her eyes, tightly. So tightly, her cheekbones were almost united with her eyebrows as she blocked out terror and the final onslaught that was about to come. Waiting for hands to grasp her throat, holding her breath – waiting for death!

The man watched his lunch-box float away upon the waves and turned towards the little girl about to admonish her, but the anguished expression on her face caused him to soften his tones. He shook her arm gently.

Jedda opened her eyes and gazed at the man, mesmerized in the fashion that a rabbit does when its limbs are frozen into fear by the hypnotic stare of a stoat.

The man spoke in deep country tones, "See that lunch box-box floating out to sea? That could have been you. You should be wary of yon waters, they come from side to side and form a horseshoe without a body knowing it. Then you're trapped! Finished! Drowned!" He paused and surveyed his wet overalls and sand-stained boots, "Where's you come from? Haven't seen you before?"

Jedda remained silent.

"Oh, I know," said the man. "You're one of them evacuees, aren't you?"

Jedda nodded, making the man smile. "Be off with you then, and if you go o'er that railway crossing before going back, make sure you wait for a signal saying its safe. Otherwise, you could end up with a leg off."

Jedda sped off murmuring thanks, oddly embarrassed for being the cause of the man's wet garments and swept-away lunch. The man watched her disappear over the dunes and shook his head from side to side, whilst making a mental note to inform the vicar that he had better hand out safety advice to the village's recent arrivals. City folk? Dear, oh dear, oh dear!

Jedda bumped into some of her school friends on the way back to the vicarage – had she a tale to tell... that of "the old man and the sea".

She entered the vicarage in time for elevenses, exhilarated after her recent adventure, glad to be alive and to have escaped an untimely end, only to be greeted by a grim little gathering seated around the wireless. Fingers were swiftly placed on lips to request her silence, and though too young to grasp the absolute significance of the event, it was a moment in history of which she was to be part. One that would live on in her memory for **ALL TIME!** Neville Chamberlain's announcement on the third of September nineteen-thirty-nine, at eleven o'clock precisely: Britain was at war with Germany. It was a speech full of pathos and regret, one that was equally reflected on the faces of the listeners. Most people in Britain would remember what they were doing the exact moment of Mr Chamberlain's historic speech that fatal day, and their whereabouts at that time. Jedda would recall it as the day she met, "the old man and the sea."

Mona burst into tears at the dreadful news and George was quick to comfort her, while Miss Bevan drew Jedda and Lily close and stroked their hair; something she had never done before, being a restrained kind of character. Matt looked grim and lit a cigarette, whilst Mrs Clayton wiped her eyes on her pinny and said she had better "brew up", the cure for all English ills.

Jedda's spirits sank. She was not sure what war meant exactly, but immediately thought of her mother, all alone and stranded in the city. Why hadn't she gone home to Cheshire? Why wasn't she herself there with Zizzie? Alex maybe? What would aunt Dora and uncle David think about the war living in Canada away from it all? They'd worry, she knew that. A hard tightness, like a hand, gripped her chest, filled her with a kind of helplessness over which she had no control. This she hated more than anything and prayed for the years to pass and allow her an adult freedom.

Mona, having recovered herself sufficiently, left George free to consider the children; comfort them. He found Jedda to be a more complex soul than Lily. Lily was a child who was happy as long as she could indulge herself in a cake or a packet of sweets. Jedda? A very different matter! As far as he could surmise, there seemed to be no sign of stability in her background. She was quite a novel individual as far as he was concerned, which puzzled him. And even more than this, something about her troubled him. Not that he could put a finger on what was wrong. When questioned about anything concerning religion, she avoided giving him a straight answer. He suspected she was like Mona in some respects. He'd become a good judge of people's strengths and weaknesses since becoming a vicar of God. From now on he was determined to keep an eye on Jedda.

Alone in the blue room, a place used by everyone for whatever activity they chose to indulge, music or card games etc., Ferdie wound up the gramophone, remaining oblivious to the tides of war. War was just a word without meaning and he could no more understand the evils perpetrated by man than he could Darwen's *The Origin of Species*. The sounds of "Mona you shall be free...ee...when the good Lord sets you free" resounded loudly across the room to be eventually replaced by, "Wheezy Hanna, Wheezy Hanna... down where the watermelons grow..." or "Ramona, I hear the mission bells above". Known around the household as "Ferdie's Choice" – being mainly the only three records he played in a most continuous fashion. If any other records were placed on the turntable he would consider this a personal affront and immediately throw a tantrum of such proportions it was enough to waken the devil in his den.

Jedda and Lily were unaware of this fact and, once he had left the room in search of a snack in Mrs Clayton's absolute domain – the kitchen – they ventured to play Lady of Spain, which was part of a medley of many others. In the midst of a tango, which Jedda and Lily were trying to perfect, a creaking of the door drew their attention, but looking outside and finding no presence beyond, they continued with their dance. They did several turns, and upon hearing a knock at the door crossed the room once more and opened it to welcome in anyone who chose to join them. They were immediately treated to a bag of salt being thrown directly at their eyes. It stung and the girls, naturally upset, began to cry. This affected Ferdie so badly he began to scream, "I want to play Mona. I want to play Mona..." The girls meanwhile, blinked behind literally, salt-shed tears.

The running of several pairs feet, eager to find out the cause of such a commotion, brought things to a head.

Matt, Mona and George arrived on the scene, together with Mrs Clayton close behind. Once the reason for the disturbance was understood, Mona slapped Ferdie's hand, which had the immediate effect of making him worse and he threw himself on the floor in a childlike tantrum.

Jedda and Lily were confused by Ferdie's actions, never having seen a grown boy behave in such a fashion before. Yet at the same time, both felt guilty at the pain they had caused him. George was quick to note the girls' dilemma. "Don't worry about him. It's because he doesn't like anyone playing records unless they are those of his choice. Only three of them, I'm afraid. Anyway, I must attend to your eyes. Do they hurt?" He drew them both into the light and examined Jedda and Lily each in turn. "I don't think it will cause any lasting damage. Good job Ferdie didn't take it into his head to use pepper. Not that he knows the difference." He turned to Mona and Matt. "This can't go on, you know. Not now there are children in the house. You'll have to keep a closer eye on him."

"We won't play the records any more, will we Lily?" Jedda was worried in case they were made to leave – such was the depth of her insecurity.

George, sensitive to her feelings as always, imagined what her fears must be. He put his arms around both she and Lily and told them not to worry. They could play music anytime Ferdie was out for a walk, which would be more often now. He gave Mona and Matt a searching look and went off to finish writing a sermon which had been so rudely interrupted, leaving them to sort out any further difficulties. There were none! Jedda and Lily had vacated the room, quickly!

With only two days to go before Christmas the vicarage was a hive of activity. Mona helped out with the village children's choir practice, in which Lily had been included. Jedda, it seemed, was not suitable. Though she had a nice voice, she seemed incapable of keeping in tune with the others – either that, or drowning the rest of them with her high-pitched trilling.

George had somehow guessed as much, considering she appeared to be out of step with most things, anyway. Only the other day he had caught her in his study deep into one of his many books. She had blushed, but he had refused to accept any form of apology saying she could sit in his study away from the hustle and bustle of domesticity anytime. In seeking to gain her confidence he hoped bring her out of herself, to come to terms with life and, sad as it may be, her parents' divorce.

As time went by Jedda came to be as fond of him as he of her. In a sense, she reminded him of Mona with her love of poetry, only Jedda seemed to prefer a different kind of venue. Mona wrote her own kind of prose that he found difficult to relate to. He was, in spite of his deep leanings towards his Creator, very much of this world. So much more so than Mona, whom he suspected lived in some romantic world of her own making. She was almost as much a problem to him as the young evacuee to whom he now offered so much devotion, and along with the difficulties Ferdie and Matt brought with them, he was well aware he had his work cut out. He was relieved that with the New Year approaching, an innovative young curate was to replace old Mr Sutton who was about to retire.

The New Year Festivities were over and it was in mid-January, early one cold blustery night that the terror appeared. A cold moon illuminated the gravestones and cast shadows on the old grey stones of the church and the old bell tower. Jedda had just stepped outside, alone. She had left the library because George had returned to write his evening sermon. He asked her to stay and insisted she was not disturbing him, but she had informed him she needed some air and that Mona had asked her if she could find Ferdie because he was outside somewhere and dinner was almost ready.

She had only just stepped outside when she saw it! The black fox! He snarled and sneaked up towards her, slyly, his eyes fixed on her with a baleful stare. Of Ferdie there was no sign and she did not care for the dark, certainly not in the churchyard. Now she was being stalked by a creature from the mouth of hell!

George, when it was discovered that Ferdie had been hiding in a cupboard in one of his hide-and-seek moods, had come in search of Jedda to inform her of the same, almost on her heels so to speak, and now he stood watching the scene before him just a short distance away. Jedda's face, reflected in the moonlight, was alabaster white, the terror in her eyes unmistakable.

"It's all right, Jedda." George stood behind her, "It's only a fox. It won't harm you." He drew her behind him, aware of her fear, and stamped his foot. The fox remained stationary, its pale water eyes fixed on them, unblinking. George had never known such fearlessness. Foxes usually ran from humans, afraid of attack. This one had no qualms whatsoever! George called out loudly for Matt, but still the creature did not budge. Not even when Matt came running gun in hand and fired a shot in the air. It began to retreat, but not as quickly as expected, standing its ground for a while, its mouth drawn back in a snarl, its eyes fearlessly trained on Jedda in absolute defiance before it turned tail and sauntered casually away. After it reached the end of the drive it looked back, as if in contempt at man's intervention, angry at losing its quarry.

"Well! Did you ever see anything like that for a fox? Evil-looking thing. Cheeky with it too!" said Matt.

"It wasn't really a proper fox," said Jedda, "I've seen it before somewhere. Its face changes into one of us."

Matt laughed. "What an imagination she has," he said to George.

George was not so sure, he'd never come across anything like it before. He imagined it was what a creature conceived in Hades would resemble.

They went indoors and everyone sat down to dinner, George and Matt still pondering on such a strange happening. They were about to discuss the arrival of the fox with Mona and Miss Bevan when Mrs Clayton interrupted them and announced a visitor: The new curate had arrived.

John Spencer was a most affable young man and charmed all who met him. Thirty years old, tall, dark and most attractive in a languid kind of way. Quite an asset in his profession and most people in the village took to the young curate immediately. George introduced him to all the company present and Mona was immediately attracted by his magnetism. George and Matt were most cordial towards him, and Lily? – well she was in love. Only Mrs Clayton and Jedda were evasive, as if something about him didn't quite click into place.

Strangely enough, Ferdie took an instant dislike to him too, which was odd, because he always seemed to deliberately oppose anything that pleased Jedda.

Chapter Seven

Winter drew her cloak around her, crept away and spring danced in. And now, at last, the hazy days of summer had arrived and the sun shone brightly just to prove it.

Mona seemed to spend more time than was warranted with John, lost in a whirl of poetic endeavour, which he, a lover of the arts, encouraged. George, conscious of Mona's happiness, and realizing how dull the vicarage must be for so mercurial a creature, was more than pleased to see the bright change in his some-times depressed looking wife.

Matt, though not thinking anything amiss between them, was less at ease with the situation. He told his sister to take care, that people might talk, and it wasn't a good thing where a vicar's wife was concerned to spend so much time with the curate. Also, that it put George in an unenviable position.

Mona had merely dismissed the idea and declared he was being ridiculous.

Mona and John fell in love without being consciously aware of it. Neither gave way to fleshly desires, their love was more a meeting of minds and things spiritual to begin with; then one day, without thinking, Mona was so entranced by a poem John had written for her she threw her arms around him and proffered a kiss, only on his cheek, but things began to escalate from then on and they could hardly bear to be apart from each other.

One of their favourite meeting places was the belfry, almost as high up to the heavens as earthly beings could aspire. Nothing untoward ever took place, their love was too pure. They merely held hands, eyes misty with a love that would not be denied. It was a situation both were sad about and, to their credit both were sensitive to the welfare of others, especially George. These were feelings that the village gossip, Mrs Marigold Smedly, would not have related to: a fact not at all surprising, as Marigold had had more affairs than the whore of Babylon.

She was well known and much talked about around the village, so was her husband, for the fool that he was. They had come to live in the village just before the advent of the war, an unwelcome fact, from a villagers' point of view. They did not take too kindly to strangers. Mack Smedly drove a van of sorts and used it for all sorts of excursions in the dark hours of early morning. People were suspicious of his activities and swore he dabbled on the black market. In between her various affairs with different men in the village and outside of it, Marigold Smedly dealt mainly in scandal. As one villager remarked, "She's only lived here for five minutes and she knows more than me that's lived here all my life, and most of that's made up. If I repeated the awful lies she tells about people, I'd cause a riot in this village."

After a time people avoided her. It was rumoured that wherever Marigold Smedly had lived she was soon made to move elsewhere.

She had often tried to target Mona when she wished to scandalize someone or other, but Mona was always as equally determined to ignore her barbed tongue, avoiding her at every turn possible. She was also not really interested in discussing the fact with Marigold that Mac Smedly wore a truss, something laughed at by the villagers when Marigold hung it on the washing line for all to see.

Mac's lack of sexual ability was the main reason for Marigold's regular ventures into illicit passion. Mainly with the milkman, but sometimes with the window cleaner or any of the repairmen who frequented her house from time to time when Mac was away involved in his own doubtful practices. Marigold was obliged to cover her own moral lapses by trying to bring to light flaws in others sprinkled around the village.

Her favourite pastime was hiding behind the Venetian blinds that covered all the windows of her house; her hated next door neighbour, Miss Pringle, took note of this, and, because Miss Pringle often smiled surreptitiously when passing by her window, Marigold knew she had been caught out spying on others and was very much annoyed by the fact.

Miss Pringle would often point out to people that they were being watched and Marigold's undersized figure would be noticed peeping from within.

Now it was poor Mona's turn to be subjected to scandal, Marigold just hated anyone who would not fit into her scheme of things. Decency in others was beyond her comprehension and her main ally when it came to joining her in any character assassination was Aggie Phelps, who helped out at the Post Office and a bitter adversary of the lovely Mona. She had long ago had her eye on George with no positive result, the vicarage having been the main attraction, and to her way of thinking, tantamount to being the lady of the manor. Yet here she had remained, a mere counter hand.

It was Lily, unfortunately for Mona, whose innocent ears picked up the scandal about she and John by listening to the babblings of Aggie and Marigold; they themselves, completely unaware of the small interloper hovering in the background.

Lily had gone to change the sixpenny postal order her mother occasionally sent her, wishing it to be turned into hard cash. Her mind was dwelling on lollipops and ice cream while waiting to be served by the chattering Aggie.

70

Her postal order eventually changed, ice cream long devoured and lollipops secreted in a pocket for later, Lily strolled at her usual slow pace along the lane and met up with Jedda.

Jedda noticed wisps of chocolate from Lily's recently eaten ice cream still present beneath the curve of her mouth.

"I see you've changed your postal order, then," said Jedda, hopeful for a share of Lily's bounty.

Lily reached inside her pocket, ever generous, and retrieved two lollipops. She handed one to Jedda. "I was saving them until I saw you." she said, speaking in the manner of someone who had committed a deed of great charity, which was true on her part. She was greedy, as well as generous, and had had to put up quite a fight with her conscience to restrain herself from devouring both treats.

Jedda thanked her and they continued on their way talking.

"I wonder what affair means?" said Lily.

"Don't know, said Jedda, "Oh, yes I do. It's swings and roundabouts and all that."

"Oh, then that's where Mona and John must be going. That's what the two ladies in the Post Office said. I heard them say so while I was waiting for my money."

They were filled with delight at the thought of visiting a fairground, neither had been to one for ages, both ignorant of the fact that there were better things to do during a war than to guide the enemy by the flickering lights of hundreds of flashing bulbs on twirling carousels.

Entering the vicarage in an exited manner they immediately approached the vicar. It had been a long time since anything so wonderful had happened and now a fair was coming to the village. The country was fine, but very little happened in the way of entertainment.

Mona had gone shopping on her old bike. The car had been put into mothballs for the duration of the war and when first Jedda and Lily had arrived they had been taken rides in it, but such luxuries were no longer possible.

Matt had taken Ferdie for a walk, and only the vicar was home seated in the library busy composing his Sunday sermon. The girls knocked on the library door, gently as was expected of them. George shouted come in and they entered brimming over with excitement and asked him about the fair.

"I haven't heard anything," George smiled back at them, conscious of their excitement. "I think you must have got the message wrong. Anyway, the lighting up of any form of entertainment is out of the question; we are at war, you know."

"Oh, no, I heard that lady behind the counter say to that lady called Marigold that Mona and John were having a fair." Lily was adamant.

George's face crumpled into a frown and Lily began to feel upset. "Was it a secret do you think? Have I spoiled a surprise?" she said.

George did not answer her, merely waved his hand as if wishing to finish the subject, then called them back as they ventured to leave. "Don't be upset about this Lily, just don't mention it to anyone. Promise!"

Lily and Jedda nodded, not wishing to defy him, worried because he looked so sad. They decided to go for another walk before lunch, see if they could find any pretty shells on the seashore to add to their burgeoning collection.

Jedda's favourite place if she wished to be quiet was just below the belfry at the back of the organ. It had also come to her notice that just above her head had become Mona and John's special meeting place, too. Once free of their individual chores, they would climb up into the belfry with sandwiches and a flask, and spend many hours there totally unaware of Jedda's existence.

At times, when the vicar had vacated the library, Jedda liked to snuggle down in his favourite chair with a book and smell the mixture of leather and tobacco that lingered there; odours reminiscent of Sandy as she rested content within its warm and cosy interior. But once George returned to write his sermon she would venture into the church, if only to find peace from Ferdie's constant gramophone playing of "Mona you shall be free..."

Even Lily did not know of her secret, private little place. Often, she could hear Mona's reciting of her latest attempt at some kind of verse, sentimental and self-indulgent, all about love and the loss of it. John knew it could never be construed as great, but was nevertheless flattered by it. He absolutely adored Mona with a pure and undying love. That's all it was, or ever would be, in spite of any scandal attached to it.

A gnawing at Jedda's stomach told her it was dinnertime and, that at seven o'clock, in spite of the food shortages, special friends with whom George and Mona had not dined with for quite a while were to be their guests.

Jedda and Lily had worked hard that day helping Mrs Clayton to clean the vicarage, give it an extra spit and polish, especially the hall with its fine parquet floor. The two girls waltzed briskly about the dining room setting the table to perfection. The damask cloth complimented the silver which was reflected in the wine glasses and cut glass rose bowls, these filled with pink and white flowers selected from the greenhouse that very morning by Mona. As an added touch, three pale pink candles had been placed in each of a beautiful pair of silver candlesticks, which now adorned either end of the long refectory table.

Mona placed petite trays of olives on small tables conveniently placed in front of sofas and at the sides of easy chairs. A large sliver drinks tray had been positioned on the sideboard in readiness for guests to have aperitifs while they waited to be summoned in to dinner.

"Those are the last of the olives. Don't know when I'll be able to obtain any further supplies with this nuisance of a war. Though I do suppose it will be over by next Christmas, if not before," Mona spoke vaguely both to herself and Jedda and Lily. It was something she was prone to do; Jedda was used to it and took it in her stride... grownups again.

Mrs Clayton came in carrying some chocolate biscuits along with the crisp water and cheese ones. "I don't think I'll put all of these out," she said referring to the tit-bits in general.

"I quite agree," replied Mona. "As I was just saying to the girls, with so many shortages, we had better be on the side of caution. I think we had better put at least half back in a tin in case they're are needed for another time."

Jedda and Lily couldn't recall Mona saying any such thing but let it go. They were aware by now of Mona thinking things and imagining she'd said them. Especially Jedda, whose maturity knew no bounds.

"I've baked plenty of scones anyway," said Mrs Clayton. "And three apple pies and four meat ones for supper later, should any one decide they are hungry. Though with such a large main meal of roast beef and all the trimmings, I can't see that they will." She paused and studied the table as if it could give her an answer. "And I've some nice cheese. Two kinds. Lancashire and Stilton. Don't know when I'll manage to get any more, though." she wandered back to the kitchen looking doleful.

Matt had called at the pub with Ferdie before deciding to go home, vowing not to stay too long, but as usual, he always broke his vows. It was a warm evening and he and Ferdie had joined a group of acquaintances, outside in the small pub garden seated by rustic tables, enjoying a laugh and a chat. They also included Ferdie in their banter, tried to add a little colour into his dry existence. The district nurse passed by, peach skinned and pretty, a bundle of curves. Ferdie whistled because he had often heard the men whistle and formed his hands in a figure eight to represent her shapely charms, something he had often observed them doing.

The nurse laughed, pinched Ferdie's cheek, unabashed by his actions, while the men joined in the laughter. Matt realized he'd had a few too many and decided Ferdie and he had better be on their way home.

Half way through the village he realized he was hungry and called for some fish and chips, the evening's dining arrangements and the special guests invited for dinner having completely left his mind.

The family, including guests, were all seated round the large dining table. The meal served up by Mrs Clayton was absolute perfection.

"How do you do it, Mrs Clayton. In these dreadful times too." Mrs Brown's several chins quivered with delight. If there were food shortages they hadn't to date affected her obese frame. She was a terrible snob, something George was well aware of. He also suspected she had heard rumours about John and Mona by the suspicious way she kept eyeing them. He was not in a pleasant frame of mind and wished the evening to be truly over.

Mona was in a convivial mood, smiling at everyone, making polite and charming conversation and Mr Brown was more than intrigued by his pretty hostess and though his blowsy wife was put out by his lack of attention to herself, she did not show it in an outright fashion. She tried to draw John into the conversation as much as possible, trying to detract from all eyes being drawn to the delightful Mona.

Julia Phillips was a tall, mannish type of woman, outspoken with a rather loud voice. Her cuddly, rotund husband Jack, whom she bossed unbearably and made bring in the washing and play nanny to their spoilt brat of a child, Evelyn, joined her.

Julia more than made herself heard. In opposite, Jack, who spoke in a Midlands accent so low that it barely rose above a whisper, would demur most of the time to his wife's commands with a rather silly titter.

Their actions caused Jedda no end of amusement, which she politely refrained from showing. Watching George's face she recalled that the whole scene reminded her of Sandy and Viner, and the thought saddened her, made her wonder when Sally was coming to visit. In spite of her mother's promises it was now late August, almost a year since she had first arrived in Cumberland and still no signs of Sally's presence.

After a decent interval, the dinner wine seemed to mellow the rather dull company, and the conversation became more sparkling; until something happened to really liven things up. Matt, forgetful of those assembled around the table came sliding forth, completely out of control and landed in their midst. Right in the middle of the dining room table to be precise, the simple reason being, helped on his way by two enthusiastic girls who had not only polished the hall, but also under the carpet!

Glasses went flying as Matt glided across the table, and Mrs Brown ended up with Matt's fish and chips in her hair, whilst Mr Brown took the brunt of most of the wine.

The company's state of shock was so evident, that for several seconds everyone appeared to be in a state of paralysis, the whole scene resembled a freeze frame; then, just as quickly, it moved, and everyone started talking together, gesticulating as they went along. The invited guests were furious and Mrs Brown cried out, "Oh what a mess Mr Sutton-Brown," – when agitated she always became hyphenated – "Whatever shall we do? Look at my dress!"

Their hosts were apologetic, while the children tried to contain their giggles. Poor Ferdie stood in a trance behind a reeling Matt, watching his older brother in amazement as he tried to gain a foothold. His confusion escalated further as Matt collapsed in a drunken heap, closed his eyes, becoming oblivious to the whole sorry proceedings. Thus ended the evening's entertainment as Mona and George escorted the Browns and The Phillips to the door midst a stream of apologies and, "Do come again, it isn't always like this," fully aware that their offer would definitely not be taken up again as their guests marched off with no desire for a repeat performance.

Later, George, secretly amused, explained to the girls that it was sweet of them to help out, but would they in future refrain from polishing under the carpet.

The newly labelled Mrs Sutton-Brown – as she had suddenly become – would relate the whole fiasco to the rest of village by noon next day.

George was made well aware of the controversy the ill-conceived dinner had caused when it was rumoured by some uncharitable souls that the vicarage was a place, if not exactly one of disrepute, was certainly not one of respectability in the finest sense of the word.

Autumn was at its height, leaves falling down in a cascade of orange, brown and gold, the tumble of which, Jedda and Lily enjoyed sweeping up and placing in small mounds ready for Matt to burn. Saturday was their favourite day, free from the ties of schoolwork and the trudge to the village school. Though they liked the village children who were nice in return, they liked contact with other evacuees, for they were homesick and playing with others from their own background helped to keep dark thoughts at bay.

Jedda never thought she would miss the city so much, but had been proved wrong, often wishing she could go and visit Addie and Gingo. She missed the succulent smells of the Tobias's bakery, playing on the pianola and the sound of Billy's jazz records. She also wished for the peace and quiet of her own fireside and the neighbours who visited the shop; and of privately being able to sit and listen to the *Third Programme* with its beautiful music and poems. She could not always follow what some of it meant, but found it intriguing, beautiful to her ears. Also being away from Fergie's endless doling out of his favourite tunes would be heaven.

Jedda stopped dreaming and she and Lilly managed to get the leaves in little bundles ready for Matt to burn. Ferdie came outdoors and started to dance about in a most annoying fashion dispersing the leaves hither and thither so that the girls were obliged to re-gather them. His actions were something they were reluctant to chide him about, because he did not know any better. Poor Ferdie, Jedda despaired for him at times and had grown quite fond of him in spite of the way he tormented her. They did have one thing in common though – regardless of his sweetness towards them both – they could not feel any affection for John Spencer.

He took up too much of the time Mona had meted out to them before his having arrived on the scene.

75

Matt built the fire from twigs and old newspaper and stood back and watched as the blaze grew steadily hotter, keeping a keen eye on Ferdie and the two girls at the same time.

"Don't come too close, Jedda. We don't want your pretty face burnt... don't do that, Ferdie." Matt leapt forward and took his hand. "Don't you girls go near that fire until I return. I'm just taking Ferdie to Mona, he's too much of a handful when I'm busy."

The girls continued to sweep the leaves while Matt searched for Mona and eventually found her in the belfry with John. "Must you always be up there with 'John Keats' Mona?" he remonstrated with her in an angry, sarcastic fashion. "I don't know what George is thinking of letting you behave so foolishly. People are talking."

"People! What people? Silly narrow-minded villagers, I suppose. Well I don't care about them." Mona shrugged her shoulders dismissively, "As long as George trusts me, that's all that matters."

"Does he? I've watched him lately, and he does not seem too happy with the situation, to me. We men are strange creatures, once made jealous."

"George is not the jealous type," said Mona.

"There is no such thing as a non-jealous man. Only if he no longer loves you, and George loves you dearly, anyone can see that. Anyway, don't you think he has enough to put up with? Ferdie and I are not his relatives, we're yours."

"I'm coming now. Goodbye John, Ferdie needs me," said Mona, tripping daintily down the belfry stairs.

With the onset of October the weather changed drastically and so did the atmosphere at the vicarage. The whole mood of the place became gloomier day by day, and Jedda, sensitive soul that she was, noticed a distinct difference of attitude in the vicar. He was becoming absent minded – a deficiency that seemed prevalent in most of his flock, for very few attended church nowadays – and his sermons lacked the fire they had once possessed.

Jedda was seated in her favourite place in the church enjoying some peace and quiet. Ferdie had been playing "Mona you shall be fre...ee..." all morning, and it had been getting on her nerves. Lily, made of stronger stuff, had remained helping Mrs Clayton clean up after breakfast, something Jedda was none too keen on doing. Lily, she thought, would make a good housewife with lots of children and live in sweet contentment. She envied Lily at times and wished she were more like her, she was always so restless herself and downright unhappy.

She was well into Dickens' *Great Expectations*, feeling worried in case Pip did not get over his illness caused by burns received whilst trying to save Miss Haversham. She could hear faint murmurings from the two poets in the belfry above, but was not disturbed by it. After Ferdie's noise, the rest seemed silence.

She looked up from time to time noticing Mona's small feet come out of the square boxed in staircase, revealing themselves through the rickety spindles that surrounded the staircase, and the occasional glimpse of John's black shoes, shiny as always and tapping to the rhythm of each spoken piece. Sometimes, one of them would lean on the balcony, and it would make her nervous. She was always afraid they might fall over; it was quite a depth.

Close by to where she was sitting, behind the organ and unobserved, the sound of a pair of feet was heard and by the swish of his cassock she knew it to be the vicar. It was most unusual, she had never known him come this way at this time of day. She was about to acknowledge him, but something in his demeanour made her act otherwise. Soon, she caught the sound of his feet, making the wood creak as he ascended the rickety stairs that led to the belfry.

She did not quite know what happened, only that George's voice was raised, something distinctly unusual for him. She looked up to see John move backwards, stumble, and fall with a sickening thud to the ground below. When Mona reached out to save him, the vicar made a grab for her – in vain it seemed – she too followed John to a sickening death as she cracked her skull on the hard surface of the church floor as it met her bones.

Close to the base of the organ, Jedda remained mesmerised as the vicar only just managed to hang on for dear life, clinging to the broken spindles that surrounded the platform of the belfry.

Jedda stared at the broken bodies only a few feet away, horrified until her mind broke free; then she ran in terror from the church, her heart pounding, while the vicar remained silent, frozen, gazing down at the two lifeless bodies below, totally unaware of Jedda's recent presence.

Jedda ran into the library, snuggled down quickly into an armchair trembling. Looking out of the window she perceived the vicar walking up the path towards the vicarage, his face a white sheet. Not aware of Jedda's witnessing the recent scene he need not have worried on her part anyway, she would not say a word. It was to be their secret but one she would keep even from himself. She'd make sure of that.

What happened next, seemed to Jedda, to occur out of the blue. It all happened most swiftly and all she and Lily knew was, they were at last going home.

Sally arrived at the Vicarage post-haste, with Lily's mother close behind. Fathers no longer seemed to feature in children's lives any more, most seemed to be in the services except for a few on special war work. Jedda would never see hers again and was greeted with terrible news from her mother that Alex had just died of pneumonia and that he was soon to be buried.

Still in a state of shock over Mona's death, she and Lily had sobbed uncontrollably into their pillows, for several dark, continuous nights. The police had visited the vicarage, come and gone several times, probing into the events of that fatal day. George had protested his innocence. bewildered by the loss of his beloved Mona, filled with regret at losing his temper and for listening to the foolish gossip that had led to such a tragic turn of events. The police remained highly suspicious, eventually taking George away with them to the police station, never to have him return, charged with double murder. When Jedda had questioned Matt and Mrs Clayton about George's arrest, they had not been able to give any complete answers to her futile enquiries.

And now her mother was telling her about Alex. That he was dead and she would never see him again and she felt guilt-ridden because she had been angry with him – bitter at his continued absence from her life. In her childlike fashion she had been so hurt. Angry with him, and she had told Lily she didn't care if he was dead because he no longer loved her. Now she had got her wish – she had killed him and the shock, on top of Mona's untimely end, was making life unbearable.

The loss of Alex pushed all thoughts of George out of her mind completely. A fact made even worse by Lily taxing her on the subject and asking her if she were glad Alex was dead. She had rounded on the hapless Lily in such a fashion that her small friend had almost lost her balance.

"Of course not, you fat stupid thing," had been Jedda's tart reply.

A rude and enraged Jedda was something Lily had never encountered before and she was visibly upset.

Jedda had not recognised her mother at first, she appeared to be someone else attired in a natty mustard coloured suit, and a little hat shaped like an artist's palette on top of her head. It sported a long brown feather, though she wore her usual furs draped across her shoulders. Red fox!

Surprisingly, she did not cry upon receiving the news of Alex's death, it had been so long since she had heard from him – he had not even sent her a card for her birthday in March. She had been angry, her pride hurt, and through her childish outburst to Lily wishing him dead, her conscience hurt so much she felt at war with herself believing her evil thoughts to have been the cause of his demise.

The woman who had come to take her home, the one who did not seem to be her mother and who, by her own confused state of mind, made her wonder if a stranger was impersonating Sally, left her feeling in mid-air. Yet, in spite of this conjecture, she nevertheless recognised that these were false thoughts. But somehow, she never felt the same towards her mother again, considering herself a complete orphan.

The vicarage was empty. Cleared of all who had ever loved, laughed, or lived there. The rooms echoed with the final reproach of the deserted and the sound of Ferdie's "Mona you shall be free" was silenced forever. Only the ghost of a late October breeze whispered through an open door as they all trooped out into the forecourt, each individual waiting for a taxi to ferry them away.

When two taxis eventually arrived – one for the mothers and children to ferry them to the station – the other to transport Ferdie and a social worker to a place unspecified, Mrs Clayton locked up the vicarage for a final time amidst tears and sorrowful embraces from the group standing outside.

Matt was the first to say goodbye as he ushered a bewildered Ferdie into the waiting social worker's car along with his gramophone and favourite records. Ferdie continued fretting for Mona and kept saying he didn't want her to be in heaven, only with him. Matt could not take care of him, the fact was obvious. Since Mona's death he had sunk lower and lower into the oblivion of drink and merciful forgetfulness. Murder was not something he could quite relate to where George was concerned, yet John and Mona lay in the mortuary until the inquest could be held. George, in the meantime, lingered in a prison cell, so poor Ferdie had to go into a home, and as Jedda and Lily observed him leave, it was with an unbearable sadness in their hearts. They each prayed silently that he would be granted the freedom to play his favourite records, something he was always been allowed to do at the vicarage.

Jedda never mentioned what she witnessed that fateful day, partly from shock and definitely in the misguided belief that she was helping George. She had seen the police and heard people talk, but she had remained faithful - silent!

Soon she would be home and hopefully, as Sally stated to Mrs Clayton, her poor daughter would forget about the carry-on at the vicarage.

Now the taxi had arrived to take the mothers and children to the station, Mrs Clayton, eyes red from the constant tears she had shed over the last few days, came forward to kiss the children goodbye; an unusual show of affection on her part as she informed their mothers that it had been a pleasure to know them and that she hoped they would write to her.

Jedda and Lily promised they would and handed her a gift they had bought with their pocket money, a sixpenny pair of earrings from Woolworth's from Lily and a necklace from Jedda. They both matched and were made of paste emeralds. Mrs Clayton was so touched she started to cry all over again.

As the taxi pulled away from the vicarage Lily and the two mothers sat looking ahead, but Jedda glanced back and in doing so perceived what she hoped she would never see again – **THE BLACK FOX**! Catching her breath she studied its black fur, shining in the October sun. It stared back at her, balefully; instinctively, as if joyful of a crime recently committed. Conscious of the knowledge that some atrocity had occurred and that it was pleased with the results. Delighted by the pain that was being heaped upon her. She had not cast her eyes upon its evil presence since that first morning when George had comforted her. Now George had vanished in the same way that everyone and everything connected with him had vanished. It was to her as if the time spent at the vicarage had never been.

Her attention was elsewhere for just a second and when she focused on the fox again it was only to find it too had disappeared along with one more disrupted chapter in her life.

The saga of the village was not yet over, much more terrifying events were to follow but Jedda still remained ignorant of the fact that she could have been of help to George in his time of great need. Her sense of misguided loyalty was to be his undoing and in spite of his protestations to the contrary, belief in his innocence was never established. As far as the authorities were concerned he was guilty and two years later, after a long and much publicized trial, George Webb was found guilty and hanged. Jedda was kept in complete ignorance of the fact and it was so well kept from her, it was too late for her to intervene when once she had found out about a most terrible case of injustice.

The evacuees slowly but surely drifted back to the cities. The war was just a joke and would be over shortly, everyone was sure of that.

Though Sally and Miss Bevan knew about George being arrested for the murder of Mona and John, they decided not to mention it to Jedda thinking it most unwise, and that it might upset her unduly. So she continued to remain ignorant of the matter, unaware of the dire consequences that her self-imposed silence had brought about.

Nor, thankfully, was she aware that the wagging of evil tongues by the villagers - especially Marigold, Aggie and people of that ilk who had been indirectly responsible for the tragedy that had occurred in the first place; and who in so doing, had laid a non-existent crime at the feet of poor George. But Jedda never bared her soul to anyone. It was not until she was much older that she realized the enormity of her misplaced loyalty and the tragedy that had resulted from it.

They say revenge is sweet and the gods are not mocked! So it seemed, when Mac Smedly came home one evening unexpectedly and found Marigold in bed, not only with Fanny from the post office, but also a land-girl with whom Mac and Marigold were both acquainted; though in Mac's case, it was for black-market reasons only.

Sleeping with the milkman was one thing, sleeping with the milkmaid was another. It was well noted in the village that, not only one woman had taken to wearing dark glasses, but three of them. After all, in those times swinging both ways was not a matter subscribed to. Girls were girls and boys were boys. A fact that could make a man also take up swinging, only in this instance, with his fists. So had it been the case with Mac Smedley.

Chapter Eight

Spring had arrived early, bright, but rather cold. A few flowers bloomed gaily in the park, but in the uncharitable climate of the city nothing flourished with much vigour.

Minus the railings that had once surrounded the park's tatty interior, children were allowed the complete freedom to roam where they chose, run as wild as they may. At the far end of the park, where a scant tennis court had once reigned and was seldom used by residents nearby, was based an air-force crew who were at that moment busy fixing up a barrage balloon which, along with the battalion, would become a permanent fixture. Jedda was amazed at the size of the balloon when grounded. It resembled a whale out of water, a very huge, restless fish that needed strings to keep it in place. One of the W.A.F.F.S was very nice and smiled a lot at children but told them to keep their distance because they were not supposed to be there.

The children were having a great time in what amounted to legalized truancy. Most of the schools had become almost empty when the teachers and pupils had been shunted off to the country. Now, many children had drifted back, but not all of the teachers, and the children were being allowed to drift in a sea of ignorance. The lean years of the depression were becoming a mere, dreadful memory. Fortunately, jobs would be plentiful once the children reached fourteen, which was now only two years away as far as Jedda and Addie were concerned.

Gingo and gang had all been due to leave at Christmas but not before the return of the teachers brought them back into the educational fold. Miss Bevan, once more home and established in her teaching position at the school, passed by on her way to class one day and, observing them all at play, told Jedda, Gingo and the gang that school was to open next week, though only part-time at first until things got organized. Gingo cursed and said he wished she hadn't seen them, even Jedda was beginning find her interest in the academic world was beginning to fade. A week later and much to their chagrin, they were all seated at their desks busy scribbling away.

Things were not too bad when Miss Bevan took the lessons but Peppercorn seemed to be taking the classes much more often.

He seemed to have a distinct dislike for Gingo and Jedda and, because of the difference in their ages, thought Jedda should be in a lower group than Gingo.

Miss Bevan disagreed and always achieved what she wanted, and though Miss Lomax, as headmistress, always had the last word, she generally agreed with Miss Bevan and Jedda was allowed to remain where she was. A fact that pleased Jedda very much; Gingo wasn't sure, being older. He thought her too clever for her own boots.

Come Monday morning in the large main hall, seated at the piano in her usual stiff-backed Barbara Stanwyke fashion was Miss Lomax, very much in charge, tutoring all her pupils with their music lessons.

All the teachers were present, including Miss Daltry and Miss Kershaw. Gingo said they were a female version of Peter Lorre and Sidney Greenstreet. Jedda was inclined to agree. Daltry and Kershaw were also very fond of each other, this she knew because whenever she went in the small room reserved for the teachers break period to pick up a cup of tea for Miss Bevan, Sid and Peter were always kissing one another. She thought it rather sweet but Gingo didn't agree with her when she informed him about it. He just doubled over laughing in a very strange way that she thought cruel.

She did not like it either when Gingo teased her every time Miss Lomax said, "All sing except Jedda Markham," with the excuse, "You have a lovely voice, I'm sure dear, but you're inclined to drown everybody."

Gingo would torment her all the way home with, "I'm sure you have a lovely voice dear, it's just that it's bloody terrible."

She would be cross and tell him not to swear, envious also of his angelic musical renderings - the one thing that he excelled at more than she.

Jedda and the gang spent their holidays at their usual rendezvous, the park; even shabbier since the advent of war, neglected, like most unnecessary pursuits. The men who tended the flowers were more intent on manning the guns; all that remained was covered by sparse grass. A murky paddling pool and an even murkier duck pond tried their best. A piece of grey concrete that passed as a recreational ground, boasted only a slide, plus several swings. The cake was a strong favourite, especially with Jedda and Addie. Gingo and co; Once Addie and she were seated on its fat wooden round, they would cling to the rails and the boys would push it round extremely fast and she and Addie would pretend to scream, which would make the boys push it faster, much to the secret joy of the two girls.

A new kind of entertainment had also formed itself in the guise of the underground shelter; one that ran like a long winding snake through the whole length of the park, as yet unused by the populace, the reason it had been built for in the first place.

It was the correct venue for spies and secret agents, or any other make-believe characters present in the fertile minds of incorrigible city children.

Even Dr Fu Manchu lurked in the shadows, though most of the time he ran the

Chinese laundry in the guise of Mr Wing. A kindly, respectable, hard working man and a Chinese father of eight children to date; he had given his wife a gold sovereign for every one born. She attached the sovereigns to a gold bracelet after each happy event. Mr Wing would always smile and give Jedda and Addie sweets when they collected the laundry for their respective mothers, but come night – in the imagination of Jedda, Addie, Gingo and Co; inclusive – he changed dramatically. No longer Mr Wing, he would become Dr Fu Manchu, Arch Demon – a devil of Chinese torture. A dealer in white slavery and a smoker of the poppy.

The children saw his shop as a place riddled with tunnels leading to China, well equipped with instruments to make even the bravest man scream. These tunnels had now expanded and ran under the park to join the other recently made burrows. Only true logic could prove how this came to be, after all, Mr Wing only possessed a small backyard and was not aware he was Dr Fu Manchu anyway. He was far too busy looking after the laundry and adding sovereigns to his wife's bracelet. Sax Rhomer had a lot to answer for.

In spite of it being well lit, the children would venture only so far into the tunnel's entrance. Wooden forms, placed all along the walls and ready to be used by citizens during prospective air raids, featured in great numbers, but the gang showed little interest in these. They would venture, stealthful as always, towards the edge of the tunnel and whisper, "We have come to get you, Fu Manchu," and slight moan of another child in hiding or the distant rustle of a mouse would send them all scampering out in to the daylight screaming, a combination of fear and delight, happy, in a last peaceful summer.

Autumn faded away. Winter arrived, described by the weather forecast as the coldest in forty years, Siberian in its wake. Whilst outdoors the children's toes soon informed them of the freezing weather but did little to deter their wild spirits. With two pairs of socks pushed down in their wellies Jedda and Addie braved the cold regardless and to add to her ensemble Jedda wore a pair of fur gloves, one brown the other black. She had another pair at home, twins of the ones she was wearing, but could not trouble to find them.

Generally, once their bodies had reached freezing point, the gang's main location was the neighbourhood church. Like young heathens they would shelter in the vestry until warm and, having made use of God's house, once thawed out, would be off outside to face the elements.

Christmas was only three days away and though goods were becoming much more scarce in nineteen-forty things seemed stable enough regarding the phoney war. By next year everyone was assured it would be over and the shops would be back to normal. Dunkirk was a thing of the past and soon, save for a few men declared unfit to serve, most were in uniform, but they too, everybody believed, would soon be demobbed in no time.

Women stayed busy in the factories to boost the war effort as long as circumstance remained unfavourable. Mrs Albertini had obtained a job in a factory and Gingo told Jedda she was going to buy him some new clothes.

Jedda was singularly pleased, especially as she had heard her mother and Mrs Tobias discussing the sad plight of Mr Albertini and, that being Italian, he could be picked up and interned at any time. He was a cobbler with five children to keep, not "the spy in black" was Mrs Tobias's view. Sally was inclined to agree with her. Jedda had a soft spot for him and his family as a whole. Poor, but most generous, Mr Albertini had a beautiful singing voice – a tenor, similar to one he had handed down to his son. He delighted in singing Neapolitan songs and had a passion for Puccini, which pleased Jedda no end.

Snow had been falling steadily all day, and the pavements had been subjected to drifts swept there by high winds. Nowhere does it look prettier than a city blanketed with snow, the tiny terraces huddled together and covered in virginal whiteness; the black wounds, caused by years of industrial discharge bandaged white at least, for a small space in time, making the dim surroundings a thing of beauty.

The moon was a large silver-blue disc in the sky and, though the lamplighter was no longer allowed to light the old street lamps, the shine of the moonlight reflected in the glass and gave the impression that something glowed there. Children still threw ropes over the bars, attached them to the old lamp standards and swung on them; laughter and swinging where light no longer shone, in happy ignorance of an even greater darkness about to engulf them.

A special Christmas school party was in progress and all the children had been invited to enjoy themselves. The desks in each classroom were covered with red paper and not a pen or paper was in sight; only a cracker, a trifle, a cake and two sandwiches, which was all that food shortages would allow. Even the blackboard had streamers hanging from it. All the pupils in Jedda's class had arrived with the exception of Gingo, who was always late. His arch enemy Peppercorn took to task those who failed to arrive at times specified, even more so if their name happened to be Gingo. Still, the whole class was aware that Peppercorn would not have liked Gingo had he arrived ten minutes earlier than quoted.

Jedda wore a red and white dress. A creation Sally had put together on her small sewing machine and thought herself rather swish. Dressmaking was one of the talents Sally excelled at.

Gingo must have thought himself quite a dresser too! As he entered the room, at last allowing all assembled there the pleasure of his company, as far as Jedda could make out at that time was, he must have wanted to make an impression, and he certainly did. He was garbed, the top half that is, in evening dress. Though his grey shirt had grown shorter with time; nevertheless, it still showed beneath his elegant coat; also, he had dispensed with his grimy trousers, which were always of a hue unrecognisable, for genuine black ones. His hair was slicked neatly back and, contrary to his usual murky complexion, his face shone clean, bright as a rosy apple. To complete the whole composition he had added a dickie-bow and encased his feet in a brand new pair of black patent leather dancing shoes, the sound of which heralded his entrance with a succession of squeaks.

"Oh, who's for posh?" thought Jedda.

Peppercorn, meanwhile, elbows on desk, face resting on hands, surveyed this apparition with deep distaste. Eyes darting like twin rats, he awaited Gingo's decision to be seated, pausing for several minutes before saying in measured tones, "Why are you so late, Albertini? Don't you think you should honour us all with an explanation?"

Gingo paused, stroked his chin like a wise old sage deep in thought and said, "I was busy with my paper round, sir. It was icy underfoot, and it held me up with my deliveries, sir."

Jedda began to feel worried and wondered what was about to occur. Two "sirs" in a row was not like Gingo. Peppercorn did not seem too keen on the undertones, either. His nostrils began to twitch, which bade ill for the lordly arrival. He leaned forward and snarled, "Come out to the front, Fred Astaire. Let your explanation be heard loud and clearly by one and all."

Jedda became even more worried especially when Gingo moved forward meekly, shoes squeaking like a nest of mice.

"Go on then, Fred," declared Peppercorn. "Explain away! Inform the class! They're the ones you've kept waiting."

The class in general didn't give a fig if their favourite wild boy was late or not, hating to be included in any form of criticism, but kept wisely quiet rather than disagree with Peppercorn.

"I was up all night, sir," answered Gingo, in a most charming manner.

Things were getting dangerous, Jedda could tell! She had seen him in action like this before, but only outside of school when he was ready to reap vengeance.

"Up all night Albertini? Why?" Peppercorn preened himself for a moment, innocent of what was about to follow.

Gingo offered him a sweet smile, "Why, I was dancing the night away with Ginger Rogers, SIR!!!"

Peppercorn did not mind handing out sarcasm, but he certainly didn't like taking it back. Jedda studied the whole affair with trepidation, watched, breath held, as Peppercorn's face turned from pink to puce. Peppercorn reached for a cane hanging on the wall, the thickest he could find.

"Hold out your hand, Fred Astaire," he said, his breath coming in rasps. "This will make you dance.!"

Gingo held up his hand as a temporarily measure, before lowering it just as quickly allowing the whole force of the cane to swish down. Peppercorn howled as he received the full force of it onto his groin. If he had turned from pink to puce before, he now resembled a rainbow. Red! Black! Purple! Green! Name it, he was it! He continued to let out with what was both a combination of a groan and absolute rage as he reached out and tried desperately to grasp the elusive figure of a parting Gingo.

Too late! Gingo was far too quick for him! He was across the room swifter than a mouse chased by a cat, but before he escaped through the classroom door he offered Peppercorn a parting shot, "Touch me, and I'll put your bloody head through the railings."

The children tried to contain their laughter but it was an up-hill task and they continued to titter until Peppercorn brought his cane down on his desk with re-sounding bang – a warning for those who did not wish to conform.

Jedda noticed on the way home from school that railings no longer surrounded the school and that they were probably part of some tank somewhere, which made Gingo's outburst even more laughable.

The school nativity play took place two days before Christmas but Gingo did not honour the school with his presence. Miss Bevan thought it was a pity and his angelic voice was much missed by teachers and pupils alike, apart from Pepper-corn, who was still suffering from bruises in an unmentionable place. Miss Bevan recited a poem for Christmas instead of her current favourite *The Ancient Mariner*. It was from her devoted teaching that many children had learned to love poetry and Jedda was no exception.

Pupils each took part in a nativity play performing accordingly. Jedda, being tall, had been chosen to represent Joseph, while Sylvia Jones, a small, pale, dark-haired girl with a quiet gentle face, played Mary. It was in the middle of this seasonable act that the sirens screamed forth with a wild and terrifying sound and, though as usual, it was assumed to be only for reasons of practice. The children and teachers descended the stairs swiftly so that they could shelter beneath the school held up by strong large columns that protected its foundations.

Jedda lost her beard in the scramble – a white one made of cotton wool. In the end it didn't really matter, the play was all but over and wouldn't be repeated anyway.

The phoney raid lasted but a short while, and once the all clear had sounded it was decided by the teachers to send the children home.

Jedda heard the warden say to Miss Bevan that it was a false alarm as usual, but he had a suspicion that aerial photographs had been taken. He had spotted German planes two days running, and as no attempt had been made to drop bombs, they must be on a reconnaissance flight.

Miss Bevan said she sincerely hoped they wouldn't attack them and that the war would soon come to an end. "It's all clearly ridiculous," she added.

Jedda did not come across Gingo until the night after the school play. School had broken up because the next day would be Christmas Eve and the end of term had come as a relief to pupils and teachers alike.

Chickens were not plentiful and Sally had ordered a piece of pork from the butchers. She had recently been called upon by the powers that be to attend an interview for a job at a factory that made planes, and that she would be obliged, whether she liked it or not, to help with the war effort. She declared it was just as well. What with shortages and things, the shop wasn't making much profit.

Jedda was well aware that things were in short supply. She and Addie had to keep going up to the wholesalers for groceries now the men were not there to deliver the goods. The Tobias's would still continue on with the business no doubt, being allowed a certain amount from the suppliers to continue baking. And besides, with Mr Tobias being declared unfit to serve in the forces after being wounded in the last war and Billy not due to be called up until next year, there would be three wages coming in. Sally, with only a schoolgirl daughter, was the lone breadwinner.

Jedda accepted this information in her usually fatalistic, uncomplaining way. She would be sad, she knew, that living in an empty shop would be dreadful thing, but her mother was powerless to stop the escalation of events the war had brought in its wake. She was overcome by a deep-seated fear concerning the future, but as always, found them to be unexplainable. As far back as she could remember, the feeling had always been there...something dark, waiting in the shadows.

The weather was becoming colder. Arctic cold. The snow was not just white, it had a silver edge to it. This made everything sparkle and small glaciers hung from the roof tops where the heat of chimneys had caused snow to soften and slide down, only to freeze there and dangle in icy blades from the gutters. In corners, where careless hands had failed to brush them away, spiders webs glowed silver, embedded with flies turned to snow white pearls, the last of the summers catch.

The moon, high in the sky, was even fuller than the night before, a complete circle, lighting the streets where her mantle chose and leaving the rest in shadows.

With nature's light in mind, Jedda and Addie decided to go for a walk, enjoying the crunch of packed snow beneath their feet as they teetered across its solid mass. The night was silent in the eerie fashion that snow gives heir to, and only fools and children braved it, as did the two of them in eager anticipation, laughing together beneath a flurry of white confetti; until, as time passed, the bitter cold became so intolerable that even they began to think sitting near the fire was the better option. They bid each other goodnight and parted company, each hurrying away to their separate homes.

Jedda had almost reached her own shop when she chanced on Gingo. He had almost bumped into her and was holding something live and clucking under his coat. He had dispensed with his evening dress in favour of his usual garb.

Jedda challenged him, "What's that you're holding?" she said, knowing full well it was some kind of a bird.

"It's a duck," he said without sarcasm. "I've just found it."

Jedda smiled... He lied! He lied!!!

"I'm taking it back to the duck pond. It must have wandered away from the park," he suggested, smiling sweetly.

Jedda returned his smile even more deeply: He lied! He lied!!! It must have worn skates to come this far? She did not argue the point knowing his temper when roused – something recently witnessed by his foray with Peppercorn held her tongue in check.

"Come with me," he said, "I must take the poor thing back to its mother. She'll be worried."

Jedda protested that she was on her way home and quite cold, but he refused to take no for an answer, so she followed him like a fool.

Minus its railings, access to the park was easy. It helped the war effort, true! It also obliged secret lovers to tryst there, and in the summer, long past, had encouraged midnight bathers to indulge in a dip in the duck pond. It also granted naughty children the right to return stolen ducks to that selfsame water.

The tapping of a stick disturbed their illicit actions and, when the shuffling of feet caused them to drop "Donald" they did a quick turn about and left the park a lot more quickly than they had entered it.

They had reached the concrete, were homeward bound and just about to part when Gingo planted a kiss on Jedda's right cheek. She blushed, unaware of its significance, unsure as to whether it meant Merry Christmas, or thank you for escorting my duck home, when a drone from above caused them both to look skywards to behold a myriad of planes! So quickly had they presented themselves, it was difficult to understand where they had come from. They shone silver in the moonlight, so low the children could perceive their bellies. Planes! Hordes of them! Not English! Jedda was to become familiar with the sounds they made. Hum! Hum! Hum! An evil sound! Bomb-filled! And, to their horror, the Hun had decided to dispose of them.

A sudden hail of gunfire from the docks, the dropping of flares by the enemy and the play of searchlights jerked the children into action; they moved swiftly, as fast as frightened legs would allow – Gingo's quite bravely! Jedda's like jelly! But move they did! Each their separate ways – Jedda home to mother, Gingo home to mamma.

Upon Jedda's arrival home, Sally all but dragged her wondering daughter through the door, fear on her face obvious as they both dived together beneath the table; it was the only offer of shelter open to them and there they remained through fourteen hours of incessant bombing. Doors blew in, and from the smashed frames of broken windows, glass hung in tiny shards clinging to the tape, that fortunately,

Sally had placed there. The fire in the small iron grate began to die out through lack of fuel, without any given warning Sally had been unable to bank it up with coal. The snow blew in through unhinged doors as they trembled together – mother and daughter – in the blessed approach to Christmas. Cold, hungry and terrified they stuck it out! They had no choice!

Once the all clear – like some wailing banshee – sounded at seven the next morning, those who had lived to tell the tale, along with many another sad-hearted survivor, made their way out of their battered homes. A spectacle of fire sweeping through mills, cinemas, shops and homes greeted eyes half open through lack of sleep.

Sally said it resembled, *Dantes' Inferno*, then bit her lip knowing that Alex's answer would be: "You should know, being a stupid devil yourself," as would Sandy's, had he also still been around.

Bemused, saddened and despairing, people stood and beheld the city, a city in flames amidst crumbling masonry, dust and destruction. A disorientated populace, who complained that the siren had been sounded too late to warn them to take cover

It was like the man said, "They always get you in the end." Adolf won, where Peppercorn had failed. It was Addie who informed Jedda of Gingo's death. Having died not far from his destination, not long after having given Jedda a final parting kiss, he had been almost home when a house he was passing received a direct hit.

"I saw him," said Addie, "not ten minutes ago. Watched them dig him out. he wasn't marked, the air raid warden said the blast must have done it. He looked a bit dusty, that's all."

Though Addie sought to comfort Jedda in her own way, Jedda refused to be comforted. She did not shed a tear, but something inside of her curled up instead. She did not wish to hear Addie's explanation of the death of Gingo. She knew instinctively that poor down-to-earth Addie's well-meaning chatter was lost on her own over-imaginative self. If she did not believe Gingo to be dead, then he would not be dead. What's more, she had no intention of going to find him wherever he was just in case she should find him to be so. Her ostrich complex was at work. She only knew she hated that innocent duck and wished Gingo had wrung its neck. Later, when speaking to Ince, she found out that the trouble was, he had not been able to kill it. He had stolen it as for a surprise Christmas dinner, but in the end, the softness of his heart had not allowed him to wring the helpless creature's neck. But then, Gingo had never really been Public Enemy Number One!

Later that day Jedda accompanied Addie to the picture house. Not to see a film but to contact Mr Eric Tobias with a message from Mrs Tobias. Eric Tobias was not in the foyer as he usually was, nor in the outer office. The two girls

89

decided to try inside the cinema itself, walked directly through the outer doors, lifted the curtain that draped the inner sanctum and entered the interior of the Pleasure Dome.

From the dim light within a spectacle greeted their eyes that could only be described as a gothic nightmare. Upright in the seats and covered by white sheets were the bodies of people recently killed in the blitz. The empty screen, silent and unmoving, mourned a lack of moving patronage. Patrons that had once laughed and cried, watched, as actors had flitted across a screen – now a white, blank square that remained mute. Those who slept in this makeshift morgue had once bought ice creams and told their children to be quiet and not wriggle. In the distance behind were seats where back row lovers had kissed in the welcome darkness. Now all were silenced – mothers, children, old folk and young lovers – joined in a macabre togetherness. No usherette now paced the isles to show patrons – eager for a few hours' entertainment to light up often-tedious lives – the way to their seats. The isles and the front of the silent screen no longer boasted an ice cream lady selling her wares... only bodies lay there, and they too, were covered by winding sheets.

The girls stood transfixed, only delivered from a petrified silence with the arrival of a man wearing a white coat, his expression filled with horror at the thought of two small girls witnessing such a scene. He told them they should not be there and they should leave immediately and explained Mr Tobias was absent because the cinema was out of bounds for the duration. In fact, it was never to open to the public again.

Addie and Jedda made their way home silently, their usual endless chattering brought to an end by what they had just witnessed, a charnel house on Christmas Eve day. They had not been warm because of the bleak weather conditions, but now a shivering of a different kind took hold of them, a shaking of young bodies, uncontrollable, suffering from shock. A few steps more and they stopped, leaned over a grid in a united fashion and held hands before being violently sick. Neither related the events of that day to their parents for fear of being shouted at and for being in the wrong place at the wrong time. What they had observed had been an experience so dreadful, so ghoulish, their poor young minds temporarily blocked it out. Jedda especially refused to contemplate that one of the unseeing patrons seated in front of the blank screen could possibly have been her adored Gingo.

Christmas Eve did not deter the Germans. They came once more, guided by the beacon light of the still burning fires evoked by the previous night's bombing. Mills that still smouldered in spite of firemen's efforts to control them.

The sirens went on time and Jedda and Sally joined the Tobias's in their cellar. From their point of view a safe place, but foolish by all accounts. An incendiary bomb on all the coal heaped there would soon have put to the torch those assembled there. They saw it as being underground, and as frightened people do, plumped for what was on offer.

Billy Tobias was late home and Milly Tobias was worried. Eric tried to comfort her. Assure her all was well; but she would not be comforted. When Billy eventually arrived home he rushed down the cellar steps, blood flowing profusely from a wound in his hand. He had been riding his bike and had been vulnerable to flying shrapnel, a large hot piece of which had pierced his flesh.

Mrs Tobias invaded the first-aid box, bound up Billy's hand and informed him he would receive proper medical attention at the hospital once things had quietened down.

Next morning found them all alive and Billy's hand was attended to at the hospital. It needed six stitches.

Though he had attended a Protestant school, Gingo's earthly remains were taken into the bosom of the Catholic church and a mass was performed. The sound of Mr Albertini's voice singing Ava Maria was heard amidst the tears of the mourners present.

Jedda and Addie sat at the back of the church with Sally and Mrs Tobias, there to pay their last respects; something even Sally agreed they should do. Fear and grieving held Jedda in its grip as flowers and incense, hypnotic in themselves, filled her with a sense of absolute foreboding. It seemed to her that in her short life there was no end to death and the loss of those you loved most in the world forever prevalent.

She did not know if Gingo wore his princely evening suit or a newly acquired shroud, because she had not chosen to see him in his small coffin. He just continued to live on in her mind as he had always been; sometimes laughing with her, others laughing at her – mocking her! And she knew she would remember him always as being that way.

Once all the rituals concerning death were over and the Albertinis had thanked she, Addie, Sally and Mrs Tobias for coming and showing their respects, the girls were left shy and confused. Not really knowing what to say in return they eventually departed leaving the Albertinis to their own private grief. Jedda then deserted Addie on some pretext or other, and hurried off through the heavily falling snow to the park, to be alone.

Upon arrival there, she ran up to the cake and pushed it round, just as Gingo had pushed it. One foot on the floor, the other on the base, and once it started to spin she jumped on. Just as Gingo and she had done so many times, she simply sat there, letting the wind rush past her ears. She stared into space, ignoring the feel of the snow that covered the seat beneath her, oblivious to its icy dampness as it seeped through and reached her underclothes and, in spite of the pain of it caused, continued to hold on to the freezing metal of the iron bar as it bit back with a cold heat deep into her fingers. And the cake kept turning, and turning, and turning ... like the world keeps turning.

Chapter Nine

Almost two years had passed since the Blitz. A few raids, including one in the following Easter and one at Whitsuntide were terrible, but not on the same scale as at Christmas. The Germans did blow up the cemetery and there were some gruesome sights of bodies tragically exhumed; also, there was the dreadful killing of many very young nurses at the near by hospital.

Addie and Jedda wanted to see Jeannette McDonald and Nelson Eddy in a film at the local cinema. They arrived promptly and were so engrossed in the film, Noel Coward's *Bitter Sweet* that, in spite of an air-raid warning coming up on the screen, they continued to watch, mesmerised by the romantic setting, Jeannette McDonald singing "I'll see you again," to Nelson Eddy, whose spirit was looking down from the clouds as he sang along with her.

At the end of the film, and out on the street, they headed for home beneath the glare of flares and searchlights tracking the enemy planes, one of which, guided by so much light, swooped low and turned a machine gun on them. They made easy targets on a night that more resembled day from the illuminations beaming overhead. Jedda froze in the midst of running, a form of paralysis striking her legs making them feel like two ice lollipops. She remained unmoving in the middle of the road, completely out in the open, until sensible Addie reached out and dragged her down by a wall. Fritz missed her by a hair's breadth.

When, eventually, they reached the top of the street close to home, Sally and Millie were waiting for them at the bottom end of the street, looking angry, and yet relieved at their safe return.

Months passed by, life continuing at a quiet, steady pace; and war, and all it represented, fading from their young minds. One day Addie suggested they both went skating. Only roller-skating of course, and they could hire the skates for sixpence. Milly Tobias said Birch Park Rink was a long way from where they lived and they must be careful not to miss the last bus, especially in the blackout.

At almost fourteen years of age they considered themselves adults and they said of course they would not miss the bus.

Upon arrival at the rink they each hired a pair of skates resembling something belonging to Klondyke Kate – black with pointed toes. They had quite a struggle to contend with laces on boots that reached halfway up their slim legs.

Skating lessons were not part of the deal, so they compromised by being in reach of the wooden barrier that circled the length and breadth of the rink. It was as if it was for their sole purpose that these implements had been fixed: very few other skaters appeared to be balancing themselves on these worthy structures.

They each went round the rink holding tightly onto the bars, envious of the able skaters who danced by with a confident grace.

Jedda thought she'd brave the rink without support and sailed on for a while. Soon it became obvious to her that she was unable to stop! Afraid, she grabbed the most solid object close by. It turned out, unfortunately, to be the lap of an Air Force Officer's shirt. The poor man was leaning on the bar with his back to her, talking to a very smartly dressed girl. The airman was immediately dragged down to the floor by Jedda's wild clutching.

The airman lay stunned for several seconds before seeing the humour of the situation, "I say, I think I've fallen for a pretty girl here, Doreen," he remarked to the girl he had been in conversation with.

The girl smirked back and Jedda noticed she was rather curvy – too curvy – and that she was dressed in a very fetching costume and white buckskin skates. Older than Addie and she, and quite self-assured, she made Jedda feel like a poor cousin on a day out from the slums.

If this was a fact, the officer appeared not to notice her poor attire and be- haved like a gentleman. Rising to his feet he bent down and lifted her up, noticing her cheeks flushed with embarrassment. "Are you all right? Are you hurt? Broken any bones?"

Jedda could hardly breathe he was so good looking. " No, I'm quite all right, thank you. I'm terribly sorry... your shirt... I..."

He intervened quickly trying to put her at ease, "Don't worry, my shirt's come to no harm. I've plenty more if it has."

How kind he was, thought Jedda, so handsome. She loved the way his mouth went into an enchanting curve when he smiled and the way it made his eyes crinkle at the sides. And his eyes, so blue, so bright, so smiling... oh, God she couldn't speak... also, she didn't care for the girl who was weighing her up with obvious contempt in her eyes. She began to move away, slowly, holding onto the bar for support, wishing to join Addie. Wishing the floor would open up and make her disappear.

"Take care," said the officer, with a wave of his hand.

She joined Addie, not daring to look back, her evening spoiled. "Let's go to the Ladies, shall we, Addie. I want to bathe my face, I'm so hot. Very hot!"

"You look it... I saw you looking moony-eyed at handsome over there. Fancy pulling his shirt out...What did he say?"

"He just said, it was all right ... my pulling his shirt out, I mean. I didn't like that girl, though."

"No she looked mean... I want to go to the toilet too, Jedda."

Jedda looked bemused, "I need to spend a penny, too, though I suppose it might be difficult in skates – still, we'll have to chance it."

Both found it difficult to manoeuvre themselves into the toilets, both giggling insanely from their separate cubicles as they clung on to the chain to stop themselves from falling.

"I'll never make a Sonja Henie," cried Addie between giggles.

"Me, neither," said Jedda, "what a trial."

"Let's get back," said Addie.

They'd paid their money, so they wanted their money's worth. They returned to the rink, stayed on, and persevered, clinging to the bars, trying their best. Not being the kind of girls to give up easily, they eventually managed a few paces.

Jedda looked across the rink and saw the officer watching her, a smile on his lips. He probably thought her a stupid teenage fool and she decided she'd had enough. She suggested to Addie that they had better leave in case they missed the bus. The officer remarked to Doreen that the young girl who'd tripped him up would grow into quite a beauty – indeed she was one now.

Doreen shrugged and said, "She's all right, Adam. I don't think either girl will come to much."

The officer pulled Doreen's hair and called her a snob.

The queue to return the skates took a while and by the time it was their turn to hand them in Jedda and Addie were becoming quite worried.

"If we don't hurry we'll miss the bus," said Jedda.

"Then we'll be in trouble," said Addie. "We promised we wouldn't be late."

They missed the bus as foreseen and started to walk. A mist was rising and the darkness did not help. Twin lights came up behind them, dipped, to hide being noticed by the enemy.

A voice called out to them, "Do you want a lift? We noticed you'd missed the bus."

Jedda and Addie expressed doubts to each other. They had been told by their mothers not go with strangers.

"You'll be all right, I'm not Jack the Ripper. Doreen's with me and you'll be much safer than wandering about in the dark on your own. I'm Adam Templer, by the way."

Jedda had a hunch she could trust him and moved towards the car, Addie following immediately behind. Adam lunged out of the car, held open the passenger door in the most gentlemanly of fashions, ushered them both into the back seats, dropped back behind the wheel and asked them which direction they were taking.

"That's a long way past our destination, Adam," said Doreen tactlessly.

"Not that far! Anyway, I'm not leaving these two lovely ladies to struggle all that way in this weather... don't worry girls, I'm not going to throw you out."

Adam. So that was his name. Adam of the lovely blue eyes and dark brown hair. Jedda was bewitched. He was quite old, of course, at least twenty-two, and she was of the view that both he and Doreen were far richer than she and Addie; also, deep down, her common sense told her she would never see him again. He'd called Addie and she lovely ladies, too. That night she lay awake and thought of him; slept deeply, dreamed of him.

Jedda was in trouble. Deep, deep trouble. She was going to have Gingo's baby. Addie had informed her indirectly of the fact. She had been listening to her mother and some ladies discussing Annie Jones, a young teenager who lived close by. Annie Jones, most shameful of hussies, was having to get married. "Shotgun," they said.

Jedda asked Addie what Shotgun was, and Addie replied, "That's what boys are forced to do when they get girls into trouble."

When Jedda asked her what "getting in trouble" meant, Addie informed her in the most knowledgeable manner that, "If you kissed boys in the moonlight that was what happened and, indeed, that's what had!"

Jedda had felt sick with fear. Hadn't that been what had happened to herself. Gingo! He had kissed her that night before he had died, and now, she, Jedda, was also to have a baby and no Gingo around to be shot gunned!

She didn't know what to do. Soon she would have a baby. Addie had told her you swell up and they cut it out with a knife, and if you don't want it, they give it away. She'd be fourteen soon and the youngest mother in the world.

The weeks passed but she didn't seem to get any fatter. How long did it take? Years maybe, before it showed. Annie Jones was fat; she'd seen her. Maybe she should ask her what to do?

Next day, knowing Annie would pass on her way to the shops, she waylaid her in the only way she knew how – she grabbed Annie's arm, her heart pounding, eyes wide with fright.

"Excuse me. I hope you don't mind me asking, but how long does it take for a baby to be born? One year, two years?

Annie started to laugh, "Not unless you're expecting an elephant."

"Elephant?" Jedda was nonplussed.

Annie reached for Jedda's arm. "Come and stand round this corner, you seem to have a problem."

Jedda explained her predicament and Annie said in an amazed tone, "You didn't go that far, did you?"

Jedda had answered, "Yes. He kissed me in the moonlight like your boyfriend did and it jumped in my mouth."

Annie was beside her self with glee. "Jumped in your mouth? You don't get babies that way, you ninny. I'll tell you how," she said, and explained the facts of life to Jedda there and then; on the street corner to the most shocked little audience she'd ever seen.

"People don't really do that do they? Ugh!" Jedda pulled a face that registered disgust.

Annie stroked Jedda's faced gently, "They most certainly do. How do you think you got here?"

Jedda didn't answer. She didn't care to. She merely thanked her informer and left, determined never to listen to Addie's half-baked ideas again. She smiled to herself. Tonight, when she and Addie were alone she would tell her ignorant friend the true facts of life. That would give Addie Tobais something to think of. She sang to herself as she went into lunch, something Sally took note off. "You seem in a happier mood that of late," she said.

Jedda sat down at the table and gave her mother a sweet smile. "I'm hungry," she said and at the same time thinking, "I'm really part of you after all, aren't I mum?"

Another move was imminent. Sally had decided to sell the shop. Goods were in short supply and her finances were far from buoyant. She had managed to rent a tiny, terraced property about three miles away, close to a park and less rough than the area they now dwelt in. The following week they were to leave the tiny shop and with it, the memories of all that had occurred there.

The employment Sally had sought out to supplement their income was at a factory in Trafford Park, an occupation she felt obliged to take up in an attempt to help out with the war effort. When Sally was on the night shift – which seemed to Jedda to be a regular thing – she was left to her own devices, a situation she was none too keen on and she wished her mother were home more often.

Winter was in its depths, bitter cold and by all intents and purposes, had no intention of improving. She studied the little shop in detail. Its shelves were empty, an absolute reminder of their final departure. So barren looking it made her aware that once more, another chapter in her life was about to end with more ghosts to put to rest.

She returned to the living room and turned on the wireless.

Dorothy Carless was singing, Sand in My Shoes accompanied by Geraldo and his orchestra. The song amused her because it wasn't only snowing outside, it was blowing a gale. She made herself a cup of coffee and some Symingtons soup. She was always surprised how large a beverage could come from so small a packet.

The fire was low and she added a few more coals from the brass coal scuttle at the side of the fireplace – it had always seemed to her such a grand item for such inadequate surroundings. Fiddling with the knobs of the old wireless that always seemed effected by interference, she tuned into the *Third Programme*. Orson wells was reading Walt Whitman's *Song of Myself* from *Leaves of Grass*. She found it most informative and, just as equally fascinating. Of course she had always suspected everyone was everybody else and here was another human being stating it most clearly, sending a message out that any fool with a scrap of imagination could understand.

How cleverly Orson Wells communicated Walt Whitman's view. To put one-self in the shoes of the hunted, the holy, the child, the old, the good and the evil, the soldier and the dying. So finely expressed in Orson's hypnotic voice, that it was a case of what life doled out to one as an individual.

An hour later it was announced that Verdi's *La Traviata* was to be performed, and that the story was about a lady of ill repute. One who fell truly in love for the first time but was obliged to give up her lover at his father's request, and it all ended with the heroine dying of consumption in her beloved's arms. The music was beautiful and she listened entranced – her first full opera and she fell in love with it.

The hour was late and she was tired, but dreaded going to a cold bed in an icy bedroom. She did not possess a hot water bottle and decided to use a shelf, which rested in a small oven adjacent to the fire. First wrapping it in newspaper, she added an old cardigan as an outer binding to keep the soot from soiling the sheets. Remaining thankfully ingenuous to the different contrasts between poetic culture, plus a night at the opera and the object poverty of her surroundings, she made her way upstairs.

Soon her schooldays would be over and at fourteen – though her mother de-clared at times that, to her way of thinking, her daughter was forty-two – she knew she must find work. Until then, though, she would try to relax by snuggling up in bed with a book, her favourite way of inviting sleep.

She slipped her hands into a pair of old woollen gloves, covered her head with a scarf, wrapped her feet in thick socks then read a chapter of a most appropriate book *Hard Times* content to ignore real life for an hour or two. And though she could in a sense equate real life with fiction, she also found it difficult to discern between the two – forget a past, so like the literature in which she was now engrossed, the coming to an end of one more tempestuous episode.

Suddenly, and for no particular reason she could fathom, thoughts of Gingo entered her head and bringing tears to the fore, giving way to deep emotion and finally, sleep.

As she slept on she was oblivious to the wind as it rushed around the little shop, blowing through gaps in the window frame until the small candle by her bedside also flickered, comparable to a tired eye, before it, too, gave way to slumber. And in the silent, murky streets, snow curled about in wraiths, mimicking ghosts from a haunted past. Cruel memories sadly demonstrated by the dampness showing on her young cheeks. Her schooldays would finish in April and a new home was on the horizon, a fresh beginning, bringing a newly turned chapter in a disjointed life.

Part Two

A Walk Through Summer

I saw you today, whom I once loved.

You passed by, close to me as a shadow on a lake

Bearing a corsage of dead leaves,

wearing the Shoes of October...

I stand unrecognised...

Chapter Ten

It was one bright May evening in the year of Our Lord nineteen-forty-eight that Joe Baker first set eyes on Jedda Markham. He would recall the event in later years as a time that could only be described as a twist of fate. One that would in effect alter three people's lives – for good or for evil – in the most drastic way possible.

Joe and Toro had just arrived in England from Ireland. They had arrived via Dublin and having landed in Liverpool, caught the train to Manchester. Upon arrival in the city they had boarded a bus and reaching the right area, made their way to Joe's sister Kate's house in Stretford. Once they reached Kate's house they expected to make contact with two of their friends, Patsy and his wife Eileen, with whom they were to take up lodgings.

Kate had invited them to join in a buffet she and her husband Charles were holding for a few of Charles's business colleagues.

Having alighted from the bus, and with his usual Irish charm, Joe inquired of a lady who was passing, the way to reach the avenue Kate had written to them about.

Toro retained a stony silence throughout the conversation; he was always apt to do this with anyone English.

The woman pointed out directions, for which Joe thanked her, and the two of them made their way down the road indicated. Finally, upon reaching Kate's residence, they noted the house number, but were obliged to ring on the doorbell several times to enable themselves to be heard above shrill music coming from within.

Kate finally answered the door, a smile as wide as half a melon on her lips. As she ushered them inside she chatted constantly: "Come in Joe." Kate offered her cheek to be kissed, her accent as Irish as the men. "I can see you're tired from your journey. Quite a way to travel, too. First a boat, then a train, and how many buses did you have to catch?"

Joe's smile was constrained. "Two to be precise. We're not feeling too bad though, are we Toro?"

Kate slipped her arm through her brother's, practically ignoring Toro, their dislike of each other mutual. In all the years they had known each other it was a feeling that had lingered – no festered – since the early childhood. Kate had never felt any empathy towards Toro and only tolerated him for Joe's sake.

"Hang your coats up there," said Kate. She waved her hand to indicate the hallstand. "Come and sit by the fire awhile. I knows it's May, but the evenings get chilly," she added, as she escorted them into the living room.

A welcome fire burned in the grate, but it was not upon its glow that Joe focused. It was the girl sitting beside it gazing down thoughtfully into its flames; and he often recalled across the years that it must have been from that moment – foolish and romantic as it seemed – that he could never have loved, or ever would love, anyone else as long as he lived.

Kate introduced both he and Toro to the girl, "This is Jedda Markham, a friend of mine. We work in the same office."

The girl looked up, gave them both a dimpled smile, displayed white even teeth, appraising them with the darkest and most beautiful eyes he had ever seen. She extended Joe a small white hand, which included a queenly turn of the head and a polite, "How do you do," withdrawing her hand as quickly as it was proffered.

Joe had taken her hand eagerly, amused by her sense of old-fashioned dignity, fascinated by her evident sex appeal and the candid brightness of her eyes.

Toro was less than impressed. A fact shown by the lack of cordiality present in his manner, an act Joe was made aware of by the way the girl turned away from them – abruptly – and let her gaze rest once more on the flickering firelight.

Kate intervened tactfully and tried unsuccessfully to hide her vexation at Toro's obvious and instant dislike of Jedda: "Would you care for something to eat Joe? Toro? There's a buffet in the dining room ...oh, that sounds like Eileen and Patsy have just arrived." She teetered towards the door. "Charles should be home soon, too. He's bringing a few friends from his office and some business colleagues along, as well."

Having furnished them with this information, she skipped lightly out of the room, returning almost immediately, ushering Eileen and Patsy before her.

Both parties rushed towards Joe. Eileen kissed him on both cheeks. Patsy remained his usual smiling good-natured self and declared, "It's been ages since last we saw you and Toro." He turned to Jedda seated by the fire, "Hello, Jedda my love."

Jedda smiled back, but remained silent.

"Let's eat," said Kate. There's a nice buffet in the dining room."

Toro allowed himself a faint smile at Patsy's greeting, but refused to be cajoled into joining the buffet despite Kate's insistence that he should. He had his own reasons for staying where he was.

Joe, hungry from the journey, merged with the rest of the company as they wandered into the dining room. He had hoped Jedda would join them too, but she had remained seated, her body relaxed, almost indolent beneath Toro's cool gaze.

Head held high and stance arrogant, Toro stood with his back to the fire. From time to time he let a superlative eye wander over Jedda; despising her instantly, judging her out of hand, especially when her attention was elsewhere.

Once, when she had looked up and met his gaze in full, she was shocked by a gimlet stare that seemed to declare instant war on her. She felt an immediate disquiet. Stranger though he was, his image seemed familiar. A feeling she could not fathom, something that seemed to permeate the atmosphere. It was, by its very nature, not particularly unique to her. Many eyes had met Toro's, and having conceived what they witnessed there, had been as equally concerned upon encountering the cruelty that lurked in those deep, cold-water blue orbs. Eyes of such infinite paleness, that they seemed in conflict with the beetle black of the eyelashes and smooth, dark brows above.

When Joe returned a few minutes later, his plate piled high with sandwiches and cakes, he was amused to observe Jedda no longer relaxed, but taking an unwarranted interest in the plaster cupids above the lintel on Kate's living room door. Toro often had the effect of making people uncomfortable and Jedda, it appeared, was no exception.

He smiled at her, offering her a drink, trying to put her at her ease. She refused his offer, but thanked him anyway.

Patsy bounced in behind Joe, seating himself down next to Jedda. He gave her a roguish look. "How you doing Jedda? All right? Haven't seen much of you in the draughtsmen's office lately?" He placed an arm round her shoulder. "Where have you been keeping yourself? Hiding from Hardman?" He squeezed her hand. "Hardman by name and hard man by nature... I shouldn't like to tangle with him."

She began to relax in the company of an old friend, smiling at him. "I haven't had reason to, Patsy. Mr Hardman doesn't seem to notice me, he thinks he's so superior." She continued, "It's often the way, with some people; especially when they've struggled to make it up the ladder." She patted Patsy's hand and smiled, "I'll be coming upstairs in the next week or two, though. Regularly."

Patsy agreed, "I know what you mean, Jedda. Just because he's chairman of the board he thinks he's the tops. And that daughter of his – phew – she does fancy herself – riding about in that sports car of hers, hair flying in the breeze. Thinks she's a film star or something." Patsy stroked Jedda's hair, "No one would even notice her though, not if you were in the room."

"Your very kind, Patsy," said Jedda and blushed in a becoming way. "More than some at Canada Brights."

"No; I'm not kind, just truthful. Joe and Toro are taking up positions at Brights, did you know that?" Patsy kissed her hand while Eileen pretended mock jealousy.

Jedda started to laugh and removed it from his grasp. "Kate did mention her brother and his friend were coming to work at Canada Brights. So you'll have company. And lots to talk about, no doubt."

Joe loved the sound of her laughter, immensely carried away by her charms. "Have you worked at Canada Brights for a long time, Jedda? Is it your first job?"

"Since I left school," she demurred.

Joe laughed, "That can't be so long, can it?"

She lifted her chin proudly. "I was eighteen in March."

"Sorry I wasn't there; we could have celebrated."

A quizzical look entered her face. "That would have been nice," she said politely, as if not sure whether to take him seriously

As they conversed, Toro eyed Joe and Jedda suspiciously, a cold expression on his face; as if to suggest that Joe had no right to even smile at Jedda, let alone talk to her.

"Are you sure you're not hungry, Jedda?" said Patsy, holding a cake aloft.

Jedda demurred but Patsy still insisted: "Have some Jedda. It tastes more exciting than it looks."

The sound of newcomers in the hall heralded Charles's arrival home with a group of associates. Once he had made them all comfortable in the dining room, eager to indulge in Kate's potluck, he had sauntered off into the lounge to greet Joe and Toro.

He walked right over to Joe and seized his hand, but was less enthusiastic about Toro. Jedda wasn't in the least surprised at Charles's attitude towards him. By what she witnessed to date about Toro, she did not like the look of him either. She also wondered how a person like Joe, who seemed gentle and giving, could possibly have anything in common with such a cold personality. She had only just met Toro, knowing nothing whatsoever about him; yet she was well aware something in his demeanour spoke volumes. She also had the odd perception that, though she had only just met him, there was something familiar about him; try as she may though, she just could not quite place it.

Patsy excused himself from Jedda's side, and left the room to join Charles and his partners in the study. They had business to discuss and plans to arrange. It was part of some new strategy they all had in mind, and extra money on top of his position at Canada Brights was something Patsy was prone to appreciate.

Left alone, Joe, Kate and Eileen reminisced about prior times in Ireland, amusing Jedda no end with regard to their childhood involvement. Toro remained silent throughout, as though not part of these long passed escapades.

After a while, business completed and their associates having finally departed, Charles and Patsy returned and joined the company for the remainder of the evening. "We'll settle things tomorrow. I think Wilkins will come round to our way of thinking, anyway," Charles informed Kate. "I explained we had guests."

"Are you sure we're not interrupting anything of particular importance?" said Joe.

"No, of course not," Charles assured him, noting the doubtful look on Joe's face. "It's just as I've stated; honestly. I'm not merely being polite."

Kate poured the wine and handed it round, allowing Jedda only two glasses. "I won't have it said that I permitted young girls to go astray," she said, whilst pouring herself whisky for the umpteenth time. She had a strong head and could hold her liquor better than many a man.

"Give her another and don't be tight. One more won't cause her any harm," said Patsy. "And I wouldn't mind a whisky, while you're at it."

"Sorry, Patsy." Kate poured him a generous measure of Johnny Walker. "There's Grouse and Teachers if you want it and good old Irish, too. Joe's brought some poteen over with him."

"I think Kate's right," said Joe, intervening hastily.

"Oh yes, and since when did you start caring whether a girl was sober or not?" Patsy's eyebrows rose with an impish tilt. "Watch out for his Irish charm, Jedda. He has a way with the girls and many a heart he's broken."

Jedda blushed and Kate scolded Patsy for teasing her. "I don't think my brother goes in for cradle snatching."

Joe changed the subject. "What have you been doing with yourselves in England. Do you and Eileen go out on the town?"

Patsy smiled. "Depends on how broke we are. Last night we went to the Flea Pit."

Joe seemed puzzled, "The Flea Pit?"

Eileen laughed loudly. "You know, go in wearing a blouse and come out with a "jumper". He means the local cinema. It's where we go when we can't afford to go up town. We saw some out-of-date film."

"Yes, years out of date. It was called *The Gentle Gunman*. Dirk Bogarde was in it. These IRA men put a bomb in a biscuit tin."

Toro, who had shown little interest until now, was suddenly alert. "What was it like? Describe it to me."

Patsy shrugged his shoulders as if unsure. "I don't know. It could have been Crawford's or it could have been Peak Freans."

Toro was furious. "I meant the bomb! Not the bloody biscuit tin!"

Kate curled up laughing, "For God's sake, Toro! Can't you see he's pulling your leg?"

Everyone joined in the laughter. Toro didn't. He was not amused. Certainly not with that English girl sitting there staring at him in an astonished fashion.

Kate decided it was time to break up the party. "I've ordered a taxi," she said.

The taxi finally arrived, late and in the midst of kisses, many a "goodnight" and "I'll see you tomorrow", all round.

Jedda, Joe, Eileen and Patsy managed to squeeze into the back seats and Toro, a loner as usual, sat up front with the driver. After a final chorus of goodbyes to Kate and Charles, the taxi finally sped its passengers on their way.

Jedda's was the first port of call – the other four travellers were destined for the other side of the city. Joe stepped out ahead of her holding her arm and assisting her to alight. "That was a tight squeeze. I hope your dress isn't too crumpled?"

"Now Jedda. You know you enjoyed having a tight squeeze," cried Patsy, drunk as a lord and not caring.

"You'll be all right here, will you Jedda? Or shall I walk you to your door?" said Joe, perplexed.

"No, but thanks anyway. I'll be all right. I only live round the corner," she said, gazing into the darkness of the entry beyond.

Toro spoke for the first time since leaving Kate's. "Do you kiss all your boyfriends here?" he said with heavy sarcasm, indicating the entry in a roundabout fashion.

Jedda, her expression inscrutable, was quick to reply, "No, I usually take them right down the entry, sometimes we sit on the bin."

Eileen and Patsy started to laugh so hard Jedda was fearful they might crash through the taxi's window... Joe managed to contain himself, lost between the desire to take her in his arms and kiss her, and at the same time being taken by surprise by her pert answer. He was also filled with a sense of unease – danger even. No one had ever got one over on Toro like that before!

Patsy thought Toro's rudeness was beyond belief at times. "I don't know Toro! Do you have to be so bloody peevish? Insulting the girl like that – she's only a kid!"

"Precisely. She's only some girl," Toro sneered. "And an English one at that. Isn't that proof enough she won't be up to much?"

"No," said Patsy. "But one thing is sure, I've plenty of spare cash in the bank... I'll pay to enrol you at a charm school, if you like?"

Through the wing mirror situated at Toro's side, the taxi-driver, about to join in the laughter, changed his mind when he perceived the cruelty reflected in the man's eyes. Upon arrival home later that evening he related the incident to his wife. "You know, Vera. I looked into a man's eyes tonight and wondered to myself, does anything live in there?"

His wife laughed, placed his supper before him and said he was imagining things.

The taxi-driver was adamant. "For God's sake, it's the truth I tell you! The very truth! The man was evil personified!"

Having been employed at Canada Brights for several months, Joe often saw Jedda moving around her downstairs office but could never catch her attention.

From time to time she visited the drawing office situated on the floor above her own office on some pretext or other. He often smiled to draw attention to himself, but all she ever offered him was a polite nod, showing a distinct lack of interest.

He wished she would be more friendly – unused to the female of the species ignoring what he imagined to be his obvious charms – he was not sure about which way to go about approaching her. Certainly not asking her for a date.

Luckily for him, a week or two later, Charles invited him to share a private box at Haydock Park. Charles was meeting some important clients there on the pretext of encouraging them to invest in a new project he had in mind.

Joe asked him if Kate would be going, too.

"Yes," was Charles's reply, followed by a knowing smile. "Yes, Kate's asked Jedda to come along, too. Does that answer the question that's so obvious in your eyes?"

"I asked no such question," Joe replied sheepishly.

Charles had laughed at him. "You didn't need to, it's apparent by the way you keep fudging about that it's her you're interested in." Charles frowned. "She's a lovely girl and Kate and I are fond of her... be careful about how you treat her or there'll be hell to play!"

"I've no intention of hurting her. Anyway, it's not serious."

A dubious look came over Charles's face. "Isn't it? In all my years of knowing you, I don't think I've ever seen you more serious over a girl before."

Patsy brushed his suit with a tortoiseshell-backed clothes brush, humming "Golden Earrings" as he disposed of stray hairs from the shoulders of his jacket.

Joe, intent on looking smart himself, busied himself in front of the mirror trying on first one shirt, then another. "Is this tie all right, Patsy?"

"I don't know. You've tried on so many Joe, that I'm becoming confused. You're becoming as vain as a peacock... what's the matter with you? Are you in love or what? If it's Jedda, watch out! She's very young, you know. An impressionable age."

"What's the matter with you all? First Charles warns me off her – now you!" Patsy ignored him and started to sing a chorus of the lovely song Catherine.

"Lets go and see *Man about the House* one night this week shall we? You look a bit like Keiron Moore, Joe, come to think of it?

"What's all this talk about Jedda?" said Joe, refusing to be sidetracked.

"You know damn well what I'm talking about; so don't come the innocent with me. I've known you too long, Joe."

"I've only met her once – face-to-face – that is. So how can I love her?"

Patsy looked troubled. "I've never notice you make so much fuss about your appearance before... she isn't of our persuasion, you know."

"Persuasion?" Joe straightened a recently swapped tie.

"Catholic, like us." Patsy cleared his throat. "As a matter of fact, according to Kate, she's a little heathen. No religion of any kind. I think they're called agnostics or something."

"I'm no missionary, Patsy, and even if I were, there's no need for you to concern yourself with it. I'm not out to convert her... or marry her. No woman's going to tie me down, no thanks."

"Just warning you to take care... remember how upset Rory and your mother were when Kate married Charles and left the church?"

"Rory's a beloved brother, but he's better sticking to the priesthood rather than interfering in Kate's life. She has her own way of doing things, and I'll always love her no matter what she does." He paused and tried on yet another tie. "Kate's better than Ida, just the same. I know she's my sister too, but I've never liked her in spite of her supposed holiness. She's another one who can't mind her own business."

"That tie looks fine... anyway, don't look too beautiful Joe, you'll have the girl fainting with desire." He tousled Joe's hair. "Come on! You're taking more time to get ready than Eileen and she's a woman!" Everything Patsy said was tempered with humour, so much in opposite to Toro's dark intentions.... "God damn it! The taxi's here to take us to the station!"

When they all met up on the platform close to the booking office Jedda did not faint at the sight of Joe's beauty, as Patsy chose to put it, but was pleasantly entertaining and her usual vivacious self, smiling at everyone as they boarded the train.

They made their way – all five of them – consisting of Jedda, Patsy, Eileen, Joe and Toro – from Central Station via Haydock Park, preparing to meet Kate and Charles, who had gone on ahead.

The railway carriage was deserted except for one man. He was wearing a pinstriped suit and carrying a rolled umbrella. A bowler hat rested on his knee. He was engrossed in reading the daily paper until they all clamoured in and disturbed him. He gave them a look that suggested they were inferior beings and did not care for their accents in the least when they said good afternoon. He merely mumbled back something unintelligible.

Eileen moaned to herself and knew the man was asking for trouble.

"I just love your Liverpool accent, sir!" said Patsy, out to infuriate the man for being a snob.

The man looked as if he had been hit by a cannon. "I'm from Cheshire," he protested, in a beautifully produced and well-modulated voice.

Patsy remained silent for a while and all seemed to be going well until he said, after a good interval, "Work on the docks, do you?"

The man's eyes started to bulge out at what he considered an insult.

Patsy's expression remained one of bland innocence. " That's a lovely hat you have there, sir. I'm sure your fine hat is instrumental in spiriting away the good-ies." He winked at the man as if they were conspirators in some great plot when it came to filching off ships. "I don't know; you dockers are a crafty lot, to be sure. Aren't you sir?"

Sir and docker remained a strange combination for all those seated there. There was no one more subtle than Patsy when it came to being offensive.

Two nuns joined them in the carriage and Patsy was on his best behaviour for the rest of the journey.

"Instrumental, indeed!" Eileen sniffed. "That's a fine word for a summer's day." They all laughed and the nuns did too, but didn't know why.

As the train drew up at the next station the man kept his voice on an even keel. "I must leave you here," he said. "Most fortunately for me." The fancy docker walked briskly away, his rolled-up umbrella pushed tightly under his arm.

Patsy refused to be drawn. "And for us too, that's for sure!"

"Patsy. What on earth got in to you. You shouldn't have spoken to him like that!"

"He asked for it! Bloody snob!"

When they at last alighted from the train they made their way – crushed together in a large taxi – to the racecourse.

It was a fine June day for racing and a special outing.

The sun shone down and blessed them. It was just the right temperature; kind enough to keep them comfortably warm, but not hot enough to burn them.

They all joined Kate and Charles in a private box and were soon surrounded by Charles's business associates. Considering they were still in the midst of a supposed food shortage, good fare was abound and champagne flowed freely. It had been such a long time since Jedda had tasted such goodies – chicken, salmon, roast beef and all kinds of assorted savouries including club pies, salad and sundry sweets, so she just dived in and made a pig of herself.

Joe kept teasing her and calling her a gannet; nevertheless, the assembled company soon followed her lead.

The company at large, having eaten and drank their fill, was summed up by Kate: "Eat drink and be merry! Tomorrow we die."

"You know I've often given that a great deal of thought," said Patsy, and ended it there and the rest chose to do the same, knowing Patsy.

But Jedda was intrigued. "About what, Patsy?"

"How terrible it must be to wake up some morning and find yourself dead."

"I suppose I asked for that," said Jedda, amidst shoals of laughter from her friends.

Introductions were called for all round at the late arrival of their host – a Mr Harry Gordon. After several drinks they all soon had the urge to do a little speculating.

Jedda, who had never gambled before, knew little about horses. Joe soon showed

111

her the ropes, "I'll put something on first and if I win, we'll share; then try our luck again."

He was proud of her company. She was beautifully turned out, apart from her shoes, which could have done with a good polish. He was almost tempted to comment but held his counsel.

He backed the first winner, and Patsy ended up literally kicking himself for not having taken Joe's advice. Eileen had backed the same horse as Joe, and was laughing at Patsy as he stood there cursing.

Kate, Charles, and Toro, recently engaged in talking to Harry Gordon, came over and joined them. They had all backed a loser, but were pleased with Joe's success. Harry Gordon managed to slide his way round to Jedda's side and was eying her in a fashion Joe was far from pleased with; a scene Toro watched with obvious pleasure.

Kate smiled at Jedda trying to diffuse the situation. "That's Joe for you, an absolute winner when it comes to horses."

"It was a tip. I couldn't lose," said Joe, taking hold of Jedda's arm and drawing her away from Harry Gordon's side. Toro noticed his shrewd action and sneered.

Patsy swatted a fly that kept buzzing close to his ear. "I think this fly fancies me, it won't give up biting me."

"They always land on bad meat," quipped Eileen.

"You must be fond of it then," he sallied back, pulling her close to him.

Eileen remained unperturbed. "If you think I'm sharing my winnings with you, I'm not."

Joe laughed, took hold of Jedda's hand and drew her further away from the rest the crowd. "We'll see you all later. Just want to show Jedda around the place." He had taken control of her completely, and apart from Toro and Harry Gordon, the others smiled, knowing Joe wished to be alone with her.

"Be careful Jedda. Never go off with a stranger; not even if you know him," cried Patsy as they moved away."

Joe and Jedda waltzed off giggling. Patsy was quite a card.

They passed the time strolling on well-kept lawns in complete harmony.

Joe spoke to Jedda in low tones, "It was good of Charles to include us in a day out, but I'm none too keen on this Harry Gordon fellow – strikes me as something of a spiv." He steered her towards the ring and they studied the horses for a while. "I don't want Charles and Kate drawn into anything illegal –especially not my sister. And what's more, I didn't like the way he was eyeing you up."

Jedda answered, "Kate's no fool – nor Charles for that matter. I enjoyed the food, but not Harry Gordon. Where he is concerned, I'm no fool either."

"English Heathen. You'll do anything for food. You eat more food for an eight-stone girl than I've ever known."

Jedda kept up the banter: "Shut up, bog-face. You've not suffered shortages in

112

Ireland like we have. There have been times when I would have done anything for some sweets or an orange."

He smiled wickedly. "Anything? Wish I'd been around during the war, darlin'."

She smacked his arm. "I didn't mean it literally! Anyway, how do you know if I weigh eight-stone?"

He squeezed her arm. "You couldn't be more?" He led her back towards the stands. "Come on, I think I'll put another bet on, you bring me luck. We'll split the cash as promised."

"No! Really!" Not having any money to bet with, she could not see how winning applied to herself.

"It's as agreed," he insisted. "Pay your stakes back out of the winnings and no more arguments, Miss."

"What if it doesn't win?" she said.

He winked at her. "It will!" he said.

They went right through the card. Talk about the "luck of the Irish!"

Joe drew her to him and squeezed her. "You're my mascot. My lucky charm – La Markham!" He pondered for a moment and frowned, "I've often watched all the men in the drawing office fancying you."

She laughed, "Of course they don't!" tripping over a stone and losing her balance.

Joe reached out and steadied her, holding her as never before, but it seemed the natural thing to do and she felt at ease leaning close to him. As if it was something that had always been, spontaneous – not artificial.

"Yes, they do all fancy you. And you know they do, you Jezebel! You make men mad with desire, you minx."

She blushed in self-defence. "It's all in your imagination."

He nodded his head gravely. "No, it's not."

Once the last race was over they joined the others, who had mainly cut even.

"Lucky devil," said Patsy. "How much did you win?"

"Quite a bundle between us," said Joe, including Jedda in his windfall.

"Joe did," she corrected him, embarrassed.

"Either way, we're all taking a taxi home," said Joe, ignoring Jedda's prostests, leading them all to a taxi rank.

It was almost seven by the time everyone had been dropped of at their respective homes. Joe asked Jedda if he could take her out that evening – perhaps to dinner and maybe the theatre. He suggested he would pick her up at eight, smiling with pleasure at the thought as he did so. Toro, seated beside him, gave Jedda a sullen look, and she noted a flash of intense dislike radiate from pale blue eyes under the droop of tar-black brows, an expression that made her shudder. It was a look reminiscent of something once again familiar, yet difficult to place.

Later, whilst gazing in the mirror, preparing her face to meet Joe, a thought suddenly occurred to her that the look Toro had given her had been identical to that of a fox - a black, dangerous and very rabid fox.

Joe kept his promise, arriving at eight o'clock sharp. After Jedda had introduced him to Sally, whose face registered neither dislike nor pleasure, they left the small terraced house, walking along the street at a leisurely pace. Joe mentioned Sally's lack of interest after their introduction. Jedda explained that it was her mother's way not to fuss. Indeed, that she never even made a fuss of Jedda herself and she was her own daughter at that. "I'm afraid we're not as emotional as the Irish; nor as friendly."

Joe held Jedda's hand as if it was something he had always done. A fact which left him feeling both pleasantly surprised and proud when she allowed it to remain there. He had been worried in case she had chosen to withdraw it, but her hand remained resting in his, smooth as satin.

They caught a bus at the top of the street and rode steadily towards the city. Joe thought it was a little late for the pictures and suggested that perhaps she would care for dinner and they could go on to somewhere else later; maybe The News Theatre and watch snippets of the news and short comedies or, failing this, take a walk somewhere, just browse.

They cut though the Parsonage, a little parcel of green, an unexpected oasis in the heart of the city. Joe was feeling hungry and asked Jedda if she felt the same.

He need not have concerned himself. Ravenous, Jedda fell in with his plans immediately, at the same time refusing to mention the fact that there was little food to be had at home, anyway. Before they had left Sally had mentioned quietly, out of Joe's hearing, that she had to attend a Union Meeting and would be home quite late. She also hoped Jedda would manage to dine out, for there was little food in the larder. She was going on to the house of one of the members and had also been invited to supper. Jedda had not been included and found nothing unusual in that; she also took the view that there were times when she would have been better off living alone.

It was early evening. The restaurant was not very crowded considering it was a Saturday night. People usually drifted in later once the dance halls had closed and the pubs had emptied. Apart from themselves only three sets of couples were present.

The menu had little to offer, really. They chose Vienna steaks, small potatoes and new peas, followed by a sweet of redcurrants and mock cream.

"What is this?" said Joe, studying the steak.

"Don't know, really," said Jedda, laughing. "I just eat it. Be staunch and hope for the best. I suppose I'm used to it. It must be a state secret."

"Must be a steak secret as well by the taste of it!"

"You sounded a bit of a Patsy, then. I've never heard that said before."

He felt jealous and his face showed it. "You've been here before then? And with whom?"

"Who with?" Unable to fathom his reason for such a question she continued to be amused. "Who with? Why lot's of people! Friends! Girls from the office! Boys from the office! Boys I've met while out dancing. Why?"

Noticing the seriousness of his face she began to get annoyed and he could tell by the tone of her voice she was beginning to distance herself from him. Had he, after all, gone too far? He had only known her for few weeks. He didn't own her.

He felt distraught and began to struggle for words. "I didn't mean to be inquisitive," but he did, and she was well aware of it, remaining cool towards him. Of course there must have been others, she was a beautiful girl. Other men must have pursued her, of that he was certain. Even now, the man at the far table, in spite of being with a female companion, had been casting sly glances her way since their arrival.

He tried to pull back from feelings so foolishly displayed. Feelings of jealousy so extreme he could hardly credit it, but he could tell he was vexing her further from sarcasm that was evident when next she spoke: "Of course! What am I thinking of? There wasn't any life before Joe, was there?"

From the cool expression she now exhibited he sensed he had gone too far and became overwhelmed by a feeling of apprehension. He could have kicked himself but instead he reached for her hand, gently pressed it, and was pained when she did not squeeze it back.

"It just took me off balance. I'm sorry, none of my business." He put on his best melancholy look trying to cajole her into being friends again.

She regarded him more softly, yet cautiously. "It never occurred to me to ask if you'd been in this restaurant with anyone."

"I haven't," he said, in all honesty.

His truthfulness broke the ice and she started to laugh, low at first an then an octave higher in the way he loved. He felt so relieved by its intensity that he vowed to himself that he would tread more carefully in future.

And of course, he should have guessed by the jealousy broadcast on the faces of some of his colleagues at Canada Brights that he was lucky to be dating her at all. Often, he had seen them admiring her. Offering to take her to dinner etc., and their crestfallen faces when, with a shrug of her shoulders, she had refused their advances. For all he knew she could have been out with everyone of them; well, not the doddering ones, at least.

A crumb rested on the side of her mouth, so he reached over with his napkin and brushed it away. "I have to take care of you all the time," he said, smiling like a good father.

"I'm quite grown up, I can assure you," she said.

Waving for the waiter to fetch the bill he reckoned it was a timely gesture in which to leave the restaurant.

"Where would you like to go?" he inquired of her as the waiter hovered.

She suggested some outrageous pub, a place in which a lady would not be seen, reaping revenge upon him. The waiter's eyebrows shot up and the hand holding the bill began to tremble as he averted his gaze. She smiled up at the poor man mischievously.

Joe remained shocked out of his mind, whilst the minx winked at the waiter, teasing him unmercifully. There were times when she was worse than Patsy, and he knew she was trying to retaliate for his having so recently tried to pin her down. Served himself right, he supposed. Damn it! After all, he didn't own the girl. She'd got even and he backed down. "Where do you really want to go?" he conceded.

"The ladies room, at present," she said, as they rose from the table together. She walked away still laughing, watching Joe as he bumped into the waiter in passing.

"She was only kidding," he explained.

"A lovely young lady, I'm sure," acknowledged the waiter.

They left the restaurant, both in a lighter frame of mind.

"Would you like to spend an hour in The News Theatre?" he said, as suggested earlier. "They'll have some cartoons on. Give us both a bit of laugh," said Joe, smiling down at her.

She beamed back up at him, smiling from the side of her mouth, teasing him again, dimples going in and out.

"I know, I've been there before – don't ask me with whom, though." She tripped slightly as she said it and held onto his arm.

"Serves you right for being wicked to Joe," he chided her, at the same time concerned. "You didn't hurt yourself, did you?"

"No, just stubbed my toe a bit," she answered.

He looked down at her feet. "You've very small feet for a fairly tall girl. What size are they?"

"Threes," she answered. "My grandmother only takes twos, but she was smaller than I. I'm five-foot-five, thereabouts."

Joe grinned. "Your shoes are dirty," he started to laugh. "All glamour on top... yet dusty shoes."

She flushed slightly. "Sorry, I never noticed... still, love me love my shoes... I only have these and a pair of work shoes."

"Good God," he exclaimed. "If these are your best ones, what do your every-day ones look like?" He held her arm and veered her towards the picture house. "No matter; I'd love you barefoot, even naked... then it dawned on him what he had said. "I'd most certainly love you naked."

Her eyes became bright and her cheeks flushed. "I think you're very naughty," she said.

He squeezed her arm tightly. "I know, but who, if he's made of flesh and blood, wouldn't be? Not with La Markham at his side." He noticed the doubt in her eyes. "Only kidding. I don't take advantage of little girls."

"I'm not a little girl," she said.

"No, I don't think you are. Looking down into your eyes, I think you're a thousand-year-old goddess in disguise."

Having spent about an hour in The News Theatre, once outside, they sauntered at a leisurely pace to the bus stop.

"Shall I try and find a taxi?" Joe inquired of her. "That way I can see you home."

She smiled at him sweetly. "No, but thank you anyway. I've some revision to do if I'm to catch up on my English – the way I want to, that is."

He wanted so much to make the night last longer and felt peeved. "You're English and still don't know the language? Why do you need to be so proficient at it, anyway?"

She frowned. "There you go again. Questions, questions," she continued, half angry, half mocking. "If you must know, Mr Snoop, I wish to become a writer one day. It's my profound ambition. That all right with you?"

"Writer? You want to be a writer? What makes you think you have it – the ability, that is?" He was walking on thin ice.

She was at her snootiest. "I don't think I'll be good as an author – I know I shall! Even if I didn't make it to university, like you."

Contrite at having behaved like a jealous fool, he was conscious of not having believed in her, also of having hurt her pride... and now, she was shying away from him. "I didn't mean to offend you. I was taken by surprise, that's all," his face twisted with emotion. "I've never met a young girl who wanted to be a writer before. I'm eight years older than you; still, it's no reason to disbelieve you. I'm sorry."

"I'm eighteen, but believe me, if you will – I'm very, very old." She gave him an old-fashioned look.

"So you've informed me before, but you don't even look it, and sometimes, I feel like a cradle snatcher... but I think its too late now to retract."

"God," he thought, "I'm in love with a baby."

She started to laugh as she always did when lost for words, bringing him more enchantment.

"I'll see you again sometimes then, if you can spare the time between lessons and flirting with the boys?" said Joe sarcastically.

"I don't flirt –I'm just being friendly, the way I am with you."

Friends? So that's what they were. She and he were friends. Certainly he was her friend, he knew he would always be that, but he also knew it would never be enough. Yet how do you tell someone so young, so carefree, that every time you look at her, or she looks at someone else, you're terrified you might lose her. He had never felt like this before; he had always mastered his emotions when it came to the opposite sex. "Take 'em or leave 'em" had always been his motto and as he watched her walk away it was with a feeling of desperation. A man had no right letting a woman – no, a child – have so much power over him and he felt she'd bilked him.

Jedda Markham sat on top of the bus smoking a cigarette in what she believed to be the height of sophistication, oblivious to the passions she roused in one man, and the hatred she had unleashed in another. A man named Timothy "Toro" O'Riley.

Joe occasionally bumped into Jedda in the course of his duties at Canada Brights and though she smiled at him politely, it seemed to be as far as it went, and he began to wonder if he no longer interested her. Not that they had ever been serious, he had not even kissed her, yet.

That same evening, he called in on Kate, and asked if they would be going anywhere in particular soon, in the way of entertainment, he stressed.

She eyed him warily. "How would you like to join us at the Opera House this Wednesday coming. Ring up and see if there are any seats left. We're going in the front stalls, but whether you'll have any luck or not, I can't say."

It annoyed him immensely when she continued to whisk some eggs in a bowl, declining to mention Jedda. First adding sugar and having beaten the mixture further she began slowly to add the flour, spoonful by spoonful, teasing him unmercifully by refusing to be drawn over his new passion in life. Not wishing to be tormented further he shrugged his shoulders, refusing to be drawn, and made his exit, not adding that he would be desperately seeking tickets.

Kate smiled to herself when he had gone and started singing, "People will say we're in love."

Kate had not said who "we" were but he was hopeful, and had managed to obtain two tickets for Toro and himself.

Once he had left the office, which was late – he had some plans to finish for head man Kilburn – he and Toro still managed to arrive at the foyer of the Opera House early, but to his disappointment, Jedda was not there. One of his favourite operas, *Tosca*, was being performed and if she arrived, his joy would be complete.

Eileen and Patsy arrived and informed him they were waiting for Kate and friends, and the thought occurred to him that maybe it might give him the opportunity to meet Jedda once more.

His despondency soon disappeared at the immediate arrival of Kate and Charles, only to be resumed by the sight of Jedda accompanied by another man.

Patsy grinned, suspecting his predicament at seeing his beloved escorted not only by another, but so beautifully turned out. She wore a smart black suit under which she sported a pastel blouse; she had even cleaned her shoes, bless her. He had never set eyes on her escort before and tightened his jaw to control an overwhelming desire to hit him.

Kate introduced him as John Trundle, an associate of Charles, not Jedda's. She spoke to Joe on the side and informed him that he was married, and staying with she and Charles until some project they were into was settled. His wife was expecting a baby and had stayed home in Essex because the baby was due anytime. At Charles's request Jedda was just being polite and accompanying him for the evening. Joe began to breathe again.

Kate and her entourage sat two rows in front of Toro and himself, thus enabling him to keep his eyes fixed on the back of Jedda's head. She turned round a couple of times, conscious of his gaze, until at last, the curtain rose and they all became lost in the magic of Puccini.

Drinks were more than welcome during the interval, along with the desire for a cigarette; definitely not allowed in the theatre on account of the delicate throats of the singers. Patsy started to behave in the fashion that English men expect Irishmen to do by asking the barman, who had an expressionless face, for a whisky and hot water, and would he put some ice in it, please? The man remained unperturbed and did as requested, much to laughter of all who stood around.

"Would that be all sir?" he said.

"Why did Patsy do that?" said Jedda, still laughing.

Eileen nodded her head. "He must think it's expected of him. To pretend to be naive."

The interval over, they all made their way back to their seats. Jedda, Joe, Kate, Charles and Eileen were walking behind Patsy and Toro when Eileen exclaimed, "Oh God, look at him now! Patsy stop it...stop it for goodness sake."

Patsy was dancing on the way back to his seat with a slow kind of jigging movement, his arms held out from his sides in graceful fashion. The last act would be most serious in the opera with no cause for laughter so Eileen grabbed his arm. "Either sit down or go home," she half turned to Jedda. "It's like dealing with a naughty child."

The opera and its many curtain calls over, the group meandered for a while.

Patsy attempted to sing again, much to Eileen's despair. "For God's sake shut up Patsy. People are looking at us."

Laughingly, in good spirits, they all wandered over to an all night cafe. Much to Joe's delight John Trundle, having made his excuses, had left early, and all seven of them now were pushed together round one table discussing the wonders of opera between coy vulgarities such as "do you want stuffing" as an adage to roast chicken or "would you like a bit of crumpet" with equally youthful relish. Filled with a naive desire to be slightly ribald, yet on the other hand charged with a strict morality – the very essence of Catholic guilt – they could not quite decide how far to go. Patsy, mischievous as ever, did, and went even further by asking the waitress if she could supply him with a left-legged chicken drumstick because those were the only ones he was allowed to eat.

The poor girl was quite bewildered until Eileen smacked Patsy over the head with a spoon and told the girl to take no notice of his shenanigans. The girl said it didn't make any difference anyway, because chickens were in short supply and they were lucky to get what little breast they had on their plates.

Eileen decided to take revenge and in front of the waitress declared: "You're all nice boys and it was good of you to rescue us from Lewis's Arcade. We were just doing our midnight window-shopping. I'm Vera by the way and these are my two friends Gladys and Aggie."

Charles turned puce. "Stop her for goodness sake, Kate," he said, noticing the waitress's eyebrows shoot up.

Patsy was in his element. "We picked three nice girls up there last night. Hope you're all as affectionate."

This wasn't the reaction Eileen wanted. Hoist by her own petard, she hit out with a spoon. "Get on with the ordering," she said.

After such a fiasco, discussion about the opera continued regardless amidst the heady smell of cappuccino as it assailed their nostrils in concert to the fog of tobacco smoke and steam issuing from between the kitchen doors.

"I love Tosca," declared Eileen, tapping ash off the end of her cigarette with a scarlet fingernail. "She was so brave, yet so compassionate. The way she put those candles close by once she'd stabbed Scarpia was quite touching."

"Just like a woman," mocked Patsy.

"Be serious for once, Patsy!" continued Eileen, scratching the back of his hand with one of her talons.

"That hurt," he said.

Eileen pulled a droll face. "It was meant to. Anyway, as I was saying, it was most christian of Tosca, once she'd killed Scarpia that is, to have the kindness to leave a candle near his body and guide his soul to heaven."

Jedda's eyes widened to the size of saucers, "Guide him to hell, more like. I certainly wouldn't have lit a candle for him! Horrid man!"

Apart from herself and Charles, the rest of the party looked shocked...even Toro's face showed expression for once; though mainly cruel delight at her causing such offence, an affront to the Catholic faith.

"You can't treat the dead in such a cavalier manner, Jedda." Patsy's usually cheerful face was grave.

"I hate men like Scarpia. Taking advantage of the power invested in them and pretending to be holy in church," she declared with a pert turn of her head. "Seems hypocritical to me anyway, to care about someone like that! Throw him to the wolves, I say."

Joe spoke directly to her in an angry voice. "Don't talk like that Jedda! God forgives us all. It's what he's there for. We all sin! I suppose you have sometimes, in spite of your youth."

She eyed him coldly. "Can't think of any sins offhand, but I'll try to make a few up just to please you." She gave him a scathing look. "No one tells me how to think – nobody tells me how to do anything."

The company grew silent, as if not wishing for further confrontation, with the exception of Toro, whose face showed delight at Jedda's downfall. She stared back at him, unflinchingly, battle lines drawn, and she knew from that moment, instinctively, that between them, Joe was prized territory. She used her woman's wiles and sulked.

It worked! Joe was more terrified of losing her than he'd ever been of losing anything in his life. Convinced he should never have spoken to her in such a manner he said, "We weren't trying to tell you how to think, only how we, as Catholics, feel." He half smiled seeking appeasement, conscious they may all have gone much too far, that they might frighten her away. He did not know what he would do if he lost her. He gave in to her, soothing her indignation, reaching for her hand.

With a quick glance Jedda observed the look of contempt Toro awarded Joe for having surrendered to her and it made her want to laugh out loud, but she was much too clever for that, and Toro, quite rightly, suspected it. No one can fight love. She had played her cards well for the time being. Joe thought she was his, but the reality of the situation was, he was hers.

They made their way to the bus station – a giggling crowd of ninnies. Patsy, being the main cause of their merriment, put on an upper-class English accent as he slipped an arm around Eileen. "Oh, do look at that moon, darling. One can only think in terms of Ginger Rogers and Fred Astair and toothache music coming from an invisible orchestra again."

"What the hell's toothache music?" said Joe, puzzled as the rest of them.

"You know," said Patsy. "Ah, ah, Eee, eeh. They always have it in romantic pictures."

"Oh, yes," said Joe, dreamily. "I can picture it now. Fred and Ginger dancing on air across a mirrored surface with swans floating by."

"Come down to earth, Joe," declared Patsy impishly. "All we've got is the River Irewell. No swans; just rats as big as cats!"

They all fell about laughing, especially when Patsy tried to croon a romantic ballad and Eileen gave him a push with her elbow. "For God's sake, Patsy, shut up. It sounds like someone dragging a fender. He's part German and part Irish you know; doesn't know whether to goose step or jig, poor boy."

Patsy stroked Eileen's face." You, know," he said, a grin breaking out on his face. "Beauty is in the eye of the beholder. It's just that some people have bad eyesight and need one of those white sticks."

"What are you getting at, now?" questioned Eileen.

"It means I should take a trip to the opticians," he parried.

"Don't you mean the chiropodist?" That's where your brains are situated. In your big flat feet."

"My feet are quite dainty." Patsy gave a twirl to verify the fact.

"The night has ended," said Joe. "I'm taking Jedda to the bus stop."

Summer shared with Joe seemed eternal to Jedda. Sometimes, the two of them were alone, content with each other's company. Sharing interests like soul mates. Joe had never known anyone who pleased him more. Her intelligence, combined with a fresh young charm, was more than he had ever dreamed or hoped for. Just the same, to his way of thinking, such a bounty was something so wonderful, he was fearful of the fact that, not only might he lose her, that the gods would be jealous and go out of their way to destroy them.

In spite of their compatibility, there were other things to consider – religion, for one thing and nationality for another; also the fact that she was very young and also very wayward. And more than this, the truth was, she held him spellbound. She had a power over him, an uncomfortable notion on his part, something he never imagined could have happened to him. He was walking on glass – sharp, broken glass.

Other times Kate, Charles, Eileen and Patsy would meet up with them, with Toro only putting in the occasional appearance. Lively, fun-loving periods, times, which in their entirety, only youth can aspire to. And, though the brooding figure of Toro began to materialize with less frequency, causing less of a blot on the horizon, his brief appearances caused Jedda a great deal of aggravation.

Jedda had begun to notice Sally was becoming more and more absorbed in matters concerning the Union and, with her mother showing little interest, having no time to spare for her offspring, mother and daughter proceeded to drift further and further apart. To be truthful, more out of disinterest than enmity.

When Kate suggested that she should come and holiday with Charles and she to a country house they had invested in, Jedda more or less jumped at the chance, especially as the rest of her friends would be joining them, but mostly because Joe would be there. She mentioned the trip to Sally and asked if it would all right if she went to the Yorkshire coast for a couple of weeks. Sally, having thought the matter over, conceded to her request on the premise that Jedda behaved herself.

When Kate called that evening to discuss their venture with her mother and ask permission for Jedda to join them, Sally repeated the same warning on Jedda's behalf. Kate had answered in a most serious manner and told Sally not to worry, that they were all very fond of Jedda and would not have her hurt for the world. And besides, the Yorkshire moors and trips to the seaside would put some colour in her daughter's cheeks.

The journey across country had seemed endless. The constant motion of the train made them all sleepy and it was a relief to all of them when, at last, they reached their destination.

Loading their luggage into the boot of two taxis, they squeezed, rather than sat, in the old black boxes on wheels that passed for cars and drove away from the station.

The house, situated on the Yorkshire moors, and only a few miles away from the coast, was a pleasant revelation to the invited guests. On the south side of the house a veranda extended itself to meet large sweeping lawns, and the September sun glinted on mullion windows, latticed, and of high proportions.

Kate slid a key into the brass lock and they all trundled in behind her resembling sheep behind a weary shepherd.

Once the fires were lit, courtesy of Charles and Patsy, the first thing the weary travellers did was to drape themselves before the fire of one of the two spacious sitting rooms, letting the flames toast them; tempting them to spend an hour over a glass of wine and a long leisurely smoke.

Kate took them on a tour of inspection, showing them first the small library, dining room, lounge and lastly the kitchen, a cosy room, across the middle of which was a table big enough to serve a king's banquet. Jedda noted the dining room, an elegant chamber with warm mahogany furniture. It impressed Jedda as a room Zizzie would have appreciated and it occurred to her that it had been an eternity since she had last encountered her grandmother and the thought plagued her.

The house boasted eight bedrooms and, after Kate had showed each of them to the rooms appointed to each guest, she left them to do their unpacking while she went down to prepare dinner.

All through the first day of their holiday it rained miserably and, though only early autumn, mists were beginning to form.

Kate suggested that Charles lit the fire in the large kitchen because it was cold once they withdrew from the sitting room, leaving the dining room unused. Charles declared, "We'll need a forest of our own to keep the damn place warm." And he and Patsy went to fetch more logs that were piled up near the shed outside.

"Miss Otis regrets she's unable to lunch today," sang Patsy... "When the gang came and dragged her from the jail, Madam they hanged her on that old willow across the way... and the moment before she died she lifted up her lovely head and cried, Madam... Miss Otis regrets she's unable to lunch today."

"Goodness, that's a weary song, Patsy," said Charles.

"I love it," said Jedda, not mentioning she was reminded of Billy and Addie Tobias.

Patsy paused from using bellows on the fire, a difficult task; it had been some time before anyone had attempted to tangle with its rather blocked chimney.

"It's strange isn't it?" said Patsy, out of the blue.

They were all used to Patsy's strange thought processes.

"What is it now Patsy?" said Eileen.

"Miss Otis."

"Well, what about her," Eileen was becoming impatient.

"Well, if she had a thick rope strung around her neck how could she come out with such a long sentence as, "Miss Otis regrets she's unable to lunch today...agh! agh! agh!"

"Oh, Patsy! Whatever will you think of next!" said Toro.

Patsy gave him a sour look, "Well, at least I think."

Miss Otis having difficulty in speaking? Patsy had brought the song home in a new light for Jedda. She smiled to herself at the thought.

While Eileen and Kate prepared the evening meal, Jedda, who was no cook herself, went into the garden and collected some flowers, and having done so, arranged them artistically in a series of vases. As she busied herself placing the flowers at different angles round the room, sadly, the whole action became reminiscent of Zizzie in that happy time so long ago; so much so, it made her want to weep.

Joe asked her what was wrong but she felt unable to tell him. He suspected a sadness about her but she never spoke of the past, while he himself could never talk of anything else.

She had often offered a sympathetic ear to tales of his troubled past. All about the tragedy of his parents' mixed marriage and of how the Protestants had turned on his father, first ostracizing him verbally before turning to physical violence, and all because he had dared to marry his Catholic mother. His father had gone to his grave earlier than he should as the result his injuries, a trauma from which he had never quite regained his health because of the beatings he had received.

His subsequent sacking from the shipyard forced the family to leave Belfast in exchange for Dublin where they felt much safer. Not long after the event – to be precise the week after which some men had crept into their backyard and even murdered young Joe's pet rabbits – they had abided in Dublin ever since.

Sometimes, on long walks upon the moors, Joe had tried to delve into Jedda's mind, but to no avail.

"You never speak of your family. Surely there wasn't just you and your mother, was there?"

"No, but there is only my mother, now. Apart from my grandmother, Zizzie. She and mother are estranged and have been for years. I wish they weren't. They are all I have in the world since my aunt and uncle went to Canada."

"Don't you ever see her?"

"No. Mother wouldn't like it."

"It's up to you now, you're old enough."

"I know. But it's been so long since I've seen her and besides, she lives so far away. I'd have some difficulty going by bus. By the time I arrived there, it would be time to leave."

Joe squeezed her hand gently. "I'll take you then. We'll take a taxi – it's a nuisance this taxi business, though. Once I'm on my feet I'll invest in a small car; that way we can drive out into the country far more often."

When he tried to investigate her background further, all she would say, and briefly, was that her father and grandfather, Sandy, were dead.

She had to his mind stated it factually, even coldly.

"What was Sandy like?" he had asked.

"He was my step-grandfather and I loved him dearly," she burst out, "and I don't want to talk about him, nor about Alex, any more. I miss them so."

"Alex?"

"My father. As I told you, he's dead too! Lots of people have died and left me... I don't want to talk about it any more." She started to stiffen her shoulders and look extremely upset.

"I'm sorry. I didn't mean to pry."

"You're not. It's just that it was so long ago and I don't like to talk about it. Bring it all back, that is. Other things happened in my childhood... bad things, I don't want to talk about either."

"How bad?"

She pressed her fingers to his lips.

He relented. "Let's go and find the others. I'm getting hungry anyway. Are you?"

"Yes, I am," she said, looking more composed.

"I knew the mention of food would cheer you up!"

She smacked his hand playfully, and grasping hers in his, he hurried her on across the moors. Besides, the wind was picking up and he didn't want her "blowing away".

A gale was sweeping across the moors by the time they reached the house.

Patsy was waiting for them in the doorway. "I don't know where Eileen and Kate have got to, there's quite a storm brewing by the looks of it. They went to the village to do some shopping ages ago and I'm starving. Can you cook, Jedda?"

"Not very well."

"Chuck her, Joe! A girl who can't cook is no good to any man."

Joe laughed, "Neither is one that looks like the back of a cab."

Patsy nodded his head. "True. True. Only kidding Jedda. You'll just have to marry a rich man who can afford to employ a cook. If you marry Joe, it's the workhouse for you... ah, here they are now," he cried, noticing Eileen on her way her way up the path with Kate. "Ist that thee Kathy love, hast come ta haunt from mi oer moors."

"Aye, Heathcliff lad. Ast put kettle on? Am bloody ungry with all this hauntin business a ave ta get up too," cried Eileen answering him back in kind.

Charles shouted, "Come in an shut doer, all o ye! Tis blowin a mighty gale in ere."

"Aye let's put wood int ole," parried Patsy.

Hurrying into the warmth of the interior they all warmed their hands by the kitchen fire, indulging in a cup of hot cocoa before starting to prepare dinner.

"Why is it?" said Jedda her eyes taking in the company at large, "that we females sit on this side of the table and you men all sit on that side?"

"So that we can play footsie with one another," quipped Patsy. Or is it that you prefer being alone with Joe before getting up to some nonsense or other?"

Joe's expression began to darken. "What does that mean?" He was, as always, quick to come to Jedda's defence.

Eileen intervened quickly, "Listen who's talking! Just because you've got barefoot gossams running around the length and breadth of Ireland, Patsy, doesn't mean Joe is about to follow suit."

"I haven't got gossams as you call them, running about the length and breadth of Ireland"... he paused and placed his hand loosely over his mouth, "only across the half of it."

The tension eased as they all exploded into laughter and Eileen swiped at his face with a cloth she was holding.

"Your hair smells nice Jedda," said Patsy. "Like Lilacs."

Eileen pulled a face, "Oh, yes and what about mine?"

Patsy leaned over and kissed her, "Mmm, yours smells even better."

"Like what?" said Eileen, pleased.

"Patsy grinned. "Cockles and mussels." He winked at Jedda. "You didn't know her grandmother was Molly Malone, did you Jedda?"

Eileen swished at him once more with a cloth. "None of my family came from Dublin, so there!"

"She was still Molly Malone though," said Patsy, teasing her further. "Her other old Granny was named Clementine, Jedda! The one that wore kipper boxes for shoes."

Everyone laughed at Patsy and agreed he was a nut case; they also acknowledged it was out of the question to venture out in such weather, spending the rest of the night safe and snug round the fire telling ghost stories. When they ran out of imagination they listened to the wireless. Bing Crosby sang, "I'll be seeing you," followed by Dinah Shore's "You'll be so nice to come home to. You'll be so nice by the fire... while the breeze on high sang a lullaby..." which made it all even cosier.

The Ink Spots sang I'll Get By and they all got up and danced together, with the exception of Toro. Jedda began to feel sorry for him until he gave her one of his icy stares, then she changed her mind.

Patsy nuzzled Eileen's hair and murmured in a deep "Ink Spot" voice, "I'll get by honey bee... boop a do... as long as I have you. Honey lamb... sugar plum... pickled herring feet..."

"Now you've spoilt everything, Patsy." Eileen was a cross between anger and amusement. "I was just feeling romantic then... everyone was..."

Kate stood in the middle of the floor, her legs crossed, her face a shade of puce. "I want to pee," she screamed out laughing and made a dash for the door without ceremony.

Joe winced as Jedda dug her fingers into his hand but it was all so hilarious he was unable to tell the love of his life about his pain, not when she was doubled up giggling, stamping her feet unable to contain herself. Charles was having a fit and even Toro was laughing for a change.

Jedda looked up and her eyes met Toro's. It seemed for a second a fondness gleamed there, then the look died just as quickly, but not before she had caught him unawares.

Toro gazed out through his bedroom window at the beautiful scenery below, his expression as miserable as the early autumn mist. Not that it had ever been otherwise, it was not in his nature; but he was honestly concerned for Joe. His fascist heart was a hard one, but ever since Joe and he had been boys – he the elder by two years – he had run Joe's life for him. Helped and loved Joe after his fashion which, though from his own point of view may have seemed genuine, to those other than himself, appeared oppressive.

He had been married once to a Spanish girl, until the communists had chosen to kill her. Youthful days at the time of the Civil War when he had been barely out of his teens and Franco had been his idol – the keeper of the flame known as the Catholic faith – yet, for all their vigilance, the evil of communism still reared its ugly head.

America was aware of it, but the stupid English were soft as usual having fought on the wrong side. It wasn't that he'd cared for Hitler or what happened to Germany, Adolf seemed too deep in a love affair where the English were concerned, and he knew that had they sided with each other they could have held the world in the palm of their hands. It was only when Germany had turned on the Brits that he had become useful against Ireland's enemy. Mussolini and Franco had the right idea but that had got squashed. Senator McCarthy wasn't asleep though. Good old Joe McCarthy.

Now she was here to try to destroy him! Him! His Joe! The one he had always looked out for from his early childhood and now she had come, to wreck all they believed in. Jedda thought she was clever with her easy-going ways and "live and let live" attitude; well, he had ways of dealing with people like that. Sometimes he hated her so much he could barely stand to look at her, never mind be in the same room. And that stupid fool of a Kate! She was just as bad! Giving up her religion after all the trouble a mixed marriage had caused her family. Joe had not proposed to Jedda yet, but he suspected things were heading that way. And if they did... watch out Jedda Markham, that's all! Yes, he'd soon sort that bloody heathen out.

When he arrived downstairs Kate was preparing breakfast in her usual relaxed way. She never hurried, but always seemed organised. Even he had to admit that it was something he admired about her. At least even she wasn't like that flibbertigibbet Jedda, who couldn't even boil an egg, let alone cook a decent meal.

He walked over to where Kate stood stirring the porridge. "Are things getting serious with Joe and Jedda?" he inquired of her.

Kate shrugged and added salt to the porridge. "I don't know. Why?" and was immediately suspicious. Toro hardly ever spoke to her, so why was he suddenly so friendly? Indeed, she was on her guard against anything that involved Toro.

"I just think she's too young for him."

Kate pulled a face. "You think too much. Anyway her being young isn't the real reason for your being inquisitive, is it?"

"What do you mean?"

Kate's temper flared. "You know damn well what I mean! Hanging about like some old woman... anyway what business is it of yours – you don't own Joe! You don't own anyone!"

Charles sauntered in. "What's all the racket about at this time in the morning? My head's splitting."

"You shouldn't drink so much wine then… and nothing's wrong and if there was, the matter's closed as far as I'm concerned." She bestowed a sour look in Toro's direction. "You two want porridge?"

Charles was so sweet, so expansive. Kate watched him as he smiled. His large mouth invariably swept up into a generous curve as it was doing right now; cautious, as he tried to evaluate what kind of mood she was in. Though well acquainted with her early morning temper he pondered for several seconds and having disposed of two aspirins with a glass of water, placed the vessel onto the table. "Yes, I'll have a bowlful my dear, but just a small one."

"How can a bowl be full and be a small portion? I thought only we Irish were supposed to say things like that."

"Stop nit picking, you know what I mean. And stop being so sensitive where you Irishness is concerned."

"I'll forgive you this once," said Kate, determined to have the last word. "And what's more, I'm proud of being Irish, not that it's anything to do with you."

The two men seated themselves at the table and ate breakfast in silence and were almost finished before the others joined them.

Patsy went straight to the kitchen door. "It's steamy in here. We could do with some air." The door refused to stay open so he strode about the kitchen looking for something to use as a doorstop. "I can't find anything thick enough," he said, falling for one of Eileen's jibes.

"Try using your head," she said, teasing him. "Literally!"

Everyone smiled, amused as always by Eileen and Patsy's banter.

Kate became more cheerful and as her mood brightened she spoke to Jedda. "Did you have a comfortable night? That bed's rather narrow."

"She's a narrow girl," said Patsy, refusing to be outdone by Eileen's form of repartee, lightening up the atmosphere with his easy charm.

Kate used her best tactics, mainly for Toro's benefit. "Nevertheless, I must invest in a three quarters one for the next time you come, Jedda; though if you're married to some rich, handsome man by that time, I'll offer you the best front room...especially for the view... even let you have the house to yourselves." She paused and looked at Joe. "Not if you marry my brother though. I'll book you a room at the local asylum instead."

Jedda smiled and consulted her breakfast. "Do you mind if I don't eat this egg, Kate? I don't care for eggs."

"Here," said Joe. "You have my bacon and I'll have your egg."

Jedda accepted the sacrifice of the favourite part of his breakfast without turning a hair. Without so much as a thank you, as though it was the most natural thing in the world for a man to do.

He'd thought she wouldn't have; that she would have demurred on the behalf of her beloved, but he had been proved wrong. He knew that kind-hearted Mary McGloughlin who loved him dearly and, whom he often thought of with a guilty conscience, would have said, "Oh no Joe, you keep the bacon as well."

But Jedda Markham wasn't the sweet Colleen he'd left behind. No, she was selfish, but she was very young. He didn't know why he loved her really, except she made him smile more than anyone he had ever known and that he counted the hours when she wasn't around.

His mother had often suggested he married Mary McGlouglin and that he would live happily ever after. Be content. Content? Well, the dead were content and with Jedda Markham he would never be that. Exasperated, yes! Confused! Of course; but never, never content! Of course if he had never met Jedda Markham he knew he would definitely have married Mary McGlouglin and the fact not only drove him mad, it made him feel guilt-ridden too. Loving an enemy wasn't exactly his idea of married bliss.

Toro watched Joe and Jedda with a look of distinct contempt. He despised Joe's weakness where Jedda was concerned. The performance over the bacon was to him a betrayal. It was as if Joe had joined the Orange Order.

After lunch the weather seemed fine and they remained seated on wicker chairs on the veranda listening to records being played on an old gramophone Kate had brought along. Charles said it must have been made in the year dot.

Kate put on a record of Irish music and when the Londonderry Air came softly through Toro became sentimental for once and sang Danny Boy.

Jedda was mesmerised by the beautiful sound that came from his vocal cords. She'd never heard anyone sing like that since Gingo. The thought of him affected her so much it took her breath and she thought her lungs were about to burst.

Joe looked at her, concerned, but said nothing.

"I love the Londonderry Air," said Jedda.

"We call that the Derry Air," said Toro coldly.

"We English refer to that as a bottom," quipped Jedda

They all laughed in spite of the insult, except Toro, who was furious. If he'd had a gun he would have shot her.

The Kerry Dancers streamed out next. Nostalgic. Pining for lost youth. Patsy took to the floor as expected. After a while he took Eileen's hand and the rest of them followed suit, dancing in a ring in a wild, abandoned fashion, apart from Toro, who was standing in the doorway, one arm leaning on the jam, dark thoughts racing through his head.

The evening meal was consumed in a leisurely fashion interposed by conversation, the drone of which continued as they all deserted the house and made their way down to the village pub.

The wine, having reached Patsy's head, made him try to kiss Eileen across the pub table. She shoed him away.

"Persona non grata," cried Patsy.

Eileen shrugged. "So? You went to University?"

"I'm very good at French," he said, teasing her unmercifully.

"It isn't French! It's Latin. Though I suppose they're Latin, too." said Eileen, falling in to his trap.

"Wrong again. The French are Celts, like us... Do you know, Ireland used to be attached to France... before the water divided us."

"That was the Welsh, Oggy! Oggy!" said Kate. "Actually England was once joined to Dublin, believe it or not."

Eileen pulled a face. "Oh, God! Here comes a history lesson again. I often wondered why you hopped rather than walked, Patsy."

"What do you mean, hop?" said Patsy.

"Eileen looked at him askance. "It must have been all those frogs legs your honourable ancestors ate."

"Yours must have been Chinese speaking like that," said Patsy, having the last word.

"It's true anyway. We were once attached to France. England as well." Patsy smiled at Jedda as if it was an honour to include her.

"Thought they'd be around somehow," said Joe. He grinned at Jedda. "We can't get away from them, no matter how we try." He reached for Jedda's hand and kissed it. "Not that I want to get away from this one."

Jedda smacked his hand playfully. "Enough of the blarney, Joe."

They spent a good two hours in the good company of the locals. Nice people with strong Yorkshire accents and sound knowledge of the surrounding countryside; information they shared freely with tourists.

Charles said that tomorrow they would explore the area thoroughly before taking a trip in a charabanc to the Yorkshire coast. Jedda smiled at the word ... Gingo always referred to the vehicle as a "charo".

Early morning and before breakfast, Eileen, Kate and Jedda did their exercises, each leaning with one arm against the doorpost. Eileen cocked her leg in the air in an abandoned fashion and invited Patsy to join them in their antics.

He studied her for several second then answered sagely, "Don't think so. The position you're in, I'm relieved – if you'll pardon the pun – I'm not a tree or, even worse; a lamppost."

"No need to be vulgar, Patsy." Eileen's face wore a cross expression and she refused to join in the laughter expressed by the rest of them. Even Toro smirked, secretly.

The phone rang repeatedly, allowing no further levity at Eileen's expense.

Charles went to answer it and returned several seconds later a scowl on his face. "Wilkins is being pig-headed again," he awarded Kate a look of profound apology. "Sorry, dear. I'm going to need you to come along too; we've been invited to dinner of all things – you and Patsy also, Eileen."

"So it's goodbye to Yorkshire for Eileen and I," protested Kate. "Between you and me Charles, I'm far from pleased."

"I'm afraid so! Business is business," Charles was adamant.

"What about Jedda and Joe? Do you two want to stay? Toro?"

Kate questioned them deeply; concerned by the change in the arrangements. Jedda looked perplexed, Joe bewildered.

Toro was definite. "We'll come with you," he said, making everyone's minds up for them.

"When are we leaving? said Joe.

"In about three hours; I'll arrange for taxis to the station," said Charles.

Joe took Jedda's hand, "Come on, that leaves us at least an hour to enjoy the last of the scenery."

When Joe and Jedda arrived back late the others were waiting, ready and packed.

Joe looked sheepish. "We've decided to stay on, if it's all right with you, Kate?"

Kate looked dubious.

Patsy looked naughty.

"Jedda will be quite safe with me, I can assure you." said Joe and slipped an arm round Jedda's waist.

"I bet she will," said Patsy, grinning mischievously.

"Oh, do shut up, Patsy," said Eileen. "Not everyone's a sex maniac, like you."

"It's you! You lead me astray, Eileen," Patsy pursed his lips inviting Eileen to kiss him. She declined with a sniff.

Toro's face was a picture to behold. His usual detached air had completely evaporated, nostrils quivering as he imparted a look of complete disgust towards Jedda and Joe.

Kate wanted to laugh outright. "Of course you can stay. No use letting all that stock of food go to waste; certainly not in times like these," she stated, as if she were innocent of ever having purchased anything on the black market. "Well, we'd better be off or we'll miss the train. Coming, Toro?"

Toro scowled and followed the rest of the party through the door, but not before giving Jedda a look of a hellhound about to pounce.

The next ten days were to decide how things stood between Joe and Jedda.

With no ambiguous thoughts to deter them, they grew closer and closer; something, which unconsciously, they knew they had always been.

By day they roamed the hills or visited the little teashop in the village to save themselves from Jedda's cooking. Seated at their usual small table they would indulge in the delicious hot pot the proprietors served and for pudding, usually apple pie, or little cakes and delicious preserves. Jedda found it reminiscent of Mrs Tobias's shop but did not mention the thought to Joe. She had not felt so content and at ease with herself in a long time.

In the evenings, they lingered by the fire, leisurely drinking wine between intermittent kisses and innocent desire; they smoked endless cigarettes that did them little good.

Joe, his passions roused, wondered how he stood it. Only his promise to Kate, along with his Catholic conscience suppressed his desire not to overpower her. Though, to his way of thinking she seemed only a child, there were other moments when she seemed older that himself. At times, there seemed to be something of the seer about her.

Often, when on their many walks amongst the hills, he had chanced upon her gazing into the distance as if she dwelled in some other place – a secret place – one he was not allowed to enter. When he inquired about her thoughts she would shrug her shoulders and say, "Nothing... I'm not thinking of anything!"

But he suspected that she was, and felt frustrated at not being able to share in her every thought; then, she would come down to earth again and kiss him in a way that made him quite dizzy.

On one of the many nights that they sat by the fire he told her that he had often lay in bed sighing and murmuring her name," Jedda... Jedda... Jedda... and that it was a wonder she hadn't heard him."

She said that she had – Truly! Truly! And that if ever they drifted apart, she would call to him through her mind, even though he had he ceased to love her."

"I'll never stop doing that," he assured her, taking a piece of her hair in his hand and letting it drift slowly downwards. "La Markham," he had said, "you're my first love and you'll be my last, and I'd better be yours."

She had smiled up at him and said, "Is that a threat?"

"Yes," he said. "I will come riding on my trusty steed, sword in hand to capture you from your latest lover." His eyes darkened. "Really though, Jedda, seriously, and I hate to say this, I'm a proud man. But if I lost you, I don't think I'd want to go on living. I know if my body continued to exist, my soul would be dead."

At first she laughed at him and said the moors were getting at him, and he sounded like that silly old Heathcliff. Then she had frowned and looked at him with that thousand-year-old look in her eyes. "People get parted from each other. It's something that's always been my greatest fear. And what about your God? Could you leave him for me? Love me best of all?"

"I could never betray – and he's your God too, whether you believe it or not – but that doesn't mean I don't love you. Only that I love you more."

"I've never worshipped anything or anyone."

"That's sad. Never? Hey, what about me?"

"Not even you. Put people on pedestals and one gets hurt. I suspect that's what you're trying to do with me, aren't you, Joe?"

He stroked her hair, "Probably. Where you're concerned I can't help it."

She kissed him quickly, softly. "Well, you must. It isn't healthy. Even dangerous."

"Ah, knows that, mi Kathy luv. Tis the heather ant moors what done it."

"I never cared for Kathy and Heathcliff," she said. "I've always thought them selfish; and the Lyntons so much nicer. Emily Bronte was, nevertheless, a great writer. I wonder where she got the idea for Heathcliff's character?"

"I don't know; but the Lyntons, they were soft," said Joe.

"No they weren't; just civilised. Heathcliff was petty and vengeful."

"He had a bad childhood."

"Hardly the Lyntons fault. Why couldn't he grow up and come to terms with it?"

"Most women seem to fancy Heathcliff."

"I don't," she leaned forward and kissed him. "So remember that; always be kind to me."

He drew her closer. "I'll always be that. You know, when Emily Bronte wrote *Wuthering Heights* she mustn't have been far of from dying. She didn't get to finish another novel."

She stirred in his arms. "A dying swan's final dance is always its best."

He drew her face round so he could look right into it. "Where on earth do you get these sayings of yours? Do you make them up yourself?"

"Of course I do. I can't help it, they just come into my head." She looked nervous, suspecting criticism.

He moved his head from side to side and pursed his mouth into a mischievous grin. "I don't know, you're unbelievable at times; but at least you're an original." He drew her close stroking her hair as if she were a child. "My inventive Jedda."

The sun shone brightly on their last few days together. Joe went into the village and booked a charabanc for a day's outing to the sea. The ride was comfortable and allowed them access to delightful scenery as they rode along.

Upon arrival at their chosen destination they alighted from the charabanc and made their way to the seashore. They walked along hand in hand, oblivious even to the few people present on the beach.

She asked him again about Ireland and what Dublin was really like. Was it modern? What was its University like? What were the shops like?

"Hey! Hey! Hey! Not so fast. I can only answer one question at a time; anyway I don't live in Dublin. I live just outside. At a place they call Curragh."

"Curragh?"

"Yes. It's mostly known for its racecourse. It's called "The Curragh" as a matter of fact."

She laughed. "I suppose I should have guessed. Where else would my Joe have lived?" Then she grew serious. "Don't you worry in case gambling becomes an obsession."

"I think it already is, or was. I've won and lost enough money to have married you three times over, come to think of it."

"I wasn't aware that I'd proposed to you yet," she said, deriding him and turning up her nose.

"What a minx I have in this English girl. You heathen, leading me astray."

They kissed and talked in the familiar way reserved for lovers, so engrossed in each other they ignored the incoming tide until, fast and swirling, it poured in around their feet. Joe grabbed her arm tightly so that it hurt. "We'd better get out of here and fast."

Jedda seemed unnaturally calm about the situation, as if nearly drowning was an everyday occurrence, so Joe put his arm around her waist and pulled her to safety.

He looked down at her concerned. "We nearly got more than our feet wet then."

She didn't seem to hear him. "The old man and the sea," was all she muttered, recalling a time long distant.

"What was that?" he said.

"Nothing. I was just thinking out loud."

They had lunch in a small, but excellent cafe. The tablecloths were pristine white on which cut glass wine glasses had been placed next to pretty flower arrangements. It was quite a romantic occasion, but more so, because they were madly in love, sharing a passion that only first love can bring.

They walked slowly through the afternoon, savouring the delights of a sea flecked with golden sunlight; listening to the murmuring of the waves as they rolled gaily in, sobbing as they receded like a quick intake of breath from a tearful child, merging from time to time with the chorus of mournful seagulls overhead.

Joe bought her a pretty silk scarf, a little leather purse and a bunch of flowers, things that delighted her because they were from the beloved.

They went back to the same small cafe for an evening meal, served by a quiet waitress, as they ate dinner by the soft glow of candlelight. They sat and gazed at each other, each entranced by the other. Joe, fascinated by the unusual damson shade of her eyes, gazed endlessly into them and was obliged to remark, "My sloe-eyed temptress. Who bequeathed you such lovely orbs?"

"What?"

"Your beautiful eyes?"

"Oh, my eyes. My father. Who else? Certainly not my mother."

"No, hers are a true blue, aren't they."

"Are you disappointed because mine are not?"

"No! Certainly not. I adore your eyes." He tweaked her hair, teasing her. "I'll never look into any others in quite the same way."

She laughed, "Flatterer. Why do you speak such nonsense?"

His face darkened, his brown eyes serious, almost sad. "I'm not speaking nonsense. I'm telling the truth. Why do you always doubt me?"

She smiled, trying to ease his pain, and reaching for his hand sighed, "You're an incurable romantic. You could get hurt... I'd never want that."

"Not by my Jedda, I hope? I, being poor, have only my dreams. I have spread my dreams under your feet. Tread softly because you tread on my dreams..."

"Who wrote that, you?"

He laughed, "No, W. B. Yeats. Ireland's greatest poet. He was a romantic too."

"It's very beautiful. A lovely poem... I'd never hurt you, even if you are a romantic. Not if I could help it, that is. But I have hurt people. Not intentionally – yet in a manner beyond belief. You'd hate me if you knew."

"What do you mean?" Joe was nonplussed. "I could never hate you, Jedda. Not even if I tried."

"Not here, not now." She consulted her watch. "Hadn't we better be moving? We'll miss the ride home."

The hours driving back to the village lulled them into cosy reverie, sitting close together, unspeaking most of the time. Content with the other's proximity.

The driver obligingly dropped them off close to the house, saving them the walk from the village.

Once inside "Kate's castle", as they all jokingly referred to it, Joe lit a fire in the living room; just in case it became chilly later in the evening. Jedda left him to his chores and went upstairs to freshen up.

She came down into the living room wearing a pretty dress; her tied back in a bun. Joe was coaxing the wood into an orange glow. "You don't want to eat anything, do you?" she said, hopefully.

Joe was forced to smile. "No, dinner at the cafe was quite enough for me. How about you?"

She shook her head. "No, let's go and sit on the veranda, have a glass of wine and watch the summer say goodbye."

"You have a flowery way of talking at times, miss. Is that the writer in you coming out?"

She didn't answer and walked out onto the veranda and sat on a cane chair. Joe followed suit, a bottle of wine in one hand, two glasses in the other.

Joe sat down close to her. "When you are old and grey and full of sleep and nodding by the fire, take down this book and slowly read and dream of the soft look your eyes had once, and of their shadows deep."

She gave him a perplexed look – questioning.

"Ah, then there's something madam doesn't know? One of our greatest Irish poets, W. B. Yeats again."

"It's very nice – tell me more."

Joe continued, pleased. "How many loved your moments of glad grace and loved your beauty with a love false or true." He cupped her face in his hands and said with emphasis, "But one man loved the pilgrim soul in you, and loved the sorrows of your changing face... There's more, but I'll not say it now...did you like it?"

"I think it's the most beautiful thing I ever heard."

She clasped her hands round her knees. "Quite, quite beautiful."

"That's because it's Irish," he said smugly, tormenting her with a roguish glint in his eye.

"Yes," she said, "but isn't that the golden promise of autumn in an English sky?"

His gaze followed hers and took in the beauty of the sunset. "Yes," he said, "I have to agree with you."

With the unexpected swiftness of autumn, dusk began to fall and, feeling slightly chilly, Joe suggested they went indoors, spending their last evening hugging the fire. The deepening night had brought a distinct dampness to the place.

"I wouldn't like to live here in winter, Joe. It's no wonder those poor Brontes went to an early grave."

"Their father didn't. He lived to be quite old. They inherited their mother's weak lungs, from what I gather."

He rose, placing another log on the fire. "I don't suppose it would be so bad living up here now with all the mod cons. Anyway, they didn't live near here, they lived in a vicarage called Haworth in Keigthly."

Jedda snuggled closer to him. "I've read their life story, it was very sad... most depressing. There were two other sisters, Elizabeth and Maria, who died even younger. No wonder they did nothing but write, isolated like that."

"You're beginning to get depressed, let's talk about something else," he held her closer enchanted by the softness of her body and the smell of her hair, which was beginning to overpower him.

She knew his desires, but in spite of the heady wine and warmth of the fire, her kisses, though passionate, did not lead her into being seduced. Not wishing to excite him further she withdrew from his embrace.

"What shall we talk about?" she said, bringing the conversation back to where he had started it.

He sensed her rejection. "Why me of course. Of what a strong character I am and of how I could never hurt Jedda Markham. He paused for a second. "Would you ever hurt me?"

She examined his face closely, her face serious. "No, not purposely. I've already told you that. But I once was the death of someone. Someone I held in high esteem and much affection. I killed him, as a matter of fact. Unintentionally; but nevertheless, I killed him."

He laughed, "There you go. Teasing Joe – see, I'm a poet after all."

She didn't smile as expected.

"What's wrong?" he said tormenting her as always. "Didn't you like my rhyme?"

His teasing brought a smile to her face. "It was the most beautiful rhyme ever uttered, from the most beautiful voice I ever heard."

"Steady on old chap," he mimicked a high-class English voice. "I think my Irishness must be rubbing off on you, considering all that blarney you've just come out with." He took her face in his hands and turned it towards the firelight. "Come to think of it, with those dark looks you could be Irish."

She shook her head. "I'm Norman. Certainly on my father's side. He traced us back. He was always keen on things like that."

"So that's how you came to conquer me, you wicked girl. Anyway, they were probably Irish Normans," he said, determined to have the last word. "And what's more, at that time in history they were certain to be Catholic and so you may not be as heathen as you think, after all."

Jedda didn't answer, the last thing she wanted on the last evening alone was to talk about religion.

"Anyway, what's all this nonsense about killing someone?"

Jedda related the events that took place at the vicarage. So long ago, but still leaving her guilt-ridden.

Joe drew her to him. "Poor child. But you mustn't grieve. I'm sure that's the last thing the vicar would have wanted. You protected him for the wrong reasons, of course. But you meant well. You loved the man. What more could you do? You were only eleven."

So that was it. That was the torment that drifted across her face from time to time. He stroked her face. Life had treated her pretty badly... even English heathens suffered.

"I wish I'd known earlier, that's all." She frowned like someone truly betrayed. "If only they had mentioned he was going to be hanged. Mother! Mrs Tobias! After all, they didn't keep Gingo's death from me."

"Gingo? Who devil was Gingo?"

She related Gingo's untimely death to him. It was all coming out now, the past. Unravelling itself from the reams of woolly mists of long ago.

Joe was unprepared for it all. He was so amazed by the hurt she had suffered his voice became sharp. "Anything else I should know?"

She stiffened, moving from his embrace mistaking his concern for anger. "Your angry with me. Don't you like me any more? Does my past upset you too much?"

"Upset me! God damn it, no!" He reached out and drew her close. "I'm not angry with you. Only at the circumstances that made you suffer, and the fact that I couldn't have been there to help; or, at least helped you sooner. How could people be so stupid treating a child like that?"

"You still like me then." Concern made her eyes appear even darker.

"LIKE YOU! Nothing in this world could ever stop me doing that. Like you?" He smiled down at her. "I love you, let alone like you. I love you so much that sometimes when I look at you I can hardly breathe." He reached down and pressed his mouth to hers and murmured, "If it ever comes about that some cruel twist of fate takes you from me, I promise... I promise with all my heart I'll never love anyone else... be impossible anyway."

"I did try to get George Webb exonerated, you know. But they wouldn't believe me."

"Who were they?"

"The authorities. But they wouldn't listen. I think they were afraid to believe me because it was such a horrific mistake. They said I was too young at the time to understand the facts. That my mind had only taken in what it wanted to accept."

"Maybe they were right. Perhaps it wasn't as you thought it was at the time. Especially with your extreme imagination."

Joe stroked her hair, trying to comfort her.

Jedda shook her head. "No, I know what I saw. It was an accident, that's all. A sad and terrible accident. I knew the vicar's character – knew it well! He wouldn't hurt a fly. He was good. Very good."

Joe held her close, tried to sooth away bad memories as they sat quietly for a while by the glow of the firelight.

"Isn't it lovely to gaze into a fire with so many pictures to be seen?" she said, dark memories beginning to fade. "I'm beginning to think I would like to stay in this house forever, that something might part us if we leave."

"Us! Never! No, it could not be! Nothing would drag me away from you, my love."

"What about your God?"

He refused to answer her question. "I think it's bedtime for little girls. You go up and I'll attend to the embers, we don't what the place going up in smoke."

"All right then," she said. "I am rather tired. Goodnight..."

"Don't move," he said. "Just stay like that... I'll be back in a minute." A few seconds later he returned carrying a drawing pad and pencil. "I want to draw you just like that. Something to keep with me forever. Something personal, only created by me."

"I didn't know you could draw," she said, tongue in cheek.

"I'm a draft..." He paused, catching the gleam in her eye. "Now that's enough of that, Markham, we'll have no more teasing Joe."

She sat quietly for a while then began to wriggle, and he warned her to be still or he'd draw her like the witch she was.

A few minutes later he finished her portrait and handed to her with a flourish. "There you are La Markham – caught on paper for all time."

It was an excellent portrayal of herself. "Can I have it?" she asked.

He nodded his head solemnly. "No. Never. But I'll draw another one and give you that." And proceeded to do so.

A few minutes later he handed the portrait over and she thanked him saying that she, too, would keep the picture forever.

"I'm going up now," she said. "It's late and I'm tired." She leaned over and kissed him and went up stairs.

Once in her room she undressed and drew back the curtains. A large September moon was revealed shining down in a friendly fashion as she crept slowly into bed. Tired by the day's journey she lay back exhausted and when Joe came up to kiss her goodnight, she was already asleep, her hair flowing in dark veils across the pillow. He kissed her cheek, softly, and pulled the bedclothes over her exposed shoulders before quietly leaving the room.

Dawn rose without a pause, giving birth to little, fat clouds that danced around the heavens, mischievous bundles watched over by an exhausted progenitor in the guise of the sun. Jedda stretched her arms above her head and yawned, having no desire to leave a comfortable bed, so pleased that the world was only just awakening. Her world anyway, now that Joe was entering the room with coffee, toast and grapefruit balanced on a tray.

"Come on lazybones! I know it's early, but rise you must, fair maiden, if we're to catch the early train.

"We've plenty of time," she said, sitting upright and accepting the tray.

"Not at the rate you go once you're in the bathroom...I've cleaned your shoes by the way." It was his bone of contention.

"You're a kind servant, my love. Whatever shall I do without you once we leave here?"

Playfully and without respite, he leaned over and smacked her on the bottom causing the tray to shudder.

"Be careful," she cried. "We don't want Kate's pretty quilt ruined!"

"Behave, then! And less of the servant, Madam!"

It's an old adage, but a true one. Happiness doesn't last forever. It was a fact Jedda had learned early on in life; it was an instinct deep within her that could never be assuaged.

Upon arrival home from Yorkshire, Jedda suffered a traumatic shock, worse than any ever previously meted out to her... her mother was dying.

Jedda could hardly countenance it. Of course they had never been close, but Sally was all she had to call her own. A child in some senses, but still her beloved mother. True, what she had done with her life had been caused by her own foolish disregard for propriety, leaving her daughter fatherless. Susceptible, when a child most needed a role model. A solid base on which to build character. Now she too was deserting her child, and though through no fault of her own, Jedda once more, felt herself betrayed.

Even before she had walked through the front door, Mrs Harper from next door had waylaid her with the message that her mother had suffered an attack of some kind only that morning.

Joe behaved wonderfully. Taking charge. Ordering a taxi. Holding her hand as they had walked hurriedly down corridor after corridor through the hospital until finally, they reached the ward where Sally was waiting out her last hours.

The doctor was already present, leaning over Sally and feeling her pulse. Unaware of Jedda and Joe's presence, he was nodding his head and looking gravely at the nurse in attendance.

Jedda rushed forward. "Mum! Mum!" she cried.

"Are you her daughter," asked the doctor, unnecessarily.

Jedda did not answer him, just stared at her mother, deeply in shock.

Joe intervened, "Yes, her only daughter... her only relative apart from the grandmother... I've no idea where she is though. Jedda?"

"In Cheshire... I'll have to think... my mother, what's wrong with her... will she be all right?"

The doctor's expression did little to console her as he reached out and placed a hand on her shoulder. "I'm so sorry to have to tell you this my dear..." he said, "but it's her heart... has she ever suffered from a fever at any time in the past...scarlet or maybe of the rheumatic kind?"

Jedda said, "My mother told me she had had rheumatic fever as a child."

"Well I'm afraid it's very serious indeed." He looked across at Joe, warning him in advance for Jedda's sake. His next words were, "I'm sorry, young lady, but your mother may not even last until morning."

Jedda's face turned white and Joe stepped forward and took her in his arms, suspecting she was going to fall into a faint. She leaned on him for a few seconds then stood up straight, her face a frozen mask. "I'll be all right," she said. She walked over to where Sally lay, seated herself close by the bed and took her mother's hand in hers. There she remained, unmoving; silently, as if there were only Sally and she in the room.

Joe stayed alongside her all night, only vacating the room from time to time for a cup of tea and a welcome cigarette. The death of a loved one was an awful thing. He knew that. He had suffered it himself when his father had died, and though he had been much younger than Jedda at the time, it was also something they had in common, for she, too, had endured the loss of her father in childhood.

Comfort her? He had tried. She was lost, poor girl, he could see that, but he vowed he'd take care of her in the dark days ahead. Death, he knew, was a merciless adversary, absolutely without compassion.

Sally slipped away at daybreak, leaving Joe to have to almost carry a distraught Jedda from the hospital. Once home, he spent the night with her staunching her tears.

The next day he made all the funeral arrangements, keeping the promise he had made himself.

The funeral was a bleak affair. Fortunately, Joe had managed to contact Zizzie. Jedda remembered her grandmother possessed a phone, so he had informed Zizzie in the kindest way possible of her daughter's sad and untimely death. He said he was sorry he and Jedda were unable to tell her in person, or able to inform her of Sally's illness beforehand, because it all happened so quickly; and anyway, Jedda was in deep shock at present and to travel would not be helpful to her at this time.

Zizzie had thanked him, her voice trembling with shock, while informing him that she would take a taxi in the morning and come and join them. "To try and comfort my poor granddaughter," she said.

Zizzie attended the funeral with misgivings, having been so long out of touch with a daughter whom she had truly loved. A daughter, who for the life of her, she had never been able to make sense of.

She fussed Jedda no end; pleased at last to have contact with a granddaughter she thought she might never see again. The years had been lonely since Sandy had died and, with David and Dora being abroad, even more so. Now she was in her element taking Jedda under her wing; though she suspected her granddaughter was already under the care of somebody else in the guise of an Irishman.

Sally was interned with Alex next to the family plot; one that held Sandy's remains, a place in the quiet Cheshire countryside where Zizzie herself wished to reside. It was a wet autumn day, the rain falling unceasingly. The trees surrounding the churchyard, already the colour of flame, dipped and swayed beneath the endless assault of a boisterous wind.

Zizzie declared later that Sally must be happy where she was because rain at a funeral was proof of the matter.

This was of no comfort to Jedda, who sobbed all through the sermon. Joe, an arm wrapped round her waist, did his best to comfort her, concerned about the trembling of her thin, delicate frame; afraid at some point she might collapse.

Deep down, Jedda wasn't really sure whether Sally would care for prayers being said over her grave; nor the churchyard burial arranged by Zizzie. But Zizzie and Joe had talked her into it, saying Sally would be in heaven whether she wanted to be there or not and her place was with her husband.

Several of Sally's friends and colleagues came in large numbers; also members of the Union she belonged to and which she had worked for with much diligence across the years. Jedda had been unaware of how popular her mother had been with her associates; people whom she had said hello to from time to time, but only in passing.

Kate, Charles, Patsy and Eileen came along to swell the ranks of the mourners, but Toro was nowhere to be seen.

After the funeral was over, those assembled there all went to Zizzie's; the main reason being that Zizzie was paying for it all, including Sally's funeral as a whole. Also, the house was quite large, making adequate room for such a large number of guests.

142

Joe was impressed by the size of Zizzie's property, and after all the mourners had gone and only Zizzie, Jedda and himself remained, he remarked on the fact to Jedda, saying that he never knew La Markham was so well provided for or that she had evolved from the ranks of the middle classes.

Jedda nodded her head sagely. "Grandmother was only a Tiller Girl. She landed lucky when she married Sandy. My own grandfather was quite something himself, though."

"Your own grandfather?"

"Yes. He was an Hussar. He's buried in India."

"Oh, one of the Empire Builders," he sounded vaguely perturbed.

Jedda noticed his change of attitude. "You sound like my mother, she was anti-Empire."

"The more I hear about your mother, the more I like the sound of her. Her friends certainly liked her."

Jedda fell silent, then after a while said, "I think my mother loved anyone in preference to me. I once heard her say children were a hindrance to one's existence. The termination of one's freedom more or less."

"All mothers say that. Mine still does, whenever I go home. Get from under my feet, Joe, she'll say."

Jedda retained a stony silence, unconvinced. She then pointed to her real grandfather's picture on the dresser. He wore a smart uniform and stood soldier-straight, his eyes slanting slightly upwards, like her own, but blue like her mother's. He also possessed a jaw that was a duplicate of Sally's, square and set in the same determined way.

"The other picture is of Sandy, my step-grandfather and the only grandfather I ever knew." She smiled a sad smile. "I loved him dearly."

"I bet you did," said Joe. "I'm sure they were both very nice after their fashion or your grandmother would never have married them."

"That's very sweet of you considering – after all, I don't suppose you're very keen on Empire Builders."

"Well." He squeezed her hand gently. "Well, who can blame an Irishman for that? But one thing's sure, I certainly love the granddaughter of The Regiment."

Jedda laughed for the first time that day. "You do say the wildest things at times, Joe Baker."

Zizzie came in and said, "Sorry to disturb you, but I must do a bit of tidying up in here. There are flower petals everywhere and bits of crumbs from the buffet."

"We'll do that," said Joe gallantly. "You put your feet up. Er... how do I address you?"

"How polite you are. Zizzie will do. If I'd known such a handsome young man was about to visit I'd have worn my best frock and dyed my hair blonde."

An amused Joe got busy with the Hoover and Jedda made Zizzie a cup of tea, insisting that she sat down and did nothing.

Zizzie had asked Jedda to stay overnight, Joe too if he wished. Perhaps Jedda would come and live with her permanently? But Jedda had refused her offer and explained that they had work to consider on Monday, at the same time, feeling guilty for leaving Zizzie alone, especially after Sally's recent death.

Chapter Eleven

The months following Sally's death were not good ones for Jedda. Though Joe was ever supportive, and her final contact with Zizzie did much to ease her predicament, she was conscious that, to have had to endure everything without Joe was something she could not, and would not have contemplated – and the thought bothered her. She hated weakness. Joe suspected this and thought she was too hard on herself.

Zizzie declared she was becoming frail in her old age and her arthritis did not help, but in spite of this, for a seventy-four-year-old, her skin was comparatively unwrinkled and not touch of grey had invaded her hair.

On one of their now frequent visits, Joe had commented on it. "Most unusual," he said. "No wonder you're so beautiful with a grandmother that looks like this."

Zizzie had slapped his hand, given him an old-fashioned look and said, "Stop the blarney." Then added seriously, "I hope you're looking after my granddaughter. With what she's had to put up within her life, she needs to be fussed a little."

"Don't start to go on about mother, Zizzie. You know you loved her in spite of your differences."

"Differences. David and I never forgave her for taking you away, and all those lefty ideas of hers...ridiculous. She must have ruined your education with such nonsense. I hope you've got more common sense, Jedda. That's all."

"Whatever her mother's done or hasn't done, Jedda seems fine to me. She's very clever and certainly quite educated ..loads of character, too. Has she inherited it from you?" said Joe at his flattering best.

"But of course she has. Bound to have. Her mother possessed it also, but in the wrong way."

"I didn't know your daughter very well... Zizzie... but she struck me as being a fine lady, too."

"Would you care for some tea, Joe?" said Zizzie, changing the subject and putting on her best performance for him. "Perhaps some sandwiches and a cake or two? Maybe you'd prefer some salmon? It's only tinned, though."

Jedda asked how she had managed to obtain tinned salmon with the shortages being so severe. Zizzie rose from her seat, beckoned them to follow her and all three traipsed to the kitchen. She opened the pantry door inviting them to look inside.

Jedda was aghast. "How on earth did you arrive at all this lot?" she said, surveying whole cases of tinned salmon, corned beef, hams and different selections of fruit. "What a hoarder you are granny, it's a wonder you haven't been shot!"

Zizzie seemed unconcerned. "I bought them all in nineteen-forty, just in case there were shortages and I was right. Things were certainly in short supply since and still are in spite of all the time that's passed." She gave them both the sweetest of smiles. "I was saving them for a special occasion, but one never arrived until now."

"I think there is enough there for many a special occasion," said Joe, amused and stating the obvious.

They returned to the sitting room conversing as they went.

"May I have a look at your garden?" said Joe, glancing through the French windows as a matter of interest.

"Open the French windows please, Jedda," said Zizzie.

Jedda did as Zizzie bid her. The way clear, they all walked out onto the terrace. Zizzie hovered in the background for several minutes then tactfully withdrew. "I'll go and prepare a nice lunch for you," was her comment.

Joe and Jedda walked together down the steps to the sunken garden below, hand in hand, slowly, with measured steps. The trees had changed from summer green to shades of red, gold, brown and amber. It was quite clement for October and the whole scene was set on fire by the bright leaves of autumn caught in the radiance of the midday sun, except for the silver sheen on the blue cedars.

Many of the summer flowers had disappeared and those that weren't, were gradually fading. Not so the roses, even at this late stage of their existence, sweet scent assailed the air and captivated them both with its delicate perfume.

Joe went to pick one.

"Watch out for thorns," warned Jedda.

"Don't spoil my big moment, not when I'm out to impress my very own lady-love."

"I don't want you hurt on my account."

"Don't be so quick to jump the gun, sweetheart," he said with a Humphrey Bogart snarl. "I wasn't referring to you." He continued giving a wicked lopsided grin, "My lady love is indoors preparing me a special lunch of ten-year-old salmon... goodness knows what other kind of poison she's cooked up."

"Of course, I forgot I'd been jilted for the Queen of the Borgias."

He squeezed her hand, first letting it go before grasping it once more and holding it tightly. "You're lovelier than any queen – certainly more than any princess I've ever seen." He remained silent for a while taking in the scenery. "This place suits you, La Markham, Queen of the Castle. And there was I thinking you

146

poor. And you turn out to be a poor little rich girl instead. I think I'll marry my heiress after all."

"It's as I've said before, I haven't proposed to you yet. Anyway, this is all grandmother's, not mine; also, she has a son."

"In that case, I will have to jilt you for your grandmother."

The lady in question hailed them from the balcony, inviting them to an illegal feast.

Being highly entertained was a distinction Joe liked to play along with. A similarity earmarked by Zizzie to a high degree as she spoke of entertaining tales of past glories; times when once she had tread the boards with remarkable talent and encountered many a strange happening. Even going through the motions of kicking her height even at her age. "I never had a good voice, though," she explained. "That was Viner's prerogative," and both she and Jedda smiled at the memory.

"Why the smiles?" inquired Joe. " Who was Viner?"

"Oh, poor dear Viner. She was a dear friend and died a few years back." She looked at Jedda. "You know, I swear she had a secret passion for Sandy. You won't remember what happened at his funeral, of course."

"Only vaguely, grandma." Jedda smiled at her kindly.

"Threw herself upon my husband's coffin, she did. In an even worse state that me, and I wasn't in a good one," declared Zizzie.

"We have to take our leave now, grandma," said Jedda, trying to bring Zizzie back to the present.

"So soon?" Zizzie looked disappointed. "Stay a little longer. Stay the night?"

Both of them rejected her offer once again and, though they had promised themselves the visit would be a brief affair, the hours had passed all too quickly. Now that it was time to leave they assured Zizzie they would visit her again and soon. When she implored them once more to stay, as she had on many occasions, though expressing their regret, they were adamant about having to leave. They admitted, nevertheless, that though they both hated to exchange the lovely Cheshire suburbs for the dark streets of Salford, work was where the body belonged, even if the heart didn't.

Once they arrived back at Jedda's, Joe expressed his delight at having got to know Zizzie. "What a charmer and such a fraud. All that 'I'm feeling old and arthritic' indeed. I've never seen a young woman kick her height like that, never mind an elderly one."

"She's a complete show off. You should have known she and Sandy when they were younger. All those parties and aunt Viner singing – well screeching – but we were all too polite to complain."

He squeezed her hand. "They sound as though they were good fun and I'm glad we've visited your grandmother. It seems to leave you more relaxed. I don't think I've heard you talk about the past and smile at the same time before."

She put the key in the lock. "I'm very tired though. Do you want a drink or anything before you go. You should have got off the bus at your stop and gone straight home. It wasn't necessary to bring me to the door."

"I worry about you living here alone. Why don't you go and stay at your grandmother's? It's much nicer than this shabby place."

"My mother lived here, remember. Anyway; it's too far from work, as you know." She wagged a finger at him, "And besides, love grandmother as I do, always will and always have, I've quite outgrown Zizzie. Goodnight, Joe."

Almost home, Joe paused on the bridge above the murky old river Irwell, which despite its shortcomings, viewed at this time of night by a full moon and a myriad of bright stars was quite romantic. He wished Jedda were close by, standing by him in the gleam of starlight, to hold his hand and linger awhile. He was dreadfully worried about her, also what the future might have in store for both of them; concerned also about the fact that his brother Rory was paying him a visit from Ireland shortly and wishing to speak with him on a matter of some urgency. Depression hung heavily upon him, and his greatest wish at that moment was that it could be summer again back in Yorkshire. Jedda and he alone again and free from all intervention. Happy. Just loving his girl. Late as it was, he felt an insane desire to return to her, run all the way if necessary. But he knew it to be a foolish ruse and walked swiftly over the bridge and made for home, surprisingly unaffected by Zizzie's toxic feast.

Where Joe was concerned Rory's arrival in England was a complete pleasure, yet underlined with a nagging doubt that all was not well at home. Had Rory unwelcome news concerning his mother? Was his mother ill? Or was it Jedda he wished to discuss? Who'd been telling tales out of school? Or was it merely a social visit? A priest's holiday. No, he didn't think it was. Now Rory sat facing him seated in a high-backed chair on the opposite side of the fire from himself in Eileen's sitting room, a grave expression on his face as he took intermittent sips of tea from a bone china cup. He spoke out in a worried tone of voice. "What's this I hear about this English girl, Joe? And a heathen at that." He put down his cup on a small table close by. "Toro says it's serious. Is it?"

Joe felt his hackles rise. Toro! He might have guessed as much.

"You haven't answered my question, Joe." Rory frowned and straightened a fold in his cassock nervously.

Joe shrugged his shoulders. "Should I? Am I obliged to explain to all and sundry the company I keep?"

"I don't want you to get hurt – the girl either!" Rory was becoming even more aggravated.

"That's good of you," said Joe bitterly. "Her name's Jedda, by the way, and she's from England, not another God damned planet!"

"Don't be blasphemous. No good can come of it."

"No good can come of what? My being blasphemous or being involved with some heathen enemy ...that's your view of her, isn't it? She doesn't have two heads you know!" Joe bounced one fist against the other. "You're judging her before you've even met her!"

"You know full well what I mean Joe. First our parents mixed marriage – then Kate! Are you next on the list?"

"They all loved one another to death, so what are you bothered about?"

"And death is what our father was made to suffer in the end, wasn't he. And mother? What about poor mother? Hasn't she had enough burdens in her life without you adding to them?"

"We live in Dublin now, not Belfast. As for Jedda, once you've seen her you'll adore her. Mother will too!"

"But by all accounts, this girl's an agnostic. It doesn't bode well for any of us."

"Nothing will ever make me give Jedda up; so you're just wasting your time. She's a thousand times better than Ida for all her church going...What's wrong? What's wrong? Why are you looking at me like that?

"Only that you may have a point about Ida. She's in trouble. Deep trouble."

"Yes? Well? Go on?"

"She's going to have a baby."

"Ida is? I don't believe it! Are you sure?"

"I'm sure all right. A woman can't hide her shame for long."

"Whose is it?"

"Need you ask?"

"Not old fancy pants from the town hall?"

"No. Pat Owen's."

"God, who'd have thought he had it him in?"

"He wants to marry her but she won't have him. At least he's trying to play the gentleman."

"The fool... the fool of a woman. What happened?"

Rory ran his finger through his hair. "She got drunk at this party they were attending. Jerry Fagin's cooled on her and I think she did it either to spite him or on the rebound."

"So why doesn't she marry this chap Owens. She certainly won't get Gerry now."

"Say's she doesn't love him. After all that, too. She slept with him soon enough, though."

Joe became even more angry. Jedda would never do a thing like that. Too much pride in herself. She would never set out to trap him. He knew that. "And

149

you're worried about my girl?" He shuffled his feet impatiently. "Why, she's that intelligent! That sincere! That beautiful...you'll just have to meet her, religion or no religion."

Rory smiled in spite of the seriousness of the situation. "I think you've made your point, Joe. When?"

"We're coming here to Kate's for dinner tonight. Jedda will be coming along, and you'll be here, so I gather?" He paused, reflecting on the matter. "And a word of advice, don't go preaching to Kate. She's made her decision in life and you couldn't find a better man than Charles for your sister to have married. So think on."

"I'll be on my best behaviour," said Rory.

"Well, what are we going to do about that my feckless sister of mine?" Joe fiddled with his tie nervously, afraid of what Rory was about to ask of him. What form would his petition take? He bit his lip waiting for the news like a condemned man would from a messenger of doom. The answer came as expected, turbulent, leaving him cold, unable to cope with its magnitude.

"I was hoping you'd go home and sort the situation out. I hate to impose... I know you have a life here now. Good employment; and you're obviously in love with this young girl, Jedda." Rory looked crestfallen.

Joe smiled. A bitter, helpless smile. "Madly in love...So it's all down to poor old Joe. I'm damn sick of it. I've spent most of my youth and even my childhood trying to cope with our family situation and now, just when I'm at my happiest, that stupid bitch has to spoil everything."

Rory looked sympathetic. "There's little I can do once the church gives its orders. I've been posted here like a soldier of God and there's little I can do about it...and though I know you're upset, she is after all, still our sister."

"That's my bad luck. And am I under orders, too? What will Jedda have to say about my leaving her, and for the sake of my sister at that? Sounds odd! Bloody odd!"

"I suppose it does, but surely she'll understand. It isn't forever, is it?" Rory twiddled his thumbs. "I can't wait to meet Jedda this evening."

Joe didn't answer. The hours were ticking away and his world had been plunged into darkness. He reached over for the teapot, his hand trembling – wishing at that moment he could throw it at Ida – and poured Rory and himself another cup of strong tea.

Joe and Rory met up on the corner and made their way to Kate's house. The trees along the avenue were almost bare and the leaves of late autumn played about their feet, blown by a high wind, and there was a distinct chill in the air.

Once invited into the house and embraced by a smiling Kate, they both made for the fire and were soon indulging in buttered crumpets accompanied by hot coffee spiced with rum, courtesy of their hostess.

"That was good, Kate," said Rory with a sense of satisfaction, at the same time searching for the presence of an absent Jedda.

"If you're watching out for Jedda she's often late. I don't think she takes notice of time," said Joe fondly.

Kate laughed. "That'll be the day. It's a good job you love her." She turned to Charles, "Would you like some more coffee, darling?"

"No, thanks. I have to hurry, I've a meeting at seven and it's twenty-to-seven now. Anyway, any more of your coffee and I'll end up drunk."

Kate gave him a peck on the cheek. "Poor Charles, always in demand."

"I need to work hard to keep my wife in frivolities," said Charles, for the express attention of Rory, his attitude signifying "see how well I treat your sister, even if I am agnostic."

Rory accepted the hint and answered, "I'm sure you do."

Kate sniffed, good humour coming to the surface. "Frivolities indeed." Someone rang the doorbell. "I think Jedda's here."

Charles passed Jedda on the doorstep and promptly kissed her on the cheek. "Don't give way under holy Rory's interrogation," he whispered. "See you later, if I'm back in time. Maybe give you a lift home. Bye." He was proud of the fact he now owned a car.

Rory looked up as Jedda entered the sitting room and wished, quite unwillingly, he wasn't a priest, also understanding why Joe loved her. What a beautiful creature she was. He rose from his chair to greet her, enchanted in spite of his reservations about her being an agnostic.

Joe introduced them. "Rory, this is Jedda. Jedda, my brother Rory."

Both agreed they were pleased to meet the other, each feeling ill at ease. Jedda wished she was elsewhere and that the priest would not stare at her so intently – not in the awful way Toro did – but as if she were some lost soul in desperate need of help.

Rory expressed his sympathy over the loss of Sally. "I'm so sorry you have recently lost your mother. Joe told me all about it...How are you feeling now?" Or isn't that the correct question to ask?"

So they'd been discussing her? Meaning well, she supposed, but finding it impossible to answer she merely mumbled her reply, "I'm all right, thank you."

Joe saw she was not at ease and went and sat beside her and attempted to take her hand.

She refused to let him, embarrassed in front of a priest.

Joe, amused, and suspecting how she felt, deliberately seized her right hand and held it fast. "He's only my brother, not the Pope. He won't send us to purgatory for holding hands."

Rory laughed and the ice was finally broken. "I'm certain you won't go there

Jedda, but I'm not so sure about my brother – the things he got up to in his time."

Jedda, relaxed though she was by the warmth of Rory's smile, remained protective towards Joe. "I can't see Joe doing anything really bad, not ever."

Rory smiled with added warmth. "I'm sure you're right, Jedda. I'm sure you're right."

"Aren't Eileen and Patsy coming tonight, Kate?" said Jedda.

"No. I think they've gone to the pictures. To see *Jane Eyre*, I think."

"Oh, I'd love to see that," said Jedda.

"We'll go tomorrow," said Joe.

"Not if your brother wishes to see you though," said Jedda, thoughtful as ever.

"What a considerate child," thought Rory, for child was all she seemed.

"That's very sweet of you, Jedda, but just call me Rory, if you wish," he said, conscious of her not being sure of how to address him.

She beamed back at him, dimples going in and out, teeth flashing. "Rory it shall be," she said.

Rory continued to be enchanted by her and Joe was well aware of it. Jedda victorious! His Jedda!

They dined at eight. Just the four of them, lingering at the table, deep in conversation. It was the lull before the storm and only Jedda was ignorant of its complications. Rory did not want to spoil the evening by mentioning any family troubles and Joe and Kate remained silent, determined to enjoy what might be "the last supper", so to speak.

Charles arrived home, late but considerate, wishing to drive Joe and Jedda home. They refused, saying if they hurried they would catch the last bus.

Once they had departed Kate showed Rory to his room and, before he removed his surplus he knelt down and prayed deeply for his family and Joe in particular. Joe would never willingly give up Jedda, he sensed as much, and he was glad when his head sank into the pillows and lulled him into sleep. It had been a long day.

The last bus, due in at the depot, had only a short run left to do, and it dropped Joe and Jedda off close to the local cinema before they reached their destination. To their surprise, they bumped into Eileen and Patsy.

"We've been to see *Jane Eyre*." (He pronounced the surname Airee.) "Quite good it was, too. Joan Fountain and H G Wells."

"Orson Wells and Joan Fontaine, silly. Stop fooling about Patsy and grow up." Eileen pushed his shoulder with her fist.

Feeling more light-hearted, Joe felt better than he had all evening. Patsy always had this affect on him. It was the same with Jedda.

"Jedda and I are going to watch it tomorrow... Rory's come over, by the way. Going to be a parish priest in Salford."

"That's good, I like Rory," said Patsy. "But I'm not going to confession, not with him around. He'd do anything to get the church roof fixed. Might even sell my story to The News of the World."

Their frames shook with laughter whilst Eileen implored Patsy to be more respectful, catching her breath between giggles.

"It's only gone eleven. Come home with us and have drink and a chat...the night's young," said Patsy.

They waltzed down the street together in rhythm to Patsy's rendering of Danny Boy which wasn't anything like as good as Toro's version. Eileen constantly chided him.

Jedda, happy because the evening had gone better than expected, and Rory was more or less won over, wanted to dance! Even do cartwheels down the street she felt so exhilarated. If there had been trees she felt she would have climbed them.

Observing her lively face, Joe felt the glow of her sweep over him; yet remained conscious that he was man on a tightrope, a very dangerous tightrope – one without a net.

They called for chips on the way to Patsy's and ate them out of the paper as they strolled along, giggling, happy, with the carefree abandonment of youth.

Once they had turned the key in Patsy's door, Joe and Patsy settled down in easy chairs, while Eileen and Jedda busied themselves making a cup of tea for them all. Darling Patsy, thought Jedda, as he acted the fool and placed four cigarettes in his mouth and lit them all intending to hand them round. The first three were easily removed, but the last one stuck to his lip, and as he pulled it away, the tender skin attached there came with it and he cursed out loud.

Eileen bent over laughing. "Serve you right, Paul Henreid."

Patsy left his chair and dragged Eileen over to the window forcing her to gaze out. "Why should a we a reach a for the moon my darlink, we have a the staras."

"There isn't any moon and if there were we couldn't see it from this backyard view... you sounded more like an Italian than Frenchman, anyway."

"Would you like to be my mistress Jedda," Patsy spoke, out of the blue."

"Not this week; I'm rather busy at present." Jedda rallied to the moment. "He's always pulling my leg, Kate."

"I'm not touching your leg... did you hear that Eileen? She's accusing me of molesting her. The Vixen! The baggage! Unhand me from yon damsel, she's trying to break up our marriage."

Eileen grimaced. "I don't know. Whatever shall I do with you? I think I'll have you incarcerated somewhere... preferably the Bastille. You'd have to perfect your French accent though... by the way, were there any mad people in your village, Patsy?"

"I didn't live in a village. I lived in a town; you know that. And it was a large town and to my knowledge only four people ever went mad."

"Who were the other three?" said Eileen, quick of the mark.

"Oh, dear, you left yourself wide open to sarcasm there Patsy boy," said Joe, joining in the laughter.

The night passed quickly amidst much merriment, making them unaware time was passing, and when next Joe consulted his watch it showed two-thirty. "I think I'd better take Jedda home," he said. "We do have work tomorrow."

They all parted, swearing constant love each for the other, amidst showers of kisses with the eternal optimism of youth and endless happiness.

"Well; what did you think of my Jedda?" It was Saturday and Joe had arrived at Kate's for lunch. The meal over, Joe was sat facing Rory across the room, each of them seated in an easy chair drawn up to the fire in the lounge. "Did she pass muster?"

"Sweet as a nut. She has charm and she's very self-possessed; extremely self possessed, considering her youth. She's also very intelligent, and there are only two things to be said against her – for one she isn't Irish – and the other, and I must stress this most importantly – she isn't Catholic."

"Jedda's no bigot. She doesn't even focus on religion." Joe bit his lip unmercifully.

Rory shook his head. "Precisely! That's my whole point. Can you imagine taking her home for instance? What would our mother's reaction be? Maybe she'd be lenient. I'm sure she'd like Jedda, who wouldn't – apart from Ida, that is."

"Maybe Jedda would turn Catholic..."

"No, she wouldn't." Rory was adamant. "You know that, too! Deep in your heart, you know she would never, never take to our religion – any religion. And you could never give up yours." He paused in reflection. "The Catholic religion is like riding a bike. You can put it in a shed and leave it for many years; but having been learnt the mechanics of it, there it remains, always in your head."

Joe smiled. "What the bike? Be a bit uncomfortable. Anyway, Kate's managed up to now."

"I pray for her all the time in pretty much the way the church prays for all the lost Protestant souls. God knows it isn't their fault they've been led astray." He paused and poured another cup of tea from the pot recently furnished by Kate and placed on a small table at the side of his chair. He continued in a serious manner. "Jedda, and we must come to terms with the fact, is an agnostic. She no more believes in God than say, we believe natives in certain parts of the world do when they worship idols, or the moon or the sun. God or mammon! It's all the same to her." Rory gave Joe a wise look. " I know she's only eighteen; and though that seems young, it's too old to learn new tricks."

154

"If you think her beliefs are that entrenched, then let the matter be. But I love her and if she doesn't pass scrutiny, so be it. Did you pray for our father by the way, with him being a Protestant?"

Rory looked angry. "No need to be facetious, Joe. If it's scrutiny you're talking about, she's certainly different. She had an indefinable something about her. Can't put a finger on it really, but to me she comes over as a child with a wise old lady's expression in her eyes."

"So you noticed it too; I've seen it many times." Joe smiled, thinking about her.

"Yes, most distinctly. Wonder what put it there?"

Joe looked up taken aback by Rory's assessment of her.

"I don't know," said Joe. "It's something I can't get to grips with and I think I know her pretty well as far as she'll let me know her... something in her childhood, I think."

"Do you believe she's the kind of person who's so enigmatic one will never know what she's thinking?" queried Rory.

"I know she's definitely elusive, but I love her. I love her more than anything else in this world and I'll never give her up... she'd have to leave me."

"I know you love her Joe, I can see that, but tread carefully. Eighteen is very, very young; and what's more, I think something incredibly awful must have happened to her at some time. Something that stole her childhood."

"Why do you assume that?"

"I don't assume it; I know it. After all, I am a priest. The things I've heard in the confessional are beyond belief and it's taught me an awful lot about human nature."

The word "confessional" made Joe think of Patsy and he found it difficult to suppress a smile.

"Why are you smiling," said Rory.

Joe explained Patsy's refusal to attend any confessional Rory took part in.

They both had a good chuckle and when Kate entered and inquired if they were ready for more coffee the atmosphere was considerable lighter.

Kate left the room wondering what was in the air, making ready to prepare Charles's supper.

Joe visited Patsy's house next day and found it to be a warm oasis. Eileen and Patsy were sympathetic, but cautious about Rory's attitude towards Jedda. Anyway she was due to join them any minute, so discussion about the current situation was vital before she arrived.

"I love Jedda, said Eileen, "but I do suppose things are difficult for you... especially you. She's nothing to lose. Nothing to give up. No one pressurising her... I suppose one could describe her as a free agent, really."

"A free soul more like it," said Patsy, " I love her too, but she isn't one of us.

155

Remember also, she's very English from a way, way back; though I suppose even the Church of England could hold up their hands to heaven as far as she's concerned without much success of wooing her... In other words she's a complete pagan."

"Not a pagan, silly. An agnostic. She believes in nothing; even pagans worship something," said Eileen.

Toro had remained silent through their conversation, lounging in a chair at the far side of the room, but Joe knew his mind was like an antenna, reaching out and drawing things in. He also wished he weren't present.

"Nothing can keep me from Jedda." Joe was adamant. "Nothing! Nothing at all!" He looked towards Toro, defiance in his eyes. "Not even people who discuss me with my brother behind my back."

The company retained an embarrassed silence.

Toro ignored Joe's barbed remarks and Joe became more enraged.

"Yes, I mean you Toro! Mind your own damn business in future!"

"I understand your point about Jedda, Joe," said Patsy. "If I hadn't met Eileen first, I'd have chased her myself; but I've been lucky and married one of my own faith."

"Oh yes," said Eileen." So that's why you're always mooning over her. I'll never leave you two alone again."

"Chance would be a fine thing... she wouldn't entertain me. She loves that wild bugger over there, God help her, heathen that she is."

Jedda arrived late as usual, sweeping in full of youthful enthusiasm, unaware of the debate being conducted on her behalf.

Charmed by her smile, Patsy relieved her of her coat and conducted her to a fireside chair, plying her with coffee, feeling guilty as hell about what was to befall her; wanting to smack Toro in the teeth for sitting silently sneering. Angry with Joe for having taken things too far with Jedda. He should have tried to nip their affair in the bud before it went too far... to his knowledge no woman had ever reigned so long Joe's affections, now it was too late. Something had happened that was escalating out of control. Something from which there was no turning back from the disaster threatening to embroil them all.

Later, when Jedda and he were alone and walking home, Joe explained the situation in detail and said he had to leave for a few weeks. That he would be staying with his mother in Ireland and had to sort out some family affairs.

If she were in the slightest degree upset by his proposal she did not show it, merely nodded her assent and added, "These things happen from time to time."

Joe thought her a clever old sage.

"But first, I'm treating you to the opera. *Madame Butterfly* is on at the Opera House. James Johnstone and Joyce Gartside are in it, so it's bound to be good."

"Oh, I love James Johnstone."

Joe laughed wickedly. " Maybe it's because he's Irish."

Jedda looked back at him in disbelief. "Is he really?"

They held hands through *Butterfly*. Jedda, sometimes intensely, stirred by the emotion of Butterfly's faithful sufferings and a fate imposed upon her by a fickle man like Pinkerton and the sad, inevitable death of one so young.

They had supper at the usual cafe they frequented, sometimes alone, sometimes with Patsy, Eileen, Kate and Charles; also Toro if he happened to tag along. Jedda was glad they were alone and especially that Toro wasn't there.

They sipped coffee and smoked cigarettes. For once Jedda wasn't particularly hungry, a fact that worried Joe. He reached for her hand. "You're not ill or anything are you, Jedda?" He knew that she had suffered these last months since Sally's death.

"No. *Butterfly* was sad, wasn't it."

"I hope it didn't upset you unduly."

"Most operas are sad."

"Perhaps I should have taken you to see a comedy. Cheered you up."

She smiled at last. "Don't be silly. I loved it and thank you for taking me. Though it did remind me of my grandfather."

"Why? Did he used to dress up as a Geisha Girl?"

She smacked his hand with a spoon and immediately thought her action reminiscent of Zizzie and wanted to cry.

"No, you wicked Irishman. My grandfather used to shake the cherry blossoms on my head when I ran around the trees." She looked into the distance as she spoke. "He said it was like the flower scene from *Butterfly*. He was the first person to introduce me to opera. He loved opera."

"I hope your memories are happy ones."

"She smiled sadly. "They are. But Butterfly's weren't, were they?"

"She seemed to think so. She waited for him long enough."

Jedda looked stern. "I wouldn't have. And fancy her giving up all her friends and her religion like that."

"You haven't got a religion."

"I know. But if I had, I wouldn't give it up."

Joe was worried. What was she trying to tell him? Was she about to set him free? He shuddered and took a sip at his coffee to steady his nerves.

"If their love had been really strong it would have survived. I hope ours does." He felt cold again, as though someone was walking over his grave.

"Me too," she said. "But marrying outside ones culture or religion is not a good idea. Supposing he had decided to take her to America before the onset of the war." She frowned. "Especially when the Japanese are so evil – Pearl Harbour and all those atrocities they committed against the Chinese and the British and American Prisoners of War."

"You dropped the atom bomb, don't forget."

She shrugged her shoulder. "Not personally; anyway they asked for it. They started it."

"We Irish didn't ask for anything."

"We never dropped bombs on you."

"No, you just slowly starved us to death."

"Starved you to death. I don't believe you. We're English, we don't do things like that."

"Oh, yes you do. Not only Germans and Japanese commit atrocities." He grinned, aggravating her. "I bet your grandfather knocked a few Indians about when he was over there."

"My grandfather wouldn't do that. He was a gentleman."

"You never knew him"

"My grandmother said he was. She loved him and wouldn't have if he'd been cruel."

"I don't know about that. Eva Braun loved Adolf Hitler and Stalin's wife must love him."

"Stalin looks a lovely person to me. Like a kind uncle of sorts."

There was an innocent cruelty about her that was beyond comprehension. "Carry on with your beliefs. Who am I to spoil your fantasies?" He smiled, forgiving her and had the terrible feeling he'd forgive her anything he was so far under her spell. Concerning Butterfly's love for Pinkerton, he supposed in a way she was right. To love someone of a different race or culture was not always a good idea.

"Anyway, why are the English depicted as cruel? In the second and third centuries the Irish used to kidnap the Britons, take them to Dublin and sell them as slaves."

"I don't believe that," said Joe.

"Well they did. Saint Cuthbert only just managed to escape. And look what you did to the Jews in Limerick! Chased them out in fear of their lives – talk about Hitler."

"Nonsense. I've never heard such nonsense."

"That's because you're ill informed about your own shortcomings. The Romans used to feed us to the lions, but I don't go to Italy complaining about it. They'd think me nuts and say that was centuries ago. And they'd be right. Cromwell had nothing to do with me."

"My Jedda knows more than I imagined."

"Everyone was badly treated in the old days. Think of all the English who were sent to Botany Bay straight from being in prison. They weren't criminals, just broke, and if they did steal, it would have been only a loaf of bread." She sipped her coffee thoughtfully. "People of our time shouldn't be made to suffer for the misdeeds of the past. We're all of mixed blood, anyway. I think my great grand-mother was Irish on my grandmother's side."

They left the café and walked companionably through the city, in close proxim-ity He squeezed her hand, called her a wise old sage and that she probably got it from an ancestor way back. "Your Irish one," he teased. Sometimes, in the shad-ows of a dark corner they would pause and kiss, passionately, each filled with the desire not to let the other go before continuing on their way.

"Anyway, at least I can take in some good scenery while I'm in Ireland. I'd like you to see it. You'd love it," said Joe, still overcome by her kisses.

"I'm not a country girl. Not even a suburban girl any more." She smiled up at him. "I love the night-haunted city."

"Haunted?" he laughed and went, Oooh! Oooh! There goes my writer." He rolled his eyes. "Who's about? Count Drac? A whole nest of Ghouls?"

"I don't mean it in that sense," she chided him. "I mean haunted by the past. By the memory of the people who once lived, loved, worked and mostly died here." She waved her hand towards the area in general. "Look at the old build-ings. The cobbles in the roads. The old lamps... Look!!! A Roman Soldier just passed and you missed him!"

He became cynical. "Never mind the Romans; Irish labourers probably took a hand in those buildings... and definitely the roads." He frowned. "The Romans may have started to civilise you, but we did the rest."

Jedda became angry. "There you go again. Who's living in the past now? Why do you always spoil things, the moment when I'm feeling poetic about my city."

"Oh, pardon me ma'am. Don't let a bunch of poor Irish labourers interfere with your strange imaginings."

"You sound just like my grandfather chiding my grandmother."

"I like the sound of him," Joe grinned. "No wonder you're crazy with your kind of upbringing."

"I was well brought up," she protested.

They were near a dark alleyway and he drew her close to him. "No, you weren't," he said gravely. "Your life was a tragedy."

"A tragedy?"

"Yes, and then you met me."

She started to protest again and he grabbed her face between his hands, roughly. "Shut up and kiss Joe."

His mouth left hers and he stroked her face, "It will be an even bigger tragedy if we let things get us down." He looked pained. "We mustn't let anything come between us; certainly not national differences."

"Not even God?" she said hopefully.

"I don't know about Him," he said.

When they finally arrived at her house they had stood on her doorstep and he had held her and kissed her a final goodnight; their differences forgotten as a tide of emotion swept over them at the immediate loss of each other. Joe cursed Ida, his mind in turmoil at all she was costing him.

The train was not long due. Joe stood on the platform at Liverpool Street station holding Jedda close to him. He wished with all his heart he could take her with him, but caution had persuaded him otherwise.

A visit to Ireland on her part while he had problems to sort out at home would not be practical; anyway, Ida and she would never relate to each another. He knew it to be a fact, so the idea had died as quickly as it blossomed. Ida and his Jedda? The thought was incomprehensible; they would soon be daggers drawn; especially where Ida was concerned, as bigoted as they come. She hadn't spoken to Kate in years. No, he would be dragging Jedda into the lion's cage bringing her to Ireland; that was for sure. His mother? Well, she was different. She'd come round where Jedda was concerned – Rory had.

Anyway, Jedda had her own career to consider. He was sure the firm would never sanction her having time off from work, too. Canada Brights had allowed him only a month's leave to sort out his affairs, emphasising in most stringent fashion that two of these weeks must be sacrificed as part of his holidays.

The sound of an approaching train was being ignored by both of them. He could not bear to leave her. He felt like giving in there and then, grabbing her hand and leaving the station. To hell with Ida! Let her do her own dirty work – fix up her own mess! He suddenly pictured his mother's face, hauntingly clear and he knew in spite of his reluctance to leave Jedda, he was duty bound to return home.

He drew Jedda close to him, weeping inwardly as he did so. "Remember whatever happens in our lives, no matter what! I'll always love you. You only, no one else. Never!" He put his arms around her tightly, hurting her in his desperate need to assure her. "I'll be back. Don't leave me Jedda! Don't forget me... I love you so very, very much."

An icy chill of fear assailed her. What was he saying? Why did he seem so fearful? His mood rubbed off on her so that she too became anxious.

"Why would I?" she said. "Don't you trust me?"

"Of course I trust you. I just don't trust fate... I've been uncomfortable with the whole situation from the beginning, but what can I do, Jedda? My religion! Everything! There's so much that's not been discussed... I wish we'd spoken about our differences more, now it's too late."

"We can't do anything! Anything at all! But the problem only lies with you; I don't have one. I know you love your God but I can't relate to religion in any form, you know that... have known it all along. I've never tried to hide it from you, Joe."

160

The train drew up with a shushing sound and the opening and banging of carriage doors. Too quickly for Joe's liking... too soon for Jedda's as she clung to him desperately. They needed all the time in the world and there seemed only seconds left.

Passengers started to board the train.

"Oh, God! So soon!" Joe held her for one last tender moment. He felt like a soldier going to war. Going into battle – maybe never to return! They were forced to pull apart as the whistle blew and "all aboard" was heard from a voice, which to them, seemed like the voice of doom.

As the train slowly departed one pair of lips left the other; yet, as the train gathered speed, he still continued to lean out of the window, holding her hand until that last vital second when the movement of the train made it impossible to retain even one beloved finger; then, he was obliged to relinquish even that last little cherished bit of her.

She remained on the platform unmoving, hands clasped to her breasts, waiting; then he laughed, a grin as large as half a moon on his face and cried jokingly, "Bye, Bye Butterfly."

The train began to draw away, faster, and she continued to wait until it became a mere dot in the distance. Sadly, slowly leaving the station she sauntered off into the city, moving along swiftly, the evening air heavy with mist of October's final day.

Three days after she had seen Joe off at the station Rory paid Jedda a surprise visit, and though he was unexpected, she was more than pleased to see him – a delight that quickly changed to irritation when he explained the seriousness of his mission.

Rory was decidedly uncomfortable with the task he was about to perform, especially when it involved one so young and vulnerable. Also, knowing the words he was about to impart would hurt her terribly; nevertheless, he felt obliged to say them.

"Jedda, I'm more than delighted to see you, too," he said, when faced with her tender greeting. "But there are things I must discuss with you before Joe returns, and I think it my duty for both your sakes, to say them now."

"Have a seat," said Jedda, gracious as ever. "Would you like some tea? I've no coffee, I'm afraid."

"No thanks, I'm not staying long. I have church matters to attend to." God, how could he wound her and accept her offer of tea at the same time?

She smiled her slow, beautiful smile and as if reading his mind stated, "It sounds ominous."

How quick she was, this beautiful English girl. How lucky Joe was and how terrible he felt that he had to cajole her into to giving him up; yet persuade her he must.

"I've come to ask something of you. Something that you will perhaps hate me for. You may even show me the door, because of it."

"You want me to give Joe up, is that it?"

Rory was taken off guard. So much so, he was relieved he was not holding that cup of tea she had so much wanted to offer him.

"I think you've guessed the measure of it, Jedda. You must have all along. You must hate me for it."

"That's true. Ever since I was first introduced to you I've known it... but I don't hate you, Rory. I could never do that. I know you think you are doing what's right for Joe, myself also, even if you do think of me as some unholy vessel."

"I don't think of you as an unholy vessel! Just a naive, unthinking meteorite innocently descending upon my church. And I must protect my church at all costs. It's what makes me a priest."

"Even at the cost of breaking our hearts? Both Joe's and mine?"

"Even that."

"Toro's tried it too, but it hasn't worked. It's only drawn Joe and I closer together."

"I am aware Toro's one of my flock, but though I am a man of God, I don't necessarily like him. But then again, it's not my place to judge."

"Yet you judge me?"

"No I don't, and what's more, I like you a thousand times more than I do Toro. All I want to do is put the facts plainly and truly before you. I know Joe will never listen to me, so in the end, I suppose it's up to you to persuade him otherwise."

Her lips tightened. Rory sounded like Alfredo's father pleading with the lady of the Camellias. "I know that. I know you think I'll be unhappy in the end; that we both will. But if we're strong enough, I think we'll survive."

"My parents thought that, and look how that turned out."

"This is England; not Ireland. Such bigotry does not apply here. Even Toro's hatred of me will not put me off."

"Anyway I must be going, Jedda. I'd love to stay; and I mean that. But I have church business to attend to." He took her hands in his. "Just try to think things through; that's all I ask. I'll not force the issue on either of you, but I really don't want Joe to desert the church." He paused and looked at her quizzically. "By the way, as for Toro hating you, hatred is often akin to love, so take care on that score." He stroked her hands gently before releasing them, like a father comforting a child. "Wise as you think you are, you may be way out in your estimation of Toro. Take care where he's concerned."

"No, I think I'm right about him. More than right! He just can't stand me." She rose from her chair. "I'll see you to the door."

"Thank you Jedda; kind as always. I hope to see you from time to time." He stroked his chin thoughtfully. "This discussion doesn't alter our friendship you know. After all, I still love Kate in spite of her rejecting our religion."

"I know you do," she pecked his cheek. "Goodnight, and take care."

"You too, Jedda. Goodnight." He paused at the door. "Do be careful living here on your own. One never knows if there are villains about... why don't you go and live with your grandmother?"

"I love my grandmother, most dearly. But I also like my independence; anyway it's too far away from my job, and although I did spend the happiest time of my life with her when young... well, too much water has flowed beneath the bridge since then."

"I understand. One can only go forward. Something I suppose we all learn as old age takes its toll." He smiled mocking her as he tickled her under the chin. "Goodnight old lady; sweet dreams." He stepped out of the door soon to be swallowed up by the night.

The office was ablaze with gossip, especially the drawing office, as they discussed Joe's disappearance. Joe had flown like a bird, unwanted, at least by the males in the office, and now many were eager to take over where he left off – certainly where Jedda Markham was concerned.

Johnny Tobin in sales. Tony Drew a draughtsman, just like Joe, and even Kurt Vane, a good looking accountant, who, though not employed by Canada Brights, called in on a regular basis to check the books and sort out the tax.

He had stopped by Jedda's desk one morning and asked her to marry him, which at first made her laugh, only making her cease when noticing the hurt on his face. "Can I at least take you to the firm's anniversary dance that's coming up," he had implored of her.

"I'll definitely have a dance with you," she had promised, trying to make up for her cavalier treatment of him.

Seated at her desk, absentmindedly chewing a pen, thoughts half on Joe, the other half occupied by the occasion of the firm's fiftieth anniversary dinner dance, she was wondering what to wear. She had no clothing coupons to spare, certainly not for any kind of ball gown or even a long dress. And Joe? Would he be back in time? She knew she would not enjoy it if he weren't there to attend. Still, there were three weeks in which to consider things, so not to worry.

Mr Kilburn brought an invoice across to her. "Do be careful, Jedda dear. You've forgot to enter this in the daybook. It's not like you to be lax. Dreaming of your boyfriend?" He patted her shoulder in a fatherly fashion. "Don't worry, he'll be back. I know I would if you were mine... I'd soon come running."

She smiled at him sweetly, thanked him, and apologised for her error.

She knew she must pull herself together and wished Joe would hurry up and write to her. True, he had answered her first letter, but not her second. She had written to him a third time with her name and address placed clearly on the back of the letter, yet still received no reply.

She had also asked Kate if she had acquired any information concerning him but she too remained in the dark about her brother's affairs. Perhaps from Rory? Perhaps from Patsy? But no, they had all drawn a blank. Joe had written to none of them. There was one good piece of news though – Toro was going back to Ireland that coming week and was taking up a very good position there. It would be a relief not to bump into him around the place.

Upon arriving home that evening she decided that after dinner – such food as there was in the larder, of which there was little these day – to retire early. Heating was another problem too. She placed some newspaper and a few sticks of wood into the small grate and tried to bring life to the dull coal bricks by balancing a shovel against the bars and covering it with a large sheet of newspaper. The results were tragic. The heat coming forth was so inadequate; one could have sat on what served as a fire without even receiving a blister for one's pains. With coal shortages and one thing and another, even with these poor offerings she was obliged to queue at the coal-yard. No deliveries? No sir!

Once she had eaten she decided she would phone Zizzie with the view to asking for her help with an evening dress. She rooted through the proverbial cupboards, because that was just what they were – bare! She wished Joe were here to take her out to dinner – even Vienna Steak would have done – but this not being possible, she made do with powdered soup and what was left of a loaf of grey bread.

Later, she put on her thin coat and walked at high speed through the early November mist to the telephone box and phoned Zizzie. When she explained about a dress for the dinner dance Zizzie laughed and said, "Come over Cinderella, I'll see you fitted out fine for the ball. Come now! Come to dinner. Stay the night. It's Saturday tomorrow."

"I work on Saturdays Zizzie," she said. " So I just can't suit myself."

"You can if you're ill, and you soon will be the way you keep shaping. Living all alone like that and no food. Get a taxi. I'll pay for it on arrival. I want to take care of you and fatten you up."

"Oh, all right, if you'll allow me to get a word in… you're a chatterbox, do you know that?"

"Don't be cheeky; and hurry along."

Upon arrival at Zizzie's, Jedda was welcomed with open arms – literally. Her grandmother led her to the warmth of an open log fire, sweet smelling and the odour of which was combined with the delicious smell of real food cooking.

"Where did you get that chicken? And the logs, grandma?"

Zizzie gave a mischievous smile and tapped the end of her nose with her forefinger. "I have my special source of supply."

"You're incorrigible! Where do you think supposed Christians like yourself will end up? Are you are completely without conscience?"

"Never mind that kind of talk." Zizzie wagged a finger at her. "I haven't noticed you refusing to eat it?"

"It doesn't matter where I'm concerned; I'm a heathen like mother, remember?"

"Ah, your poor misguided mother...never mind, lets not go into all that. Regrets don't help." She lifted a tureen of vegetables. "Have some more of these, they'll keep your skin lovely. Nice and clear. Though I don't suppose it could be more perfect; that of course is because you have me as a grandmother."

"Don't be so vain; still I'm glad you're my grandmother, if it's only for your cooking...May I have another of those delicious roast potatoes?" She was feeing cosseted and it came to mind once more of how wonderful life had been in those far-of days when, as a child, she had lived here. Days when the table had groaned with food and the world had been a safer place and fate had treated her more kindly.

"My granddaughter has lovely manners, praising me for my cooking; maybe one day, when rationing ends, you'll make a good cook, too?"

"No, I won't. That's one thing I'm certain of."

"You'll have to marry a rich man then – hire a cook. How's Joe by the way?"

"Don't know. I haven't heard from him, apart from the once. My last two letters have met with silence."

"How odd. There must be a specific reason. I could tell at a glance how much he adored you."

"Maybe he's met someone else?"

"Oh, you of little faith. It must be something more than that. Something very, very serious to keep him away from you."

"There's trouble at home. That's why he left so quickly. But I think perhaps a letter; or even a phone call to the office wouldn't go amiss."

"Never mind, have some fruit and cream and I've got a bar of chocolate stocked away; you can have it later to go with your coffee."

"I haven't grazed my knee grandma; only my pride."

Zizzie gave her a squeeze. "I know; I don't think I'll ever allow you to grow up... she gave a twirl round the room. "Come on little girl, dressing up time for granny."

Once in the vicinity of Zizzie's bedroom, the bed became ablaze with a mix of bright colours as Zizzie draped dresses and gowns across the counterpane hiding its pretty pattern. All her fine wears ready for Jedda's inspection.

"I'm spoilt for choice Jedda, as I know you must be, but I'm sure they'll fit. I was just your size when I was your age."

She swept a gown up in her arms and held it up. "This I never wore. Do you like the shade? Gold will suit you with your colouring. Do you like the cut of it? The way it falls away at the top?" She held it against herself for Jedda's inspection. "It would make a lovely frame for your pretty shoulders."

"Why have you never worn it?"

"Couldn't bring myself to. I bought it for your grandfather's and mine sixth wedding anniversary to wear at the Regimental ball; then the news came that your poor grandfather had been killed. His poor neck broken. He was always so wild! So brave! But also, most impetuous when on a horse." She sighed, caught up in memories. "All those battles he fought and then to end up being killed when playing polo. You know, that was the very reason I put a stop to your mother's horse riding. I don't think she ever forgave me for that. But she was always impetuous too."

"I'm so sorry, grandma. See, I'm making you sad. It's a very lovely dress, but I don't want to spoil things for you by bringing back sad memories."

"You won't. Nothing could spoil my memories of your own grandfather; and I'm sure he would have been pleased had he been able to see you in it... there's no love like your first love, Jedda. Mark my words. And mark them well."

"What about granddad Sandy?"

"Oh, I loved him too; but differently. But I was older then. I did not marry for quite some time after granddad Markham died, but one cannot live in the past forever. Life must go on, as they say."

"They are all such beautiful dresses, grandma. Oh, I'm so lucky. I'll be the belle of the ball."

"Who knows, you may meet Prince Charming. A rich one, who can buy you a cook!"

They behaved in an animated fashion together as Jedda tried on gown after gown, shawl after shawl, and jewellery after jewellery, until Jedda became dizzy with delight. Goodbye austerity! A new age is dawning!

Jedda slept until eleven next morning, waking up exhilarated and with more energy than she had known for a long time. The only thing missing in her world was Joe.

When Jedda appeared downstairs for a very late breakfast, Zizzie had already informed the office she was ill and that she wouldn't be coming into work that day. The patient ate a hearty breakfast of unbelievable quality: brown toast, beans and mushrooms, followed by a large portion of tinned grapefruit – whereas most people at this time would be obliged to struggle along with dried eggs on grey bread. Jedda refused the real eggs on offer to her, hating them.

166

She spent a happy Saturday chatting to Zizzie and playing cards, and later, after Zizzie had raided her store cupboard, partook of a delicious lunch of tinned ham, which Zizzie first grilled and served up with creamed potatoes and two portions of vegetables.

It was quite bright for November and they decided on a walk round the garden after lunch. The flowers and bushes were not quite as trim as when Sandy had looked after it, but Zizzie still managed to hire a man to cut the grass and keep it weed-free.

"The roses are still in bloom, grandma."

"They never seem to completely fade until the frost comes, even at Christmas some still struggle on... I think they must have Sandy in mind."

"I loved Sandy."

"You love everyone; always did. Sometimes I think you love too much. Expect too much! We humans are fragile creatures at the best of times." She looked straight at Jedda, her expression grave. "Be careful, you may get hurt. Deeply hurt."

Jedda didn't answer; life had hurt her too much already.

At precisely nine o'clock, and after an excellent dinner, compliments of Zizzie once more, Jedda was now seated within the cold interior of a waiting taxi and armed with parcels of clothes and boxes of food.

Zizzie kissed her one more time. "Take care darling and come and see me soon. Anytime you wish; I'm not going anywhere." She turned to the taxi driver. "Take care of my granddaughter and drive carefully. You'll have me to answer to if you don't."

Jedda blushed. "I'll be fine grandma; I'm sure the gentleman knows what he's doing."

The taxi driver remarked to Jedda as they drove away, "Don't be embarrassed. My gran was just like that, God bless her. It's their way of showing they love us."

Jedda shared a taxi with Kate, Eileen, Patsy and Charles, making their way to the large Manchester hotel in style. Once over the threshold, the ladies made their way to the Queen Anne suite to repair their make-up and make adjustments in general.

It was an extremely luxurious suite furnished with pretty bow-fronted dressing tables covered with chintz, above which elegantly shaped gilt mirrors framed the walls; hand mirrors had also been furnished, placed on the tables in readiness for the ladies, enabling them to view the backs of their heads.

Toilet complete, they joined the men, obliged to run the gauntlet of hand shaking with their hosts, Mr Hardman and Mrs Hardman. Both were waiting at the entrance to the large dining/come ballroom, to greet each guest as they emerged

167

from the foyer. Each participant smiled and thanked their hosts in an uneasy fashion; an action returned with the same feeling of insincerity on the part of their hosts. Very few people liked the Hardmans.

Jedda couldn't help but question whoever it was that had allowed Mrs Hardman to wear that gown. Puce coloured, cut low at the back, it made no allowances for her putty-tinted skin and excess fat that flowed over the top like dumplings pushing their way out of an over steaming pot of stew. The woman was obviously at the mercy of Hardman and hardly allowed to open her mouth. Jedda felt a sting of pity for her in spite of all her wealth.

The room they had entered echoed nothing of the austerity from which Britain was at present suffering. Long tables, over which pristine white clothes had been carefully arranged, were complimented by fine cutlery. Placed upon individual tables, and before the chair of each guest, were cards with their names swirled on in gold writing. For ladies, an individual posy, plus pin, had been placed enabling them to attach the flowers to their dresses. Embroidered napkins and the gleam of cut glass bowls filled with pretty flowers completed a dazzling picture.

Kate was seated opposite Charles and Eileen opposite Patsy. Jedda sat across from Kurt Vane – she had a suspicion he'd arranged it so – but then, he was very well in with the son of one of Hardman's friends. She had seen them chatting to one another earlier.

Kurt offered Jedda a welcoming smile, enchanted by a golden vision wearing Zizzie's anniversary dress. Kate had remarked early that she was green with envy and that all the other girls would be too.

"Those flowers go well with your dress, Jedda," said Kurt, glancing at the cream and yellow roses that made up her posy. "You look all together lovely."

"Thank you," said Jedda politely, finding his compliments irritating. She wished Joe were there to make them instead; though he would probably have joked and told her it was like dancing with a prickly rosebush.

Soup was served. A delicious concoction that did not cry "austerity". This was followed, first by trout in a rich cream sauce, then turkey breast accompanied by sauté and roasted potatoes, two veg, stuffing and cranberry sauce – well, it was close to Christmas. Waiters regularly filled glasses with well-chosen wines and pudding was a chocolate ice cream bomb glace, with rum truffles to follow and an assortment of cheeses.

Jedda smiled thoughtfully to herself. And Zizzie thought she had plenty of stock in the pantry; she also wished her grandmother was there with her, able to enjoy it all.

Even the cigarettes, placed at intervals along the table, were in positive numbers. Jedda took a quick glance at Patsy to see if he would fill his mouth with them, lighting up for the whole table, but he seemed to be on his best behaviour – still, the night was young.

Kurt captured her for a dance and danced divinely, but held his unwilling partner much too tightly.

From the distance a figure watched with interest as she and Kurt cavorted round the floor.

"May I cut in?"

Jedda looked up and beheld a sun-kissed, tall, brown-haired stranger with blue eyes, ones that crinkled when he smiled. Kurt released her unwillingly, a scowl on his face.

The stranger swept her across the floor without speaking, his eyes so intent upon hers that she missed a step.

"Don't slip! I don't want you pulling my shirt out again!" he said, in a well-modulated, well-educated voice. "I wouldn't like it in front of all these people. I'm the shy type."

He seemed anything but shy to Jedda. "I beg your pardon?"

He gazed down at her, a grin on his face. "Don't make me fall for you again; though I must say it's too late. I've done that already."

"I'm afraid I'm not with you."

"Have you done any skating lately?"

"I don't skate; I can't skate!"

"I know that, much to my sorrow. I've still got the bruises to prove it." He started to laugh. "You don't remember me do you? Then, why should you? It was so long ago."

Jedda continued to look confused. The stranger tried to make her feel at ease. "But I remember you. A little girl lost in the blackout with her little friend. I made sure you arrived home safe."

Of course, she understood now. Of how enchanted she had been at that time and how enchanted she was once more becoming. She blushed and started to laugh. "Of course I remember. But fancy after all this time and such a small incident... though I must say at the time, I wished the ground could have swallowed me up."

"I disagree."

"Disagree?"

"It wasn't a small incident. It was meant to be. I've been searching for you ever since. When will you marry me?"

His attitude was quite hilarious to her way of thinking and she started to laugh out loud. Too loud, much to the consternation of those close by. People started to stare and murmur to each other. What was Jedda Markham up to now?

"I'm not laughing, I'm serious. But I do hope to spend the rest of my life laughing with you." He pulled her closer to him. "You're Jedda and I'm Adam. See, I even remember your name. Go on. Marry me."

169

"How do you do," she said politely, ignoring his forward request. The band stopped playing and she said dancing with him had been pleasant and attempted to join Kate and co; but before he allowed her to do so, he said he'd be back for another dance with her.

Jedda was about to join her friends when a girl crossed the room in front of her, challenging her with an icy stare. Jedda thought she had seen her before, but could not place her.

"That's Hardman's daughter," said Patsy.

"Who?" Jedda was taken back by Patsy's remark.

"The girl that just gave you an ugly look. I think you must have monopolised her boyfriend," said Patsy in answer to her question. "She's been tanning herself in the South of France by the looks of her. So has he." He squeezed Jedda's hand as a warning. "Be careful Jedda. Her family have pots of money and she can be quite nasty from what I've heard about her."

Jedda glanced across the room to where the girl was standing. She was deep in conversation with Adam and she did indeed look tanned. A look that contrasted well with the white, expensive off-the-shoulder gown she was wearing. She was a younger version of her mother with mousy hair and pale eyes. Then Jedda remembered where she had seen her before. It was the girl who, so long ago, had objected to Adam offering Addie and she a lift home. "Whoops!"

"I'm not even interested in him," she lied, aware at the same time she wasn't fooling Patsy.

"You are," said Patsy. "You're a born flirt and can't help it. Joe's certainly got his work cut out where you're concerned, Jedda."

Kurt came across and asked Jedda for a dance, he was becoming quite possessive. She was relieved when Patsy came over and rescued her, at the same time conscious, that for Patsy, he seemed in a more sombre mood than usual; none of his Irish humour had come to the surface – not even once. Jedda remarked upon it and Patsy looked crestfallen:

"I've something to tell you, Jedda. Eileen and I are going back to Ireland."

Jedda stopped dead in her tracks on the dance floor. "Back to Ireland?" She almost shouted it and people began to look their way. "You're leaving me too, Patsy? Why?"

"Toro's managed to get me a job at the same firm he works for and Eileen's been homesick for Ireland for quite a while now."

Damn and blast Toro! Was he the reason Joe had not written?

"Toro! Does he have anything to do with Joe not having written to me?" she said it at last out loud.

"He isn't the reason Joe hasn't written to you. I phoned home and Toro says he hasn't seen him around."

Jedda was all concern. "I wonder if Joe's ill or if something dreadful has happened to him."

"No, Kate would have heard and his mother would have written. Personally, I think you had better forget him, Jedda. He's not for you, and to be honest, I don't think he ever was."

Jedda took a sharp intake of breath. "I think you're hiding something from me."

"No, I'm not. I'd never do that. I respect you too much. Love you too much. So does Eileen. So does Kate... and there's another piece of bad news for you...Kate and Charles are emigrating to Canada. Charles has been offered a very good post there, one he'd be foolish to refuse. Part of his business interests lie there."

Jedda felt angry, let down. "She never told me."

"I know, but she's about to. I think she's working up courage. She doesn't want to leave England; but Charles is insistent... he doesn't want to give up such a great chance to succeed."

Jedda looked cross. "So that's how I'm loved by you all?"

Kurt came over to ask her for a dance but she said she was sitting this one out and walked mournfully towards Kate and sat down beside her.

Kate took her hand. "Patsy's told you hasn't he? I can tell by your face. I'm sorry. I hate to leave you at such a bad time. You've had it rough, I know. Still, there's a few weeks to go and we must get together as often as possible... maybe you could come with us."

"Go abroad? I shouldn't like to leave my grandmother at this time. She's all I have... I'm all she has."

Adam came over and asked her to dance; she accepted, but her heart wasn't in it. Not at first that is, but as the dance continued she relaxed a little, happy in his company.

Mr Hardman was not very pleased at their attraction towards each other; neither was Doreen, but Jedda was past caring about other people or their opinions. Her world was in ruins and she was disinclined to count the feelings of others.

It was early December and the ensuing weeks were far from happy as far as Jedda was concerned. Kate and Charles were ready to leave for Canada. Patsy, Eileen and Jedda had accompanied them to the railway station for the first leg of their journey. They had all parted amid tears and promises of keeping in touch. Kate and Charles had hugged Jedda tightly in the special way of true friends, tearfully and regretfully.

"Promise you'll come. Promise you'll join us Jedda. It's going to be damn lonely without you in a strange country." Kate's eyes began to fill with tears. "Do come Jedda! Do come! They have more food over there, too. And better wages."

"I would if it was possible, but I can't. And remember, England was once a strange country to you and you soon made friends here. Plenty of them." Jedda kissed her cheek to comfort her.

"I hope there are a few Irish there."

Jedda started to laugh. "There will be – there will be! They're everywhere."

"Of course there will. Anyway, if Ireland doesn't suit Eileen and I; who knows? We may follow shortly ourselves," Patsy had added to cheer them up.

Once the train began to chug away, taking Kate and Charles with it, it was to a flurry of wild waving and tears abound from three desolate souls left standing in a cold, deserted station.

Two weeks later Patsy and Eileen left for Ireland but Ireland was not so far a way. They could visit Jedda they said, but not for a while. Money was tight and they had to settle in and find a house; they did not want to stay with Patsy's folks forever. And this time, when the train pulled away, only one slight figure remained left behind on the platform, crying on a bleak December day – Jedda Markham. No mention had been made of Joe... Joe it seemed was lost to her forever.

A shock awaited her at the office the next morning. There was a phone call for her, and would she be quick in answering it, said a grumpy Mr Hardman. He'd been very terse with her since the firm's anniversary dance, picking on her for the slightest thing – if she arrived just one minute late for work he would make a right fuss. On top of all this, she had been feeling rather ill of late. "Completely run down," her Jewish doctor had informed her. Dr Zimmerman, plump, fatherly and in his fifties had wisely advised her to give up smoking or else, and that her chest was rather weak and she should try eat better; and, that though there were shortages she should be able to get fruit from the greengrocers from time to time. Zizzie had tried her best to coax her into eating more, but to no avail. She simply had no appetite.

The police were on the other end of the line. A lady living in the detached house down the road from her grandmothers had asked them to contact her to tell her that her grandmother was in hospital gravely ill.

She had had a heart attack, they said, and could she – Jedda – come quickly!

She asked Hardman for permission to leave. This he granted, his manner indifferent; chilly. His eyes expressed no sympathy, only a threat.

In the traumatic hours and days that followed her grandmother's attack she missed Joe immeasurably. David and Dora had booked a flight over, but at present she felt completely alone in the world with absolutely no one to turn to, and, though many of the men in the office had tried to attract her interest, she was not inclined to return it.

As she rushed to and fro from the hospital, the cold December weather bit through her thin clothing. She was aware of the need for more substantial gar-

172

ments and that she needed a warmer coat, but money was in short supply without Sally's wages to supplement her income.

She was also having a desperate time paying the bills, and she knew if she did not pay the electricity account soon, she would end up in the dark. An unpleasant thought in the midst of winter; the house itself was lonely and creepy enough for a girl living alone. She knew she could have asked Zizzie for money and that she would have helped her without thought of repayment; she could even have gone and lived with her – Zizzie had asked her often enough – but her pride would not allow it.

Making her way to the hospital, feeling tired, her footsteps were becoming less fleet. The drizzle of the cold December rain, though kept at bay by the nylon mackintosh she wore, its thin covering was not enough to deter a dampness enhanced by a chilly wind, making her even more aware of the deeper elements of winter. She was conscious also of the affect it was having on her body. A deep pain, starting at her shoulder, was becoming quite unbearable. She was thankful when she reached the hospital gates without collapsing.

Zizzie was in intensive care and each time Jedda saw her wan colouring, having so recently observed the same pallor on her mother's face, knew her grandmother was nearing the end. She grasped Zizzie hands in hers – hands that were her grandmother's pride and joy; she'd been so vain about them. The long fingers, once white and nails always varnished pink, were now tinged blue; her face, once so lively, resembled a grey mask, her breathing shallow, where once it had been so deep.

She sat by her grandmother's side through the early evening and into the early morning. Unable to bid Jedda goodbye and, without ever gaining consciousness, Zizzie died at four o'clock in the morning.

When a doctor came in and pronounced Zizzie dead she was devastated by having captured Zizzie's love once more, only to find it so cruelly snatched from her on this dark December day.

Desperate with grief, she clung to her grandmother's hands, refusing to be parted from them until a very understanding nurse came along and gently prised them away.

The nurse took her in a side room and, having placed a steaming hot cup of tea in her hand, spoke softly to her to her coaxing tones. She asked if there were any other relatives or friends she could contact and about her grandmother's funeral arrangements etc;

Jedda, answered, "No," but said there was her grandmother's solicitor.

The nurse seemed doubtful and rang the almoner, a gregarious lady, who turned out to be most helpful with the advice offered. She declared Jedda was in no fit state to travel by bus and arranged a taxi out of special funds. She informed her that once she had rested she would visit her in particular and help her to sort out her affairs.

Mr Braithwaite was Zizzie's new solicitor – her old solicitor had died several years ago. He was young, brisk and much more efficient in some ways. Having been informed of Zizzie's demise, he soon brought things into perspective; nevertheless to Jedda, he was just another stranger who, even if kind and helpful, was not someone upon whose shoulder she chose to weep. She wanted Joe or her mother, but both had deserted her. That it was something beyond the control of both of them, made her more miserable. It was as if God – if there indeed was one – had punished her for ignoring him and banished her to some uncaring planet; or at least ousted her from the rest of humanity. It was as if some wicked magician had waved an evil wand and caused everything she had ever loved or known to disappear, literally, before her very eyes.

The almoner, whose name was Mrs Jenkins, with the help and understanding of Mr Braithwaite, made all the funeral arrangements between them just in time for David and aunt Dora to arrive the day before the burial itself.

David and Dora arrived at six o'clock on a stormy night and, once having kissed Jedda, declared she was so grown up they hardly recognised her. David was grey at the temples and Dora was a little plumper than Jedda had remembered; apart from this, they seemed not to have changed at all.

Jedda asked how they liked Canada and that two of her friends had just emigrated there. David and Dora informed her it was lovely and she should join them once things had been settled in England. Jedda said this was the second time she'd been asked by someone and said she'd think about it.

Dora smiled, guessing her thoughts. "I know all about your lost love, Joe. Zizzie wrote and told us. I'm sure he still loves you best in all the world," she said.

"I'm beginning to doubt it," answered Jedda mournfully. "Everything and everyone I love seems to have deserted me."

Both David and Dora took her in their arms.

On a cold dank day in mid December they buried Zizzie next to Sandy. In the churchyard a few evergreens braved the cold and the sparse grass that encircled the graves struggled to overcome nature. The trees stood stark and bare, black frames etched out against a grey sky. Few people attended the funeral and that included a lack of Sandy's relatives. They were infirm themselves and unable to travel. Many of Zizzie's friends had also passed away, including Viner and the three "E's".

The mourners stood around Zizzie's last resting place; a sorrowful group trembling in the wintry rain and, once the interment was complete and the vicar thanked for his kindly administrations, David invited them – especially the elderly – back to the house to defrost their old bones with hot punch.

Once the company had left, "To top it all," as David remarked, Zizzie's only remaining stage friend Lily had ended up intoxicated and David and Dora had been obliged to tuck her up in Zizzie's bed and spend the night over with Jedda and themselves. Lily had woken at three in the morning to go to the bathroom and, unaware of where she was, had ventured into David and Dora's room and tried to get in bed with them. David could not stop laughing in spite of Dora being so cross.

Morning dawned with rain hurling down mercilessly. Beating on the windows amidst claps of thunder, remaining just as cold as the previous day.

Once breakfast was over, to David's infinite relief, he was able to manoeuvre Lily into a taxi and send her on her way. "Thank God she's gone," he declared. "I wouldn't want to put up with that again tonight."

Jedda smiled for the first time since the funeral. It was a little like the old days, having intoxicated people staying over. "Nor should I," she said. "I had difficulty sleeping last night, as it was."

"David asked, *The Three Bears?*"

"No," said Jedda. "*The Snow Queen*. Like always."

David smiled at her softly. He was feeling sentimental. He pulled her hair playfully. "Perhaps uncle David had better read you a story tonight then. What would you like? *Hansel and Gretel?*"

Mr Braithwaite arrived at one o'clock sharp and was invited to join them for lunch.

He expressed his thanks sincerely and complimented Dora on her cooking. "Very good food indeed," he exclaimed, ignorant of Zizzie's food store. Jedda smiled to herself, secretly amused, and guessed Joe would have done the same.

When Mr Braithwaite read out the Will it came as something of a shock, especially to Jedda. Zizzie had left her the bulk of her estate, which was quite large.

"Don't worry on my part, Jedda," declared David "As a matter of fact, Dora and I agreed on it when we heard of Sally's death. Zizzie was worried about your lack of funds, and did not wish to leave you all alone in the world without maintenance of any kind."

"It's terribly good of you – to let Jedda have the house and quite a substantial amount of money. You are, after all, her son and heir," said Mr Braithwaite.

David laughed. "With our kind of money we won't even miss it. If you want to do well, come to Canada."

Taken by surprise Jedda remained silent for several minutes. "Are you sure, uncle David? Surely you're entitled to something. At least half?"

Dora reached for her hand. "We are sure. Quite sure. As matter of fact, you can come over to Canada with us next week if you'd like to; for good, that is? We can arrange to sell the property through Mr Braithwaite."

Times were changing; her luck was changing. Dora's offer was wonderful and what's more, Kate and Charles lived close by to where David and Dora were settled. Yet something held her back – Joe of course. Joe Baker!

"You're very kind and I'd like to think about it, but not just now. It's all too soon. I hope you'll both understand, but I feel rather mixed in my feelings and I've things to sort out."

A week later she saw David and Dora off at the station and thought parting with loves ones at railway stations was becoming a habit she would very much like to break. She was also becoming quite fatalistic about it.

She walked through the city and made her way to the bus station, conscious she was once more completely alone. Perhaps she should have gone to Canada as her aunt and uncle had suggested, but something deep within had told her she was on the wrong track.

She had had a pain in her back for a day or two recently but had not liked to bother Dora and David about it and make them worry when they were due to make their long journey back to Canada. They may have wanted to stay and, in doing so become inconvenienced, so she had remained silent. But now, much to her consternation, the pain was becoming quite intense, almost unbearable. She was finding breathing difficult.

An easterly wind began to bite through her nylon Macintosh, reaching the thin coat beneath. A damp fog hung around, a sickly yellow and the glow of the lamplight gave everything an eerie air. Her freezing feet were beginning to hurt unbearably. She was glad when at last she reached home.

It was late December and though Zizzie had been buried two weeks, the ache in Jedda's heart refused to leave her. She had, after all, no one with whom she could share her grief – certainly not Joe Baker. She had written to him three times and received no reply. That was as far as her pride would allow, and no further. She had come to the conclusion he no longer loved her and she must consider a future without him.

Her day spent in the office had been a miserable one. Hardman's manner was becoming more intolerable by the minute. He was after an excuse to be rid of her – the reason she had attended work today, in spite of feeling extremely ill.

Once work was completed she made her way homeward, wobbly-kneed, stumbling rather than walking in an almost desperate fashion. It was beginning to snow, only lightly but joined by a cruel wind.

Turning the key in the door with cold fumbling fingers, she walked cagily up the narrow lobby. Hardman's need for her to stay extra time had not helped her situation or the necessity on her part to leave early. Canada Brights. A strange thought suddenly occurred to her: that the word "Canada" seemed fated to enter her life, always stealing something beloved.

She had not felt very well for some time and though Mr Kilburn had been more than kind to her, Hardman had been quite off-hand lately. The name Hardman suited him down to the ground she thought – Hardman by name and hardman by

176

nature. The reason for his coolness had not escaped her and she knew only too well the incident at the anniversary dance, in which Adam had danced with her, was the main cause of his abruptness. She could not understand why. She had not seen Adam since; nor, as far as she herself was concerned, was she likely too. Men. They were all alike! Stupid and jealous.

The house was cold, miserably so and she did not really feel up to lighting a fire but was obliged to unless she wished to freeze to death. All that had been obtainable to her during the coal crisis was a few coal bricks; three of these she placed on top of some newspaper scrunched up into balls with a few sticks of wood on top, struck a match and lit the paper, which she constantly fanned with a piece of cardboard. After several minutes the flames began to leap towards the bricks but not much heat came from them; they remained dull and uninviting so she balanced a shovel on the bars and, as per usual, was obliged to stand guard in case the newspaper covering it caught fire.

Well, she thought, the situation wouldn't last forever. By next week, Zizzie's affairs would be classified; put in order, and she would be able to move into her grandmother's house and be comfortable...leave this poor miserable house and the dark brooding neighbourhood.

But at this moment, feeling ill and down as she was, she would have done anything to have Zizzie back preparing a hot meal and fussing over her. To sit by her grandmother's log fire, first having enjoyed a hot, tasty meal from Zizzie's non-austerity hoard, and then, be packed of to bed with a hot water bottle, even have a fire in the bedroom as she snuggled down under a feather quilt of the finest eiderdown.

She still wore her coat – her very thin coat, which even indoors, brought no warmth to her trembling body. She needed food but found little in the cupboard apart from beef cubes and some very, very old biscuits. How stupid she had been. All that food at Zizzie's. All those naughty tins her grandmother had hoarded and here she was, her granddaughter, without a piece of bread. She had looked in the bread bin first and all that had caught her eye had been a hard as iron lump of grey bread. A lump of unappetising austerity when fresh, it was positively uneatable now. She felt so weak she did not even have the strength to venture into the cold outdoors and throw it into the bin.

She made a cup of beef tea from one of the musty cubes she had found in the cupboard. It tasted far from delicious and the heat from it did nothing to melt the chill from her bones.

The long wait in the icy weather waiting for a non-existent bus had not added to her comfort. Or the snow itself, at first a faint powdering, thickening as it continued to fall. It had also done little to help her breathing problems and once she had reached the vicinity of her where she lived, she had had great difficulty in manoeuvring the streets.

A weak body, accompanied by irritating thoughts whizzing round in her head, brought her to the point of making her dizzy. In one instance she had to cling to a chair – a shabby armchair with wooden arms and fading upholstery.

Mr Kilburn and his wife had visited her just after Zizzie died and had been very sweet to her. Mrs Kilburn had glanced about the room and invited her to stay with them for a while, which of course she refused, but the memory of their kindness lingered. She knew little of friendship nowadays and very much appreciated their concern.

She looked through the small sash window and out into the backyard, but nothing came into view. The snow hung in heavy wraiths of ghostly white, marrying the evening darkness.

She glanced at the clock. It showed eight-thirty. Though hunger filled her body it was not as deep as the hunger that filled her mind. Hunger for love and human companionship. Hunger for Joe Baker.

An excruciating pain came without warning down her right shoulder and spread into her lungs. She felt hot and sick but even through the pain she still clung to the thought of Joe. His very presence seemed to fill the room and she could have sworn she heard him call her name. It was as if he was physically there and that she could have touched him...then the cup she was holding slipped from her fingers as she fainted over and downwards to the floor.

Chapter Twelve

Joe Baker left the Curragh and rode into Dublin to visit some old friends of his named Collins. He'd known Kevin and Carmel since childhood, and more than this, it was an excuse for a break. Mainly from Ida, not his mother. He was sick, heartily sick of her moaning and the bitterness that ran through her like a second spirit.

That's how he perceived her anyway, as two people. One minute the clinging sorry vine – next minute, the bitch for all seasons. If Gerry Fagin at the town hall was already married why had she bothered with him. Hardly the actions of a good Catholic girl, yet Joe knew that Toro and even Rory would have placed her above his beloved Jedda if it came to the crunch.

Jedda. His beloved Jedda. His first love and certainly his last. But was she still his? Why had she not written? Answered his letters?

He paused at the bridge and gazed down into the Liffey, dark without a reflecting moon or bright stars; only the lamps on the sides of the bridge offered a pool of light. No snow was present as in his Jedda's England, and as he thought about her, and the dreadful situation that was keeping them apart, he suddenly felt close to her in spite of a sense of ambivalence. Yet even with doubt in mind, it was as if she was about to rise, reach out from the river and drag him down. He could have sworn he heard her calling him from a great distance.

Finding it all too much to bear he stepped back from the river's edge; afraid of his own weary thoughts as her image vanished as quickly as it had appeared; and he guessed at that very moment, he had lost her.

He was quite sure that he would never spend his life with her. That he would be alive but not truly living. He placed his head against the stone parapet and wept. She'd betrayed him. He, who had loved her more that life itself, was to be no longer part of her existence, nor she part of his.

She had drawn the rose coloured damask curtains back to let in the winter scene. The large picture window made the garden appear to leap into the living room. The garden was swathed in virgin whiteness and leafless trees, their nakedness garlanded with inches of snow vied with bushes turned into fat, white, snowmen.

How silent it was; not even a breeze to stir nature into any kind of reproach.

How hushed the dead of winter; not even the birds searching the hedgerow for food twittered or sang, and only a lone robin, hopping and bopping from bush to tree brought any form of relief against the density of a deep, ashen background. How distinct was the robin's coat. Like blood against white flesh. Like the dress she had worn in that fatal winter of nineteen-forty; the one that Sally had made so lovingly for the school party, red and white; blood on snow – Gingo! A time when her childhood had disappeared and whose memory had now returned to her, brought back like an instant echo.

She shrugged her shoulders and smiled a bitter smile. Winter indeed! What price October and its cruelty by comparison? A time that had stolen Sally! Joe! Zizzie! Even Patsy was gone. No longer there to cheer her up and bring a smile to her lips. Neither were Kate and Eileen, confidants whom she missed most terribly.

She had not even been able to go to Zizzie's grave she'd been so ill. Close to death, the hospital had informed her once she'd been found and rushed to intensive care. The Kilburns, visiting her on a whim, only to find found her unconscious, close to dying.

Worried about her absence from the office, Mr Kilburn had declared he was off to investigate. Worried with her living alone he had first phoned his wife and picked her up on the drive down to Jedda's. This was fortunate because Mrs Kilburn was well versed in first aid. They had rushed her off to the hospital without even waiting for an ambulance, saving her life.

The fact that Sally's and her grandmother's grave lay forlornly bare troubled Jedda deeply and as soon as she was well enough she'd take flowers there – hundreds of them. She was only comforted by the fact that at least Zizzie was not alone buried with Sandy and next to Sally and Alex.

Hardman had sacked her first chance he'd got. He had coldly informed her that he couldn't put up with people who let the firm down and, what's more, he didn't think her strong enough to stand the pace. He informed her he was sorry, lying through his teeth, his tongue cleaving to the top of his mouth but the business had to survive and paying out good money for bad work didn't amount to much. Goodness, she'd been with Canada Brights for four years without putting a foot wrong... why Mr Kilburn had always said how bright she was. Without Zizzie's money to protect her where would she be now? Sleeping on the streets? In a hostel? God, it didn't bear thinking of.

She fixed several cushions behind her back and stretched out on the window seat; the window seat which she had so often shared with David when she was not sitting on the back stairs braving winter's elements. A time when she had snuggled up in a car rug, turning snowflakes to stars with Sandy's magnifying glass. All her memories of times so joyful had turned to sadness – turned into ashes.

Vera, the young lady allotted to her by the kindly almoner until she was strong enough to cope alone, had built a fire of logs and stacked another pile close by in a cranny next to the large fireplace; ready for use throughout the day and evening, until she was able to return again the next morning. Vera served Jedda lunch and prepared an evening meal for her to heat up later; then, having tidied up in general she departed in a flurry of energy that left Jedda feeling deflated.

Though the ornate clock on the mantelpiece showed four o'clock Jedda was still wearing her dressing gown. She had bathed late and her hair was still swathed in a towel. The weakness she felt from her recent illness left her disinclined to take on the routine of dressing.

The warmth of the sitting room, the friendly crackling of logs as they threw out heat from the familiar old grate was something her weary body appreciated. She'd always preferred this room to the morning room with its unassuming gas fire.

Feeling thirsty she went to the fridge for some cold milk. The doctor had insisted on lots of cold milk and no cigarettes. "Your lungs are too weak my dear. Mustn't indulge. Not after such a bad bout of pleurisy that threatened to turn to pneumonia."

She opened the fridge door recalling Zizzie's pleasure and infinite surprise at such a handy gift, compliments of Sandy. Her grandmother had been in her element and they all had to suffer the consequences by having cold jellies and drinks forced upon them; plus a succession of pressed meats and chicken in aspic. She'd shown off so much that Sandy insisted on calling her "Mrs Fridge".

Was this what life was to be from now on – memories? No warmth? No human contact? Nothing? Had Joe's God forgotten her?

Would he not even show mercy to a heathen girl whose heart was surely breaking? The sorrow of losing Joe transcended all that she had suffered before.

She searched through some old recordings, mostly Sandy's, and placed one on the turntable. The music was sad and did not help any. She switched on the wireless and the sound of Christmas Carols filtered through, which made her feel melancholy; that her life, though she was not yet even nineteen, had invariably come to an end, denied all hope of happiness.

When she awoke – having unintentionally fallen asleep – the fire was at its lowest and the room in darkness. The music coming from the wireless was familiar. "When day is done," sang Richard Tauber.

She rose from the window seat, retrieving some logs from the pile close by and threw them onto the embers, hoping she had not left it too late to encourage a flame. After a while, once the fire had sprung to life, she switched on a lamp at the far side of the room. Shadows danced across the walls from place to place, and the wide fringed lampshade took on the form of a wild dancer that did some kind of a dervish on the ceiling. Even chair legs began to creep slowly across the rug, helped by intermittent flickering from the firelight, and ornaments formed a pantomime of both elegant and ugly creatures. She watched carefully, on her guard, but no fox appeared.

She carefully removed the towel from her head and, well rested from a welcome sleep, began to brush her hair.

"This yearning, returning, to hold you in my arms..." sang Richard, making her feel sad. Then suddenly she was feeling much better – stronger. She decided to dress. Why not? Christmas was still Christmas, even if one was completely alone. She ambled up the stairs and rooted out some warm clothes. A tweed skirt and a bright red jumper to cheer her up. She had only just finished dressing when the doorbell rang.

She walked downstairs, nervously. Who could possibly want her company at this hour? She was not well acquainted with the neighbours, apart from the elderly lady in the detached house, a long way further up the road: the one who had kindly informed her that Zizzie was ill.

She reached the hall and, upon doing so, perceived a tall shadow reflected in the lead glass window that covered part of the door. Etched in deep relief from the lamp outside, the figure proved not to be female. Joe? Joe? He'd come back to her? She rushed to the door and opened it wide. A man was standing on the doorstep, tall and brightly smiling. But it wasn't Joe. It was Adam Templer.

Hiding her shock upon the appearance of such an unlikely visitor she suddenly remembered her manners and politely asked him in out of the cold.

"I'm sorry if I frightened you," he said. "But then again, do you think it wise to open a door so eagerly in the dusk? Especially when you're all alone. I think you're alone, aren't you?"

Jedda retreated back inside, Adam following.

"Please sit down. Would you like a hot drink? The weather's very cold, isn't it?"

She was being overly polite, a little nervous. "How did you find me? I never gave my address to you. I only danced with you a few times." That was it! "Why are you here? Is something wrong at Canada Brights?" She suddenly felt fearful. Was Joe all right? Had something terrible happened. Oh, no! Not more bad news? How could she bear the thought?

Adam, conscious of her dilemma, reached out and took her hands in his.

"I'm so sorry," he said, noticing the instant pallor of her face. Of course nothing's wrong. Why are you so concerned about Canada Brights? From what I've been hearing, they treated you very badly."

Jedda relaxed a little. "What is it then?"

He laughed. "What is it? I just wanted to find you, that's all. I've been in the United States. We have a subsidiary there. Then I went on to South America to look into plans for a bridge we are constructing there. It was only when I arrived back in England that I heard of your illness." He paused and frowned, "And of your sacking, of course."

182

"So you build bridges?"

"Not personally. I just help to design them and take care of the paper work. Sort out the details. In other words, I'm the boss." He smiled at her gently. "I'm sorry you lost your mother and grandmother in such a short space of time."

She wondered how he knew so much about her. "Thank you," she said, then looked at him quizzically. "The boss? What do you mean by the boss?"

"Yes. Why, did you think Hardman was?"

"I suppose so."

"Well you're wrong. My father owns Canada Brights. Hardman's gone anyway, so you wont be seeing him again. Fancy sacking you when you were ill."

"I don't think that was the true reason. He never really liked me. His daughter doesn't either."

"I don't believe that was the true reason, either."

"Why weren't your parents at the anniversary dance? You do have a mother, don't you?"

"Too true I do; and she's quite a lady. You're going to like her."

"Like her?"

"She's going to be your mother-in-law, so you'd better."

"Stop teasing me... are you sure you wouldn't like a drink?"

"No just pack a bag and lock the doors, we must off before it gets any darker... mother's expecting us for dinner."

"What are you talking about?"

"Oh, I forgot. I've told mother all about you and she wants you to stay over for Christmas so that she can take care of you." He squeezed her hand. "I'm serious, you will come, wont you? I've explained about your illness and losing your mother and grandmother in quick succession."

And my lover she thought; and my friends. Why didn't he mention them? Someone must have talked about them in the office.

"I've no wish to impose, but I do hope you'll join us for Christmas." his blue eyes darkened with concern. "Are you coming then?"

What a gorgeous looking man he was. "Why not?" she said.

Then, smiling at him truly for the first time, "I'll sort out a flask first."

Richard Tauber sang "Can I forget you," and temporarily – as regards Joe Baker – she did.

The journey into deepest Cheshire was much more countrified than the one she resided in. Visions of foxhunts came to her and red-coated riders chasing Reynard across the countryside. She was not cruel by nature, but if the huntsmen killed her black fox, and hers only, then it would not matter any more and the kill would no longer have to proceed.

When she and Adam had set off on their journey the snow had been falling steadily, but finely. Now it was coming down so thickly, the road before them was barely visible as its feathery whiteness clogged up the windscreen. A keen wind, coming in wild gusts from the east, pierced between the gaps in the roof of the car. Adam glanced at Jedda, a worried look on his face, concerned about her frailty due to her recent illness – one from which she had barely recovered. He could tell by the wannest of her cheeks she was cold and inquired if she was warm enough.

He wished he'd come in a bigger vehicle instead of his sports car; the roof was tightly closed but the car was an icebox. His mother had insisted that he took the Rolls, but like a fool he'd ignored her wise counsel, and now he was in danger of causing Jedda to be ill again.

"I'm fine," she said, truthfully. "This car rug is very warm. It once belonged to my grandfather. Are you all right, Adam? Can I pour some coffee for you?"

"I wouldn't mind. I'll just slow down a bit. I don't want you to scald yourself."

Once the car had steadied Jedda unscrewed the lid of the flask and poured out two beakers of coffee; steaming hot, inviting, in the cold dead of night.

She tried to consult her watch but could not make out the figures. "What time is it? I can't tell by my watch?"

Adam rummaged in the glove compartment and retrieved a small torch. He shone it on his watch. "Eight-thirty precisely; though it seems more like midnight, it's so dark."

"Is it much farther – the journey that is? Will your mother be worried?"

Adam laughed at her concern. "I shouldn't think so, I'm a big boy now; so don't concern yourself any further on my part. She'd laugh if she heard you talking like that, especially when I've made it without a scratch through a terrible war... or are you so young you didn't notice what was going on?"

She'd noticed it all right, but it was the last thing she wanted to discuss on a Cheshire lane hemmed in by the pitch dark. They drank their coffee in easy silence, the warmth of the liquid making them more alert.

They drove on, the windscreen wipers making a jogging sound as they continued on their journey through the swirling snow. Adam felt a sense of disquiet in case they became snowbound, and should his precious bundle became ill again, he would be powerless to help her; conscious of his crass stupidity – filled with an overriding sense of shame.

Lulled by the beat of the engine and the falling snow, the bundle he was so concerned with had fallen fast asleep. It was with distinct relief when, having reached their destination, he managed to turn into the driveway and manoeuvre the large gates; thankful they weren't yet blocked by ever-escalating snow. Half a mile later found them in the forecourt that graced the front of the Templers' splendid residence.

The car drew to a halt and as Adam alighted, a rush of cold embraced a sleeping Jedda and she woke with a start. Adam told her to stay where she was, left the car and struggled, rather than walked, as he ascended the vast set of steps that led to the main entrance of the house.

From the depths of the small car in which she was seated, Jedda studied the massive building in alarm. Zizzie had left her comfortably off – but not veritably so – certainly not to the same extent as the Templers. Why, her grandmother's large house faded into insignificance by contrast to the looming spectacle before her. What a pile of bricks! Did the Queen visit from time to time?

Lights shone from within and streamed through French windows, bringing into relief an elegant room. A room as festive as the hall and first perceived by her through the opening of the front door. A very, very huge Christmas tree festooned with lights and decorations stood at a splendid height in the drawing room, and holly and mistletoe hung in profusion from crystal chandeliers.

Jedda wanted to run. It was all too much! How could she be made welcome in a place of such magnitude, surely not by its inhabitants? The whole process must be an idea of Adam's. She was someone Adam wanted, but would his parents? She doubted it.

Three people made their way towards her, all male. One solitary figure, female, remained at the head top of the steps. Jedda waited with bated breath.

One, a man who appeared to be a servant, was carrying a pair of Wellington boots which, once the car door was opened, he insisted on putting on her feet. Adam had a large mackintosh, which he threw over her head and shoulders. The other figure was a silver-haired, middle-aged looking gentleman who immediately offered his hand in greeting and smiled. "Hello Jedda. Pleased to meet you. I'm Adam's father... I'm sorry you've been ill – welcome to "The Dump!"

Once they had reached the top of the long flight of steps the woman waiting there stepped forward and embraced a trembling Jedda as she stumbled on the top step. The woman grasped hold of her to offer support and said in an apologetic tone of voice, "I'm sorry I didn't come down to meet you. I was afraid I might slip...goodness you're trembling with cold," she said, mistaking Jedda's fear for the inclement weather. "Let's go indoors and sit by the fire. Adam! Get Millie to bring hot drinks and some muffins or something."

Adam smiled and winked at Jedda. "Right madam. Just as you say madam."

Jedda relaxed a little, her fears at last unfounded by the welcome she had received from the whole household.

Mary Templer began to make a fuss of her again. "Let's get you warmed up; we don't want you falling ill again." The eyes, deep blue, resembled her son's, twinkling with warm affection towards one who was a stranger, evidently trusting her son's judgement.

Mary Templer squeezed Jedda's hand and guided her to the sitting room with a sense of relief; thankful it wasn't Doreen she was escorting. Adam had been right, the girl was not only a beauty, she was a charmer as well.

185

Jedda entered a hall big enough in which to hold a fancy dress ball and knew instinctively that she had come home; also, that she would be was safe and loved here and that life and happiness were not over – they were just beginning.

Seated by the fire in the cosy sitting room and subjected to Mary's kindly ministrations, Jedda sensed with all her heart she had found another Zizzie.

Christmas morning dawned with a difference. Jedda had not relished such contentment in many a long year. She was being coddled; spoiled beyond what she thought she deserved. A state of mind on her part that the Templers strongly disagreed with.

"Of course you deserve the best we can offer. You've suffered a great deal for one so young. How you coped with such tragedy all alone, I've no idea," said Mary affectionately.

John Templer nodded his head in agreement. "You never will again," he said. "We'll see to that."

Jedda did not answer – it was as if the Templers had adopted her.

Strangely enough, Doreen, and Adam's best friend Gilbert, came to Christmas lunch. To Jedda's surprise, it was a pursuit they adopted frequently, in spite of the Templers' dislike for Doreen's father.

"Hardman would definitely not be welcome," Mary remarked to Jedda later.

Chapter Thirteen

Spring was here! "Beautiful spring!" thought Jedda, delighted with the flowers and bright, if cold, sunshine. How alive she felt! How happy she was; her health was so much improved. Positively blooming!

Life at "The Dump" suited her. If this was a dump, she surmised it was a dump most people would certainly appreciate living in.

She had inquired of Adam that, if they called it "The Dump", how did the postman find it? He'd replied that he knew it all right, and so did the whole village. His father, he explained to her, had bought the place when it was half falling down and then, having refurbished it when it was in such a mess, it had taken so long to finish that he had exclaimed at the time, "It looks like a dump!" and the name had stuck ever since.

"It's a very beautiful dump. I adore it."

"Good, because one day it will be all yours and our son's."

"Steady on boy; I haven't said I'd marry you yet."

"And I haven't asked you; but I'd like to buy you a whopping big engagement ring. How's about it, Jedda Markham?"

"A very big ring?"

"A very big ring."

"All right then."

"Gold digger."

"That's me."

He reached over and started to tickle her. "I'll chuck you in the lake if you don't behave, madam." He scooped her and carried her down the garden steps as she struggled and screamed in protest. John and Mary Templer watched from the terrace, amused; pleased with their son's happiness.

He paused by the lake. "Shall I? Or shan't I?"

Jedda lifted her nose in the air and sniffed elegantly, the way Zizzie had taught her as a child. "Please yourself. If you want me to catch pneumonia, do so, murderer."

"Ah! A cool creature, eh. One who is detached, eh!"

Adam turned, made his way up the steps and deposited her on a wrought iron bench on the balcony in mock irony.

"There, I told you I was fearless; you gave in most quickly, sire."

"I gave in because I love you. Come on, get your coat. We're going for a ring."

"I love you too," she said. "It's my birthday next week, by the way."

"We'll have a party, I'll tell mother. We'll have lollipops and a clown and invite all the kids from the village."

"All right. Can you hire some swings?"

He laughed. "You always like the last word, don't you?"

"Yes, I suppose I do."

They had a party as promised, but it turned out to be dinner at eight for a dozen people.

Doreen arrived accompanied by Gilbert, seating themselves at the table close to Adam and Jedda.

Adam introduced them both to Jedda again. "You remember meeting at Christmas, don't you, Jedda?"

"We have met," said Doreen. She seemed a little friendlier than last time, as if admitting defeat on her own part. She took hold of Jedda's hand. "Let me see the ring...um, what a sparkler! Look Gilbert isn't it a beaut?"

Gilbert said, "Yes, expensive things, rings," and shied away as if nervous of Doreen trying to make him invest likewise.

Mary made a fine hostess and was really charming. She adored Jedda and showed it. "Well, everybody," she said, once the assembled company were all seated at her magnificent table, "let's all drink to the future happiness of our son and his lovely fiancé." She turned to Jedda, seated to the right, and took her hand. "It is also Jedda's birthday; she has reached the old age of nineteen today and I'm sure we all wish her much happiness. She raised her glass. "Congratulations, Jedda."

The assembled company raised their glasses. "Congratulations and much happiness," they chorused.

"I think I like this congratulations business; this champers is very good. Can we toast anyone else?" said Gilbert merrily.

No one answered, but they all looked amused.

"Oh, very well. Worth a try." He winked across at Jedda. "Adam's a lucky man. A very lucky man, indeed."

Jedda liked Gilbert, he reminded her of an upper-class English kind of Patsy. Not that he was better than Patsy, just a hell of a sight richer. Patsy, as far as Jedda was concerned, was in a class of his own.

Mary took Jedda's hand in hers, eyes twinkling. "I'm sorry there are no swings and lollipops, perhaps another time."

Jedda burst out laughing. "You're worse than your son."

"What are you two laughing at?" declared John from the far end of the table, his silver hair twinkling by the light from the candles.

"I was just apologising to Jedda for not having given her a party with lollipops and swings and clowns and things."

"Oh, yes. Well, we'll have another party. Just a small one," answered John, starting to look tipsy.

"Stop teasing," said Jedda blushing. "You'll have people believing it's true."

"Well, you've got your clown, Jedda. I'm here," said Gilbert, on the way to joining John in the drunken stakes.

Jedda smiled at him fondly. "Thank you, Gilbert, but I'm sure you're far from being a clown."

Gilbert raised his glass. "You're a lady, Jedda. A real lady."

"I'll second that," said Adam, his eyes softly appraising Jedda.

"Thank you," said the object of their praise.

It was a delightful evening spent with charming people to whom life had been kind, a state of existence which made them gentle and happy in return. Jedda walked out onto the balcony to take some air, to be alone and think awhile. Considering how fortunate she had been, the way her life had eventually turned out. Still, she wished her mother was there and Zizzie, and that how nice it would have been if Alex had been able to walk her up the isle and hand her over to her dearest Adam.

Then another face came to mind; unexpected, not desired at this time – Joe Baker; his dark eyes smiling, black waves of hair glistening in the spring moonlight…

Suddenly, Adam was standing next to her whispering, "How about a June wedding? Would that suit you?"

She said, "Yes" and kissed him before they both strolled indoors, eager to inform the company at large.

Mary and Jedda shopped all through April and May, and even the end of it, did not think they had shopped enough.

"They've taken all my coupons and left me with only my old morning suit to wear," complained John.

"Some of mine too," teased Adam. "I think mother's been round the whole village begging.

Mary pursed her lips. "I've plenty of cloth. Trunks full, from before the war, and I'm having them made up by a really good dressmaker. I feel so terribly guilty at times, as though I've been hoarding them. But what could I do?" she said, addressing them all in general.

"Ooh, ooh," mimicked John. "I am aghast! I really am. Your mother feeling guilty about some rolls of cloth. Would you feel better if I reported you to the authorities, dear?"

Jedda started to laugh. "If you think mother hoards, you ought to see my grandmother's stockpile. I suppose all those tins would come in handy for the buffet."

"Tins?" Mary almost jumped towards her. "Tins, you say? What kind of tins? Or rather, tins of what?"

"Ham, salmon, fruit, vegetables – lots of different things: corned beef, olives and loads of the old booze."

"Really?" Mary's face took on a wistful look and Adam and John curled up laughing.

"How shows the greed in a woman's face at the thought of such bounty. Even your eyes have turned from blue to green!" said John.

"Don't be ridiculous," said Mary, blushing.

"Grandmother had lots of clothes before the war, too. Many are brand new and of pure silk and she owned lots of lovely shawls. Some are Spanish and quite exquisite. She had lots of pretty beads as well; some are coral."

"Really," said Mary, all agog.

"There she goes again; she'll never sleep tonight thinking of your Aladdin's cave, Jedda," said John, grinning.

Jedda smiled. "She's more than welcome to them, considering her kindness to me."

Mary moved towards the drawing room with an air of composure she was far from feeling; excited by the thought of such treasures. She could hardly wait till morning for an eagerly awaiting visit to Zizzie's house. "Let's relax with a bottle of fine wine and a game of cards. That suit you all?" she said.

They all agreed and sauntered up to the card table to take part in a game. Adam brought a decanter of wine from the sideboard along with a box of chocolates achieved without coupons.

"This is wonderful. Just the thing and so cosy," said Mary. "It's quite cool for spring, though. John, be a dear, throw another log on the fire."

Everyone agreed that it was indeed chilly and a cup of hot chocolate would be welcome prior to retiring.

I'm all for that," declared John, dishing out the playing cards.

The sun shone down its blessings on the day of Jedda and Adam's lovely June wedding. Jedda wore a gown of Brussels white brocade and carried a bouquet of cream and white roses interposed with tiny white stephanotis. Adam's two young nieces wore bridesmaids' dresses of pure silk, a delicate shade of pink flowers traced on a white background. As chief bridesmaid, Doreen wore a dress of white muslin patterned with pale green sprigs, all compliments of Zizzie's hoarded material.

Everyone looked beautiful. Jedda blessed her grandmother under her breath before thoughts of her absence brought a rush of tears and she found herself crying, her head pressed to Mary's ample bosom.

Mary was the belle of the ball in a grey silk suit, her head swathed in one of Zizzie's large hats; a gorgeous confection of pink roses dotted here and there with sweet little violets.

John helped an eventually composed Jedda into the waiting limousine and, once seated beside her, held her hand comfortingly. Once upon their arrival at the old Norman church and a little late, he walked a trembling Jedda down the isle, all the time secretly hoping his old morning suit did not look too shabby. Mary had previously assured him he looked fine, stressing the fact that it was common for men to look too newly attired, anyway.

Adam had borrowed a very smart morning suit from a friend of Gilbert's and looked most distinguished but kept wishing he had had enough coupons so he could have kept it as a reminder of this special day. He was fed up with austerity and wished it would all come to an end. His main thoughts were, "what's the use of having loads of money and nothing to spend it on?"

Dressed for the occasion the church was a riot of colour, thanks to plenty being obtainable in the Templers' garden. The gardener had picked them early that morning and given them to the ladies who tended the church, thus allowing them to decorate the vicinity of St Matthew's High Church of England.Garlands lay on the main alter, the sides of the pews were draped at intervals on each side of the aisles and at the base of large white, glittering candles.

Upon entering the church Jedda paused for a few seconds in the centre of the aisle, feeling her heart skip a beat. This, she thought, must be how actors felt in a fit of stage fright.

John sensed her nervous reaction and squeezed her arm tightly until she gradually grew calm before continuing to escort her down the aisle. Fear departed, gradually receding, especially when Adam looked round and smiled at her.

When she arrived at his side close to the alter Adam looked down at her and said, "You look beautiful." She relaxed, warmed by the love shining in his eyes.

She had not wanted to marry in church, being as it were, quite secular by nature; it seemed pure hypocrisy on her part. But Adam had wanted their marriage blessed, so she had agreed rather than hurt his feelings; besides, Mary had been in her element, loving the all glamour that a white church wedding entailed; and she would have hated to have offended her dear mother-in-law-to-be for anything.

As it turned out, as she stood there taking holy vows, she was pleasantly surprised by the whole situation; pleased that, having generously conceded to Adam's way of thinking she had made everyone happy in the long run, which, strangely enough was an extra bonus for all, including herself.

After signing of the register in the vestry, Adam led her back down the aisle and outside into the sunlit day. Now there, they were showered with a flurry of confetti – rice seemed wasteful with shortages still present – but Mary, not to be outdone threw a few handfuls anyway. How like Zizzie she was, thought Jedda. Quite a rebel!

Photographs and giggles joined forces as guests and family swapped places amidst general disorder. Indeed, they were so involved with what each or the other was doing they were totally unaware of a figure lurking out of sight in the shadows close to the church wall.

The lone figure of a male, whose lips were drawn in a vicious sneer; fox-like, at the same time triumphant. A look of derision so familiar to Jedda that, had she reason to have observed it, would have been both shocked and angered. None of the happiness associated with weddings showed on his face, only a taunting look of hatred and contempt. He had come over to England on a business matter. Ironically at Canada Brights, but soon he would return to Ireland.

News of Jedda's coming nuptials via the staff at Canada Brights had sprung him into action. It was a wedding he would not have missed for the world. When next he saw him, Timothy "Toro" O'Reily, would be more than pleased to impart the good news to his best friend Joe Baker and inform him that Jedda Markham had committed the ultimate betrayal. She had married someone else.

Jedda and Adam made their way happily to their wedding reception, taking place at the Templers' own private abode. As they drove along Adam drew her to him, gave her a long and loving kiss and murmured, "Mrs Templer, I've got you at last." Jedda started to laugh and as she did so the car drew to a screeching halt.

"What caused that?" complained Adam to the chauffeur.

The man, red in the face, looked angry. "A bloody fox! Excuse my language Madam, but it could have got us all killed...look there it is, near that hedge...the cheeky beggar's staring at us as large as life." He honked his horn but it never moved. "Can you believe that," said the man. "Hard faced as they come."

"It is odd," said Adam. "Foxes are usually more nervous of us than we are of them. Never mind, just carry on driving."

Jedda turned round and looked at the fox as they drove away, her face as white as a sheet.

"Goodness, are you all right, dear? You look as if you've seen a ghost." He put an arm round her shoulders to comfort her. "It was only a silly old fox. We are in hunting country, you know."

Jedda continued to look afraid while Adam held her close, laughing, trying to cheer her up. "Never mind. Tomorrow I'll get out my trusty gun and go and shoot it for you."

Her reaction was quite startling. "No, you mustn't! Promise me you won't go near it?"

"Of course not, if you don't want me to. There's no need to upset yourself that way."

She snuggled up to him creasing her veil, not caring if she did. A deep shudder went through her body as if someone was walking over her grave

The car drew up to the house, the large house that would one day belong to she and Adam.

On Jedda Markham's wedding day Ida Baker gave birth to a son, a screaming, nine-pound red-haired bundle, objecting to life all the way. She named him Danny.

Joe loved him right away. At his mother's request, he had stayed on at the hospital like a substitute father and waited until Danny was born. He had thought that would be an end to it, only to find to his eternal sorrow, it was not to be.

On a return visit to the hospital two days later he took his mother along with him to see her new grandson. "A child born out of shame," as she referred to him; nevertheless she loved him on first sight. Ida could not stand to be deserted by her family, a fact Joe was well aware of, even though she had been stupid enough to refuse the hand of a lover, one who had acknowledged his responsibilities by wanting to marry her.

Joe couldn't wait to sort things out, have provision made for Ida and the baby, then be off back to England and his darling Jedda. "Ida ought to marry Pat Owen," he thought. At least he'd offered and he wasn't too bad a catch at that. But no, Ida was as stubborn as a mule, clinging to the foolish notion that Gerry Fagin, the love of her life, would divorce his wife marry her. "Fat chance," thought Joe. Gerry Fagin had an eye for the ladies but he was also a Catholic like Ida herself.

Ida was bored with the strict hospital routine. Ten days confined to bed was not to her liking and as she moaned on and on Rose answered, "You shouldn't have done what you've done then, if you don't like it."

The visit thankfully over, Joe escorted his mother out into the sunshine. As they sauntered towards the bridge with catching a bus in mind he guessed by his mother's downcast expression how she must be feeling. They approached the bridge and were about to make their way over the Liffey when a figure approached them out of the June night.

It was Toro! Joe was surprised to see him and felt a sense of unease at such an unexpected visit. Was there something wrong with Patsy or Eileen? Or, even more disquieting, Jedda?

Rose suspected that Toro was anxious to discuss something with Joe and excused herself by saying that home was not far away and, maybe he and Toro wished to go for a drink. Joe refused to leave her to make her own way and escorted her to the bus that would take her home to the Curragh. Once she was safely aboard he accompanied Toro through the Dublin streets until they came to the nearest public house; one that suited them their requirements.

Seated in a quiet corner, drinks placed in front of them Joe asked Toro if he had news of anyone, hoping, but not expecting, word of Jedda from Toro's lips. He was surprised, but not in a way he would have wished, when Toro broke the news of Jedda's marriage. He imparted the news in the only way Toro knew how. Cruelly! Bluntly! Not without a secret pleasure.

Joe remained silent for a while feeling that death had entered the place to destroy him, almost wishing it had. Jedda? Jedda had betrayed him? So that was why she had not answered his letters; she'd taken up with a new love. She, who swore to love him forever. He couldn't believe it. It wouldn't sink in.

"I don't believe you. It must be some mistake. Who told you?"

"I didn't need to be told. I was there!"

Joe looked stunned. "You were there? How come?"

Toro half smiled. "She didn't invite me if that's what you mean. I went over on business to Canada Brights. Can you believe it? A girl out of the typing pool told me about Jedda and this new man of hers." Toro took a drink from his glass. "She said to me, 'Are you going to Jedda's wedding? You're an old friend of hers, aren't you?'" Toro shook his head from side to side. "That was a laugh, I can tell you."

"You're amused aren't you? You never liked her did you? Or is it as Rory often suspected? Did you secretly love her? They say love's akin to hate. Anyway, it's too late now for both of us. Whatever we think or feel, it's over."

"I certainly don't love her. Just because you thought her the most wonderful girl in the world, doesn't follow I felt the same. Far from it! I hated her! I could see what she was doing to you, Joe."

"I was never aware she was trying to do anything to me, whatever you mean by that."

"I know you weren't, Joe. That's the folly of it." Toro even looked sad.

"What was he like?" Joe's eyes held a pitiful expression, almost mournful.

"Who?"

"You damn well know who! The bloody husband!"

A sneer played across Toro's face and Joe wished it could have been a smile it was so wanton. "Mr Brillcream himself, plain and simple. A beautiful blue-eyed Englishman. Tall, upper class, public school boy. Landed herself a very rich fish there, I can tell you."

Joe remained silent; he'd never known Toro so talkative. The man was positively in his element.

"You should have seen the rest of them, dressed up to the nines and talk about la-de-da."

"Jedda was never like that, snobbish."

"No, but she soon will be with that lot. I should imagine money is something she'd like to get use to."

"She had money of her own, or will do when her grandmother dies."

"She already has, but I didn't know Jedda was loaded, you sly devil. See what you've lost?"

"Dead? Zizzie's died?"

"Why are you so shocked? I didn't know you knew her that well?"

"She was a lovely woman. Poor Jedda, all alone in the world, and me not there to help her."

"She doesn't want you! Remember? Anyway, I heard from all accounts she was very ill last year. Pleurisy, I believe."

"I knew nothing of this; perhaps that's why she didn't write?"

Toro was adamant. "She's had plenty of time since. Accept it! She no longer wants you."

"I'll never understand it. Never! I wrote to her several times, but she never answered me once. Not even once. It's beyond my comprehension. Absolutely!" He bit his lip, despairing. "Who knows, maybe she thought I had deserted her, too. I wish I'd never come back home, but it's too bloody late now by all accounts."

"Her husband's father owns Canada Brights, you know." Toro continued. "He owns a large house in the country, too. He's loaded, but then, Jedda was always a Rolls Royce and buckets of champagne person – solid silver buckets. Plenty of servants, I believe."

"I wonder if the butler cleans her shoes. Or don't butlers clean shoes?"

"Shoes?"

Joe smiled bitterly. "Just a thought."

"They say at Brights she rides around in a little red roadster. No catching the bus for our Jedda anymore; goes horse riding as well. Got a holiday home in the South of France. Takes in skiing in Switzerland." Toro paused and signalled to the waiter for two more beers. "Women are like that," he said wryly, without realizing how much he was hurting Joe, trying to comfort him. "Content with tiddlers then striking out for bigger fish."

"That doesn't sound like the Jedda I know, or at least the one I once knew."

A group of musicians started to play a sentimental Irish song about lost love and life's cruelties. It was enough for Joe and he decided it was time to leave. He wasn't in the mood to dwell on his own stupid follies and try to resuscitate the past.

Toro also agreed it was time for him to make his way back to his hotel. He had to travel North on business early in the morning, see another firm in Belfast about sorting out some deal concerning Canada Brights.

"Are you remaining here or heading back for England, Joe? If not, come and work with Patsy and me. They need more draughtsmen at O'Brien's and with your qualifications, you'll make good money."

"I'll not be going back to England now; not much point with Jedda married. I'll write to the firm and hand in my notice; but I'm not leaving the Curragh. I hate the North, it has too many bad associations for me; what with my parents and all that." He frowned and his lips tightened in a bitter smile. "Seems history has repeated itself, hasn't it Toro?"

Toro's hand bit into Joe's arm until his friend winced. "I'm sorry Joe, I really am. And I'm sorry also to have to say I told you so." Toro began to frown, gazing into the distance. "I'm not gloating over your break-up with Jedda in spite of all my misgivings about her. It's just that it wouldn't have worked out between you both, that's all... I know it wouldn't."

"You may be right. You may all be right, but I know this, I know I'll never, never love anyone else as long as I live. It certainly wouldn't be fair on another woman to pretend that I did."

They strolled away from the pub and into the June night, deep in conversation as they walked along.

"Time heals all things. You'll love again, you'll see." They paused by the bridge. "Will you live at home, Joe?" Toro showed concern.

"I suppose so. Mother needs me at present, anyway. She hasn't been well and the shock of Ida's downfall, as she sees it that is, will never go away."

"She's your sister I dare say, but she was always a silly girl. Never down-to-earth, like Kate."

Joe was forced to smile. "I never thought the day would come when you had a good word to say for Kate."

"Only because she gave up her religion. That's the only reason she offends me. It seems as if she's joined the other side."

"The other side of what, for God's sake?" said Joe as they reached the bridge.

"Those heathen English who have always persecuted us because of our true love of the Holy Father in Rome, that's whom."

Joe gazed down into the Liffey, chanced on both their images reflected on the water, pinked by the setting sun as it kissed the river. "I don't think they're heathen exactly, just misguided. It's not their fault about what happened centuries ago; no more than it's ours."

"Never mind," said Toro, missing the point. "We're home now Joe. We must put the past behind us. You'll forget Jedda in time."

Joe nodded his head in disagreement. "No, I won't." He gave Toro a quizzical look. "You won't either."

Toro ignored his last statement, frowning. "Anyway, there's the bus to take me to my hotel." He moved forward and put his hand out to stop the oncoming vehicle. "Get in touch. You've got my phone number, and if you should change your mind about the job, give me a ring. Bye."

Joe watched Toro jump on the bus, the light coat he was carrying flapping across his long legs as he did so and knew he would never ring him. He consulted his watch. It was only nine-thirty and he didn't care to go home just yet. He wanted time to himself. Time to consider what went wrong between himself and Jedda. He walked across the city until he came to the park.

Though the evening was warm, not many people were about, except for the odd couple. One pair in particular made him catch his breath, causing despair to engulf him further. The girl was dark and very pretty and she was laughing, looking up in to the eyes of the man she was with; the man also was enchanted in turn. Joe thought "Oh yes. Smile back at her. Laugh with her. I did that last June. Walked with Jedda Markham, too. In gardens. In parks. By the glittering sea, holding her in my arms all summer. Be careful young man, women are treacherous creatures. Mine has just broken my heart and it will never mend. Never! The world's full of women and I used some of them badly, now it's my turn to suffer and its bloody terrible."

He walked slowly through the park, meandered passed a playground and the tennis courts until he found a quiet haven in an enclosed garden, pleased to find a deserted spot where he could hide his face from the rest of humanity. He started to tremble. On the edge of despair since receiving news of Jedda's marriage, he was aware he was suffering from shock. A deep feeling of sadness fogged his reason and he could not seem to rise above the mist of his sorrow. He felt lost, forsaken. How could she do this to him? How could he endure life without her? It was like a death. His very soul was in mourning. No, it was worse than that! If she had died he would have known she could have not helped it; have no control over the matter. And he could have born the fact that she had died loving him alone. But now, she lived for someone else, and the thought was unbearable.

The sun still shone on this June day; yet his sun had gone out. He felt sick at the thought of someone else possessing her, holding her, loving her. He leaned with his back against a tree before slowly letting his body sink to the ground, cursing his own stupidity at having left her; of coming back to Ireland – and to what? He cursed Ida and cursed himself more as tears, previously unshed, coursed down his face washing away for all time the happiness he had once known.

Jedda Markham Templer strolled along the tree-lined boulevards of Paris, arm-in-arm with new husband Adam Templer, enjoying the raptures of newly married life, unaware a desperately unhappy man sat under another tree weeping his heart out; a tree in an Irish park, trying to bring under control bitter tears, ones that could not assuage the wounds she had innocently imparted.

Adam smiled down from time to time at the vivacious face gazing up at him thinking himself a lucky man. People seemed infected by their preoccupation with each other and smiled knowingly... two more honeymooners enjoying the romantic sights of Paris.

Joe Baker was a distant memory now. One that had hurt her for a time, but lonely orphans attach themselves to those who offer love, and Jedda knew that at last life offered her a great deal of happiness, combined with an enduring future.

Part Three

Shades of Autumn – Final Steps

...I long for a soft look...

For memories sake:

A winding sheet to heal the wounds

Of bruised desires.

But in your eyes I see the death of love,

A flickering candle at my wake...

We've reached our sad October...

Wear its decomposing shoes.

Chapter Fourteen

The March wind was blowing a gale, rushing at Joe Baker causing his fawn Burberry to flap around his knees and chilling the flesh beneath.

He pushed his hands down deep into the pockets of his coat trying to add warmth to his fingers. The trilby, drawn down well down over his head kept his hair dry, but threatened to fly skywards any time, he had to continually grasp it. Being offered no protection from the frosty rain, making exposed flesh tingle, he was well aware comfort was well out of the question in the area that he was now walking. Danger lurked in every corner as he continued to manoeuvre the unfamiliar streets, knowing he must hurry on regardless until he reached more hospitable territory. Meantime, he thought a cigarette might satisfy his needs; accord boldness to his fears.

He edged cautiously into the doorway of a bookshop situated nearby; keeping an eye out for anything or anyone that might be a threat to his safety. He struck a match, protecting the flame with cupped hands against the draft. Enjoying a cigarette he inhaled deeply, appreciating the calming effects the nicotine had on his system. While glancing casually into the window at the items on display, his heart suddenly skipped a beat. In the foreground, in a place of honour and inviting the public to buy, a notice in large print stated, "This is Jedda Markham's greatest book to date."

Her face, so familiar, featured on the cover, was even more beautiful than he remembered. Jedda Markham! Courted by the media! Admired by the public! He leaned closer. Beloved Jedda! After all these years, and at such an ill-timed moment. Back to haunt him! Emotion overtook him. Anger! Grief! Love! Hate! Despair! All combined with the endless joy of seeing her face once more.

He frowned, paused within his own foolishness. Hadn't he other things to contend with, much more serious and urgent things? Ones that didn't include the intrusion of lost love Jedda Markham? The situation was becoming obtuse, to say the least. When further desire to lament about events long passed no longer seemed feasible, withdrawing from the shelter of the shop doorway, he prepared to face the elements once more.

The wind had changed from west to east in a short space of time, combined with a mixture of rain and sleet that rushed unmercifully towards him, slashing at his face in an unbearable fashion.

He continued to box with the weather street after street, cautiously. A man of shadows! Fully conscious of the danger that surrounded him and of what kind of pressures would be put upon him should he be stopped and questioned. Although it was only early evening, the British soldiers seemed thick on the ground and made him feel dubious, wondering if something ominous was afoot. If it was, he had had no news of it.

He began to walk more swiftly, trying to push all thoughts of Jedda out of his mind, but the more he tried the more she invaded his thoughts. God, how he'd loved her. How could she have betrayed him in the fashion that she did? Money? It hadn't seemed likely from the Jedda he had known.

Seeing her face once more had jolted him dreadfully and he had to admit, brought back feelings he had long thought forgotten. He was also aware that softness was no longer his ally. In his line of business he could not afford to be sentimental; yet, through all the years of being without her, if he had to be honest, he could hardly recall a time when he had not thought about her. A strain of music. A piece of poetry. A certain colour. A pair of shoes. Jedda. He half smiled to himself at the thought of her. The top half well groomed and cared for, the tips of her toes so badly neglected. "A girl in need of a maid," he had said. Yes, he had been so unhappy with her at times but even more unhappy without her. He re-called the moment he had turned back to find her, only to be too late. How swift had been her betrayal. How unexpected! How great had been the blow to his soul.

It was growing dark, the streets almost deserted. People did not venture out late in Belfast these days, and if they did, they moved quickly, anxious to return to the assumed safety of their houses.

A cold-faced moon cast light on the left hand of the street and he made sure he took cover under the shadows on the right. He did not want soldiers calling him to a halt, searching him, asking questions as he weaved his way through the dismal streets. He passed the Clover Leaf church where some parishioners had braved the weather – or were some terrorists – such as himself? They seemed mostly Anglicans making their way home from evening service. After all, he was in enemy territory.

He quickened his steps until he reached the city outskirts, and once he arrived at a tree-lined lane, began to move even more swiftly.

Having reached the bottom of the lane he came to a gate, loose and rocking in the wind. He leaned hard on it and it made a sound like a disgruntled old dog. One more push, and it gave way, allowing him to enter an overgrown garden.

Following an uneven path he stopped in front of what appeared to be an unin-habited house and paused awhile before lifting a knocker shaped in the form of an eagle's head. Knocking three times on a solid oak door was not without a feeling of trepidation as it proceeded to boom before then echoing back at him. He wanted

202

to shout, "Does Miss Haversham live here? Or, "Is a certain Mr Heathcliff in residence?"

The door drew slowly ajar and the gaunt face of an elderly man appeared from within. He confronted Joe roughly. "What do you want?" inquired the owner of the face.

"I'm expected," said Joe, using the code.

The old man stood aside and allowed him to enter. "Upstairs! Room to the right," he said. "And watch the stairs – they're rickety," he warned, before withdrawing like a wraith into the shadows.

Joe nodded his thanks, making his way up the flimsy stairs as he did so until he reached the top landing. He hesitated before the door the old man had pointed out and tapped on it nervously.

"Come in," cried an unknown voice from some distance.

Joe entered. Facing him at the end of a narrow room, and seated at a long trestle table, were a dozen men or so, all hooded.

Joe began to feel vulnerable, uneasy in their presence. Naked! Part of them; yet apart from them when they all continued to remain silent in his presence, their hands folded in front of them on the table, unmoving. Eventually, after several seconds, but what to Joe seemed an eternity, a man seated in the middle, the one who seemed in charge, stood up.

"Good evening," he said. The voice was soft, almost melodious. He continued in the same strain of voice. "You have no knowledge of us of course; nor are you likely too. We are well aware of who you are though: Dublin informed us of your coming."

Joe did not answer, mesmerised by the man's voice that was almost a purr.

The man gestured for him to take a chair opposite himself and, once Joe had obeyed him, he also became seated.

Joe suspected he grinned at him from behind his mask and also his comrades, whose many eyes bore down on him through slits. The fact that they all sat in the shadows, while he himself sat in the full blaze of light coming from the lamp facing him, left him feeling doubly disadvantaged.

Against such odds Joe tried to remain as calm as possible and said, "I agree. The less we know of each other the better. Let's get on with the business in hand. Dublin informs me there is a special mission to be done. That we must combine forces." He paused, trying to consider the reason for his being there. "But why here? Couldn't I just as easily have done whatever I have to do from the South?"

"You'll sail from the South, but it's for our mission that we are borrowing you," said the man with the musical voice, the eyes behind the shades indiscernible, making it difficult for Joe to know if they were in tune with the softness of his voice.

Joe raised his eyebrows. "What makes me so necessary?"

For the first time since Joe had entered the room the musical voice became discordant. "England does! That land of the devil; are you not well acquainted with her?"

"Yes," said Joe, quite puzzled. "But what would I want with her?"

"You have a sister living there, have you not? And a brother... a priest?"

"That's true," said Joe, feeling edgy. "But I haven't been over there for years. Twenty or more." Not since Jedda, he thought to himself, as the memory of her face rose before him and he quickly pushed the image away, afraid that musical voice might interpret what was on his mind, shoot him on the spot for indulging in unhealthy reflections of betrayal.

"Manchester," said the man flatly, the music gone.

"Manchester?" echoed, Joe.

"Yes, that's where we want you to go. Not Southern England this time, it's much too dodgy down there. They're on to us." The musical voice became tuneless.

"There's nothing positive in Manchester. Certainly no politicians of any consequence."

Joe was feeling uneasy. "The North of England is as much at odds with the raw deal they get from Parliament as we do".

"They'll have nothing to suspect then, will they? Take them unawares. Keep them on their toes up there – then, hey presto! Back down South. Much too hot for us down there at present. They have their eyes skinned waiting for us. Too many of us getting caught."

"Couldn't bombing Manchester have the wrong effect? The people there aren't any better off than we are. What's more, like Liverpool, its full of Irish. We could end up killing our own."

"Serve 'em bloody right for living there, won't it!" Soft voice suddenly sounded harsh, dismissive.

"We haven't much work here. Where will they find jobs? No one would leave Ireland if they could help it. Bet the English would emigrate to this beautiful land if we had work for them."

"Not bloody likely. We wouldn't want them. Fought hard enough freeing the South from them, now we want the North. Undivided!"

"The ordinary English have nothing to do with it. It's like the rich Irish, co-towing to them all the time. There are only two types of people – those who have and those who have not. Anyway, why me, though?"

"I've explained already. Because not only have you relatives there – which is a good cover – you have also lived there for several years and must know the area well." The voice became eager. "Apart from that, two friends of yours are already over in England waiting to join you. Well, three actually. A Mr Patsy Dunne, his wife Eileen and a Mr Timothy O'Reilly. And may I add: stop sticking up for the bloody English – we could shoot you for less.

Toro? God! Joe felt himself stiffen. He hadn't seen Toro in years. Thought he'd gone living in Spain. Toro! Franco's friend. Eileen and Patsy? He had his doubts about them; decidedly more human than Toro; but far from reliable, though. He began to feel more and more perturbed. "I don't get on very well with my relatives," he argued. "Anyway my sister Kate emigrated years ago; so I'm afraid your information isn't sound."

The man's voice became musical again, as if sensing Joe's discomfort. "That's all right. This isn't a vendetta." He paused and added with empathy, "Your sister would have been handy as a cover, that's all. As for your brother, we all need a priest from time to time." He turned to the man beside him. "Why wasn't this information about his sister handed to me sooner?"

The man shrugged his shoulders and said, "I'll look into it."

Joe began to wonder what else they knew about him. How much more of his life had they sifted through – Jedda? Curse the thought. One thing was certain, they knew very little about the characters of both Kate and Rory. No help forthcoming there. "What's the position regarding myself?" inquired Joe.

"Jelly of course. You're an expert at it; so I believe? Dunne and his wife will keep tabs. Ring warnings. O'Reilly is there to organise." Musical voice paused for a second as though mulling something over in his mind. "Oh, yes. And another thing. You and O'Reilly will have to deliver. We have no spare people to plant explosives at present; there's too much going on here at the moment."

"I've never done that! Never!" said Joe objecting. "It's something I'm not at all trained to do."

"Well there's always a first time." The man's voice became forceful.

"When has all this to take place?" said Joe disdainfully. "When must I leave?"

"Easter, of course. To commemorate the uprising. For the love of Michael Collins and in memory of bold Robert Emmet."

With these names mentioned the men seated at the table stood up and saluted and musical voice said, "I'm afraid that's it; unless you have something else to add?"

Joe didn't answer; there was little more he could say.

Musical voice took this to signify the end of the meeting and placing an arm round Joe's shoulders in a brotherly fashion said, "It's no different than the work we do here. Just different territory, that's all. Goodnight, then. Good luck with your mission in England. And take care going back through Belfast."

Joe bade him goodnight and offered the same courtesy to the other men seated at the table. They merely nodded in return, and once he had swept out of the door and down the rickety stairs it was with the realization that of all the company present, only he and the man with the musical voice had exchanged words.

Night brought with it an even colder spell and it was with a sense of relief when he reached the Bog side with its offer of more friendly protection. The wind had dropped, but apart from that he needed the fresh air; his head felt hot, and he was extremely thirsty.

In the right vicinity he at last found the street where a friendly ally lived and, pausing in front of a small neat house, knocked on the red front door and waited.

John McNally opened the door. A true friend and believer in the cause, upon beholding Joe, held out a welcoming hand to him saying, "Come in Joe," as he guided him into the warm interior of the sitting room. He called to his wife biding somewhere in the other part of the house. "Joe's here! Get him something to eat, will you, Maureen dear?"

John's wife entered the sitting room. "Oh, there you are darlin'," he continued. "Sorry to interrupt you, but the man's starving."

"Sure, I'll get you something," said Maureen. "How are you, Joe?"

Joe answered, "Fine, and don't go to too much trouble."

Maureen answered, "No trouble at all." Several minutes later she returned with a tray full of food and drink, placed them on a coffee table, and discreetly left the room.

"You have your dinner and a rest and I'll have you in Newry in no time," said John. "I sell chickens up there on a regular basis. No one will suspect anything."

"Thanks," said Joe," and thank Maureen for the meal. I do hope no one tries to check up on me, though. Soldiers. Or the police. I'd find it difficult explaining why I'm this side of the border."

John smiled and said thanks weren't necessary regarding food, and Joe wasn't to worry about things unnecessarily. He left the room going in search of Maureen.

Joe soon dozed off, lulled by the heat of the fire, a good meal and the length of the day, and when John returned two hours later, he was obliged to shake him by the arm and wake him up. "I'm sorry to disturb you, Joe, but we need to hurry if we want to make it to Newry in good time. Especially if you want to hitch a lift South. Then, there's Dublin to get to."

"It's all right. Danny is picking me up from the hotel once I've reached Drogheda. I hope to arrive there in time for breakfast." Joe stretched his arms and tried to focus but the electric light hurt his eyes. Feeling tired he felt unwilling to move, unhappy about the whole situation, miserable about not being able to share his concern with another living soul.

Maureen fetched Joe's coat from the hall and handed it to him, her expression haunted – a look that inhabited the faces of many other Irish women in times like these. John offered a comforting smile, trying to assure her of something he was not altogether feeling. "Don't sit up all night Maureen, I'll be back as soon as possible." He gave her a kiss. "Come on Joe, let's be off."

The wind was beginning to sharpen once more, bringing rain and sleet on the back of an easterly wind, fine and damp, chilling the bones. The van was draughty, forcing Joe to draw his coat about his ears as he settled down into the cold leather seat of the ramshackle old vehicle, feeling the chill of it biting through his clothing. Not exactly a V.I.P. way to travel. No radio or heater added consolation to the journey; yet, the discomfort did not deter him from falling asleep as they rattled on through the night.

Joe awoke with a start as the van jerked to a halt and he heard the sound of voices drifting towards his ears, voices filled with a sense of urgency that caused him to sharpen his wits. A soldier made his way from the rear of the van and tapped on the window, insisting that they both left the vehicle.

They alighted from the van, unsure of themselves, and the wind, ferocious in its assault, yanked at the door as Joe and John stood there. Joe was dragged flat against it, cursing under his breath as he did so, feeling an idiot in front of such unwelcome company.

The soldier, soon to be joined by others of varying ranks, ordered John and himself to put their hands on top of the vehicle with their backs towards them. They obeyed without hesitation, and after being searched, were then told to turn around. They faced the owner of a voice who immediately asked for proof of identity. By the singing sound of his speech Joe had thought him to be Welsh but when meeting the man face-to-face, he proved to be black. The soldier held his hand out and John handed over his driving licence.

"I'm the owner of the van," volunteered John.

The soldier studied them both in depth, looking from face to face, doubtful in his assessment of them but not arrogant in his approach. He handed back John's licence to him and they both smiled thinking they had got off lightly until, two more men in uniforms appeared on the scene and their spirits began to sink. The black soldier had been polite, easy-going, but the new arrivals were a different kettle of fish. They could tell it at a glance, especially the officer in charge.

"What have we here?" he addressed the black man, his accent clipped, upper class English. He was tall, square chinned, with close cropped blonde hair, whilst the mouth issuing the words was soft, mobile, almost at war with the cool, efficient, blue eyes now resting so keenly on the captives.

This one's not so easy, thought Joe. The blonde soldier had relieved the black soldier of the driving licence and was busy scrutinising it. After some consideration he handed it back to John before asking Joe to produce some form of identification himself. Joe handed him a union card. False, but all he carried on him.

"Why are you so far from Dublin?" he asked Joe.

"He's my wife's cousin," interceded John, lying.

"I asked him, not you!" The voice was icy, the blue eyes watchful, gimlet in their intensity. "What proof have you that you're his wife's cousin?" he declared, pointing at John in a threatening manner. "Would you be willing for us to ride back home with you so that you could prove it to us?"

John had no choice but to stick it out. "Of course... but I've my chickens to deliver. Losing them would cost me a lot of money."

"Where are you going?" said the blonde officer.

"Newry," replied John.

"That's a long way for a chicken dinner," said the blonde officer, sarcastically.

The black soldier started to grin but the officer wiped the expression from his face with a withering glance, while pausing for several seconds, dubious as ever. They could be bluffing, but he had not the men to spare to go riding back into Belfast on what may well be a wild goose chase – or in this case, a chicken chase. He smiled inwardly at his own humour eyeing Joe again doubtfully. "You couldn't make it to Dublin tonight. Where will you be staying in Newry?"

"I'm not staying in Newry." Joe spoke for the first time and guessed the officer was trying to tear his alibi to shreds. "I hope to get a lift to Drogheda. My nephew is picking me up from there."

"Oh, so you can speak for yourself, then," continued the officer." I was beginning to think your friend had strings in your back and was pulling them."

The officer then turned and addressed the two soldiers that had been searching the back of the van. "Is everything in the clear back there?" he asked, whilst still clinging on to Joe's union card and at the same time motioning to the black soldier. "Search the back of the van thoroughly, then the front!" He continued to wait, his eyes still fixed steadily on the two suspects.

The men shouted it was okay at the back, then walked forward to the front and searched. Nothing suspicious was found, so the all clear was given. The officer handed Joe back his union card abruptly. "You can go; but remember, we're watching you. We also have your address."

Joe cursed as the van moved forward. "Young bastard. Couldn't be more than twenty-three. I don't know what time we'll reach Newry now. It will make you late, John. And Maureen will be worried sick." His voice remained doubtful. "That was a bad move, pretending I'm Maureen's cousin. Suppose they check it?"

"We'll cross that corner we come to it, if it ever does. Just hope they don't check on your union card before you reach the South. You've never been arrested for anything; so, they'll probably drop it. Just be careful when you catch the boat from Dublin. They may communicate with England, they're not fools."

"It's under a false name. I'll destroy it soon as I get a chance."

John stopped the van and handed him a lighter. "Do it now. If we get stopped again, we might not be let off so easily. Who knows? If that young officer takes it into his head to report us we may not make it to Newry yet, never mind Dublin."

Joe set light the union card and let it burn away, disposing of the ashes in the wind as they sped at high speed through a deserted lane.

It was gone midnight when they entered the all night cafe in Newry, feeling more than relieved once they had closed the café doors behind them, shutting out the battling wind. It was not a very smart place, but to Joe, anything seemed a luxury after John's van. It was warm, welcoming and, thankfully, empty.

A woman was standing behind the counter; plump and dark-eyed, she gave them a friendly smile. They walked across to the counter and ordered a meal of eggs and ham to be accompanied by toast and a pot of tea before seating themselves down at a corner table near the window.

After a while the woman brought their order across and they ate with relish and for a time in silence before John called over to the woman.

"Molly! Is there any chance of a lift to Drogheda for my friend here?"

"Well, there's a man comes through here regularly every Thursday; well, three different men, to be precise. Same firm though! English! They go via Drogheda, though." She studied the clock on the wall, "He's late tonight, I'm afraid. Must be the weather. May be a bit rough on the boat coming over."

"English, is he now?" said John, grinning across at Joe.

Joe had a depressed expression on his face and the woman seemed to sense his mood. "There's been a lot of trouble on the border, lots of shooting, with plenty of army about. Maybe he won't come?"

"If he doesn't come tonight Joe, you'll have to stay over until morning. They have rooms free I think. Wonder if that shooting is what saved us, Joe?" John started to look worried.

"The rooms aren't free," quipped the woman.

"Now, now," said John. "Less of the blarney, madam."

Molly smiled and left them to enjoy their meal.

The meal over, Joe lit a cigarette, but it didn't relax him any. He leaned towards the window, wiped the steam away with the back of his hand and peered out. No sign of a lorry was in evidence. Danny would worry when he was not around to be picked up; he'd think that the authorities had intercepted him in some way. Maybe locked him up. He was beginning to feel on edge, the warmth of the small room had begun to sap his energy making him sleepy once more.

He quaffed his tea in an effort to revive, think more clearly. "Thanks for all you've done John, but I think I've imposed on you quite enough. Maureen will be worried sick. Though your company is more than welcome, nevertheless, it won't hurry things on for me."

John smiled and handed Joe another cigarette. "We'll give it a few more minutes, and if the lorry doesn't come by the time we've finished our smoke, I'll be off."

They sat and smoked in silence, the way only friends can do, each musing on their own predicament, when the cafe door flew open and a man breezed in.

"Oh, there you are!" cried Molly, relieved at not having made a promise she could not keep.

The man waltzed over to the counter, confident without being brash. He spoke in a deep voice, the accent broad. "Got my supper, Molly love?" he asked, with the familiarity of a regular customer.

Joe tried to place the accent. It was not Mancunian. Maybe from somewhere outside. Definitely Lancashire. Even after so long, he could still recall its tone.

Molly laughed and joked with the man, leaning close, confidentially. Eventually, the man looked over to the table where Joe and John were seated, before walking across and addressing them. "I believe one of you gentlemen wants a lift?"

Joe looked up. The man was six-feet or more with dark hair and eyes and the complexion of one who spent much time out of doors. He seated himself at their table uninvited, as though it was the most natural thing in the world to do. In ordinary circumstances, Joe would have been put off by such familiarity, but the smile on the man's lips was so much in tune with his eyes, it was impossible to be offended. He had a commanding presence that took over the whole room.

The man turned to Molly. "Bring it over, love, when it's ready." He addressed Joe and John. "I won't be too long before I set off; but I must eat first, I'm starving." He took a sip of tea. "Some soldiers interrupted my journey; they were looking for someone, or something or other. They're very keen on tonight. There's been some shooting or other." It did not seem to occur to him that he could be speaking to anyone connected to terrorism or freedom fighters, or on whose side they were on.

His appetite satisfied he spoke to Molly. "That was lovely, especially the ham." He pushed her offer of change away. "I'll see you next time round love."

He beckoned to Joe. "Ready mate?"

Joe said his goodbyes to John, left with the man, and settled down in the cab. It was not a lorry, but a huge tanker. Inside it was all mod cons and music to boot. Behind the two front seats was a sleeping compartment, certainly spacious enough to fit the six-foot driver.

"I don't think I'll be coming via Belfast any more; the firm thinks it's too dodgy, and so do I," said the stranger. "I'll be docking at Dublin in future. Maybe I'll do a couple of turns more, I'm not sure."

Joe nodded. He was certainly glad the man had come this way tonight. "You're from the North of England, aren't you?"

"Yes. How did you guess? I live near Manchester. A place called Worsley, know of it?"

"Quite well, as a matter of fact." Jedda's face loomed up once more, haunting him. "I often walked by the canal there. It was quite a pretty place, full of boats," he said. He did not include, "With a girl I used to know. A girl I once loved and still do, dammit."

The journey was long and the buzz of the engine and snug warmth of the cab caused Joe to nod sleepily. The man glanced at him, smiled, reached for a flask, and offered him a drink. "Can't pour; I'm driving. Do one for me, if you like."

Joe sipped the beverage thankfully. It was hot, sweet and refreshing. He was beginning to take to the man. In different circumstances he knew they could have been good friends.

"I used to work in Manchester – well, Salford. Lived there for quite a while."

"So you've changed it for greener pastures. Can't say I blame a man for that. I'd love to live here in spite of the troubles. Though you don't seem to have anything much that way in Southern Ireland, do you?"

Joe struggled with his thoughts, cut in two. He only knew if he was ordered to kill this most gregarious of beings seated beside him he would do so, but not with any particular relish.

They travelled smoothly along, Joe's eyes becoming heavier with each successive mile as sleep took over. The man seemed aware of his predicament.

"Sleep if you want to. The music's soft enough. I'll wake you when we arrive at your stop."

Joe had to smile. It sounded as if he were on a bus.

When his nightmare began he was walking by the sea and in it his mother passed by him, but she was not alone. Her arms were wrapped around Ida and the two women were bent forward gathering bunches of white flowers. Filled with both pain and anger he started to walk towards them only to be distracted by another figure. A woman. Tall. Slender. Walking along the water's edge. She turned, aware of his presence. He knew instinctively she wished to speak to him, but something was holding her back. Something was in the water she wished to retrieve so she waded out and the waves began to close around her, threatening her. He was torn two ways. The woman's safety, or his mother and Ida? Both seemed to be in great distress. He looked up to the top of a cliff and a group of men wearing black hoods stood there demanding his attention.

Filled with feelings of both love and anguish, he ran towards a rope hanging from a rock. He pulled at it. It snapped, rotting in his hand. Fear and anger tore at him. He wanted to get to the water now. Desperately. To save the woman. All kinds of obstacles lay in his path. He fell, and a sticky substance like treacle made it impossible to move. He could hear his own voice crying out, but it seemed distant, as though not part of him. Huge thundering waves came up and the sky turned scarlet. He looked again for the woman, but knew it was too late – she was gone! His pain became more anguished. Deeper. He started to sob because he had lost her and the sea was beginning to turn scarlet... he was awakened by the tanker drawing to a sharp halt.

The driver was shaking him by the shoulder, gently. "That was a bad nightmare you just had, mate. You must have been overdoing it. Screaming your head off, you were!" He poured out another cup of tea. It seemed to be his cure all whatever the circumstances happened to be. "We're almost there now. So, stay awake, aye." He started the engine and proceeded to drive, trying to make good time.

Joe wiped perspiration from his brow; in spite of the cold his whole body was soaked in it. He sipped the tea the man had given him but the hands holding the beaker trembled.

"Here we are! Drogheda!" exclaimed the man. "I'd take you straight to Dublin if I could, but I've several places to go. Could mean you waiting about for hours."

"This is fine," said Joe. "I've someone waiting to pick me up, anyway. My hotel is just up the road. Thanks for the ride and the good tea."

"You're more than welcome," said the man. "Take care." Then he was off, walking up the work's yard, but not before he had turned round and shouted, "And no more bad dreams!"

Joe made his way to the hotel, musing as he went along that, in different circumstances, he would have liked to ask the man to share a drink with him by way of saying thank you. He was also aware that the man had never proffered his name, something for which he was truly thankful. He would only have had to lie about his own.

Obliged to manoeuvre a hill that wound its way up to the hotel, he found that, though the wind tugged at him all the way, the exercise was doing him good. True also that though the wind was now at its height, it was not strong enough to blow away his nightmares. He laughed to himself about his dream; put the whole thing down to travelling on a stomach full of ham and eggs, assuming it must have caused havoc with his mind.

When he reached the hotel it was to find, apart from a faint light coming from the reception desk, that the rest of the place appeared to be shrouded in darkness. At five o'clock in the morning it was still dusk. Peering through the glass doors of the main entrance, he spied a woman moving about in the foyer. He tapped on the glass to attract her attention.

The woman moved forward and opened the door. "Can I help you, sir?"

Joe smiled, excusing his appearance.

"That's all right, sir," said the receptionist, "many travellers arrive looking much the same way. Have you come far?"

"Belfast." He had assumed she might have complimented him on his appearance, saying he did not look too bad.

"Oh, all through the night?" she said, making it sound as if he'd travelled down accompanied by a Welsh choir.

Joe asked if there was anywhere he could make himself presentable.

She led him to a downstairs cloakroom. "I'll make you some coffee, sir. Are you hungry?"

He nodded and said he was.

"I'll try and find some breakfast. Quarter of an hour, all right?"

"Fine" he answered. "That's fine. Thank you."

"You're welcome," she said.

He had seated himself in the main lounge. Now he was relaxed in an armchair drinking with deepest pleasure the coffee the receptionist had brought him. Drawing deeply on a cigarette he felt so much more at ease with himself, especially since his wash and brush up.

The receptionist came towards him. "Breakfasts don't usually start until eight; but for you, we'll make an exception." She had lowered her voice when coming to the end of the sentence, as if they were conspirators in some deadly plot and led him quietly to the dining room.

Once he had breakfasted he returned to the lounge and snuggled down comfortably once more in an armchair, awaiting Danny. He looked at his watch. Seven-forty-five.

Another hour passed and still no sign of Danny. Twenty minutes later he looked up and saw the figure of a man sweep towards him across the room. Disappointingly it was not Danny, but Jack Brady, a young friend of Danny's.

Joe made as if to rise, but the young man put his hand on Joe's shoulder and told him to remain seated. Speaking softly, putting Joe in the picture right away he gravely informed him "It's Danny... he..."

Joe remained still. Something was terribly wrong He sensed it. Knew it! "What is it? Tell me what is it?" He began to get angry.

Jack Brady caught his breath, a wild expression on his face. "Danny's dead."

Joe continued to stare at him, disbelief filling his face, causing his cheekbones to tighten.

Jack answered the question put forward in Joe's eyes. "Last night. A shooting on the border."

"When?" said Joe.

"Midnight. No later. He was on his way to meet you and became caught in the crossfire." Jack lowered his head, tears in his eyes. "He wasn't even part of it. We managed to get him home, though. He died in his mother's arms an hour later."

His mother! Joe wanted to laugh. Danny had always been a burden to Ida. She looked upon Danny as the child who had spoiled her chances. "Chances for what?" he asked himself. Certainly not Gerry Fagin. Even if he hadn't been already married he didn't really love her anyway, and from what he knew of him, he definitely wouldn't have wanted a woman with a son born out of wedlock.

Well, that was Ireland for you, pure as driven snow. Strangely enough, Ida would have fared better in England. That would have been a laugh, too. She hated the English as much as Toro, even though she had never set foot in the place. Right now, he hated them too.

He was grieved by Danny's death, yet at the same time cursing the boy's stupidity. How often had he warned him? Tried to keep him away from the cause. Jack had said Danny had had nothing to do with it; he for one didn't believe him.

He asked the receptionist for the bill, praying his hurt wouldn't show. She smiled, thanked him and said she hoped to see him again sometime.

They buried Danny quietly, the snow billowing around the figures standing there before the open grave. The immediate funeral was quiet, so to speak; though all hell was soon to let loose, bitterness and accusations were to become rife.

Kate had not attended the funeral, the family rift had become too great; also, it would only have caused more upset at this time, because she had been right in saying all along that Danny would come to a sticky end if he didn't watch it! Apart from which she would have been unable to contain her contempt for Ida, in spite of her sister's sad loss.

Rory had come over to conduct the funeral, but with some reservations. He didn't care to throw his lot in with terrorists, even if they were viewed as patriots. He had always thought that talking round a table was the only answer to all political problems.

Certainly, he thought the English were wrong in the way they had acted towards Ireland, past and present included, especially as regards Bloody Sunday! He always had and always would think that way. Nevertheless, from his point of view, only successive governments who continued to make a hash of things could sort things out.

History? England itself had been invaded many times and suffered terror, one that had made its way from the continent and Viking lands in past centuries. Who were crueller to the English than the Normans? Perhaps they should all start again and rewrite everyone's history? Either side, the truth was doubtful at times. He lived among the English now and found the people, on average, quite agreeable. They had their problems too. To him the poor were the poor whatever their nationality, and from his own point of view, he found even the middle-classes to be quite tolerant.

The service was made up of family and friends and many others, whose reason for being there, Joe was not sure of.

Rory looked at Joe from time to time with eyes that were both sympathetic and accusing. After the funeral there were questions to be asked and these included those by the authorities.

Ida stood by the side of the grave, a bunch of white flowers clasped to her bosom, a bosom which moved uncontrollably as sobs shook her body and tears ran down her face. Rose Baker's frame shook likewise and she kept picking petals from a bouquet she was holding, the blossoms of which fell to the ground as she gazed at her daughter's inconsolable figure bending forward towards the hollow in which lay the coffin of her son.

To Joe it was a nightmare come true! In conjunction with the one suffered on his journey to Drogheda, now it was real – without an English stranger to wake him up with hot tea and assure him it was all a bad dream.

Rory offered a benediction. Prayers for the dead; though heaven knows, to the mind of Rose Baker, the living gathered there seemed more in need of them. When the sermon had finished and earth was thrown in handfuls onto a most untimely bier and the mourners made their way solemnly homeward.

From Joe's point of view the whole sorry situation was not only part of a bad dream, it was a continuing nightmare, and he prayed Danny's death would put a final end to an unhappy dilemma; draw the family together. But, deep down, he knew he was to face an even bigger challenge in the form of an English journey.

Joe was seated on the sofa pretending to take an interest in the conversations going on around him, conscious of the fact that, after a respectful interlude he would leave and take a walk around outside. Anywhere! Anywhere to get away from these four walls, escape the suffocating atmosphere that was closing in on him. He only resided at home strictly for his mother's sake – certainly not Ida's.

Rose interrupted his thoughts. "Joe! I've asked you twice if you would like another cup of tea?" She was feeling old today. Distant from her children. The rheumatism in her right arm had troubled her all day, her breathing felt restricted, as if a heavy weight had been placed on her heart.

Rory smiled across at her, offering a little light into her dark world. She was beginning to wish all her children had chosen to give their lives to the church; that way the Lord would have kept them out of trouble – certainly of the worldly kind. Ida was becoming more bitter by the day, heaven only knew what was to become of her, especially now, with all this trouble.

She had long had her suspicions about Joe being connected with something not quite legal, but not Danny! Her daughter had never loved her son, not really. That she knew. Ida had always been ashamed of his very existence, but that was her own fault, not Danny's. Poor boy, all because of his mother's drunken one-night involvement with Pat Owens, who had at least had the decency to want to marry her, hadn't he? And she'd stupidly refused, and for what, for heavens sake? All because of her mistaken love for that snob at the town hall, Gerry Fagin. He had not wanted to marry her. Never would, even though his wife had now passed away, leaving the way clear for him and Ida to get together. She knew Ida met Gerry on the sly, but he was only using her. She thought it about time her daughter grew up. At forty-six, you're no chicken. She began to feel ashamed of her thoughts, sorry for her daughter's grief and, no doubt, her guilty conscience.

Joe glanced across to where Ida was seated, her eyes at last dry, but remaining stony-faced. Back to her usual selfish self, probably thinking of Gerry Fagin. Would he marry her now she's free? Now he's free? Well! Well! Well!

Ida stared back at him becoming suspicious at Joe's look of contempt. It's too late now, he thought. You're too old. She had never been pretty, really. Maybe quite personable, but lacking in humour. Certainly not like Kate. God, to think he came rushing back to Ireland leaving Jedda all those years ago, just for her sake. She'd ruined his life, but not only his – her mother's also. Rose had aged well before her time. Ida wasn't worth a light and he had lost the love of his life on account of her.

He would never have believed that Jedda could have betrayed him in such a fashion. "I'll write often," she had said. Soon gave that up though, didn't she? He felt as if he would like to go over and choke Ida despite her grief. Grief? No, guilt more likely. Nothing was left for him now, except revenge. England and revenge. He looked across at his mother and wondered how he would explain his leaving.

As the day drew on Rory was the first to ask to be excused. "Otherwise I'll miss my boat back to England," he explained. He kissed his mother with a sense of foreboding and thought how much older and much more frail she looked since the last time he had seen her.

Rose felt despair rise in her heart. England? Why England? It seemed to take her children from her with a cold sense of reason. So unjustified, like some tempting harlot taking all that was best and giving little in return. Was Ireland doomed forever, constantly tied to Britain's skirts for all time?

Rory kissed Ida dutifully and blessed her, as priests are bound to do. He was sad for her loss that was true; nevertheless, he still thought her a foolish woman, one who, no matter how one tried to teach her, would never attain wisdom.

Joe carried Rory's bags to his car, placing them in the boot, not because he thought his brother incapable of doing so but as an excuse to leave the house. They shook hands and hugged one another. One, the respecter of life – the other, the taker. Rory said he hated to leave at such a stressful time, still, duty called. Easter was upon them and there was much to arrange within the church. Joe refrained from mentioning any thoughts regarding his own trip to England; he would go and return without even visiting his brother. That's as it must be, he thought. One brother to bless, the other to destroy. Joe stood in the garden and watched Rory's car drive away until it became a mere dot in the distance, then walked through the gate to take a long walk, hoping to clear his head.

Several hours later when he returned to the house all the visitors had left and his mother was busy clearing the table of what remained of the funeral feast. She left the dining room, carrying dishes as she went into the kitchen to do the washing up. Joe joined her next to the sink, relieved to be away from Ida, who was still sulking in the straight-backed chair from which, it seemed to him, she had never once stirred since having occupied it.

He wanted to be alone with his mother and break it to her as gently as he could the news of his coming visit to England.

Upset when he informed her of his intentions she dropped a cup, the clatter of which, as it crashed against the tiles, brought Ida to the scene. He cursed under his breath; the last thing he wanted was Ida's interference.

Ida retrieved the broken crockery, symbolic, like their shattered lives. "What have you done now?" she raged at Joe.

Joe felt his blood rise to the surface. "What do you mean, now?"

"You know bloody well what I mean, you murdering bastard. My son..."

Rose intervened. "That's enough of that language... and your brother, a priest! I won't have it, do you hear. I just won't have it!"

Joe spat back at Ida. "See! You've upset mother now! You're only a lady when it suits you... when your fancy man is about." He snarled at her. "He'll not marry you though," he continued to taunt her. "I take my hat off to him. There! Though I must say, it's the only bit of sense I'd give that creep credit for, you bit..." He held his words back in deference to the hurt on his mother's face.

Ida was past caring about anyone but herself. "I know things that you're not aware of. I've plenty on you... England. That's where you're going. That's where Toro, is!" She smiled slyly at Joe's look of incredulity. "Yes, that's taken you by surprise, hasn't it? You can't kid me and if it weren't for mother being involved ... I'd put you where you should be. In goal."

Joe taunted her, his reason deserting him. "Tell your squealer boyfriend at the town hall if you want to. Let him do his public duty...maybe get made a member of the Parliament? Though he could end up with a gun to his head, ever thought of that? As for mother's sake? That's a laugh. All you care about is Ida. Poor little Ida!"

"You're evil," she said. "Making threats like that."

"You're not very bright, are you? Haven't you noticed dear Mr Fagin hasn't been round since Danny's been shot. Danny was in the way while living, but he's even more harmful to your chances now he's dead. You'll never bag your lover now."

He left the kitchen, went into the living room and threw himself down on the sofa, exhausted. Ida always seemed to have this effect on him.

Ida bounced up the stairs as she always did when things weren't going right for her, but not without a parting shot. "You never got the girl you wanted either. I've watched you mooning for her all these years. She broke your heart, didn't she? Well, I could tell you the reason why, and that would start you dancing a jig, wouldn't it?"

Joe dismissed her scornfully. "I don't know what you're talking about...your innuendoes won't affect me in any way whatsoever."

Ida laughed from the distance only to return a few seconds later to throw a bundle of letters at his feet. "There!" she cried. "If you think I don't know something that you don't, take a look at those!" She took the stairs quicker than he had

217

ever known and locked her bedroom door. It was just as well; he would have murdered her after having read what the letters contained.

His mother said, "I'm tired. I'm going for a lie down, Joe."

Joe kissed her, flopped down in an easy chair and spent the rest of the night reading Jedda's letters. Letters of love and dismay at him not having answered them. He squirmed in his chair, horror and disbelief spreading across his face. That bitch of a sister of his had ruined his life. He felt sick, finding her cruelty and deceit beyond anything he had ever come across. Why, even Toro, much as he hated Jedda, would not have sunk so low as to try and dissuade him from his course by stealth.

He spent the next few hours in deep contemplation; hours filled with regret and fears for a future he had so foolishly meted out for himself. He did not want to return to England and fulfil the duties set out for him. He no longer wished to take a hand in death...in revenge. Danny's death, though it tortured him, thoughts of revenge suddenly became less feasible when faced with a greater pain, the need-less loss of his one and only love "JEDDA MARKHAM"

Chapter Fifteen

Jedda gazed across the table, past the crystal glasses filled with excellent Bordeaux, the colour reflected by candlelight as she spoke to Adam. "It would be nice to be in Provence right now; away from this bitter spring."

"Never mind, we can go in May, Jedda. It will be at its most beautiful then."

"We'll join you, of course," said Doreen, filling her glass to the brim. "This wine is wonderful. How many bottles have you in stock?"

Gilbert patted her hand affectionately. "Don't overdo it dear. You know you'll only be ill in the morning if you do."

"We're staying the night, so what does it matter. We don't have to drive home."

"Doesn't time fly? We've all been married for twenty-two years now," said Jedda, changing the subject.

"What brought that on?" Adam was used to Jedda's thoughts by now, he believed she grasped them out of the air.

"Just thinking. I don't know, we've been friends for so long now and yet it only seems yesterday since we all first met." She sighed a Jedda sigh, one that Adam was also now familiar with.

"And you and Doreen still look like it was yesterday," said Gilbert gallantly.

Adam was more than pleased as he scrutinized both women in detail. Jedda still looked like the girl he married, her hair still a dark gleaming crown, her skin smooth and flawless and she had not put on an ounce of weight. Doreen had become a little plumper, but not in the same way as her mother, and character-wise, she had grown in his estimation and been a good friend, as had Gilbert, to both himself and Jedda.

"The snow's coming down quite heavily. Thank God for a log fire and a good glass of wine," said Gilbert. "Excellent meal, by the way, Jedda."

"Thank you Gilbert, would you care for something else?"

Jedda smiled, dimples flashing. She was very fond of Gilbert.

"No thanks dear. I'm as full as a stuffed turkey."

They all laughed.

"You'll never alter, Gilbert," said Jedda. "At least, I hope you won't?"

"Don't worry, he won't," said Adam, rising from his seat and carrying a glass of wine with him. "Let's watch the news and then perhaps you'd all like a game of

219

cards – or monopoly, if you like? A children's game I suppose, but Jedda's fond of it, aren't you dear?" He walked over to the television and switched it on. "We may as well have a relaxed night. As you are all aware, it's dinner at the Midland tomorrow and the opera after to celebrate Jedda's birthday." He leaned over and smoothed a hand over Jedda's hair. "It's her favourite, *Tosca*."

Doreen pulled a face at Jedda. "News! News! News!... Men! That's all they're interested in, and nothing can be done about it."

"We can't all think like that, dear, or nothing ever would be fixed in this world," said Gilbert, filling his glass and settling down on the velvet-upholstered sofa. "And everything's going to pot before our very eyes. I blame the comprehensive school system; you mark my words, no good can some from it."

He took a quick sip of wine before continuing. " All these left wing, trendy teachers and their liberal counterparts. All they think about is sex! The stuff they tell the kids, enough to make one blush."

"I'm sure they do their best; though I do agree they are experimenting with children's education. I certainly don't agree with new way of teaching reading and spelling. All these phonetics mean they have to learn things twice – but for what, indeed?" said Jedda, wrinkling her nose in disgust.

Adam switched on the television and politics in general flashed across the screen with arguments about strikes and coal, bread, electric and other issues of interest to the public. God he thought, the ghastly trendy seventies, about as horrible as the fashions, all those horrible psychedelic colours.

The newsreader referred to Ireland and the newly-arrived troubles, and that the Gardia had cornered –but not for long – one Timothy O'Riley, known primarily as "Toro" by some, and nicknamed "The Black Fox" by others because of his dark hair and unusually pale blue eyes. Also, his ability to avoid capture, as he had now also done once more, having escaped the net.

"We have our Irish correspondent with us now. Can you hear me Paul?"

"Yes I hear you."

"What kind of a person is this Timothy O'Riley, Paul?"

"Pretty secretive. Bit of a loner by all accounts. Fought on Franco's side during the Civil War. Very right wing. Bit of a fascist – no, I correct myself there – a lot of a fascist!"

"Surely he can't be on his own altogether?"

"I can't guess at that; but no others have been connected with him as yet – though I daresay the rest of his companions will come to light. It's a newly formed group. A splinter group, but more or less taking the same view as the I.R.A."

"Thank you Paul. Now, back to the main news."

Adam switched off the television and frowned. "Didn't he work for us once? You knew him, didn't you Jedda?"

"To my sorrow, yes. Couldn't stand the man." Visions of Joe came to mind. God, surely he wasn't associated with Toro's endless pursuit of revenge against the so-called English heathens.

"What was he like?" said Doreen, her interest aroused. "Was he ugly and vicious?"

"No, to the contrary, he was quite handsome in a way and not so much out-wardly vicious as subtle and sarcastic."

"Why did you hate him so?" said Gilbert.

"I never said I hated him." Jedda drew a deep breath.

"Your face shows that you did," said Adam. He reached for her hand. "I hope he was never cruel to my Jedda."

"No, he was just part of the crowd. A few of his friends were at the dance on the night I first met you. They were Irish, but nothing like Toro. I loved them dearly."

"Like you loved Joe."

Jedda was taken unawares. "You knew about Joe?" she blurted out, without thinking.

Adam smiled at her, comforting her. "Of course I did. I know everything about you from the day you were born. The staff at Canada Brights talked about you a lot. All about Joe and your involvement with him. Surely you knew that?"

"Yet you never asked me about him. Never mentioned him in all these years?"

"I was afraid I might lose you."

"But no mention of him until now? Why?"

"I didn't feel the need to. I'm the one who won you and you're James's mother, that's all I need to know. And it's what I thank you for."

"He's coming home in three weeks. I can't wait to see him. My clever, hand-some son." Jedda's face shone with pure delight.

Adam squeezed her hand. "Neither can I. I just wish mum and dad were still alive to see him now."

Doreen and Gilbert had remained silent until now, then both said in unison, "Who's Joe?"

"It was long ago and far away. I've almost forgotten him." Long ago and far away? There used to be a song called that. Why was she thinking this way; she felt decidedly sad.

"Do you think you'll ever meet again?" Doreen's eyes were like saucers.

"There is no chance of that; so why discuss it?" Jedda felt embarrassed with Adam's eyes upon her.

"Do you still think of him with affection?" said Doreen, more intrigued than ever.

Jedda shook her head and lied, "I don't think of him at all." Except in dreams she thought, or when he calls my name, which for some reason, he often does. Certainly in these last weeks when the feeling had become stronger; but she just sipped her wine and smiled at them lovingly, glad they couldn't read her mind. "Well, who's for a game of cards?"

"I'll draw the curtains. It's blowing a gale out there. Besides it will make things cosier," said Adam, pulling the heavy velvet to with a swish.

Doreen and Jedda retired early, leaving Adam and Gilbert seated round the fire talking "men's" talk.

Jedda found that, in spite of feeling tired, sleep refused to come to her. Thoughts of Joe and Toro kept spinning around in her head and she wondered what Kate's reaction would have been if she heard the news of Toro's dreadful deeds. He'd intensified in his hatred from mere threats to murder, and she dreaded the thought that Joe was in any way connected in Toro's scheme of things.

She hadn't heard from Kate for a while and decided she must write to her. Kate had not been able to attend her wedding but had sent her best wishes. A few weeks later she had written saying she'd heard from Joe and he was heartbroken at her having married Adam and that Jedda had never answered his many letters.

She answered Kate saying Joe wasn't telling the truth and was using such statements as an excuse because he no longer loved her; and that she too, had been devastated by his lack of response to her letters.

Kate had replied that she loved them both equally and couldn't believe either of them would tell lies; so something must have gone amiss and they must surely have been at cross purposes.

Now she lay in bed thinking about it after all these years, as she had often done, when trying to figure out what had truly happened between them. On what had unquestionably happened between two people who had been so in love and who had, consequently, spent their lives apart.

The crossing on the ferry was choppy. The sea restless. Angry. In the same furious mood as he himself, as he sat drinking coffee, mulling over the recent events. Of actions in which he had been, and was still, deeply embroiled in. Yes, the sea was as restless as he himself seated in the ferry's restaurant facing a sandwich he'd ordered but did not want, heading for Liverpool amidst thoughts of Ida's deceitfulness and his mother's tears and entreaties, begging him to stay.

Even without this desperate mission in hand – one in which he was no longer keen on taking part – he knew he could not have stayed in Ireland. Revenge had come to nothing having read Jedda's letters of love and deep affection and the fact that she hadn't betrayed him – Ida had! Holy Ida. Agnostic Jedda, the much more compassionate of the two. He should have trusted her and all he had done was play the fool. She had been so straightforward, too much so at times for her own good, his beloved Jedda.

It had not been their fault, their falling in love. Each to love the unloved, that Irish and English burden that seemed so endlessly incompatible. He recalled loosening his mother's clinging arms and promising to return soon, but not to live with Ida. Not after what she did, keeping Jedda's letters like that. They would buy another house, his mother and he. A place of their own. But still his mother had clung to him, "You won't be back. Something's wrong, I can feel it! Since I married your father, once he'd accepted our faith, I've been dogged with some tragedy one way or another."

She had turned her back on him as if in some final gesture over something of which she had no control. "I wish I had never had children," had been her last words to him.

The restaurant was crowded with people who, by their light-hearted chatter, were seemingly much happier than the terrorist dining amongst them. Someone had switched on a radio and the sound of Andy Williams singing Home Loving Man wafted across. "...And I am coming home to you, ooh, ooh, ooh!" He found the words ironic. He certainly wasn't coming home to Jedda and the more he thought about the trick that fate had played upon him, the more depressed he became.

God! To think of what he had lost and how different his life might have been. Or would it? Would he have settled in England? He recalled being stubborn about that. And his religion? Jedda would never have stood for that. Something wayward in her spiritual make-up made it impossible for her to settle for half measures. He also recalled how adamant she had been about any form of belief. Not bigoted – just not interested. It had been so difficult for her to understand his commitment to religion; asking her to believe in God was like asking him to believe in Jupiter. Each, in their own way, had thought the other's view out of the question – ludicrous.

His head began to thump, his depression deepening and he felt the need for privacy. He made his way up on deck and once there, rested his arms on the side of the ferry. It was freezing cold, but absent of people, apart from an old man lolling in a chair. Solitude, that's what he wanted, and a chance to think things out.

The rolling of the vessel did little to improve his headache. Feeling nauseous he leaned over the side of the ferry and threw up several times, much to the concern of a passing steward.

The steward, a considerate young man, offered to take him down below. Joe refused, but was grateful when the steward returned several seconds later with a rug in one hand and a glass of white fizzy mixture in the other.

"There you are, sir," he said. "See if that will help." He covered Joe's knees with the rug and tucked him in. He placed the glass of mixture in Joe's hand and said, "If you must stay up here and freeze, I don't want any part in your getting pneumonia. Would you like a hot drink?"

Joe said, "No, but thank you. Anyway, I feel a bit better now."

"Good," said the steward, retrieving the glass with accustomed expertise. "I'll be back to check on you later, sir."

Drowning in the black abyss of his thoughts, Joe continued to think of Jedda. Regret twisted and turned like a tight band around in his mind, future memories of what might been. Children perhaps? A girl? A little girl like her, whom he could have spoiled. Or a boy? A boy, especially for himself, and if they had settled in Ireland he could have taken him fishing in the beautiful vales surrounded by the mountains. But no! Perhaps Jedda wouldn't have liked to have come and live in Ireland. She would have argued about religion and not allowed the kids to go to church. What was he thinking of? It hadn't, and most certainly couldn't, have happened. It was all a dream. England would have been the only place they could have lived and, in the end, what could he have done for her but drag her down? He saw it all clearly now, of how it would have ended. But then again, he wished he'd been selfish, fulfilled his own desires, given up religion and taken on Jedda Markham. If there were a God in heaven, surely He would have understood? Surely it would have been better than to be the killer he had now become.

And for what, he questioned himself? All because of what somebody's father or grandfather and great-grandfather had done to someone else's. It didn't make sense and, the more he thought about it, even less. But now he was trapped. They didn't take kindly to your leaving the association once you'd committed yourself to it; not the secret people he was now acquainted with. Besides, he'd moved on far away from Jedda Markham, from his youth and everything that had ever seemed sweet to him.

His head had cleared quite a bit by the time they reached the port of Liverpool. He left the chair and folded the rug tidily, ready for the steward to remove. He picked up his luggage, noticing that people were making their way up on deck and joining him, all ready to disembark. He hoped no one noticed the rug folded neatly on the chair, embarrassed lest the passengers should take him to be some kind of invalid.

The steward who had previously taken care of him came forward and offered to carry his bag. Joe waved him to one side, thanked him, and gave him a tip. "I'm quite well now, thank you," he said.

Once he had reached the duty counter, he found himself queuing behind a woman, a large boisterous type, built like a bus. The kind he could not stand because she kept joking with her inquisitors; trying to be fly. Joe found it all rather twee as she giggled, joked and neighed; so much so, that she did not watch what she was doing and inadvertently banged her case down so hard on his wrist that his watch bit deep into his flesh. He pulled his hand away surprised to find his watch unbroken, feeling the urge to give her a smack, but the woman remained unapologetic and continued talking, as if oblivious to her crime.

The customs officer searched his bags thoroughly, annoyed about all the extra work the "Irish Troubles" were bringing. The silly chattering of the woman had not helped his day. He inspected Joe's bag with a sneer on his face, then informed him all was well, dragging the bags of the man behind Joe towards him for inspection before Joe hardly had time to close his own.

Joe walked through the door of customs feeling a deep sense of grievance, making his way to Lime Street with a scowl on his face as he boarded the train, continuing on his journey to Manchester.

Joe walked down the city thoroughfare surveying a scene that had once been so familiar, but was now drastically changed. Manchester Cathedral stood out as a known landmark, looking cleaner from a face-lift that brought out the beauty of the lovely stonework. Other things had changed too, but not for the better. High-rise buildings had mushroomed up and out all over the place. Tall, concrete harlots making one dizzy when one looked up at them. To his mind built by men, but designed by mammon. They were certainly not his idea of artistry.

He made his way down through Deansgate feeling the cold even more, hunger gnawing at his guts. The bout of sickness he had endured on the ferry had left a yawning gap in his stomach needing to be filled. He scanned the high street in search of a place to eat until he came upon a café. He entered into the welcoming warmth, took a seat close to the window and ordered a meal from a set menu. The place was inhabited mainly by those employed in the surrounding area of shops and offices.

He ate with relish, finding the food quite good, and half smiled remembering those awful Vienna steaks he had shared with a young Jedda in the lean years of long ago. Memories. Beautiful memories. The meal finished and feeling satisfied and warm for the first time in hours, he lit a cigarette and surveyed the cafe in detail; amused by its mock olde-worlde furniture and sham Victorian oil lamps; nevertheless, he found the place pleasant and quite relaxing.

It had begun to snow, which added to the charm of his surroundings. Most Dickensian, he thought. The snow fell lightly at first but as time passed, began to fall heavily, making him even more conscious of the warmth of the room, lulled by the comfortable atmosphere and the drone of people's voices as they sat at small tables intent on enjoying a break and a good meal.

Even Danny's death, pointless as it was, was beginning to feel less painful as time passed. He was weakening and he knew it. It was as if by leaving Ireland all the hatred he had felt against the English had ceased to exist, swallowed up in the mists of that fatal land; yet, deep down, he knew he fooled himself by harbouring such notions; something ominous was about to rear its head. It was a fear that came to mind in the form of Timothy O'Riley, making him conscious of being born along on with tide. The tide of terrorism.

He lit another cigarette, aware that he smoked too much, but not caring; hating the barren field that was his life. He was on a slippery slope, longing for something to hold on to, but the way down was bereft of trees. Jedda had been the branches to which he had clung, and here he was, in her country about to do God knows what and aching to see her. Longing for the sight of her wonderful face, not on the back of a book, but in the flesh. A human form he could love and hold onto forever.

He knew that, even now, after all these years, he would give his all for her. Give up the cause and even to his shame, take no revenge for Danny's death. The dream was pointless as it stood, impractical, it would also endanger her. It would also result in his own death; any pulling out of the scheme of things, or any form of betrayal, would not easily be forgiven. Once one enlisted in terrorism there was no turning back. And to what end?

Should he betray the cause he knew Jedda wouldn't even want him now, a man without substance, appearing from nowhere out of the past. No, that rich and handsome husband of hers would never give up a jewel like Jedda. Anyway, she would have forgotten him by now; wouldn't want a nobody like himself, not after so long an absence and who could blame her?

But he would have liked to know what she had thought about him across the years. Had her love turned to hate thinking he had let her down all those years ago? Had she married on the rebound, or, even if he hadn't left, would she have fallen for Adam Templer just the same? No, she had loved him; that he knew! It had been too deep a thing, too magical to die. Unique, that's what he had believed their love to be and that it would always remain so.

Though he could have sat in the warmth of the cafe forever, he paid the bill. Decided to brave the outside. Once on the street, he drew up his collar, pulled down his hat, and started off on his destination, but was covered by a white powdering of snow before he had even walked two blocks. The cold began to bite into him, through his clothing, even through his leather gloves, so he pushed his hands well down inside his pockets as he hurried along.

He reached the bridge at Blackfriars, crossed over towards the Flat Iron, walked under the arches and caught a bus to Salford. As he journeyed along, he gazed through the window recalling a young Jedda, visualizing her with her usual desperate "I'm late" look. Her made up excuses at which Kate would roar with laughter. The quick tapping of her small feet, first on the flags, then over the cobbled road. A ghost from the far distant past...

What was it she had once said to him? Oh yes. I don't believe in heaven as you depict it, Joe. But that doesn't mean there aren't other spheres. I think there are times when I've glanced at them in passing. He smiled to himself, his thoughts tender. Well, Jedda Markham, maybe that's what I'm doing right now?

The thirty-four bus took him to Cross Lane and, once his destination was reached, he alighted only to find that here, too, things had changed. Gone were familiar landmarks appropriated by high-rise flats, all too evident were shopping complexes and car parks. Only the Old Ship Hotel, its windows vandalised and doors boarded up, was hauntingly familiar. Its old walls seeped with the memories of sailors and ladies of doubtful morals who had accompanied them. No doubt it still held onto its secrets: those and the old ship's bell, still intact on the battered roof, proved he was in the right locality.

"Can we go in there?" she had asked of him. "What's it like? I've never been in."

The shock he had felt at the time had been indescribable and he had answered, "I hope to the high heavens, you haven't?"

She had stared at him, eyes wide with shock by the way he had spoken to her, and he had continued to chastise her. "A decent girl doesn't go into a pub. Certainly not one like that! Not even with a man."

Exasperation had caused her to frown as she informed him that Polly Anders out of the typing pool had been in and she had heard her telling Kate what good fun it was; and they had laughed about it.

He recalled saying, "Kate would laugh, Jedda; but you wouldn't catch her going in the Ship Hotel herself." Anyway, he had never cared for Polly Anders' morals.

She had replied, "Polly's all right". But then, everyone had been all right to Jedda's way of thinking – apart from Toro, that is!

He saw things more clearly now. The writer in her had only wanted to observe, and he would have blocked her vision, destroyed her talent. He should have allowed her more freedom, trusted her more, but he had been afraid, even jealous of her wandering thoughts. The times when she had suddenly taken on a detached air, leaving him somewhere on the fringe of her imagination. A shrug from her shoulders had often made him grit his teeth in anger. The liberal and the catholic, what a fool he had been! They would never have made it through life together but it would have been a hell of a challenge anyway.

He moaned inwardly and continued his way down Cross Lane in search of his destination. Then he found it – a dilapidated building at the back of a cinema. One he and Jedda had visited so often and had held hands in the dark. He was beginning to wish he had never set foot in England; the memories were becoming too painful.

Many of the streets had been pulled down, but some were still standing. He went round the back of one, removed some loose boarding, and strode through. A ramshackle workshop confronted him and a figure was standing at the bottom of some rickety stairs... it was Toro and he was not looking too pleased with himself.

Joe walked towards him, at the same time sickened by the place; it smelled of dead mice and explosives. What had Toro been conjuring up? Sugar and soap powder were scattered all over a grimy bench along with batteries and empty casings which lay beside each other. Seeming to appear only as a foe, not as a friend, Toro's presence disturbed him greatly. He wanted to turn heel, run away from all that was coming to pass. But to what end? And to where? All he could muster was a weak "Hello".

Toro ignored his greeting. "You've been a long time. I'm in a mess. A hell of a mess. Patsy's been picked up by the police near the Flat Iron for being drunk and disorderly. Eileen won't deliver – not on her own, anyway. Apart from that, we need her to 'phone in the warning. I hope she comes through on that score at least." Toro spoke with a cold deliverance. "I've had a hell of a time obtaining glycerine!"

Joe gave a sigh of relief. They were going to call it off, then? But relief soon gave way to chagrin when Toro said, "We'll have to do it."

"Us!" said Joe in disbelief. "We're top men. Dublin won't like officers taking such risks. I'm here for the fixing. Not the doing."

"It's too short a notice. We can't just leave. Not without doing something. It's Easter!"

What a way to celebrate. Joe felt wearied by it all and gave vent to his emotions. "Does it matter?"

Toro's eyes narrowed. "Matter? What do you mean, matter? Of course it does! What's got into you, Joe?" His face softened for a second, an unusual thing for Toro. "I'm sorry about Danny, but shouldn't that make it all the more reason to continue with our mission, not less so?"

Joe shrugged his shoulders. To hell with it! What did he care either way? What had he to lose, when all was lost? "Danny's death isn't part of it. I just think it's reckless, that's all. I've never been on a plant job... neither have you, for that matter. We could make a hash of it. I, for one, don't want to do it."

Toro's eyes narrowed. "What's happened, Joe? You've changed since last time I saw you."

"It's been a long time, Toro. Years, in fact, and people change. There's nothing at all wrong. I just think we are making a bad move as things stand." Joe clenched his fists, lying through his teeth.

Toro stared at him, an incredulous expression on his face. "Nothing? What do you mean, nothing? I thought you hated the English apart from that slip of a Jedda you knew years ago. Wasn't she proof enough, you can't trust them?"

Unthinkingly, Toro had hit the nail on the head.

Joe winced. "True. It was years ago, so let's forget it."

228

"Why, then, the sudden change of heart? You know the terms, Joe. In for a penny! In for a pound! Once you join us there's no going back! Kill the enemy or we'll kill you. We don't take betrayal lightly."

Joe didn't answer immediately; he didn't feel he cared either way.

"Well? Are you in or out?" Toro was becoming more aggravated.

"I'm in," said Joe, despondently.

Toro gave his version of a smile. "Do you want a drink, Joe?" he said, as though Joe hadn't spoken. "Here, have a cup of tea," he said, as if offering Joe the keys to the kingdom. He took a packet of cigarettes from his jacket pocket and proffered one to his dithering friend.

Joe accepted without a thank you and lit it before blowing out quick spurts of smoke.

"You'll be surprised to see me after such a long time," said Toro. He smiled, all charm.

"Yes. I admit I was taken off guard when the cell in Belfast informed me you were over here." He rubbed an itch on his nose. "How long have you been here?"

"Longer than I care to admit. I hate this bloody country." Toro spat the words out, a look of disgust on his face.

Joe smiled wistfully. "It's certainly not home, especially this area. It has some nice places, though."

"You sound like a holiday brochure. I'd write every bit of it off from the face of the earth if I could. They're all commies that live here. Godless bloody lot!"

"Rory doesn't seem to think so."

Toro gave a short bitter laugh. "Priests. Holy Joe's always telling us to love one another. Probably told the Irish that during the famine."

Joe raised his eyebrows concerned. "You're going back a bit aren't you?"

"We'd be betraying all the holy dead that went so tragically before us if we didn't remember them."

"Yet the English are so forgetful. They don't seem to hold grudges. Make quite a fuss of the Germans in spite of two world wars."

"That's because they're run by Germans up at Buckingham Palace. The House of Lords is as corrupt as they come...when they're not falling asleep." Toro started to laugh at his own statement, highly amused. "Dodder, dodder, dodder. Not one of them under ninety."

Joe smiled in spite of himself and said, "What time are we off, then?"

"It's all done and ready." Toro placed a parcel down carefully. "This needs to be packed in that holdall over there."

"It's set already?" Joe's face mirrored dreadful thoughts.

Toro laughed. "Don't look so worried. It's set hours from now. Just be careful how you handle it, that's all."

Joe picked up the holdall and they manoeuvred the package into the place between them carefully, before zipping it up.

Toro went into the small kitchen and sidled over to a small burner, lifted a steaming kettle, mashed the tea and, once brewed, handed Joe a mug of tea. "Drink that before we go. Do you good, calm your nerves," he said, before walking into a small alcove and returning with a tin of biscuits. "Want one?" he said, as if entertaining a special guest before the main party began.

So Toro had noticed his nervousness. Joe refused the biscuits. "I've just had a nice meal in a cafe... I notice it's all set to go off at ten-past-six," said Joe, still on edge. "Will the store be empty by then? Is Eileen phoning the warning through?"

"Yes! Everything is arranged." Toro spoke with an air of indifference, as if not caring whether she made the call or not.

Joe gave him a suspicious look, but Toro continued to drink his tea, either pretending or not caring to notice. He put his cup down. "What time is it?"

"It's getting late...we'd better hurry. The traffic will start to build up soon." Joe spoke in an agitated fashion.

Toro was nonplussed and tried to calm Joe down. "It's only a ten-minute ride." He looked at his watch as he spoke. "Five o'clock. I think mine's fast. What time do you make it, Joe?" He looked at the wall. "There's no clock in this place."

"You're ten minutes fast," said Joe. "Come on let's go."

"Are you sure, Joe? I thought I set mine right."

"Positive. I set mine by the clock on the ferry and it can't be wrong. Ferries are sticklers for schedules."

Once outside in the street Toro locked the door carefully behind him and they walked slowly towards the car. Joe held on to the bag carefully and waited until Toro had opened the car door before settling down gingerly into the front seat. Toro turned the key in the ignition and they drove steadily off towards the city.

Chapter Sixteen

Jedda dressed up warmly to the Flower Duet echoing from the radiogram. It was one her favourites and she was in a very happy mood. Today was her birthday and, as previously discussed last evening she was looking forward to having dinner tonight at the Midland before visiting the Opera House. *Tosca.* Yes, it had been a long time since last she had watched it performed at the Opera House. So long ago with Joe Baker, as she recalled, in what seemed another era. Must have been twenty years ago. She had not mentioned the fact to Adam though; she had not wanted to spoil the evening by making him jealous. Just she, Adam, Doreen and Gilbert were spending the evening together.

She looked out of the window, shuddered at the weather and looked decidedly worried. She had to meet her agent at five and that left little time to rush and buy that new bag she needed to go with her new velvet cocktail dress for tonight's outing.

She put the finishing touches to her make-up, pushed her feet into a pair of hand made leather boots, snuggled into her mink coat and went into Adam's study to kiss him goodbye before leaving.

"Do you really need to go out in this weather, Jedda? The forecast isn't good. The roads could be slippy."

"I'll be all right. You know I'm a good driver." She twirled her car keys round in her hand as if to emphasise the fact, laughing at him, stopping when she saw a worried frown wrinkle his forehead. She leaned over and kissed him again. "I'll be all right, I tell you. I've never missed sharing my birthday without you since we've been married, have I?" She walked towards the study door, turned round, smiled and blew him a kiss before leaving.

An odd feeling came over Adam and he followed her outside, nervously. Once she had slid into her car, he remained in the driveway, watching fearfully as she drove away, a tender expression, a look especially reserved for Jedda beginning to chase out the fear on his face. He waited until the back of her head with its dark, shiny hair, so familiar to him now, had disappeared from view, vaguely ill-at-ease about her travelling in such inclement weather. He shrugged his shoulders as if to dismiss a dark thought, turned indoors and went back to his desk. She'd be all right. He comforted himself with the thought. She wouldn't be his Jedda, if she weren't.

Jedda rode on steadily to the strains of Manon Lescaut coming from the car radio, conscious of times when she too had been lost in a desert. Though not always literally, it had at times felt that way.

When she reached Manchester City Centre the snow was gathering momentum. She was in a cautious frame of mind but had not been subjected to any of the perils uppermost in Adam's mind, apart from some bad tempered man in a shabby old car. She thought there were two men come to think of it, but she couldn't see their faces because of the snow-covered windows behind which they were sitting. Their windscreen wipers did not appear to be working, but she thought at least one of them could have wiped them with a cloth of some kind.

She spent twenty minutes in her agent's office discussing percentages concerning her present output. Over coffee Yvonne and she talked about her new book, one of her best to date. There was much to be arranged by June, when it would be launched with the author's usual signing reams of them at a chosen bookstore. Yvonne was a nice woman, but over-subscribed at times because she was so good at her job. Jedda had been her client from the beginning of her career and had made them both rich, but they did have their differences at times; yet, in spite of this, each knew each would come to grief without the other.

The meeting over and once out on the street, Jedda consulted her watch. There was little time left for shopping and her leather boots drove rather than walked through the snow and she began to wish there had been room to park her car closer to the vicinity she was now in. The snow had become quite thick underfoot in a very short space of a time.

She made her way hurriedly to the department store, the one where she always purchased the kind of bag she needed. She contemplated that she would have to hurry; it was almost ten-to-six and little time was left to choose the item necessary to go with her cocktail dress.

When Joe and Toro eventually reached Blackfriars at a very slow pace it was to a vision of cars filled with people eager to arrive home from work; plus last minute shoppers stocking up for the Easter break. A bastion against hunger over the holidays.

The sky was as black as doomsday, a notion that made Joe feel even more depressed. He felt like a man on a tightrope who, once halfway across, any attempt to turn back would prove disastrous. He had felt uncomfortable about this English business from the start. Premonition? He didn't know. He was only aware that it had come to pass that day on the journey to Drogheda and had never left him since.

There had even been disagreement within the cell. It had been decided the North of England did not seem the right place to bomb. That it may lose them the sympathy of the British working classes; doing more harm than good. Their quarrel was with the Ulster Parliament and London, and there the cause should lie. And here he was, sat in the middle of a traffic jam, a bomb ticking nervously away on his knee.

Toro, with some difficulty, manoeuvred the car up the side of Salford bus station until he reached the vicinity of Deansgate. They were in Manchester. Across the road stood the cathedral. All they had to do now was slide into the underground car park and they would be home and dry.

Joe, in spite of the darkness of his mood, glanced towards Deansgate and could not help but note the shops were brightly lit. Easter eggs of various sizes and colours filled confectionary windows vying with flower shops advertising an array of spring flowers. Daffodils. Wasn't it Jedda's birthday around now? He could not remember the exact date, but seeing the flowers had brought it to mind. God! Fancy dreaming of the past at a time like this!

The squeal of Toro's breaks brought him to his senses as the car shuddered to a stop. Toro had to press the ignition twice before the engine noisily sprang to life. A woman, driving a shiny new Jaguar had almost collided with their front bumper, missing them narrowly. She never looked their way, as if unconscious of her near-fatal action; but she could not possibly have been unaware of her lack of judgment when taking the corner.

"Bloody woman!" Toro's hands were surprisingly steady as they grasped the wheel.

Joe looked down on the bomb-filled parcel placed precariously between his knees, sick with apprehension!

"Rich bitch!" Toro was livid at the woman's dismissive attitude and careless actions. "Why doesn't she learn to drive? She can't be short of money to pay for lessons by the look of her." He followed her up the ramp that led to the underground car park. "Any other time I'd have given her a piece of my mind. She's lucky today... I don't want our faces remembered."

After paying the toll the woman emerged into the light, casting an embarrassed look towards their car as she did so, but not coming forward to apologise.

She seemed in a hurry, as if on some last minute shopping spree, decided Joe. He left the car, watching the woman walk down the ramp whilst Toro paid the toll fee. As he peered at her through the half-light she rose, phoenix like, beneath a brighter one beyond. Even after all these years he could not have mistaken that walk... Jedda Markham! He grew cold, thanked God Toro hadn't seen her, turning away before his ally could notice the change of expression on his face. He was aghast! Stunned beyond all reason! He was thankful she hadn't recognised them either, disguised as they were through the mists of the swirling snow.

Toro pulled on his arm and said, "What's wrong?"

Joe answered, "Nothing." A wise choice of words he thought. If Toro had thought she had seen them he would have killed her instantly. Destroyed her under the cover of the heavily falling snow, put her body in the car until their mission was finished, then dumped it. Joe knew this to be so as sure as he stood there.

In different circumstances he would have found the whole thing ironic, a sick joke. Jedda of all people nearly turning the pair of them into cinders! Causing their car to crash! It would have blown them to smithereens, taking her and anyone in the vicinity with it! He took a sidelong look at Toro. No, Toro wouldn't have found it funny. No, not in the least.

They made an odd pair as they walked down Market Street. Toro, his face set against wind, the snow buffeting hard into his flesh, making him wince with discomfort while remaining innocent of the conflicting thoughts going on in the mind of the terrorist Casanova who walked so unwillingly beside him.

Joe studied his watch. It showed five-twenty-five. That left plenty of time to get it over with and be out. Finished and away. A wave of apprehension flooded his being. What was he doing here? What's the matter with you, Joe? You're behaving more like a lovesick twenty-year-old Romeo instead of a killer trying to reap revenge on Manchester. Killer? Is that what he was? There was no denying it; that's what he truly was in spite of his inner protestations. Is this how he would end his life? Is this how he was content to live? Blowing up people. It had seemed right at the time of joining, now it had all turned sour. He had never come close to mirroring his actions before and now he had, he did not care for what was reflected there.

Holding at bay the finality of the hour, he wished he were on a boat sailing back to Dublin. Free, without Jedda swamping his thoughts over and over, grinding him down and as Toro and he moved closer to their objective, the further away he wished to be. Doubt about his actions was becoming more evident. A deep foreboding, combined with recent events, seemed too much of a coincidence to make him happy with the situation. As if some kind of spectre were about to rise and overwhelm him. Try to draw him away from impending disaster. Warn him? But of what? He gave an involuntary shiver. He'd never wanted this assignment in the first place; hadn't he told Dublin that! Hadn't he explained his reservations in Belfast also, but to no avail! He had warned Toro of the same; they were not their men when it came to planting explosives, but the man walking beside him seemed as if he was taking immense pleasure in his chosen task.

He gave the object of his thoughts a sidelong look, but Toro was deep in thought and he knew that he was the last person with whom he could discuss his foreboding. Call the whole thing off? But no, not Toro. Not one so single minded and determined as he. It was as if nothing in life mattered to him. Joe, thinking back across the years, was also aware that, with regard to Toro's character, he had finally come to the conclusion, nothing, or no one, ever had.

They reached the store much too soon as far as Joe was concerned, but Toro strode eagerly ahead. A happy participant in the game of death; ready to take part in the ultimate destruction of a hated foe. Joe moved at a much slower pace, a culpable and unwilling ally. A little girl brushed past him knocking the holdall against him and made him catch his breath. The child's mother smiled and told the little girl to apologise to the gentleman, which she did with the utmost charm. An inward surge of guilt made him feel like the epitome of all that was evil.

Joe and Toro reached the bag department as planned then separated, each pretending to take an interest in the merchandise. Joe glanced at his watch. It showed five-thirty-five. The young lady assistant was busy clearing the counter of odd pieces of tissue paper and grey patterned carrier bags. She seemed in a last minute rush to put things in order; tired and bored after a long day.

"Can I help you, sir?" she asked, and though courteous, seemed as if she could hardly contain her desire to be rid of her last two customers.

Joe mumbled, "No thank you," and moved to the next counter.

Toro, meanwhile, ignored her completely, moving at a leisurely pace and when her attention was elsewhere placed the holdall amongst others of similar appearance. That done, he chose a new one and handed it to the girl behind the counter, at the same time fixing his eyes balefully upon her in the way that Toro was apt to do. The girl took the money in a hurried fashion, uncomfortable when faced with pale eyes in such a dark countenance. She wished the men would hurry up and leave; the store was due to close and she would be late for that special date she was looking forward to.

In spite of her dislike for the man with the piercing eyes, she offered a well-trained customer service smile and asked if she could offer any further help, but much to her relief, the men suddenly seemed to be in a great hurry.

Departing from the bag department, Toro skirted ahead of Joe and made for the escalator. Joe trailed along with less enthusiasm than his eager compatriot, lagging several stairs behind. Gazing down into the store he became puzzled by how deserted the store had become for such a busy a time as Easter.

Toro assumed differently, noticing with satisfaction that the place was almost empty; that their plan was indeed going well. If Eileen remained late phoning in, it wouldn't matter. People had shopped early, eager to be out of the cold, and the doorman was already standing in the foyer waiting to lock up.

Joe was gazing straight ahead. Something wasn't right. The girl upstairs in the bag department was causing him some concern; suppose she didn't leave in time? Her eyes, when she had smiled, reminded him of Kate and he started to grind his teeth, desperately. He felt absolutely at a loss, then something happened that turned his blood in to ice!

A woman was being transported upwards on the oncoming escalator, obviously late. Whilst taking the stairs two at a time her hand brushed his as she sped by, and she looked straight into his eyes, eyes that immediately widened with recognition. For the second time in less than half an hour he found himself in the presence of Jedda Markham. Only this time, she too, had identified him.

Trust her to be late, damn it. Oh, Jedda! Jedda! In that sense she had not altered then. He turned away from her, quickly! From her! The woman he had so longed to encounter and hold this last twenty years. Had longed unreasonably to take her in his arms. Jedda! Jedda! Jedda! Oh God! Not now! Not now at this moment when both their lives could end at any second. Even more than this – hers! She knew he had recognised her.

What a mess! Oh, God! What had he done? Joe glanced down at Toro, not two feet away, but still looking ahead; innocently unaware of Joe's predicament and the turmoil going on within. Frozen with fear as he stood gazing in petrified silence at the departing figure of his long-lost love. Twice in one day Jedda Markham had escaped from having a gun turned on her. Joe glanced upwards once more and in doing so noticed that she too had turned round to look back at him, a puzzled frown adorning her face. Then she moved quickly up the stairs assuming he had deliberately ignored her.

Joe hurried forward down the escalator mainly for Jedda's sake. He knew Toro, if he should notice her, would never let her live. Jedda would blow their cover completely, but the only positive thing he could think of was that he knew he would kill Toro and betray heaven and earth before he would let anything happen to her.

Joe stepped off the escalator and made his way to the foyer following in Toro's wake. Soon, they would be away and Toro would be none the wiser; then something occurred that made his blood turn even colder than when he'd first encountered Jedda...the clock on the wall above the door, unseen as he had entered, now clearly stated it was six o'clock. His wristwatch showed five-forty-five. What was wrong? God! That bloody horse-faced woman at the ferry! She must have thrown his watch out of gear when she'd banged her case down on it!

Joe trembled with a mixture of fear and aggravation! Jedda was up there and that young girl... Eileen must have phoned in by now, surely, but too late to know how far behind they were. God! He'd bungled things truly! Properly!

As he followed Toro out of the store and onto the busy street he ran his fingers through his hair and swallowed hard, trying to figure out what to do, fear and desperation etched out on his waxen face being brought into instant relief by the glow of the neon lights. A sight quickly noted by Toro.

"Don't faint at a time like this, Joe! For God's sake man! Pull yourself together!"

"It's my watch. It's wrong. It's gone five-forty... I... it's gone six..."

Toro glanced towards the store. "We'd better get out of here before it goes up, and quick!"

236

Joe did not budge. Toro took his arm to move him along. Joe resisted. "I'll go and phone," he said, making towards the road and trying to cross.

"There isn't time." Toro's jaw tightened as he tried to restrain him.

But Joe broke free, dashed across the road and entered the telephone box. His frantic state of mind forced him to move swiftly and he picked up the receiver, his heart thumping. The complete handle came away, wiring and all; loose in his hand. Vandals! The phone! A useless object in a time of great crisis!

He cursed the heavens as perspiration ran down his back, exertion causing him to breath deeply. He didn't know what to do to solve things; it was like some bad joke the English are apt to play on the Irish from time to time. Such remarks had never amused him, but this was a far from funny situation and was about to rebound on the English themselves. To hell with them! But Jedda was a different matter. She was up there and her beautiful body was about to be ripped to pieces.

Toro flung open the door of the telephone kiosk, letting a shower of snow cascade in. "What the hell are you doing, Joe? Let's get away from here!"

Joe stepped out of the telephone box like a man possessed. "Jedda's up there! In the baggage department, Toro! She'll be blown to bits."

Toro grabbed his lapels. "What are you talking about? Are you mad? What the hell do you mean, Jedda?" He was worried, fearful that Joe was suffering from shock and a lapse of memory. He softened. "Come on. No one's up there! Jedda was long ago, you must be imagining..."

Joe cut him short. "I'm not going crazy, if that's what you think. She's up there all right; so don't talk to me like that!" His breath came in gasps. "I didn't tell you because she recognised me. She was going up the escalator as we were leaving..."

"So you left her to betray us." Toro all but snarled the accusation out.

"I didn't want you to harm her."

Toro's eyes narrowed. "It's no use saying she wouldn't have guessed the reason for our visit." He paused and glared at Joe. "She knows us all too well; and the circumstances surrounding us, Joe." He gripped Joe's shoulders. "Especially me! I'm on the news something and often, even if you aren't. You've seen me quoted often enough. She knows us like the back of her greedy little hand... God, you're stupid." He paused and looked across at the store. "If she dies it solves our problem, doesn't it?...Anyway, she dumped you didn't she?"

"No, but my bloody sister Ida made sure it looked that way...but I can't discuss that now!"

Even Toro looked taken aback. "Yes, It's hardly a time to discuss the past." His jaw set in a determined line. "Let's go! That's an order, and I'm serious...I'll have to kill you if you don't."

"I'm going up there. I must warn them... her, and the girl..."

Toro froze, his killer instinct coming to the fore. "Don't make me kill you Joe.

Not after all these years of friendship, and for what? She doesn't belong to you. She never did! She never will!"

Joe pulled himself free from Toro's restraining hand and moved away from him towards the store. In spite of the icy air, beads of perspiration trickled down his forehead, his imagination going haywire. He'd heard of bodies ripped apart, but he had never done the dirty work before and now it was resounding on him with chilling irony. It had only been part of a game before. For idealism and for Ireland! But not her. Not Jedda, the mother of a child that might have been his. Not all that talent and loving, graceful beauty suddenly destroyed. She had no nationality. No sense of God or culture. She was just Jedda. His Jedda!

He ran quickly towards the store, Toro's voice ringing in his ears. "I'll kill you if you don't come back... then, an explosion ripped the air and people started to scream. He ran faster towards the wrecked building.

Toro, following swiftly on his heels, paused, his heart breaking as he raised the gun and fired two bullets into Joe's back...

Cars screeched to a halt! Women dropped parcels. Parents grabbed children, holding them close against walls to shield them. Toro stood in their midst, waving a gun, of which four bullets remained. Like a caged animal he glanced down to where Joe had fallen, blood from his wounds turning the snow beneath from white to dark red. "I warned you," he said. Pain, mixed with deep sorrow showing in his eyes, as he gazed down at his dying ally, until something unbelievable caught his eye. Out of a mist of snow and smoke she came. Wraith like, the girl he had always hated – a woman now: lovelier than ever. Emerging from the dust and rubble of the recently destroyed building... he'd have known that apparition anywhere...

My God! Jedda Markham! At last and in the flesh! Standing here before him. Really here before him, at last! His foe! God, how he despised her, how he'd longed for this moment across the years. A gun in his hand, and her in his power. He laughed inwardly. What a turn up for the books. It was his turn to gloat. To put her in her place... put her in her coffin.

Jedda had wondered at Joe's presence, also his lack of cordiality. She was in such a rush, the store was due to close leaving her no time to dally, even for old friends...no, old lovers! She also wished she had not idled so long at the confectioners where she had bought Adam an Easter egg as a joke, one with bunnies all over it. She was eager to purchase the evening bag she so desperately needed, and with no desire for further delay, had rushed up the escalator to purchase the same.

Bumping into Joe Baker had been a shock, as had been his refusal to acknowledge her, until that is, she had glanced back and seen the departing figure of Toro O'Reilly and guessed this to the reason for Joe's reticence. She also knew something must be afoot. What would Toro be doing visiting a department store on a late spring evening? Indeed, what was he doing in England at all? He was a wanted man.

She had entered the handbag department at high speed. She hoped to make a purchase before it was too late to do so and bumped into a girl in the process. The girl was carrying a holdall. "Sorry!" The girl was apologetic. "I was hoping to catch the gentleman who left here just now. He seems to have left this behind. You didn't happen to see him did you? Tall? Dark? Wearing a fawn trench coat?"

She'd seen him all right. Jedda's eyes narrowed suspiciously before they changed an expression of horror. "Put that bag down and let's get out of here, I suspect it's a bomb!"

The girl hesitated; disbelief swamped her face. "I'm sure you're mistaken. The man accompanying him was such a was such a nice person."

Jedda wanted to cry out, "But the man who planted the holdall isn't; he's from the mouth of hell!" Instead she said out loud, "I know I'm right. They are wanted terrorists; at least one is. I've seen his picture in the paper. Hurry, there probably isn't much time."

The girl looked doubtful. How could this woman know so much? Was it a trick to rob the till? She looked very rich; but you never knew. After all, she supposed that's where they got the money to allow them to indulge in such expensive clothes. "I daren't leave now. I must cash up and lock the till..."

Jedda interrupted angrily, "Damn the money. Just lock the till, and come back later. If it turns out to be a false alarm all to the good... but the men did have Irish accents, you know."

The girl marched up to the till and locked it. "I hope you don't get me fired... I'll discuss it with the under manager. He's in his office..."

"Where's that?" Jedda was getting desperate.

"Downstairs, on the way out."

"Hurry then," said Jedda, relieved that they were at last about to leave.

After the initial shock of the explosion, Jedda – with the young assistant and manager in tow – emerged dust covered, but unhurt from the trembling building, only to be confronted with the macabre scene of Joe lying fatally wounded upon a snow-lined city street.

Toro was waving a gun in the air, at odds with the world in general until he spied Jedda. All else was forgotten as he sauntered menacingly towards her.

Jedda stood transfixed, mesmerised by Toro's unhurried approach. He was enjoying himself; she sensed it. Was sure of it, as clearly as if his mind were a mirror and she herself was its only desired reflection. It was as if he was at a fairground and he was determined to take a pot shot. Not at a coconut shy, though. No, she knew she was the target and the spot was an unseen dot on her heart imagined by her executioner's trained eye. Already, a beloved victim lay at her feet.

Jedda was incapable of movement. Here it was. It was truly about to happen. Her nightmare to end all nightmares had turned into reality; her fight for survival across the years, she realized, had come to nothing. Always in the back of her mind, the fox...the black fox. Waiting. Watching. Knowing it had only to catch her unawares and it would come and find her. Come and take her. Take her life. It fitted the theme. It all came nicely together, except it wasn't nice at all. Those terrifying dreams, first evoked in childhood, had clung like a monkey on her back through the whole of her life...**of all the foxes on Zizzie's sofa the one she had feared most was the one with the water pale eyes...the black one!**

It pounced and pressed its claws into her neck snarling! Viciously! Death was here. She had smelled it many times, but to date she had always escaped it, but not this time. No getting out of it now! It was the sword that had always hung precariously above her head. It had always been there. Waiting. Evil. A soul without rest and out to destroy. For some reason, and one she could not fathom, Gingo came to mind...It's like the man said, they always get you in the end. There was always someone around to spoil it all. Drag you down into the quagmire of their own making, taking you with them, because they hated life, were determined you would share in sickness.

Toro pulled her to him, roughly. His eyes were cold fire as he pressed the gun against her heart. Jedda looked deep into his eyes and watched the hatred glowing there. Cruel! Pitiless! Apart from a giveaway second. She was a woman and quick to sense a change of thought. Sensitive. Intuitive.

Toro's eyes softened, only for a second, but too late for her not to notice what dwelled there. It was to prove to be his downfall. He pulled the trigger quickly to escape alien thoughts so at odds with the hatred in his soul.

Jedda, defenceless as she was, had tuned into his momentary change towards her and she committed the wickedest act of her life. Revenge! She reached up and kissed him full on the mouth. "I always loved you Toro," she sighed, lying with the last breath she would ever take...

Joe Baker lay helpless on the ground and watched, horrified, stunned by the murder of his beloved Jedda. Helpless and unable to intervene, he was at the same time dumbfounded by the dramatic effect her action had on Toro. He had listened with complete disbelief to her last words. The lies she had spoken to Toro when she had slunk against him, declaring her "dying" love. Toro was holding her closer now, screaming as the life flowed out of her...

It had been too late to stop the gun from firing and the pain Toro was suffering could not in any way be pacified. He kept stroking Jedda's hair tenderly one minute and cursing her for a liar the next. He shook her limp body and implored her to come back. "Come back," he said, between sobs. "Come back! Tell me that you're lying! Tell me! Tell me!"

He continued to hold her like a man in a trance, his sobs becoming stronger by the minute. Her body, limp as a doll's, was treated with tenderness one second and with absolute abuse the next.

The shop assistant, whose life Jedda had saved, was also sobbing; crumpled up in a corner, eyes half covered by her hands, watching as the terrorist's face changed from hate to grief. Why had he shot the woman? Why wasn't he attempting to get away when the police were approaching, guns in hand?

Distracted by Jedda's death Toro's gun had fallen from his hand and two policemen were making their way towards him. They acted swiftly, to secure him while he was otherwise engaged in expressing regret for having killed the beautiful woman who lay limply in his arms.

Joe watched with dying eyes Toro's final descent into madness when, like a trapped animal he suddenly sprang to life and started to struggle. The game was over, Jedda's body slipped from his grasp. It landed two feet away from where Joe was lying and Toro started to scream... Jedda!...Jedda! Jedda! The sound continued as he was dragged away, the sound of his lament echoing on the icy air and into the ears of Joe lying beside an almost lifeless Jedda.

Jedda! Jedda! His lovely Jedda, so clever, even at the end she had conquered Toro. Driven him mad. Though in a sense he had always been unstable, insecure, in spite of his arrogant pose.

He crawled to where Toro had let her slide, a small distance away on the snow-covered pavement. Her eyes were still open and he could tell she was looking at him. He also knew, as with him, her time was running out.

Blood, pumping slowly from his ruptured heart, ran from his wounds as he crawled towards her, turning the snow-covered ground beneath to scarlet. He recalled how long ago he had vowed that he would take her soul along with his. That night in the cottage when all that had mattered was their love for each other; but he had not anticipated it being like this. Not lying in the snow on a Manchester street with their life's blood ebbing away. She lay watching him, unmoving apart from her eyes and he saw love in them. His last thoughts were if only he could tell her the reason he hadn't returned. Speak about his letters being withheld from him. Explain! But he knew that time was up for both of them.

He reached out for her hand and found soft leather, but the effort was already proving too much and in his struggle to crawl across to her his heart burst, flooding his lungs as he had reached out to grasp her hand, but too late, she had already gone on ahead of him. His last thoughts dwelt on Toro and his mad protestations of love for Jedda. Rory had warned him about Toro's obsession with her. Well, they'd paid the price for it, all three of them.

It was getting darker. He couldn't see properly and someone was trying to prise Jedda's hand from his, but he held on to it, tightly. Not while there was breath in his body would they be parted again... with one last sigh he clung on to life no longer... but his hand still held on to Jedda's as he joined her in eternity.

THE END

Epilogue

At the request of the health authorities, Rory had come to visit Toro. To add some semblance of sense out of his constant rages, and now, on this October day, he was seated opposite him, the early afternoon light shining brightly through the small bars of the window.

He knew from the moment of their first meeting he was dealing with a deranged man; also, that Toro's chances of recovery were slim. He had only to look at and listen to him to assume as much. Seated before him was a soul in hell. One bereft of hope. He was a priest and must help him.

Toro, head down, glanced up from time to time, the eyes that surveyed Rory churning from a madness deep within. Rory thought his eyes looked even paler than ever, a fact he found most disconcerting.

After a long silence between them, Toro rose abruptly from the seat opposite, fists pounding at the air.

"She did it! Her!" he cried, moving from side to side in a weird trotting motion, his eyes searching the walls as if conversing with an invisible being.

"She loved me, she said. But she never told me. All those years she cheated me! Then, as she lay dying in my arms she said she loved me." He leaned forward and put his arms on the wall either side of Rory, blocking him in. "If she loved me so much, why didn't she tell me years ago? Tell me that?" His voice was emotional, so unlike his usual cold self. "All those sarcastic remarks La Jedda Markham delivered on my account and all the time hiding her love for me."

Rory knew it not to be true, but to deny it to a man who could so easily be pushed over the edge would, he knew, be a fallacy. Especially a man who now stared into his eyes with a look that suggested he would kill him if he dared disagree with his version of the matter. A man whose expression could change from gloom to absolute delight in a matter of seconds when he despaired at Jedda's cruelty one minute and at the next, declare how much he knew she loved him.

Rory found such erratic behaviour difficult to cope with, especially when he knew in his heart of hearts that Jedda Markham would no sooner love Toro than she would invite a tiger to dinner.

"She made me do it. Kill Joe, I mean. She didn't love me. Played one of her damn tricks. Always was tricky. A devil at the best of times; well, she doesn't fool

243

me now. I'll dig her up and kill her; and each time they bury her, I'll dig her up and do it again... He rubbed his hands together at the thought, his eyes narrowing. "Yes that's what I'll do. When do they bury her? Tomorrow? In a few days?"

Rory took his arm gently. "Jedda's dead Toro. Dead for all time. Buried six months ago."

"No she isn't, I've seen her. She visits me sometimes... she loves me you know... told you that already, though."

He continued to drift from one extreme to another. First love, then hate. First belief, then suspicion. Rory was fully aware that to reason with him was not possible and that he was watching a man who was slowly drifting into deeper madness. The psychiatrist had warned him about Toro's state of mind, so all he could do was pray for a man he had never particularly liked: A man who had murdered his brother. Killed a beautiful, talented woman. The fact that he felt so badly towards Toro bothered him as a man of God.

Toro sat down once more and a moment of peace seemed to settle on his face and he rubbed his forehead to dispel the dampness lingering there.

"Have you a cigarette, Rory... whew, I'm exhausted," he complained, as he paused in a moment of sanity.

"As well you might be," thought Rory, with all that baggage you're carrying around in your head. He walked across the cell and handed Toro a packet of cigarettes, placed a hand on his shoulder and blessed him. Blessed him? His brother's murderer! Jedda's murderer! He was only thankful he had the courage to do so.

Now that Toro's mood appeared more temperate Rory decided it was time to take his leave before the man's mind sunk into wherever his unbalanced thoughts seemed to plunge.

Rory beckoned to the warder to open the door of the cell and, as the guard ushered him out of the passage he glanced back, but Toro seemed oblivious to his leaving; he was leaning back smoking and staring into space.

Outside the gates, and once more in the welcome cleanness of the open air, Rory noticed autumn had already arrived. The air was sweet with the smell of decaying leaves... October leaves once green and originally so fresh in springtime had, like youth, also faded, withered and lost their promise. For him only loneliness remained. The laughter within him had died; as had the many people he had loved and most terribly at that... his father, Danny, Joe, Jedda. Only Toro, mad as a hatter, remained to remind him of what once was. Tomorrow he would catch the boat to Dublin and spend a few days' leave with his mother... the only certainty left to his knowledge... was the finality of death.